SEVENTEEN
LOST STORIES
by W. SOMERSET
MAUGHAM

SEVENTEEN LOST STORIES by W. SOMERSET MAUGHAM

Compiled and with an Introduction by
CRAIG V. SHOWALTER

Doubleday & Company, Inc., Garden City, New York

All of the stories in this volume are fictitious; the resemblance of any of the characters to actual persons, living or dead, is purely coincidental.

Printed in the United States of America

This compilation is for
Susan and Gordon Ring

—CRAIG V. SHOWALTER

CONTENTS

INTRODUCTION ix

The Punctiliousness of Don Sebastian (*1898*) 1

A Bad Example (*1899*) 17

De Amicitia (*1899*) 47

Faith (*1899*) 65

The Choice of Amyntas (*1899*) 81

Daisy (*1899*) 107

Cupid and the Vicar of Swale (*1900*) 139

Lady Habart (*1900*) 151

Pro Patria (*1903*) 177

A Point of Law (*1903*) 189

An Irish Gentleman (*1904*) 203

Flirtation (*1906*) 217

The Fortunate Painter (*1906*) 227

A Marriage of Convenience (*1906*) 237

Good Manners (*1907*) 249

Cousin Amy (*1908*) 261

The Happy Couple (*1908*) 267

INTRODUCTION

Somerset Maugham published various editions of collected stories, but all such editions consist only of stories written after 1920, for Maugham excluded all those written in his earlier years. This book now brings together seventeen stories which are entirely new to the present generation. They have not been published for over sixty years. They were written after Maugham had left England following the publication of his first novel LIZA OF LAMBETH in 1897 and when, having given up his medical career and gone to Spain, he was determined to teach himself the craft of writing. Maugham later gave a picture of his first arrival in Seville. "I grew a moustache, smoked Fillipino cigars, learnt the guitar, bought a broad-brimmed hat with a flat crown, in which I swaggered down the Sierpes and hankered for a flowing cape lined with green and red velvet." But he could not afford capes, for he referred to these years before his play LADY FREDERICK brought fame and instant success as "a constant struggle against poverty." He lived only by selling stories when he could to magazines and newspapers and the first six stories that appear in this book made up Maugham's earliest collected work, ORIENTATIONS, published in 1899. His first published short story "The Punctiliousness of Don Sebastian" which had appeared a year earlier in an international magazine was included in that collection.

Maugham himself never republished these stories in his lifetime. Indeed in a preface to one edition of his collected stories he wrote, "In my early youth I wrote a number, but they are so immature that I have preferred not to reprint them. A few are in a book that has long remained out of print, a few others are scattered

in various magazines. They are best forgotten." For Maugham, though so extremely unassuming about his gifts, set for himself high standards concerning work which he thought should be offered to the public. He believed it would have been dishonest both to himself and to the reader to reissue stories which did not satisfy him. However I believe that many readers will not only find the stories enjoyable in themselves, but that they may be fascinated to trace the development of that craftsmanship which, when he returned to the short story form in the 1920's, made him one of the most successful storytellers of his time. And I believe too that many young authors teaching themselves to write as Maugham did by perseverance and by trial and error may be considerably helped, as all readers may be intrigued, by comparing some of these early efforts with the use which Maugham later made of some incidents. Thus for instance "A Marriage of Convenience," "Cousin Amy" (under the title of "The Luncheon") and "The Happy Couple" were later extensively rewritten by Maugham and are included in his Collected Works, and "A Bad Example" was partly used in his play SHEPPEY. It is in the hope that the presentation of these early stories will serve such purposes that the executors of Mr. Maugham have permitted me to make this compilation.

CRAIG V. SHOWALTER

THE PUNCTILIOUSNESS OF DON SEBASTIAN

(1898)

I

Xiormonez is the most inaccessible place in Spain. Only one train arrives there in the course of the day, and that arrives at two o'clock in the morning; only one train leaves it, and that starts an hour before sunrise. No one has ever been able to discover what happens to the railway officials during the intermediate one-and-twenty hours. A German painter I met there, who had come by the only train, and had been endeavouring for a fortnight to get up in time to go away, told me that he had frequently gone to the station in order to clear up the mystery, but had never been able to do so; yet, from his inquiries, he was inclined to suspect—that was as far as he would commit himself, being a cautious man—that they spent the time in eating garlic and smoking execrable cigarettes. The guide-books tell you that Xiormonez possesses the eyebrows of Joseph of Arimathea, a cathedral of the greatest quaintness, and battlements untouched since their erection in the fourteenth century. And they strongly advise you to visit it, but recommend you before doing so to add Keating's insect powder to your other toilet necessaries.

I was travelling to Madrid in an express train which had been rushing along at the pace of sixteen miles an hour, when suddenly it stopped. I leant out of the window, asking where we were.

"Xiormonez!" answered the guard.

"I thought we did not stop at Xiormonez."

"We do not stop at Xiormonez," he replied impassively.

"But we are stopping now!"

"That may be; but we are going on again."

I had already learnt that it was folly to argue with a Spanish guard, and, drawing back by head, I sat down. But, looking at my watch, I saw that it was only ten. I should never again have a chance of inspecting the eyebrows of Joseph of Arimathea unless I chartered a special train, so, seizing the opportunity and my bag, I jumped out.

The only porter told me that everyone in Xiormonez was asleep at that hour, and recommended me to spend the night in the waiting-room, but I bribed him heavily; I offered him two pesetas, which is nearly fifteenpence, and, leaving the train to its own devices, he shouldered my bag and started off.

Along a stony road we walked into the dark night, the wind blowing cold and bitter, and the clouds chasing one another across the sky. In front, I could see nothing but the porter hurrying along, bent down under the weight of my bag, and the wind blew icily. I buttoned up my coat. And then I regretted the warmth of the carriage, the comfort of my corner and my rug; I wished I had peacefully continued my journey to Madrid—I was on the verge of turning back as I heard the whistling of the train. I hesitated, but the porter hurried on, and, fearing to lose him in the night, I sprang forwards. Then the puffing of the engine, and on the smoke the bright reflection of the furnace, and the train steamed away; like Abd-er-Rahman, I felt that I had flung my scabbard into the flames.

Still the porter hurried on, bent down under the weight of my bag, and I saw no light in front of me to announce the approach to a town. On each side, bordering the road, were trees, and beyond them darkness. And great black clouds hastened after one another across the heavens. Then, as we walked along, we came to a rough stone cross, and lying on the steps before it was a woman with uplifted hands. And the wind blew bitter and keen, freezing the marrow of one's bones. What prayers had she to offer that she must kneel there alone in the night? We passed another cross standing up with its outstretched arms like a soul in pain. At last a heavier night rose before me, and presently I saw a great stone arch. Passing beneath it, I found myself immediately in the town.

The street was tortuous and narrow, paved with rough cobbles;

and it rose steeply, so that the porter bent lower beneath his burden, panting. With the bag on his shoulders he looked like some hunchbacked gnome, a creature of nightmare. On either side rose tall houses, lying crooked and irregular, leaning towards one another at the top, so that one could not see the clouds, and their windows were great, black apertures like giant mouths. There was not a light, not a soul, not a sound—except that of my own feet and the heavy panting of the porter. We wound through the streets, round corners, through low arches, a long way up the steep cobbles, and suddenly down broken steps. They hurt my feet, and I stumbled and almost fell, but the hunchback walked along nimbly, hurrying ever. Then we came into an open space, and the wind caught us again, and blew through our clothes, so that I shrank up, shivering. And never a soul did we see as we walked on; it might have been a city of the dead. Then past a tall church: I saw a carved porch, and from the side grim devils grinning down upon me; the porter dived through an arch, and I groped my way along a narrow passage. At length he stopped, and with a sigh threw down the bag. He beat with his fists against an iron door, making the metal ring. A window above was thrown open, and a voice cried out. The porter answered; there was a clattering down the stairs, an unlocking, and the door was timidly held open, so that I saw a woman, with the light of her candle throwing a strange yellow glare on her face.

And so I arrived at the hotel of Xiormonez.

II

My night was troubled by the ghostly crying of the watchman: "Protect us, Mary, Queen of Heaven; protect us, Mary!" Every hour it rang out stridently as soon as the heavy bells of the cathedral had ceased their clanging, and I thought of the woman kneeling at the cross, and wondered if her soul had found peace.

In the morning I threw open the windows and the sun came dancing in, flooding the room with gold. In front of me the great wall of the cathedral stood grim and grey, and the gargoyles looked savagely across the square. . . . The cathedral is admirable; when you enter you find yourself at once in darkness, and the air is heavy with incense; but, as your eyes become accustomed

to the gloom, you see the black forms of penitents kneeling by pillars, looking towards an altar, and by the light of the painted windows a reredos, with the gaunt saints of an early painter, and aureoles shining dimly.

But the gem of the Cathedral of Xiormonez is the Chapel of the Duke de Losas, containing, as it does, the alabaster monument of Don Sebastian Emanuel de Mantona, Duque de Losas, and of the very illustrious Señora Doña Sodina de Berruguete, his wife. Like everything else in Spain, the chapel is kept locked up, and the guide-book tells you to apply to the porter at the palace of the present duke. I sent a little boy to fetch that worthy, who presently came back, announcing that the porter and his wife had gone into the country for the day, but that the duke was coming in person.

And immediately I saw walking towards me a little, dark man, wrapped up in a big *capa*, with the red and blue velvet of the lining flung gaudily over his shoulder. He bowed courteously as he approached, and I perceived that on the crown his hair was somewhat more than thin. I hesitated a little, rather awkwardly, for the guide-book said that the porter exacted a fee of one peseta for opening the chapel—one could scarcely offer sevenpence-halfpenny to a duke. But he quickly put an end to all doubt, for, as he unlocked the door, he turned to me and said:

"The fee is one franc."

As I gave it him he put it in his pocket and gravely handed me a little printed receipt. *Baedeker* had obligingly informed me that the Duchy of Losas was shorn of its splendour, but I had not understood that the present representative added to his income by exhibiting the bones of his ancestors at a franc a head. . . .

We entered, and the duke pointed out the groining of the roof and the tracery of the windows.

"This chapel contains some of the finest Gothic in Spain," he said.

When he considered that I had sufficiently admired the architecture, he turned to the pictures, and, with the fluency of a professional guide, gave me their subjects and the names of the artists.

"Now we come to the tombs of Don Sebastian, the first Duke of Losas, and his spouse, Doña Sodina—not, however, the first Duchess."

The monument stood in the middle of the chapel, covered with

a great pall of red velvet, so that no economical tourist should see it through the bars of the gate and thus save his peseta. The duke removed the covering and watched me silently, a slight smile trembling below his little black moustache.

The duke and his wife, who was not his duchess, lay side by side on a bed of carved alabaster; at the corners were four twisted pillars, covered with little leaves and flowers, and between them bas-reliefs representing Love, and Youth, and Strength, and Pleasure, as if, even in the midst of death, death must be forgotten. Don Sebastian was in full armour. His helmet was admirably carved with a representation of the battle between the Centaurs and the Lapithae; on the right arm-piece were portrayed the adventures of Venus and Mars, on the left the emotions of Vulcan; but on the breast-plate was an elaborate Crucifixion, with soldiers and women and apostles. The visor was raised and showed a stern, heavy face, with prominent cheek-bones, sensual lips, and a massive chin.

"It is very fine," I remarked, thinking the duke expected some remark.

"People have thought so for three hundred years," he replied gravely.

He pointed out to me the hands of Don Sebastian.

"The guide-books have said that they are the finest hands in Spain. Tourists especially admire the tendons and veins, which, as you perceive, stand out as in no human hand would be possible. They say it is the summit of art."

And he took me to the other side of the monument, that I might look at Doña Sodina.

"They say she was the most beautiful woman of her day," he said, "but in that case the Castilian lady is the only thing in Spain which has not degenerated."

She was, indeed, not beautiful: her face was fat and broad, like her husband's; a short, ungraceful nose, and a little, nobbly chin; a thick neck, set dumpily on her marble shoulders. One could not but hope that the artist had done her an injustice.

The Duke of Losas made me observe the dog which was lying at her feet.

"It is a symbol of fidelity," he said.

"The guide-book told me she was chaste and faithful."

"If she had been," he replied, smiling, "Don Sebastian would perhaps never have become Duque de Losas."

"Really!"

"It is an old history which I discovered one day among some family papers."

I pricked up my ears, and discreetly began to question him.

"Are you interested in old manuscripts?" said the duke. "Come with me and I will show you what I have."

With a flourish of the hand he waved me out of the chapel, and, having carefully locked the doors, accompanied me to his palace. He took me into a Gothic chamber, furnished with worn French furniture, the walls covered with cheap paper. Offering me a cigarette, he opened a drawer and produced a faded manuscript.

"This is the document in question," he said. "Those crooked and fantastic characters are terrible. I often wonder if the writers were able to read them."

"You are fortunate to be the possessor of such things," I remarked.

He shrugged his shoulders.

"What good are they? I would sooner have fifty pesetas than this musty parchment."

An offer! I quickly reckoned it out into English money. He would doubtless have taken less, but I felt a certain delicacy in bargaining with a duke over his family secrets. . . .

"Do you mean it? May I—er—"

He sprang towards me.

"Take it, my dear sir, take it. Shall I give you a receipt?"

And so, for thirty-one shillings and threepence, I obtained the only authentic account of how the frailty of the illustrious Señora Doña Sodina was indirectly the means of raising her husband to the highest dignities in Spain.

III

Don Sebastian and his wife had lived together for fifteen years, with the entirest happiness to themselves and the greatest admiration of their neighbours. People said that such an example of conjugal felicity was not often seen in those degenerate days, for

even then they prated of the golden age of their grandfathers, lamenting their own decadence. . . . As behoved good Castilians, burdened with such a line of noble ancestors, the fortunate couple conducted themselves with all imaginable gravity. No strange eye was permitted to witness a caress between the lord and his lady, or to hear an expression of endearment; but everyone could see the devotion of Don Sebastian, the look of adoration which filled his eyes when he gazed upon his wife. And people said that Doña Sodina was worthy of all his affection. They said that her virtue was only matched by her piety, and her piety was patent to the whole world, for every day she went to the cathedral at Xiormonez and remained long immersed in her devotions. Her charity was exemplary, and no beggar ever applied to her in vain.

But even if Don Sebastian and his wife had not possessed these conjugal virtues, they would have been in Xiormonez persons of note, since not only did they belong to an old and respected family, which was rich as well, but the gentleman's brother was archbishop of the See, who, when he graced the cathedral city with his presence, paid the greatest attention to Don Sebastian and Doña Sodina. Everyone said that the Archbishop Pablo would shortly become a cardinal, for he was a great favourite with the king, and with the latter His Holiness the Pope was then on terms of quite unusual friendship.

And in those days, when the priesthood was more noticeable for its gallantry than for its good works, it was refreshing to find so high-placed a dignitary of the Church a pattern of Christian virtues, who, notwithstanding his gorgeous habit of life, his retinue, his palaces, recalled, by his freedom from at least two of the seven deadly sins, the simplicity of the apostles, which the common people have often supposed the perfect state of the minister of God.

Don Sebastian had been affianced to Doña Sodina when he was a boy of ten, and before she could properly pronounce the viperish sibilants of her native tongue. When the lady attained her sixteenth year, the pair were solemnly espoused, and the young priest Pablo, the bridegroom's brother, assisted at the ceremony. In these days the union would have been instanced as a triumphant example of the success of the *mariage de convenance,* but at that time such arrangements were so usual that it never occurred to anyone to argue for or against them. Yet it was not customary for a

young man of two-and-twenty to fall madly in love with the bride whom he saw for the first time a day or two before his marriage, and it was still less customary for the bride to give back an equal affection. For fifteen years the couple lived in harmony and contentment, with nothing to trouble the even tenor of their lives; and if there was a cloud in their sky, it was that a kindly Providence had vouchsafed no fruit to the union, notwithstanding the prayers and candles which Doña Sodina was known to have offered at the shrine of more than one saint in Spain who had made that kind of miracle particularly his own.

But even felicitous marriages cannot last forever, since if the love does not die the lovers do. And so it came to pass that Doña Sodina, having eaten excessively of pickled shrimps, which the abbess of a highly respected convent had assured her were of great efficacy in the begetting of children, took a fever of the stomach, as the chronicle inelegantly puts it, and after a week of suffering was called to the other world, from which, as from the pickled shrimps, she had always expected much. There let us hope her virtues have been rewarded, and she rests in peace and happiness.

IV

When Don Sebastian walked from the cathedral to his house after the burial of his wife, no one saw a trace of emotion on his face, and it was with his wonted grave courtesy that he bowed to a friend as he passed him. Sternly and briefly, as usual, he gave orders that no one should disturb him, and went to the room of Doña Sodina; he knelt on the praying-stool which Doña Sodina had daily used for so many years, and he fixed his eyes on the crucifix hanging on the wall above it. The day passed, and the night passed, and Don Sebastian never moved—no thought or emotion entered him; being alive, he was like the dead; he was like the dead that linger on the outer limits of hell, with never a hope for the future, dull with the despair that shall last forever and ever and ever. But when the woman who had nursed him in his childhood lovingly disobeyed his order and entered to give him food, she saw no tear in his eye, no sign of weeping.

"You are right!" he said, painfully rising from his knees. "Give me to eat."

Listlessly taking the food, he sank into a chair and looked at the bed on which had lately rested the corpse of Doña Sodina; but a kindly nature relieved his unhappiness, and he fell into a weary sleep.

When he awoke, the night was far advanced; the house, the town were filled with silence; all round him was darkness, and the ivory crucifix shone dimly, dimly. Outside the door a page was sleeping; he woke him and bade him bring light. . . . In his sorrow, Don Sebastian began to look at the things his wife had loved; he fingered her rosary and turned over the pages of the half-dozen pious books which formed her library; he looked at the jewels which he had seen glittering on her bosom; the brocades, the rich silks, the cloths of gold and silver that she had delighted to wear. And at last he came across an old breviary which he thought she had lost—how glad she would have been to find it, she had so often regretted it! The pages were musty with their long concealment, and only faintly could be detected the scent which Doña Sodina used yearly to make and strew about her things. Turning over the pages listlessly, he saw some crabbed writing; he took it to the light—*"Tonight, my beloved, I come."* And the handwriting was that of Pablo, Archbishop of Xiormonez. Don Sebastian looked at it long. Why should his brother write such words in the breviary of Doña Sodina? He turned the pages and the handwriting of his wife met his eye, and the words were the same—*"Tonight, my beloved, I come"*—as if they were such delight to her that she must write them herself. The breviary dropped from Don Sebastian's hand.

The taper, flickering in the draught, threw glaring lights on Don Sebastian's face, but it showed no change in it. He sat looking at the fallen breviary, and, in his mind, at the love which was dead. At last he passed his hand over his forehead.

"And yet," he whispered, "I loved thee well!"

But as the day came he picked up the breviary and locked it in a casket; he knelt again at the praying-stool and, lifting his hands to the crucifix, prayed silently. Then he locked the door of Doña Sodina's room, and it was a year before he entered it again.

That day the Archbishop Pablo came to his brother to offer consolation for his loss, and Don Sebastian at the parting kissed him on either cheek.

V

The people of Xiormonez said that Don Sebastian was heartbroken, for from the date of his wife's interment he was not seen in the streets by day. A few, returning home from some riot, had met him wandering in the dead of the night, but he passed them silently by. But he sent his servants to Toledo and Burgos, to Salamanca, Cordova, even to Paris and Rome; and from all these places they brought him books—and day after day he studied in them, till the common folk asked if he had turned magician.

So passed eleven months, and nearly twelve, till it wanted but five days to the anniversary of the death of Doña Sodina. Then Don Sebastian wrote to his brother the letter which for months he had turned over in his mind:

"Seeing the instability of all human things, and the uncertain length of our exile upon earth, I have considered that it is evil for brothers to remain so separate. Therefore I implore you—who are my only relative in this world, and heir to all my goods and estates—to visit me quickly, for I have a presentiment that death is not far off, and I would see you before we are parted by the immense sea."

The archbishop was thinking that he must shortly pay a visit to his cathedral city, and, as his brother had desired, came to Xiormonez immediately. On the anniversary of Doña Sodina's interment, Don Sebastian entertained Archbishop Pablo to supper.

"My brother," said he, to his guest, "I have lately received from Cordova a wine which I desire you to taste. It is very highly prized in Africa, whence I am told it comes, and it is made with curious art and labour."

Glass cups were brought, and the wine poured in. The archbishop was a connoisseur, and held it between the light and himself, admiring the sparkling clearness, and then inhaled the odour.

"It is nectar," he said.

At last he sipped it.

"The flavour is very strange."

He drank deeply. Don Sebastian looked at him and smiled as his brother put down the empty glass. But when he was himself about to drink, the cup fell between his hands and the steward's, breaking into a hundred fragments, and the wine spilt on the floor.

"Fool!" cried Don Sebastian, and in his anger struck the servant.

But, being a man of peace, the archbishop interposed.

"Do not be angry with him; it was an accident. There is more wine in the flagon."

"No, I will not drink it," said Don Sebastian wrathfully. "I will drink no more tonight."

The archbishop shrugged his shoulders.

When they were alone, Don Sebastian made a strange request.

"My brother, it is a year to-day that Sodina was buried, and I have not entered her room since then. But now I have a desire to see it. Will you come with me?"

The archbishop consented, and together they crossed the long corridor that led to Doña Sodina's apartment, preceded by a boy with lights.

Don Sebastian unlocked the door, and, taking the taper from the page's hand, entered. The archbishop followed. The air was chill and musty, and even now an odour of recent death seemed to pervade the room.

Don Sebastian went to a casket and from it took a breviary. He saw his brother start as his eye fell on it. He turned over the leaves till he came to a page on which was the archbishop's handwriting, and handed it to him.

"Oh God!" exclaimed the priest, and looked quickly at the door. Don Sebastian was standing in front of it. He opened his mouth to cry out, but Don Sebastian interrupted him.

"Do not be afraid! I will not touch you."

For a while they looked at one another silently; one pale, sweating with terror, the other calm and grave as usual. At last Don Sebastian spoke, hoarsely.

"Did she—did she love you?"

"Oh, my brother, forgive her. It was long ago—and she repented bitterly. And I—I!"

"I have forgiven you."

The words were said so strangely that the archbishop shuddered. What did he mean?

Don Sebastian smiled.

"You have no cause for anxiety. From now it is finished. I will forget." And, opening the door, he helped his brother across the threshold. The archbishop's hand was clammy as a hand of death.

When Don Sebastian bade his brother good-night, he kissed him on either cheek.

VI

The priest returned to his palace, and when he was in bed his secretary prepared to read to him, as was his wont, but the archbishop sent him away, desiring to be alone. He tried to think; but the wine he had drunk was heavy upon him, and he fell asleep. But presently he awoke, feeling thirsty; he drank some water. . . . Then he became strangely wide-awake, a feeling of uneasiness came over him as of some threatening presence behind him, and again he felt the thirst. He stretched out his hand for the flagon, but now there was a mist before his eyes and he could not see, his hand trembled so that he spilled the water. And the uneasiness was magnified till it became a terror, and the thirst was horrible. He opened his mouth to call out, but his throat was dry, so that no sound came. He tried to rise from his bed, but his limbs were heavy and he could not move. He breathed quicker and quicker, and his skin was extraordinarily dry. The terror became an agony; it was unbearable. He wanted to bury his face in the pillows to hide it from him; he felt the hair on his head hard and dry, and it stood on end! He called to God for help, but no sound came from his mouth. Then the terror took shape and form, and he knew that behind him was standing Doña Sodina, and she was looking at him with terrible, reproachful eyes. And a second Doña Sodina came and stood at the end of the bed, and another came by her side, and the room was filled with them. And his thirst was horrible; he tried to moisten his mouth with spittle, but the source of it was dry. Cramps seized his limbs, so that he writhed with pain. Presently a red glow fell upon the room and it became hot and hotter, till he gasped for breath; it blinded him, but he could not close his eyes. And he knew it was the glow of hell-fire, for in his ears rang the groans of souls in torment, and among the voices he recognised that of Doña Sodina, and then—then he

heard his own voice. And, in the livid heat, he saw himself in his episcopal robes, lying on the ground, chained to Doña Sodina, hand and foot. And he knew that as long as heaven and earth should last the torment of hell would continue.

When the priests came in to their master in the morning, they found him lying dead, with his eyes wide open, staring with a ghastly brilliancy into the unknown. Then there was weeping and lamentation, and from house to house the people told one another that the archbishop had died in his sleep. The bells were set tolling, and as Don Sebastian, in his solitude, heard them, referring to the chief ingredient of that strange wine from Cordova, he permitted himself the only jest of his life.

"It was *Belladonna* that sent his body to the worms; and it was *Belladonna* that sent his soul to hell."

VII

The chronicle does not state whether the thought of his brother's heritage had ever entered Don Sebastian's head; but the fact remains that he was sole heir, and the archbishop had gathered the loaves and fishes to such purpose during his life that his death made Don Sebastian one of the wealthiest men in Spain. The simplest actions in this world, oh, Martin Tupper! have often the most unforeseen results.

Now, Don Sebastian had always been ambitious, and his changed circumstances made him realise more clearly than ever that his merit was worthy of a brilliant arena. The times were propitious, for the old king had just died, and the new one had sent away the army of priests and monks which had turned every day into a Sunday; people said that God Almighty had had His day, and that the heathen deities had come to rule in His stead. From all corners of Spain gallants were coming to enjoy the sunshine, and everyone who could make a compliment or a graceful bow was sure of a welcome.

So Don Sebastian prepared to go to Madrid. But before leaving his native town he thought well to appease a possibly vengeful Providence by erecting in the cathedral a chapel in honour of his patron saint; not that he thought the saints would trouble themselves about the death of his brother, even though the causes of it

were not entirely natural, but Don Sebastian remembered that Pablo was an archbishop, and the fact caused him a certain anxiety. He called together architects and sculptors, and ordered them to erect an edifice befitting his dignity; and, being a careful man, as all Spaniards are, thought he would serve himself as well as the saint, and bade the sculptors make an image of Doña Sodina and an image of himself, in order that he might use the chapel also as a burial-place.

To pay for this, Don Sebastian left the revenue of several of his brother's farms, and then, with a peaceful conscience, set out for the capital.

At Madrid he laid himself out to gain the favour of his sovereign and by dint of unceasing flattery soon received much of the king's attention; and presently Philip deigned to ask his advice on petty matters. And since Don Sebastian took care to advise as he saw the king desired, the latter concluded that the courtier was a man of stamina and ability, and began to consult him on matters of state. Don Sebastian opined that the pleasure of the prince must always come before the welfare of the nation, and the king was so impressed with his sagacity that one day he asked his opinion on a question of precedence—to the indignation of the most famous councillors in the land.

But the haughty soul of Don Sebastian chafed because he was only one among many favourites. The court was full of flatterers as assiduous and as obsequious as himself; his proud Castilian blood could brook no companions. . . . But one day, as he was moodily waiting in the royal antechamber, thinking of these things, it occurred to him that a certain profession had always been in great honour among princes, and he remembered that he had a cousin of eighteen who was being educated in a convent near Xiormonez. She was beautiful. With buoyant heart he went to his house and told his steward to fetch her from the convent at once. Within a fortnight she was at Madrid. . . . Mercia was presented to the queen in the presence of Philip, and Don Sebastian noticed that the royal eye lighted up as he gazed on the bashful maiden. Then all the proud Castilian had to do was to shut his eyes and allow the king to make his own opportunities. Within a week Mercia was created maid of honour to the queen, and Don Sebastian was seized with an indisposition which confined him to his room.

The king paid his court royally, which is, boldly; and Doña Mercia had received in the convent too religious an education not to know that it was her duty to grant the king whatever it graciously pleased him to ask. . . .

When Don Sebastian recovered from his illness, he found the world at his feet, for everyone was talking of the king's new mistress, and it was taken as a matter of course that her cousin and guardian should take a prominent part in the affairs of the country. But Don Sebastian was furious! He went to the king and bitterly reproached him for thus dishonouring him. . . . Philip was a humane and generous-minded man, and understood that with a certain temperament it might be annoying to have one's ward philander with a king, so he did his best to console the courtier. He called him his friend and brother; he told him he would always love him, but Don Sebastian would not be consoled. And nothing would comfort him except to be made High Admiral of the Fleet. Philip was charmed to settle the matter so simply, and as he delighted in generosity when to be generous cost him nothing, he also created Don Sebastian Duke of Losas, and gave him, into the bargain, the hand of the richest heiress in Spain.

And that is the end of the story of the punctiliousness of Don Sebastian. With his second wife he lived many years, beloved of his sovereign, courted by the world, honoured by all, till he was visited by the Destroyer of Delights and the Leveller of the Grandeur of this World. . . .

VIII

Towards evening, the Duke of Losas passed my hotel, and, seeing me at the door, asked if I had read the manuscript.

"I thought it interesting," I said, a little coldly, for, of course, I knew no Englishman would have acted like Don Sebastian.

He shrugged his shoulders.

"It is not half so interesting as a good dinner."

At these words I felt bound to offer him such hospitality as the hotel afforded. I found him a very agreeable messmate. He told me the further history of his family, which nearly became extinct at the end of the last century, since the only son of the seventh

duke had, unfortunately, not been born of any duchess. But Ferdinand, who was then King of Spain, was unwilling that an ancient family should die out, and was, at the same time, sorely in want of money; so the titles and honours of the house were continued to the son of the seventh duke, and King Ferdinand built himself another palace.

"But now," said my guest, mournfully shaking his head, "it is finished. My palace and a few acres of barren rock are all that remain to me of the lands of my ancestors, and I am the last of the line."

But I bade him not despair. He was a bachelor and a duke, and not yet forty. I advised him to go to the United States before they put a duty on foreign noblemen; this was before the war; and I recommended him to take Maida Vale and Manchester on his way. Personally, I gave him a letter of introduction to an heiress of my acquaintance at Hampstead; for even in these days it is not so bad a thing to be Duchess of Losas, and the present duke has no brother.

A BAD EXAMPLE

(1899)

I

James Clinton was a clerk in the important firm of Haynes, Bryan & Co., and he held in it an important position. He was the very essence of respectability, and he earned one hundred and fifty-six pounds per annum. James Clinton believed in the Church of England and the Conservative party, in the greatness of Great Britain, in the need of more ships for the navy, and in the superiority of city men to other members of the commonweal.

"It's the man of business that makes the world go round," he was in the habit of saying. "D'you think, sir, that fifty thousand country squires could rule Great Britain? No; it's the city man, the man who's 'ad a sound business training, that's made England what it is. And that is why I 'old the Conservative party most capable of governing this mighty empire because it 'as taken the business man to its 'eart. The strength of the Conservative party lies in its brewers and its city men, its bankers and iron-founders and stockbrokers; and as long as the Liberal party is a nest of Socialists and Trades-Unionists and Anarchists, we city men cannot and will not give it our support."

Except for the lamentable conclusion of his career, he would undoubtedly have become an Imperialist, and the Union of the Great Anglo-Saxon Races would have found in him the sturdiest of supporters!

Mr. Clinton was a little, spindly-shanked man, with weak, myopic eyes, protruding fishlike behind his spectacles. His hair was scant, worn long to conceal the baldness of the crown—and Caesar was pleased to wear a wreath of laurel for the same

purpose. . . . Mr. Clinton wore small side-whiskers but was otherwise clean-shaven, and the lack of beard betrayed the weakness of his mouth; his teeth were decayed and yellow. He was always dressed in a black tail-coat, shiny at the elbows; and he wore a shabby, narrow black tie, with a false diamond stud in his dickey. His grey trousers were baggy at the knees and frayed at the edges; his boots had a masculine and English breadth of toe. His top hat, of antiquated shape, was kept carefully brushed, but always looked as if it were suffering from a recent shower. When he had deserted the frivolous byways in which bachelordom is wont to disport itself for the sober path of the married man, he had begun to carry to and from the city a small black bag to impress upon the world at large his eminent respectability. Mr. Clinton was married to Amy, second daughter of John Rayner, Esquire, of Peckham Rye. . . .

II

Every morning Mr. Clinton left his house in Camberwell in time to catch the eight-fifty-five train for the city. He made his way up Ludgate Hill, walking sideways, with a projection of the left part of his body, a habit he had acquired from constantly slipping past and between people who walked less rapidly than himself. Such persons always annoyed him; if they were not in a hurry, he was, and they had no right to obstruct the way; and it was improper for a city man to loiter in the morning—the luncheon-hour was the time for loitering, no one was then in haste; but in the morning and at night on the way back to the station, one ought to walk at the same pace as everybody else. If Mr. Clinton had been head of a firm, he would never have had in his office a man who sauntered in the morning. If a man wanted to loiter, let him go to the West End; there he could lounge about all day. But the city was meant for business, and there wasn't time for West End airs in the city.

Mr. Clinton reached his office at a quarter to ten, except when the train, by some mistake, arrived up to time, when he arrived at nine-thirty precisely. On these occasions he would sit in his room with the door open, awaiting the coming of the office-boy, who used to arrive two minutes before Mr. Clinton and was naturally

much annoyed when the punctuality of the train prepared him a reprimand.

"Is that you, Dick?" called Mr. Clinton, when he heard a footstep.

"Yes, sir," answered the boy, appearing.

Mr. Clinton looked up from his nails, which he was paring with a pair of pocket scissors.

"What is the meaning of this? You don't call this 'alf-past nine, do you?"

"Very sorry," said the boy; "it wasn't my fault, sir; train was late."

"It's not the first time I've 'ad to speak to you about this, Dick; you know quite well that the company is always unpunctual; you should come by an earlier train."

The office-boy looked sulky and did not answer. Mr. Clinton proceeded, "I 'ad to open the office myself. As assistant-manager, you know quite well that it is not my duty to open the office. You receive sixteen shillings a week to be 'ere at 'alf-past nine, and if you don't feel yourself capable of performing the duties for which you was engaged, you should give notice. . . . Don't let it occur again."

But usually, on arriving, Mr. Clinton took off his tail-coat and put on a jacket, manufactured from the office paper a pair of false cuffs to keep his own clean, and, having examined the nibs in both his penholders and sharpened his pencil, set to work. From then till one o'clock he remained at his desk, solemnly poring over figures, casting accounts, comparing balance-sheets, writing letters, occasionally going for some purpose or another into the clerks' office or into the room of one of the partners. At one he went to luncheon, taking with him the portion of his *Daily Telegraph*, which he was in the habit of reading during that meal. He went to an A. B. C. shop and ordered a roll and butter, a cup of chocolate, and a scone. He divided his pat of butter into two, one half being for the roll and the other for the scone; he drank one moiety of the cup of chocolate after eating the roll, and the other after eating the scone. Meanwhile he read Pages Three and Four of the *Daily Telegraph*. At a quarter to two he folded the paper, put down sixpence in payment, and slowly walked back to the office. He returned to his desk and there spent the afternoon solemnly poring over figures, casting accounts, comparing balance-

sheets, writing letters, occasionally going for some purpose or another into the clerks' office or into the room of one of the partners. At ten minutes to six he wiped his pens and put them back in the tray, tidied his desk, and locked his drawer. He took off his paper cuffs, washed his hands, wiped his face, brushed his hair, arranging the long wisps over the occipital baldness, and combed his whiskers. At six he left the office, caught the six-seventeen train from Ludgate Hill, and thus made his way back to Camberwell and the bosom of his family.

III

On Sunday, Mr. Clinton put on Sunday clothes and, heading the little procession formed by Mrs. Clinton and the two children, went to church, carrying in his hand a prayer-book and a hymn-book. After dinner he took a little walk with his wife along the neighbouring roads, avenues, and crescents, examining the exterior of the houses, stopping now and then to look at a garden or a well-kept house, or trying to get a peep into some room. Mr. and Mrs. Clinton criticised as they went along, comparing the window curtains, blaming a door in want of paint, praising a well-whitened door-step. . . .

The Clintons lived in the fifth house down in the Adonis Road, and the house was distinguishable from its fellows by the yellow curtains with which Mrs. Clinton had furnished all the windows. Mrs. Clinton was a woman of taste. Before marriage, the happy pair, accompanied by Mrs. Clinton's mother, had gone house-hunting and fixed on the Adonis Road, which was cheap, respectable, and near the station. Mrs. Clinton would dearly have liked a house on the right-hand side of the road, which had nooks and angles and curiously shaped windows. But Mr. Clinton was firm in his refusal, and his mother-in-law backed him up.

"I dare say they're artistic," he said, in answer to his wife's argument, "but a man in my position don't want art—he wants substantiality. If the governor"—the governor was the senior partner of the firm—"if the governor was going to take a 'ouse I'd 'ave nothing to say against it, but in my position art's not necessary."

"Quite right, James," said his mother-in-law; "I 'old with what you say entirely."

Even in his early youth Mr. Clinton had a fine sense of the responsibility of life, and a truly English feeling for the fitness of things.

So the Clintons took one of the twenty-three similar houses on the left-hand side of the street and there lived in peaceful happiness. But Mr. Clinton always pointed the finger of scorn at the houses opposite, and he never rubbed the back of his hands so heartily as when he could point out to his wife that such-and-such a number was having its roof repaired; and when the builder went bankrupt, he cut out the notice in the paper and sent it to his spouse anonymously. . . .

At the beginning of August, Mr. Clinton was accustomed, with his wife and family, to desert the sultry populousness of London for the solitude and sea air of Ramsgate. He read the *Daily Telegraph* by the sad sea waves, and made castles in the sand with his children. Then he changed his pepper-and-salt trousers for white flannel, but nothing on earth would induce him to forsake his top hat. He entirely agreed with the heroes of England's proudest epoch—of course I mean the middle Victorian—that the top hat was the sign-manual, the mark, the distinction of the true Englishman, the completest expression of England's greatness. Mr. Clinton despised all foreigners, and although he would never have ventured to think of himself in the same breath with an English lord, he felt himself the superior of any foreign nobleman.

"I dare say they're all right in their way, but with these foreigners you don't feel they're gentlemen. I don't know what it is, but there's something, you understand, don't you? And I do like a man to be a gentleman. I thank God I'm an Englishman!"

IV

Now, it chanced one day that the senior partner of the firm was summoned to serve on a jury at a coroner's inquest, and Mr. Clinton, furnished with the excuse that Mr. Haynes was out of town, was told to go in his stead. Mr. Clinton had never performed that part of a citizen's duties, for on becoming a householder he had hit upon the expedient of being summoned for his

rates, so that his name should be struck off the coroner's list; he was very indifferent to the implied dishonour. It was with some curiosity, therefore, that he repaired to the court on the morning of the inquest.

The weather was cold and grey, and a drizzling rain was falling. Mr. Clinton did not take a 'bus, since by walking he could put in his pocket the threepence which he meant to charge the firm for his fare. The streets were wet and muddy, and people walked close against the houses to avoid the splash of passing vehicles. Mr. Clinton thought of the jocose solicitor who was in the habit of taking an articled clerk with him on muddy days, to walk on the outside of the street and protect his master from the flying mud. The story particularly appealed to Mr. Clinton; that solicitor must have been a fine man of business. As he walked leisurely along under his umbrella, Mr. Clinton looked without envy upon the city men who drove along in hansoms.

"Some of us," he said, "are born great, others achieve greatness. A man like that"—he pointed with his mind's finger at a passing alderman—"a man like that can go about in 'is carriage and nobody can say anything against it. 'E's worked 'imself up from the bottom."

But when he came down Parliament Street to Westminster Abbey, he felt a different atmosphere, and he was roused to Jeremiac indignation at the sight, in a passing cab, of a gilded youth in an opera hat, with his coat buttoned up to hide his dress clothes.

"That's the sort of young feller I can't abide," said Mr. Clinton. "And if I was a member of Parliament I'd stop it. That's what comes of 'aving too much money and nothing to do. If I was a member of the aristocracy I'd give my sons five years in an accountant's office. There's nothing like a sound business training for making a man." He paused in the road and waved his disengaged hand. "Now, what should I be if I 'adn't 'ad a sound business training?"

Mr. Clinton arrived at the mortuary, a gay red and white building, which had been newly erected and consecrated by a duke with much festivity and rejoicing. Mr. Clinton was sworn in with the other jurymen, and with them repaired to see the bodies on which they were to sit. But Mr. Clinton was squeamish.

"I don't like corpses," he said. "I object to them on principle."

He was told he must look at them.

"Very well," said Mr. Clinton. "You can take a 'orse to the well but you can't make 'im drink." When it came to his turn to look through the panes of glass behind which were the bodies, he shut his eyes.

"I can't say I'm extra gone on corpses," he said, as they walked back to the court. "The smell of them ain't what you might call *eau-de-Cologne*." The other jurymen laughed. Mr. Clinton often said witty things like that.

"Well, gentlemen," said the coroner, rubbing his hands, "we've only got three cases this morning, so I sha'n't have to keep you long. And they all seem to be quite simple."

V

The first was an old man of seventy; he had been a respectable, hard-working man till two years before, when a paralytic stroke had rendered one side of him completely powerless. He lost his work. He was alone in the world—his wife was dead, and his only daughter had not been heard of for thirty years—and gradually he had spent his little savings; one by one he sent his belongings to the pawnshop, his pots and pans, his clothes, his arm-chair, finally his bedstead, then he died. The doctor said the man was terribly emaciated, his stomach was shrivelled up for want of food, he could have eaten nothing for two days before death. . . . The jury did not trouble to leave the box; the foreman merely turned round and whispered to them a minute; they all nodded, and a verdict was returned in accordance with the doctor's evidence!

The next inquiry was upon a child of two. The coroner leant his head wearily on his hand, such cases were so common! The babe's mother came forward to give her evidence—a pale little woman, with thin and hollow cheeks, her eyes red and dim with weeping. She sobbed as she told the coroner that her husband had left her, and she was obliged to support herself and two children. She was out of work, and food had been rather scanty; she had suckled the dead baby as long as she could, but her milk dried up. Two days before, on waking up in the morning, the child she held in her arms was cold and dead. The doctor shrugged his shoulders. Want of food! And the jury returned their verdict, framed in a beautiful and elaborate sentence, in accordance with the evidence.

The last case was a girl of twenty. She had been found in the Thames; a bargee told how he saw a confused black mass floating on the water, and he put a boat-hook in the skirt, tying the body up to the boat while he called the police, he was so used to such things! In the girl's pocket was found a pathetic little letter to the coroner, begging his pardon for the trouble she was causing, saying she had been sent away from her place, and was starving, and had resolved to put an end to her troubles by throwing herself in the river. She was pregnant. The medical man stated that there were signs on the body of very great privation, so the jury returned a verdict that the deceased had committed suicide whilst in a state of temporary insanity!

The coroner stretched his arms and blew his nose, and the jury went their way.

But Mr. Clinton stood outside the mortuary door, meditating, and the coroner's officer remarked that it was a wet day.

"Could I 'ave another look at the bodies?" timidly asked the clerk, stirring himself out of his contemplation.

The coroner's officer looked at him with surprise, and laughed. "Yes, if you like."

Mr. Clinton looked through the glass windows at the bodies, and he carefully examined their faces; he looked at them one after another slowly, and it seemed as if he could not tear himself away. Finally he turned round, his face was very pale, and it had quite a strange expression on it; he felt very sick.

"Thank you!" he said to the coroner's officer, and walked away. But after a few steps he turned back, touching the man on the arm. "D'you 'ave many cases like that?" he asked.

"Why, you look quite upset," said the coroner's officer, with amusement. "I can see you're not used to such things. You'd better go to the pub, opposite, and 'ave three 'aporth of brandy."

"They seemed rather painful cases," said Mr. Clinton, in a low voice.

"Oh, it was a slack day to-day. Nothing like what it is usually this time of year."

"They all died of starvation—starvation, and nothing else."

"I suppose they did, more or less," replied the officer.

"D'you 'ave many cases like that?"

"Starvation cases? Lor' bless you! On a 'eavy day we'll 'ave 'alf a dozen, easy."

"Oh!" said Mr. Clinton.

"Well, I must be getting on with my work," said the officer—they were standing on the doorstep and he looked at the public-house opposite, but Mr. Clinton paid no further attention to him. He began to walk slowly away citywards.

"Well, you are a rummy old file!" said the coroner's officer.

But presently a mist came before Mr. Clinton's eyes, everything seemed suddenly extraordinary, he had an intense pain, and he felt himself falling. He opened his eyes slowly and found himself sitting on a doorstep; a policeman was shaking him, asking what his name was. A woman standing by was holding his top hat; he noticed that his trousers were muddy, and mechanically he pulled out his handkerchief and began to wipe them.

He looked vacantly at the policeman asking questions. The woman asked him if he was better. He motioned her to give him his hat; he put it feebly on his head and, staggering to his feet, walked unsteadily away.

The rain drizzled down impassively, and cabs passing swiftly splashed up the yellow mud. . . .

VI

Mr. Clinton went back to the office; it was his boast that for ten years he had never missed a day. But he was dazed; he did his work mechanically, and so distracted was he that, on going home in the evening, he forgot to remove his paper cuffs, and his wife remarked upon them while they were supping. Mrs. Clinton was a short, stout person, with an appearance of immense determination; her black, shiny hair was parted in the middle—the parting was broad and very white—severely brushed back and gathered into a little knot at the back of the head; her face was red and strongly lined, her eyes spirited, her nose aggressive, her mouth resolute. Everyone has some one procedure which seems most exactly to suit him—a slim youth bathing in a shaded stream, an alderman standing with his back to the fire and his thumbs in the arm-holes of his waistcoat—and Mrs. Clinton expressed her complete self, exhibiting every trait and attribute, on Sunday in church, when she sat in the front pew self-reliantly singing the hymns in the wrong key. It was then that she seemed more than

ever the personification of a full stop. Her morals were above suspicion, and her religion Low Church.

"They've moved into the second 'ouse down," she remarked to her husband. "And Mrs. Tilly's taken 'er summer curtains down at last." Mrs. Clinton spent most of her time in watching her neighbours' movements, and she and her husband always discussed at the supper-table the events of the day, but this time he took no notice of her remark. He pushed away his cold meat with an expression of disgust.

"You don't seem up to the mark to-night, Jimmy," said Mrs. Clinton.

"I served on a jury to-day in place of the governor, and it gave me rather a turn."

"Why, was there anything particular?"

Mr. Clinton crumbled up his bread, rolling it about on the table. "Only some poor things starved to death."

Mrs. Clinton shrugged her shoulders. "Why couldn't they go to the workhouse, I wonder? I've no patience with people like that."

Mr. Clinton looked at her for a moment, then rose from the table. "Well, dear, I think I'll get to bed; I dare say I shall be all right in the morning."

"That's right," said Mrs. Clinton; "you get to bed and I'll bring you something 'ot. I expect you've got a bit of a chill and a good perspiration 'll do you a world of good."

She mixed bad whisky with harmless water and stood over her husband while he patiently drank the boiling mixture. Then she piled a couple of extra blankets on him and went downstairs to have her usual nip, "scotch and cold," before going to bed herself.

All night Mr. Clinton tossed from side to side; the heat was unbearable, and he threw off the clothes. His restlessness became so great that he got out of bed and walked up and down the room —a pathetically ridiculous object in his flannel night-shirt, from which his thin legs protruded grotesquely. Going back to bed, he fell into an uneasy sleep; but, waking or sleeping, he had before his eyes the faces of the three horrible bodies he had seen at the mortuary. He could not blot out the image of the thin, baby face with the pale, open eyes, the white face drawn and thin, hideous in its starved, dead shapelessness. And he saw the drawn, wrinkled face of the old man, with the stubbly beard; looking at it, he felt

the long pain of hunger, the agony of the hopeless morrow. But he shuddered with terror at the thought of the drowned girl with the sunken eyes, the horrible discolouration of putrefaction; and Mr. Clinton buried his face in his pillow, sobbing, sobbing very silently so as not to wake his wife. . . .

The morning came at last and found him feverish and parched, unable to move. Mrs. Clinton sent for the doctor, a slow, cautious Scotchman, in whose wisdom Mrs. Clinton implicitly relied, since he always agreed with her own idea of her children's ailments. This prudent gentleman ventured to assert that Mr. Clinton had caught cold and had something wrong with his lungs. Then, promising to send medicine and come again next day, went off on his rounds. Mr. Clinton grew worse; he became delirious. When his wife, smoothing his pillow, asked him how he felt, he looked at her with glassy eyes.

"Lor' bless you!" he muttered. "On a 'eavy day we'll 'ave 'alf a dozen, easy."

"What's this he's talking about?" asked the doctor, next day.

"'E was serving on a jury the day before yesterday, and my opinion is that it's got on 'is brain," answered Mrs. Clinton.

"Oh, that's nothing. You needn't worry about that. I dare say it'll turn to clothes or religion before he's done. People talk of funny things when they're in that state. He'll probably think he's got two hundred pairs of trousers or a million pounds a year."

A couple of days later the doctor came to the final conclusion that it was a case of typhoid, and pronounced Mr. Clinton very ill. He was indeed; he lay for days, between life and death, on his back, looking at people with dull, unknowing eyes, clutching feebly at the bed-clothes. And for hours he would mutter strange things to himself so quietly that one could not hear. But at last Dame Nature and the Scotch doctor conquered the microbes, and Mr. Clinton became better.

VII

One day Mrs. Clinton was talking to a neighbour in the bedroom; the patient was so quiet that they thought him asleep.

"Yes, I've 'ad a time with 'im, I can tell you," said Mrs. Clinton. "No one knows what I've gone through."

"Well, I must say," said the friend, "you haven't spared yourself; you've nursed him like a professional nurse."

Mrs. Clinton crossed her hands over her stomach and looked at her husband with self-satisfaction. But Mr. Clinton was awake, staring in front of him with wide-open, fixed eyes; various thoughts confusedly ran through his head.

"Isn't 'e looking strange?" whispered Mrs. Clinton.

The two women kept silence, watching him.

"Amy, are you there?" asked Mr. Clinton, suddenly, without turning his eyes.

"Yes, dear. Is there anything you want?"

Mr. Clinton did not reply for several minutes; the women waited in silence.

"Bring me a Bible, Amy," he said at last.

"A Bible, Jimmy?" asked Mrs. Clinton, in astonishment.

"Yes, dear!"

She looked anxiously at her friend.

"Oh, I do 'ope the delirium isn't coming on again," she whispered, and, pretending to smooth his pillow, she passed her hand over his forehead to see if it was hot. "Are you quite comfortable, dear?" she asked, without further allusion to the Bible.

"Yes, Amy, quite!"

"Don't you think you could go to sleep for a little while?"

"I don't feel sleepy, I want to read; will you bring me the Bible?"

Mrs. Clinton looked helplessly at her friend; she feared something was wrong, and she didn't know what to do. But the neighbour, with a significant look, pointed to the *Daily Telegraph,* which was lying on a chair. Mrs. Clinton brightened up and took it to her husband.

"Here's the paper, dear." Mr. Clinton made a slight movement of irritation.

"I don't want it; I want the Bible." Mrs. Clinton looked at her friend more helplessly than ever.

"I've never known 'im ask for such a thing before," she whispered, "and 'e's never missed reading the *Telegraph* a single day since we was married."

"I don't think you ought to read," she said aloud to her husband. "But the doctor'll be here soon, and I'll ask 'im then."

The doctor stroked his chin thoughtfully. "I don't think there'd

be any harm in letting him have a Bible," he said, "but you'd better keep an eye on him. . . . I suppose there's no insanity in the family?"

"No, Doctor, not as far as I know. I've always 'eard that my mother's uncle was very eccentric, but that wouldn't account for this, because we wasn't related before we married."

Mr. Clinton took the Bible, and, turning to the New Testament, began to read. He read chapter after chapter, pausing now and again to meditate, or reading a second time some striking passage, till at last he finished the first gospel. Then he turned to his wife.

"Amy, d'you know, I think I should like to do something for my feller creatures. I don't think we're meant to live for ourselves alone in this world."

Mrs. Clinton was quite overcome; she turned away to hide the tears which suddenly filled her eyes, but the shock was too much for her, and she had to leave the room so that her husband might not see her emotion; she immediately sent for the doctor.

"Oh, Doctor," she said, her voice broken with sobs, "I'm afraid—I'm afraid my poor 'usband's going off 'is 'ead."

And she told him of the incessant reading and the remark Mr. Clinton had just made. The doctor looked grave, and began thinking.

"You're quite sure there's no insanity in the family?" he asked again.

"Not to the best of my belief, Doctor."

"And you've noticed nothing strange in him? His mind hasn't been running on money or clothes?"

"No, Doctor; I wish it 'ad. I shouldn't 'ave thought anything of that; there's something natural in a man talking about stocks and shares and trousers, but I've never 'eard 'im say anything like this before. He was always a wonderfully steady man."

VIII

Mr. Clinton became daily stronger, and soon he was quite well. He resumed his work at the office, and in every way seemed to have regained his old self. He gave utterance to no more startling theories, and the casual observer might have noticed no difference between him and the model clerk of six months back. But Mrs.

Clinton had received too great a shock to look upon her husband with casual eyes, and she noticed in his manner an alteration which disquieted her. He was much more silent than before; he would take his supper without speaking a word, without making the slightest sign to show that he had heard some remark of Mrs. Clinton's. He did not read the paper in the evening as he had been used to do, but would go upstairs to the top of the house and stand by an open window looking at the stars. He had an enigmatical way of smiling which Mrs. Clinton could not understand. Then he had lost his old punctuality—he would come home at all sorts of hours, and, when his wife questioned him, would merely shrug his shoulders and smile strangely. Once he told her that he had been wandering about looking at men's lives.

Mrs. Clinton thought that a very unsatisfactory explanation of his unpunctuality, and after a long consultation with the cautious doctor came to the conclusion that it was her duty to discover what her husband did during the long time that elapsed between his leaving the office and returning home.

So one day, at about six, she stationed herself at the door of the big building in which were Mr. Clinton's offices, and waited. Presently he appeared in the doorway, and after standing for a minute or two on the threshold, ever with the enigmatical smile hovering on his lips, came down the steps and walked slowly along the crowded street. His wife walked behind him; and he was not difficult to follow, for he had lost his old, quick, business-like step, and sauntered along, looking to the right and to the left, carelessly, as if he had not awaiting him at home his duties as the father of a family. . . . After a while he turned down a side street, and his wife followed with growing astonishment; she could not imagine where he was going. Just then a little flower girl passed by and offered him a yellow rose. He stopped and looked at her; Mrs. Clinton could see that she was a grimy little girl, with a shock of unkempt brown hair and a very dirty apron; but Mr. Clinton put his hand on her head and looked into her eyes; then he gave her a penny, and, stooping down, lightly kissed her hair.

"Bless you, my dear!" he said, and passed on.

"Well, I never!" said Mrs. Clinton, quite aghast; and, as she walked by the flower girl, snorted at her and looked so savagely that the poor little maiden quite started. Mr. Clinton walked very

slowly, stopping now and then to look at a couple of women seated on a doorstep, or the children round an ice-cream stall. Mrs. Clinton saw him pay a penny and give an ice to a little child who was looking with longing eyes at its more fortunate companions as they licked out the little glass cups. He remained quite a long while watching half a dozen young girls dancing to the music of a barrel organ, and again, to his wife's disgust, Mr. Clinton gave money.

"We shall end in the work'ouse if this goes on," muttered Mrs. Clinton, and she pursed up her lips more tightly than ever, thinking of the explanation she meant to have when her mate came home.

At last Mr. Clinton came to a narrow slum, down which he turned, and so filthy was it that the lady almost feared to follow. But indignation, curiosity, and a stern sense of duty prevailed. She went along with up-turned nose, making her way carefully between cabbages and other vegetable refuse, sidling up against a house to avoid a dead cat which lay huddled up in the middle of the way, with a great red wound in its head.

Mrs. Clinton was disgusted to see her husband enter a public-house.

"Is this where he gets to?" she said to herself, and, looking through the door, saw him talk with two or three rough men who were standing at the bar, drinking "four 'arf."

But she waited determinedly. She had made up her mind to see the matter to the end, come what might; she was willing to wait all night.

After a time he came out and, going through a narrow passage, made his way into an alley. Then he went straight up to a big-boned, coarse-featured woman in a white apron, who was standing at an open door, and when he had said a few words to her, the two entered the house and the door was closed behind them.

Mrs. Clinton suddenly saw it all.

"I am deceived!" she said tragically, and she crackled with virtuous indignation.

Her first impulse was to knock furiously at the door and force her way in to bear her James away from the clutches of the big-boned siren. But she feared that her rival would meet her with brute force, and the possibility of defeat made her see the unladylikeness of the proceeding. So she turned on her heel, holding up

her skirts and her nose against the moral contamination, and made her way out of the low place. She walked tempestuously down to Fleet Street, jumped fiercely on a 'bus, frantically caught the train to Camberwell, and, having reached her house in the Adonis Road, flung herself furiously down on a chair and gasped:

"Oh!"

Then she got ready for her husband's return.

"Well?" she said, when he came in; and she looked daggers. . . . "Well?"

"I'm afraid I'm later than usual, my dear." It was, in fact, past nine o'clock.

"Don't talk to me!" she replied, with a vigorous jerk of her head. "I know what you've been up to."

"What do you mean, my love?" he gently asked.

She positively snorted with indignation; she had rolled her handkerchief into a ball, and nervously dabbed the palms of her hands with it. "I followed you this afternoon, and I saw you go into that 'ouse with that low woman. What now? Eh?" She spoke with the greatest possible emphasis.

"Woman!" said Mr. Clinton, with a smile. "What are you to me?"

"Don't call me woman!" said Mrs. Clinton very angrily. "What am I to you? I'm your wife, and I've got the marriage certificate in my pocket at this moment." She slapped her pocket loudly. "I'm your wife, and you ought to be ashamed of yourself."

"Wife! You are no more to me than any other woman!"

"And you 'ave the audacity to tell me that to my face! Oh, you—you villain! I won't stand it, I tell you; I won't stand it. I know I can't get a divorce—the laws of England are scandalous—but I'll 'ave a judicious separation. . . . I might have known it, you're all alike, every one of you; that's 'ow you men treat women. You take advantage of their youth and beauty, and then. . . . Oh, you villain! Here 'ave I worked myself to the bone for you and brought up your children, and I don't know what I 'aven't done and now you go and take on with some woman, and leave me. Oh!" She burst into tears. Mr. Clinton still smiled, and there was a curious look in his eyes.

"Woman! woman!" he said, "you know not what you say!" He went up to his wife and laid his hand on her shoulder. "Dry your tears," he said, "and I will tell you of these things."

Mrs. Clinton shook herself angrily, keeping her face buried in her pocket handkerchief, but he turned away without paying more attention to her; then, standing in front of the glass, he looked at himself earnestly and began to speak.

"It was during my illness that my eyes were opened. Lying in bed through those long hours I thought of the poor souls whose tale I 'ad 'eard in the coroner's court. And all night I saw their dead faces. I thought of the misery of mankind and of the 'ardness of men's 'earts. . . . Then a ray of light came to me, and I called for a Bible, and I read, and read; and the light grew into a great glow, and I saw that man was not meant to live for 'imself alone; that there was something else in life, that it was man's duty to 'elp his fellers; and I resolved, when I was well, to do all that in me lay to 'elp the poor and the wretched, and faithfully to carry out those precepts which the Book 'ad taught me."

"Oh dear! oh dear!" sobbed Mrs. Clinton, who had looked up and listened with astonishment to her husband's speech. "Oh dear! oh dear! what is he talking about?"

Mr. Clinton turned towards her and again put his hand on her shoulder.

"And that is 'ow I spend my time, Amy. I go into the most miserable 'ouses, into the dirtiest 'oles, the foulest alleys, and I seek to make men 'appier. I do what I can to 'elp them in their distress, and to show them that brilliant light which I see so gloriously lighting the way before me. And now good-night!" He stretched out his arm, and for a moment let his hand rest above her head; then, turning on his heel, he left the room.

Next day Mrs. Clinton called on the doctor, and told him of her husband's strange behaviour. The doctor slowly and meditatively nodded, then he raised his eyebrows, and with his finger significantly tapped his head. . . .

"Well," he said, "I think you'd better wait a while and see how things go on. I'll just write out a prescription, and you can give him the medicine three times a day after meals," and he ordered the unhappy Mr. Clinton another tonic, which, if it had no effect on that gentleman, considerably reassured his wife.

IX

Mr. Clinton, in fact, became worse. He came home later and later every night, and his wife was disgusted at the state of uncleanness which his curious wanderings brought about. He refused to take the baths which Mrs. Clinton prepared for him. He was more silent than ever, but when he spoke it was in biblical language; and always hovered on his lips the enigmatical smile, and his eyes always had the strange, disconcerting look. Mrs. Clinton perseveringly made him take his medicine, but she lost faith in its power when, one night at twelve, Mr. Clinton brought home with him a very dirty, ragged man, who looked half-starved and smelt distinctly alcoholic.

"Jim," she said, on seeing the miserable object slinking in behind her husband, "Jim, what's that?"

"That, Amy? That is your brother!"

"My brother? What d'you mean?" cried Mrs. Clinton, firing up. "That's no brother of mine. I 'aven't got a brother."

"It's your brother and my brother. Be good to him."

"I tell you it isn't my brother," repeated Mrs. Clinton; "my brother Adolphus died when he was two years old, and that's the only brother I ever 'ad."

Mr. Clinton merely looked at her with his usual gentle expression, and she asked angrily:

"What 'ave you brought 'im 'ere for?"

"'E is 'ungry, and I am going to give 'im food; 'e is 'omeless, and I am going to give 'im shelter."

"Shelter? Where?"

"Here, in my 'ouse, in my bed."

"In my bed!" screamed Mrs. Clinton. "Not if I know it! 'Ere, you," she said, addressing the man, and pushing past her husband. "Out you get! I'm not going to 'ave tramps and loafers in my 'ouse. Get out!" Mrs. Clinton was an energetic woman, and a strong one. Catching hold of her husband's stick, and flourishing it, she opened the front door.

"Amy! Amy!" expostulated Mr. Clinton.

"Now, then, you be quiet. I've 'ad about enough of you! Get on out, will you?"

The man made a rush for the door, and as he scrambled down the steps she caught him a smart blow on the back, and slammed the door behind him. Then, returning to the sitting-room, she sank panting on a chair. Mr. Clinton slowly recovered from his surprise.

"Woman," he said, this being now his usual mode of address—he spoke solemnly and sadly—"you 'ave cast out your brother, you 'ave cast out your husband, you 'ave cast out yourself."

"Don't talk to me!" said Mrs. Clinton, very wrathfully. "It's bedtime now; come along upstairs."

"I will not come to your bed again. You 'ave refused it to one who was better than I; and why should I 'ave it? Go, woman; go and leave me."

"Now, then, don't come trying your airs on me," said Mrs. Clinton. "They won't wash. Come up to bed."

"I tell you I will not," replied Mr. Clinton, decisively. "Go, woman, and leave me!"

"Well, if I do, I shan't leave the light; so there!" she said spitefully, and, taking the lamp, left Mr. Clinton in darkness.

Mrs. Clinton was not henceforth on the very best of terms with her husband, but he always treated her with his accustomed gentleness, though he insisted on spending his nights on the dining-room sofa.

But perhaps the most objectionable to Mrs. Clinton of all her good man's eccentricities was that he no longer gave her his week's money every Saturday afternoon as he had been accustomed to do; the coldness between them made her unwilling to say anything about it, but the approach of quarter day forced her to pocket her dignity and ask for the money.

"Oh, James!"—she no longer called him Jimmy—"will you give me the money for the rent?"

"Money?" he answered with the usual smile on his lips. "I 'ave no money."

"What d'you mean? You've not given me a farthing for ten weeks."

"I 'ave given it to those who want it more than I."

"You don't mean to tell me that you've given your salary away?"

"Yes, dear."

Mrs. Clinton groaned.

"Oh, you're dotty! . . . I can understand giving a threepenny bit, or even sixpence, at the offertory on Sunday at church, and of course one 'as to give Christmas-boxes to the tradesmen; but to give your whole salary away! 'Aven't you got anything left?"

"No!"

"You—you aggravating fool! And I'll be bound you gave it to lazy loafers and tramps and Lord knows what!"

Mr. Clinton did not answer; his wife walked rapidly backwards and forwards, wringing her hands.

"Well, look here, James," she said at last. "It's no use crying over spilt milk; but from this day you just give me your salary the moment you receive it. D'you hear? I tell you I will not 'ave any more of your nonsense."

"I shall get no more salaries," he quietly remarked.

Mrs. Clinton looked at him; he was quite calm, and smilingly returned her glance.

"What do you mean by that?" she asked.

"I am no longer at the office."

"James! You 'aven't been sacked?" she screamed.

"Oh, they said I did not any longer properly attend to my work. They said I was careless, and that I made mistakes; they complained that I was unpunctual, that I went late and came away early; and one day, because I 'adn't been there the day before, they told me to leave. I was watching at the bedside of a man who was dying and 'ad need of me; so 'ow could I go? But I didn't really mind; the office 'indered me in my work."

"But what are you going to do now?" gasped Mrs. Clinton.

"I 'ave my work; that is more important than ten thousand offices."

"But 'ow are you going to earn your living? What's to become of us?"

"Don't trouble me about those things. Come with me, and work for the poor."

"James, think of the children!"

"What are your children to me more than any other children?"

"But—"

"Woman, I tell you not to trouble me about these things. 'Ave we not money enough, and to spare?"

He waved his hand and, putting on his top hat, which looked

more than ever in need of restoration, went out, leaving his wife in a perfect agony.

There was worse to follow. Coming home a few days later, Mr. Clinton told his wife that he wished to speak with her.

"I 'ave been looking into my books," he said, "and I find that we have invested in various securities a sum of nearly seven 'undred pounds."

"Thank 'Eaven for that!" answered his wife. "It's the only thing that'll save us from starvation now that you moon about all day, instead of working like a decent man."

"Well, I 'ave been thinking, and I 'ave been reading; and I 'ave found it written—'Give all and follow me.' "

"Well, there's nothing new in that," said Mrs. Clinton, viciously. "I've known that text ever since I was a child."

"And as it were a Spirit 'as come to me and said that I too must give all. In short, I 'ave determined to sell out my stocks and my shares; my breweries are seven points 'igher than when I bought them; I knew it was a good investment. I am going to realise everything; I am going to take the money in my hand and I am going to give it to the poor."

Mrs. Clinton burst into tears.

"Do not weep," he said solemnly. "It is my duty, and it is a pleasant one. Oh, what joy to make a 'undred people 'appy; to relieve a poor man who is starving, to give a breath of country air to little children who are dying for the want of it, to 'elp the poor, to feed the 'ungry, to clothe the naked! Oh, if I only 'ad a million pounds!" He stretched out his arms in a gesture of embrace, and looked towards heaven with an ecstatic smile upon his lips.

It was too serious a matter for Mrs. Clinton to waste any words on; she ran upstairs, put on her bonnet, and quickly walked to her friend the doctor.

He looked graver than ever when she told him.

"Well," he said, "I'm afraid it's very serious. I've never heard of anyone doing such a thing before. . . . Of course I've known of people who have left all their money to charities after their death, when they didn't want it; but it couldn't ever occur to a normal, healthy man to do it in his lifetime."

"But what shall I do, Doctor?" Mrs. Clinton was almost in hysterics.

"Well, Mrs. Clinton, d'you know the clergyman of the parish?"

"I know Mr. Evans, the curate, very well; he's a very nice gentleman."

"Perhaps you could get him to have a talk with your husband. The fact is, it's a sort of religious mania he's got, and perhaps a clergyman could talk him out of it. Anyhow, it's worth trying."

Mrs. Clinton straightway went to Mr. Evans's rooms, explained to him the case, and settled that on the following day he should come and see what he could do with her husband.

X

In expectation of the curate's visit, Mrs. Clinton tidied the house and adorned herself. It has been said that she was a woman of taste, and so she was. The mantelpiece and looking-glass were artistically draped with green muslin, and this she proceeded to arrange, tying and carefully forming the yellow satin ribbon with which it was relieved. The chairs were covered with cretonne which might have come from the Tottenham Court Road, and these she placed in positions of careless and artistic confusion, smoothing down the antimacassars which were now her pride, as the silk petticoat from which she had manufactured them had been once her glory. For the flower-pots she made fresh coverings of red tissue paper, rearranged the ornaments gracefully scattered about on little Japanese tables; then, after pausing a moment to admire her work and see that nothing had been left undone, she went upstairs to perform her own toilet. . . . In less than half an hour she reappeared, holding herself in a dignified posture, with her head slightly turned to one side and her hands meekly folded in front of her, stately and collected as Juno, a goddess in black satin. Her dress was very elegant; it might have typified her own life, for in its original state of virgin whiteness it had been her wedding garment; then it was dyed purple, and might have betokened a sense of change and coming responsibilities; lastly it was black, to signify the burden of a family, and the seriousness of life. No one had realised so intensely as Mrs. Clinton the truth of the poet's words. Life is not an empty dream. She took out her handkerchief, redolent with lascivious patchouli, and placed it in her bosom—a spot of whiteness against the black. . . . She sat herself down to wait.

There was a knock and a ring at the door, timid, as befitted a clergyman; and the servant-girl showed in Mr. Evans. He was a thin and short young men, red-faced, with a long nose and weak eyes, looking underfed and cold, keeping his shoulders screwed up in a perpetual shiver. He was an earnest, God-fearing man, spending much money in charities, and waging constant war against the encroachments of the Scarlet Woman.

"I think I'll just take my coat off, if you don't mind, Mrs. Clinton," he said, after the usual greetings. He folded it carefully, and hung it over the back of a chair; then, coming forward, he sat down and rubbed the back of his hands.

"I asked my 'usband to stay in because you wanted to see 'im, but he would go out. 'Owever"—Mrs. Clinton always chose her language on such occasions—"'owever, 'e's promised to return at four, and I will say this for 'im, he never breaks 'is word."

"Oh, very well!"

"May I 'ave the pleasure of offering you a cup of tea, Mr. Evans?"

The curate's face brightened up.

"Oh, thank you so much!" And he rubbed his hands more energetically than ever.

Tea was brought in, and they drank it, talking of parish matters, Mrs. Clinton discreetly trying to pump the curate. Was it really true that Mrs. Palmer of No. 17 Adonis Road drank so terribly?

At last Mr. Clinton came, and his wife glided out of the room, leaving the curate to convert him. There was a little pause while Mr. Evans took stock of the clerk.

"Well, Mr. Clinton," he said finally, "I've come to talk to you about yourself. . . . Your wife tells me that you have adopted certain curious views on religious matters; and she wishes me to have some conversation with you about them."

"You are a man of God," replied Mr. Clinton; "I am at your service."

Mr. Evans, on principle, objected to the use of the Deity's name out of church, thinking it a little blasphemous, but he said nothing.

"Well," he said, "of course, religion is a very good thing; in fact, it is the very best thing; but it must not be abused, Mr. Clinton," and he repeated gravely, as if his interlocutor were a

naughty schoolboy—"it mustn't be abused. Now, I want to know exactly what your views are."

Mr. Clinton smiled gently.

"I 'ave no views, sir. The only rule I 'ave for guidance is this—love thy neighbour as thyself."

"Hum!" murmured the curate; there was really nothing questionable in that, but he was just slightly prejudiced against a man who made such a quotation; it sounded a little priggish.

"But your wife tells me that you've been going about with all sorts of queer people?"

"I found that there was misery and un'appiness among people, and I tried to relieve it."

"Of course, I strongly approve of district visiting; I do a great deal of it myself; but you've been going about with public-house loafers and—bad women."

"Is it not said: 'I am not come to call the righteous, but sinners to repentance'?"

"No doubt," answered Mr. Evans, slightly frowning. "But obviously one isn't meant to do that to such an extent as to be dismissed from one's place."

"My wife 'as posted you well up in all my private affairs."

"Well, I don't think you can have done well to be sent away from your office."

"Is it not said: 'Forsake all and follow me'?"

Decidedly this was bad form, and Mr. Evans, pursing up his lips and raising his eyebrows, was silent. "That's the worst of these half-educated people," he said to himself; "they get some idea in their heads which they don't understand, and, of course, they do idiotic things. . . ."

"Well, to pass over all that," he added out loud, "apparently you've been spending your money on these people to such an extent that your wife and children are actually inconvenienced by it."

"I 'ave clothed the naked," said Mr. Clinton, looking into the curate's eyes; "I 'ave visited the sick; I 'ave given food to 'im that was an 'ungered, and drink to 'im that was athirst."

"Yes, yes, yes; that's all very well, but you should always remember that charity begins at home. . . . I shouldn't have anything to say to a rich man's doing these things, but it's positively wicked for you to do them. Don't you understand that? And last

of all, your wife tells me that you're realising your property with the idea of giving it away."

"It's perfectly true," said Mr. Clinton.

Mr. Evans's mind was too truly pious for a wicked expletive to cross it; but a bad man expressing the curate's feeling would have said that Mr. Clinton was a damned fool. "Well, don't you see that it's a perfectly ridiculous and unheard-of thing?" he asked emphatically.

"'Sell all that thou 'ast, and distribute unto the poor.' It is in the Gospel of St. Luke. Do you know it?"

"Of course I know it, but, naturally, these things aren't to be taken quite literally."

"It is clearly written. What makes you say it is not to be taken literally?"

Mr. Evans shrugged his shoulders impatiently.

"Why, don't you see it would be impossible? The world couldn't go on. How do you expect your children to live if you give this money away?"

"'Look at the lilies of the field. They toil not, neither do they spin; yet Solomon in all his glory was not arrayed as one of these. . . .'"

"Oh, my dear sir, you make me lose my patience. You're full of the hell-fire platitudes of a park spouter, and you think it's religion. . . . I tell you all these things are allegorical. Don't you understand that? You mustn't carry them out to the letter. They are not meant to be taken in that way."

Mr. Clinton smiled a little pitifully at the curate.

"And think of yourself—one must think of oneself. 'God helps those who help themselves.' How are you going to exist when this little money of yours is gone? You'll simply have to go to the workhouse. . . . It's absurd, I tell you."

Mr. Clinton took no further notice of the curate, but he broke into a loud chant:

"'Lay not up for yourselves treasures upon the earth, where moth and rust doth corrupt, and where thieves break through and steal. But lay up for yourselves treasures in heaven, where neither moth nor rust doth corrupt, and where thieves do not break through nor steal.'" Then, turning on the unhappy curate, he stretched out his arm and pointed his finger at him. "Last Sunday," he said, "I 'eard you read those very words from the chancel

steps. Go! go! I tell you, go! You are a bad man, a wolf in sheep's clothing—go!" Mr. Clinton walked up to him threateningly, and the curate, with a gasp of astonishment and indignation, fled from the room.

He met Mrs. Clinton outside.

"I can't do anything with him at all," he said angrily. "I've never heard such things in my life. He's either mad or he's got into the hands of the Dissenters. That's the only explanation I can offer."

Then, to quiet his feelings, he called on a wealthy female parishioner, with whom he was a great favourite, because she thought him "such a really pious man," and it was not till he had drunk two cups of tea that he recovered his equilibrium.

XI

Mrs. Clinton was at her wit's end. Her husband had sold out his shares, and the money was lying at the bank ready to be put to its destined use. Visions of debt and bankruptcy presented themselves to her. She saw her black satin dress in the ruthless clutches of a pawnbroker, the house and furniture sold over her head, the children down at heel, and herself driven to work for her living—needlework, nursing, charing—what might not things come to? However, she went to the doctor and told him of the failure of their scheme.

"I've come to the end of my tether, Mrs. Clinton; I really don't know what to do. The only thing I can suggest is that a mental specialist should examine into the state of his mind. I really think he's wrong in his head, and, you know, it may be necessary for your welfare and his own that he be kept under restriction."

"Well, Doctor," answered Mrs. Clinton, putting her handkerchief up to her eyes and beginning to cry, "well, Doctor, of course I shouldn't like him to be shut up—it seems a terrible thing, and I shall never 'ave a moment's peace all the rest of my life; but if he must be shut up, for Heaven's sake let it be done at once, before the money's gone." And here she began to sob very violently.

The doctor said he would immediately write to the specialist,

so that they might hold a consultation on Mr. Clinton the very next day.

So, the following morning, Mrs. Clinton again put on her black satin dress and, further, sent to her grocer's for a bottle of sherry, her inner consciousness giving her to understand that specialists expected something of the kind. . . .

The specialist came. He was a tall, untidily dressed man, with his hair wild and straggling, as if he had just got out of bed. He was very clever, and very impatient of stupid people, and he seldom met anyone whom he did not think in one way or another intensely stupid.

Mr. Clinton, as before, had gone out, but Mrs. Clinton did her best to entertain the two doctors. The specialist, who talked most incessantly himself, was extremely impatient of other people's conversation.

"Why on earth don't people see that they're much more interesting when they hold their tongues than when they speak?" he was in the habit of saying, and immediately would pour out a deluge of words, emphasising and explaining the point, giving instances of its truth. . . .

"You must see a lot of strange things, Doctor," said Mrs. Clinton, amiably.

"Yes," answered the specialist.

"I think it must be very interesting to be a doctor," said Mrs. Clinton.

"Yes, yes."

"You *must* see a lot of strange things."

"Yes, yes," repeated the doctor, and as Mrs. Clinton went on complacently he frowned and drummed his fingers on the table and looked to the right and left. "When is the man coming in?" he asked impatiently.

And at last he could not contain himself.

"If you don't mind, Mrs. Clinton, I should like to talk to your doctor alone about the case. You can wait in the next room."

"I'm sure I don't wish to intrude," said Mrs. Clinton, bridling up, and she rose in a dignified manner from her chair. She thought his manners were distinctly queer. "But, of course," she said to a friend afterwards, "he's a genius, there's no mistaking it, and people like that are always very eccentric."

"What an insufferable woman!" he began, when the lady had

retired, talking very rapidly, only stopping to take an occasional breath. "I thought she was going on all night. She's enough to drive the man mad. One couldn't get a word in edgeways. Why on earth doesn't this man come? Just like these people, they don't think that my time's valuable. I expect she drinks. Shocking, you know, these women, how they drink!" And, still talking, he looked at his watch for the eighth time in ten minutes.

"Well, my man," he said, as Mr. Clinton at last came in, "what are you complaining of? . . . One moment," he added, as Mr. Clinton was about to reply. He opened his notebook and took out a stylographic pen. "Now, I'm ready for you. What are you complaining of?"

"I'm complaining that the world is out of joint," answered Mr. Clinton, with a smile.

The specialist raised his eyebrows and significantly looked at the family doctor.

"It's astonishing how much you can get by a well-directed question," he said to him, taking no notice of Mr. Clinton. "Some people go floundering about for hours, but, you see, by one question I get on the track." Turning to the patient again, he said, "Ah! and do you see things?"

"Certainly; I see you."

"I don't mean that," impatiently said the specialist. "Distinctly stupid, you know," he added to his colleague. "I mean, do you see things that other people don't see?"

"Alas! yes; I see Folly stalking abroad on a 'obby-'orse."

"Do you really? Anything else?" said the doctor, making a note of the fact.

"I see Wickedness and Vice beating the land with their wings."

"Sees things beating with their wings," wrote down the doctor.

"I see misery and un'appiness everywhere."

"Indeed!" said the doctor. *"Has delusions.* Do you think your wife puts things in your tea?"

"Yes."

"Ah!" joyfully uttered the doctor, "that's what I wanted to get at—*thinks people are trying to poison him.* What is it they put in, my man?"

"Milk and sugar," answered Mr. Clinton.

"Very dull mentally," said the specialist, in an undertone, to his colleague. "Well, I don't think we need go into any more

details. There's no doubt about it, you know. That curious look in his eyes, and the smile—the smile's quite typical. It all clearly points to insanity. And then that absurd idea of giving his money to the poor! I've heard of people taking money away from the poor, there's nothing mad in that; but the other, why, it's a proof of insanity itself. And then your account of his movements! His giving ice-creams to children. Most pernicious things, those ice-creams! The Government ought to put a stop to them. Extraordinary idea to think of reforming the world with ice-cream! Post-enteric insanity, you know. Mad as a hatter! Well, well, I must be off." Still talking, he put on his hat and talked all the way downstairs, and finally talked himself out of the house.

The family doctor remained behind to see Mrs. Clinton.

"Yes, it's just as I said," he told her. "He's not responsible for his actions. I think he's been insane ever since his illness. When you think of his behaviour since then—his going among those common people and trying to reform them, and his ideas about feeding the hungry and clothing the naked, and finally wanting to give his money to the poor—it all points to a completely deranged mind."

Mrs. Clinton heaved a deep sigh. "And what do you think 'ad better be done now?" she asked.

"Well, I'm very sorry, Mrs. Clinton; of course it's a great blow to you; but really I think arrangements had better be made for him to be put under restraint."

Mrs. Clinton began to cry, and the doctor looked at her compassionately.

"Ah, well," she said at last, "if it must be done, I suppose it 'ad better be done at once; and I shall be able to save the money after all." At the thought of this she dried her tears.

The moral is plain.

DE AMICITIA

(1899)

I

They were walking home from the theatre.

"Well, Mr. White," said Valentia, "I think it was just fine."

"It was magnificent!" replied Mr. White.

And they were separated for a moment by the crowd, streaming up from the Français towards the Opéra and the Boulevards.

"I think, if you don't mind," she said, "I'll take your arm, so that we shouldn't get lost."

He gave her his arm, and they walked through the Louvre and over the river on their way to the Latin Quarter.

Valentia was an art student and Ferdinand White was a poet. Ferdinand considered Valentia the only woman who had ever been able to paint, and Valentia told Ferdinand that he was the only man she had met who knew anything about Art without being himself an artist. On her arrival in Paris, a year before, she had immediately inscribed herself, at the offices of the New York *Herald,* Valentia Stewart, Cincinnati, Ohio, U.S.A. She settled down in a respectable *pension,* and within a week was painting vigorously. Ferdinand White arrived from Oxford at about the same time, hired a dirty room in a shabby hotel, ate his meals at cheap restaurants in the Boulevard St. Michel, read Stéphane Mallarmé, and flattered himself that he was leading *"la vie de Bohême."*

After two months, the Fates brought the pair together, and Ferdinand began to take his meals at Valentia's *pension.* They went to the museums together; and in the Sculpture Gallery at the Louvre, Ferdinand would discourse on ancient Greece in gen-

eral and on Plato in particular, while among the pictures Valentia would lecture on tones and values and chiaroscuro. Ferdinand renounced Ruskin and all his works; Valentia read the *Symposium.* Frequently in the evening they went to the theatre; sometimes to the Français, but more often to the Odéon; and after the performance they would discuss the play, its art, its technique—above all, its ethics. Ferdinand explained the piece he had in contemplation, and Valentia talked of the picture she meant to paint for next year's Salon; and the lady told her friends that her companion was the cleverest man she had met in her life, while he told his that she was the only really sympathetic and intelligent girl he had ever known. Thus were united in bonds of amity, Great Britain on the one side and the United States of America and Ireland on the other.

But when Ferdinand spoke of Valentia to the few Frenchmen he knew, they asked him:

"But this Miss Stewart—is she pretty?"

"Certainly—in her American way; a long face, with the hair parted in the middle and hanging over the nape of the neck. Her mouth is quite classic."

"And have you never kissed the classic mouth?"

"I? Never!"

"Has she a good figure?"

"Admirable!"

"And yet— Oh, you English!" And they smiled and shrugged their shoulders as they said, "How English!"

"But, my good fellow," cried Ferdinand, in execrable French, "you don't understand. We are friends, the best of friends."

They shrugged their shoulders more despairingly than ever.

II

They stood on the bridge and looked at the water and the dark masses of the houses on the Latin side, with the twin towers of Notre Dame rising dimly behind them. Ferdinand thought of the Thames at night, with the barges gliding slowly down, and the twinkling of the lights along the Embankment.

"It must be a little like that in Holland," she said, "but without the lights and with greater stillness."

"When do you start?"

She had been making preparations for spending the summer in a little village near Amsterdam, to paint.

"I can't go now," cried Valentia. "Corrie Sayles is going home, and there's no one else I can go with. And I can't go alone. Where are you going?"

"I? I have no plans. . . . I never make plans."

They paused, looking at the reflections in the water. Then she said:

"I don't see why you shouldn't come to Holland with me!"

He did not know what to think; he knew she had been reading the *Symposium*.

"After all," she said, "there's no reason why one shouldn't go away with a man as well as with a woman."

His French friends would have suggested that there were many reasons why one should go away with a woman rather than a man; but, like his companion, Ferdinand looked at it in the light of pure friendship.

"When one comes to think of it, I really don't see why we shouldn't. And the mere fact of staying at the same hotel can make no difference to either of us. We shall both have our work —you your painting, and I my play."

As they considered it, the idea was distinctly pleasing; they wondered that it had not occurred to them before. Sauntering homewards, they discussed the details, and in half an hour had decided on the plan of their journey, the date, and the train.

Next day Valentia went to say good-bye to the old French painter whom all the American girls called Popper. She found him in a capacious dressing-gown, smoking cigarettes.

"Well, my dear," he said, "what news?"

"I'm going to Holland to paint windmills."

"A very laudable ambition. With your mother?"

"My good Popper, my mother's in Cincinnati. I'm going with Mr. White."

"With Mr. White?" He raised his eyebrows. "You are very frank about it."

"Why—what do you mean?"

He put on his glasses and looked at her carefully.

"Does it not seem to you a rather—curious thing for a young

girl of your age to go away with a young man of the age of Mr. Ferdinand White?"

"Good gracious me! One would think I was doing something that had never been done before!"

"Oh, many a young man has gone travelling with a young woman, but they generally start by a night train, and arrive at the station in different cabs."

"But surely, Popper, you don't mean to insinuate— Mr. White and I are going to Holland as friends."

"Friends!"

He looked at her more curiously than ever.

"One can have a man friend as well as a girl friend," she continued. "And I don't see why he shouldn't be just as good a friend."

"The danger is that he become too good."

"You misunderstand me entirely, Popper; we are friends, and nothing but friends."

"You are entirely off your head, my child."

"Ah! you're a Frenchman, you can't understand these things. We are different."

"I imagine that you are human beings, even though England and America respectively had the intense good fortune of seeing your birth."

"We're human beings—and more than that, we're nineteenth-century human beings. Love is not everything. It is a part of one—perhaps the lower part—an accessory to man's life, needful for the continuation of the species."

"You use such difficult words, my dear."

"There is something higher and nobler and purer than love—there is friendship. Ferdinand White is my friend. I have the amplest confidence in him. I am certain that no unclean thought has ever entered his head."

She spoke quite heatedly, and as she flushed up, the old painter thought her astonishingly handsome. Then she added as an afterthought:

"We despise passion. Passion is ugly; it is grotesque."

The painter stroked his imperial and faintly smiled.

"My child, you must permit me to tell you that you are foolish. Passion is the most lovely thing in the world; without it we should not paint beautiful pictures. It is passion that makes a woman

of a society lady; it is passion that makes a man even of—an art critic."

"We do not want it," she said. "We worship Venus Urania. We are all spirit and soul."

"You have been reading Plato; soon you will read Zola."

He smiled again, and lit another cigarette.

"Do you disapprove of my going?" she asked after a little silence.

He paused and looked at her. Then he shrugged his shoulders.

"On the contrary, I approve. It is foolish, but that is no reason why you should not do it. After all, folly is the great attribute of man. No judge is as grave as an owl; no soldier fighting for his country flies as rapidly as the hare. You may be strong, but you are not so strong as a horse; you may be gluttonous, but you cannot eat like a boa-constrictor. But there is no beast that can be as foolish as man. And since one should always do what one can do best—be foolish. Strive for folly above all things. Let the height of your ambition be the pointed cap with the golden bells. So, *bon voyage!* I will come and see you off to-morrow."

The painter arrived at the station with a box of sweets, which he handed to Valentia with a smile. He shook Ferdinand's hand warmly and muttered under his breath:

"Silly fool! he's thinking of friendship too!"

Then, as the train steamed out, he waved his hand and cried:

"Be foolish! Be foolish!"

He walked slowly out of the station, and sat down at a café. He lit a cigarette, and, sipping his absinthe, said:

"Imbeciles!"

III

They arrived at Amsterdam in the evening, and, after dinner, gathered together their belongings and crossed the Ij as the moon shone over the waters; then they got into the little steam tram and started for Monnickendam. They stood side by side on the platform of the carriage and watched the broad meadows bathed in moonlight, the formless shapes of the cattle lying on the grass, and the black outlines of the mills; they passed by a long, sleeping canal, and they stopped at little, silent villages. At last they entered the dead town, and the tram put them down at the hotel door.

Next morning, when she was half-dressed, Valentia threw open the window of her room, and looked out into the garden. Ferdinand was walking about, dressed as befitted the place and season—in flannels—with a huge white hat on his head. She could not help thinking him very handsome—and she took off the blue skirt she had intended to work in, and put on a dress of muslin all bespattered with coloured flowers, and she took in her hand a flat straw hat with red ribbons.

"You look like a Dresden shepherdess," he said, as they met.

They had breakfast in the garden beneath the trees; and as she poured out his tea, she laughed, and with the American accent which he was beginning to think made English so harmonious, said:

"I reckon this about takes the shine out of Paris."

They had agreed to start work at once, losing no time, for they wanted to have a lot to show on their return to France, that their scheme might justify itself. Ferdinand wished to accompany Valentia on her search for the picturesque, but she would not let him; so, after breakfast, he sat himself down in the summer-house, and spread out all round him his nice white paper, lit his pipe, cut his quills, and proceeded to the evolution of a masterpiece. Valentia tied the red strings of her sun-bonnet under her chin, selected a sketchbook, and sallied forth.

At luncheon they met, and Valentia told of a little bit of canal, with an old windmill on one side of it, which she had decided to paint, while Ferdinand announced that he had settled on the names of his *dramatis personae*. In the afternoon they returned to their work, and at night, tired with the previous day's travelling, went to bed soon after dinner.

So passed the second day; and the third day, and the fourth; till the end of the week came, and they had worked diligently. They were both of them rather surprised at the ease with which they became accustomed to their life.

"How absurd all this fuss is," said Valentia, "that people make about the differences of the sexes! I am sure it is only habit."

"We have ourselves to prove that there is nothing in it," he replied. "You know, it is an interesting experiment that we are making."

She had not looked at it in that light before.

"Perhaps it is. We may be the forerunners of a new era."

"The Edisons of a new communion!"

"I shall write and tell Monsieur Rollo all about it."

In the course of the letter, she said:

"Sex is a morbid instinct. Out here, in the calmness of the canal and the broad meadows, it never enters one's head. I do not think of Ferdinand as a man—"

She looked up at him as she wrote the words. He was reading a book and she saw him in profile, with the head bent down. Through the leaves the sun lit up his face with a soft light that was almost green, and it occurred to her that it would be interesting to paint him.

"I do not think of Ferdinand as a man; to me he is a companion. He has a wider experience than a woman, and he talks of different things. Otherwise I see no difference. On his part, the idea of my sex never occurs to him, and far from being annoyed as an ordinary woman might be, I am proud of it. It shows me that, when I chose a companion, I chose well. To him I am not a woman; I am a man."

And she finished with a repetition of Ferdinand's remark:

"We are the Edisons of a new communion!"

When Valentia began to paint her companion's portrait, they were naturally much more together. And they never grew tired of sitting in the pleasant garden under the trees, while she worked on her canvas and green shadows fell on the profile of Ferdinand White. They talked of many things. After a while they became less reserved about their private concerns. Valentia told Ferdinand about her home in Ohio, and about her people; and Ferdinand spoke of the country parsonage in which he had spent his childhood, and the public school, and lastly of Oxford and the strange, happy days when he had learnt to read Plato and Walter Pater. . . .

At last Valentia threw aside her brushes and leant back with a sigh.

"It is finished!"

Ferdinand rose and stretched himself, and went to look at his portrait. He stood before it for a while, and then he placed his hand on Valentia's shoulder.

"You are a genius, Miss Stewart."

She looked up at him.

"Ah, Mr. White, I was inspired by you. It is more your work than mine."

IV

In the evening they went out for a stroll. They wandered through the silent street; in the darkness they lost the quaintness of the red brick houses, contrasting with the bright yellow of the paving, but it was even quieter than by day. The street was very broad, and it wound about from east to west and from west to east, and at last it took them to the tiny harbour. Two fishing smacks were basking on the water, moored to the side, and the Zuyder Zee was covered with the innumerable reflections of the stars. On one of the boats a man was sitting at the prow, fishing, and now and then, through the darkness, one saw the red glow of his pipe; by his side, huddled up on a sail, lay a sleeping boy. The other boat seemed deserted. Ferdinand and Valentia stood for a long time watching the fisher, and he was so still that they wondered whether he too were sleeping. They looked across the sea, and in the distance saw the dim lights of Marken, the island of fishers. They wandered on again through the street, and now the lights in the windows were extinguished one by one, and sleep came over the town; and the quietness was even greater than before. They walked on, and their footsteps made no sound. They felt themselves alone in the dead city, and they did not speak.

At length they came to a canal gliding towards the sea; they followed it inland, and here the darkness was equal to the silence. Great trees that had been planted when William of Orange was king in England threw their shade over the water, shutting out the stars. They wandered along on the soft earth, they could not hear themselves walk—and they did not speak.

They came to a bridge over the canal and stood on it, looking at the water and the trees above them, and the water and the trees below them—and they did not speak.

Then out of the darkness came another darkness, and gradually loomed forth the heaviness of a barge. Noiselessly it glided down the stream, very slowly; at the end of it a boy stood at the tiller,

steering; and it passed beneath them and beyond, till it lost itself in the night, and again they were alone.

They stood side by side, leaning against the parapet, looking down at the water. . . . And from the water rose up Love, and Love fluttered down from the trees, and Love was borne along upon the night air. Ferdinand did not know what was happening to him; he felt Valentia by his side, and he drew closer to her, till her dress touched his legs and the silk of her sleeve rubbed against his arm. It was so dark that he could not see her face; he wondered of what she was thinking. She made a little movement and to him came a faint wave of the scent she wore. Presently two forms passed by on the bank and they saw a lover with his arm round a girl's waist, and then they too were hidden in the darkness. Ferdinand trembled as he spoke.

"Only Love is waking!"

"And we!" she said.

"And—you!"

He wondered why she said nothing. Did she understand? He put his hand on her arm.

"Valentia!"

He had never called her by her Christian name before. She turned her face towards him.

"What do you mean?"

"Oh, Valentia, I love you! I can't help it."

A sob burst from her.

"Didn't you understand," he said, "all those hours that I sat for you while you painted, and these long nights in which we wandered by the water?"

"I thought you were my friend."

"I thought so too. When I sat before you and watched you paint, and looked at your beautiful hair and your eyes, I thought I was your friend. And I looked at the lines of your body beneath your dress. And when it pleased me to carry your easel and walk with you, I thought it was friendship. Only to-night I know I am in love. Oh, Valentia, I am so glad!"

She could not keep back her tears. Her bosom heaved, and she wept.

"You are a woman," he said. "Did you not see?"

"I am so sorry," she said, her voice all broken. "I thought we

were such good friends. I was so happy. And now you have spoilt it all."

"Valentia, I love you."

"I thought our friendship was so good and pure. And I felt so strong in it. It seemed to me so beautiful."

"Did you think I was less a man than the fisherman you see walking beneath the trees at night?"

"It is all over now," she sighed.

"What do you mean?"

"I can't stay here with you alone."

"You're not going away?"

"Before, there was no harm in our being together at the hotel; but now—"

"Oh, Valentia, don't leave me. I can't—I can't live without you."

She heard the unhappiness in his voice. She turned to him again and laid her two hands on his shoulders.

"Why can't you forget it all, and let us be good friends again? Forget that you are a man. A woman can remain with a man forever, and always be content to walk and read and talk with him, and never think of anything else. Can you forget it, Ferdinand? You will make me so happy."

He did not answer, and for a long time they stood on the bridge in silence. At last he sighed—a heart-broken sigh.

"Perhaps you're right. It may be better to pretend that we are friends. If you like, we will forget all this."

Her heart was too full; she could not answer; but she held out her hands to him. He took them in his own, and, bending down, kissed them.

Then they walked home, side by side, without speaking.

V

Next morning Valentia received M. Rollo's answer to her letter. He apologised for his delay in answering.

"You are a philosopher," he said—she could see the little snigger with which he had written the words—*"You are a philosopher, and I was afraid lest my reply should disturb the course of your reflections on friendship. I confess that I did not entirely under-*

stand your letter, but I gathered that the sentiments were correct, and it gave me great pleasure to know that your experiment has had such excellent results. I gather that you have not yet discovered that there is more than a verbal connection between Friendship and Love."

The reference is to the French equivalents of those states of mind.

"But to speak seriously, dear child. You are young and beautiful now, but not so very many years shall pass before your lovely skin becomes coarse and muddy, and your teeth yellow, and the wrinkles appear about your mouth and eyes. You have not so very many years before you in which to collect sensations, and the recollection of one's loves is, perhaps, the greatest pleasure left to one's old age. To be virtuous, my dear, is admirable, but there are so many interpretations of virtue. For myself, I can say that I have never regretted the temptations to which I succumbed, but often the temptations I have resisted. Therefore, love, love, love! And remember that if love at sixty in a man is sometimes pathetic, in a woman at forty it is always ridiculous. Therefore, take your youth in both hands and say to yourself, 'Life is short, but let me live before I die!'"

She did not show the letter to Ferdinand.

Next day it rained. Valentia retired to a room at the top of the house and began to paint, but the incessant patter on the roof got on her nerves; the painting bored her, and she threw aside the brushes in disgust. She came downstairs and found Ferdinand in the dining-room, standing at the window looking at the rain. It came down in one continual steady pour, and the water ran off the raised brickwork of the middle of the street to the gutters by the side, running along in a swift and murky rivulet. The red brick of the opposite house looked cold and cheerless in the wet. . . . He did not turn or speak to her as she came in. She remarked that it did not look like leaving off. He made no answer. She drew a chair to the second window and tried to read, but she could not understand what she was reading. And she looked out at the pouring rain and the red brick house opposite. She wondered why he had not answered.

The innkeeper brought them their luncheon. Ferdinand took no notice of the preparations.

"Will you come to luncheon, Mr. White?" she said to him. "It is quite ready."

"I beg your pardon," he said gravely, as he took his seat.

He looked at her quickly, and then, immediately dropping his eyes, began eating. She wished he would not look so sad; she was very sorry for him.

She made an observation and he appeared to rouse himself. He replied and they began talking, very calmly and coldly, as if they had not known one another five minutes. They talked of Art with the biggest of A's, and they compared Dutch painting with Italian; they spoke of Rembrandt and his life.

"Rembrandt had passion," said Ferdinand, bitterly, "and therefore he was unhappy. It is only the sexless, passionless creature, the block of ice, that can be happy in this world."

She blushed and did not answer.

The afternoon Valentia spent in her room, pretending to write letters, and she wondered whether Ferdinand was wishing her downstairs.

At dinner they sought refuge in abstractions. They talked of dykes and windmills and cigars, the history of Holland and its constitution, the constitution of the United States and the edifying spectacle of the politics of that blessed country. They talked of political economy and pessimism and cattle-rearing, the state of agriculture in England, the foreign policy of the day, Anarchism, the President of the French Republic. They would have talked of bimetallism if they could. People hearing them would have thought them very learned and extraordinarily staid.

At last they separated, and as she undressed Valentia told herself that Ferdinand had kept his promise. Everything was just as it had been before, and the only change was that he used her Christian name. And she rather liked him to call her Valentia.

But next day Ferdinand did not seem able to command himself. When Valentia addressed him, he answered in monosyllables, with eyes averted; but when she had her back turned, she felt that he was looking at her. After breakfast she went away painting haystacks, and was late for luncheon.

She apologised.

"It is of no consequence," he said, keeping his eyes on the ground. And those were the only words he spoke to her during the remainder of the day. Once, when he was looking at her sur-

reptitiously, and she suddenly turned round, their eyes met, and for a moment he gazed straight at her, then walked away. She wished he would not look so sad. As she was going to bed, she held out her hand to him to say good-night, and she added:

"I don't want to make you unhappy, Mr. White. I'm very sorry."

"It's not your fault," he said. "You can't help it, if you're a stock and a stone."

He went away without taking the proffered hand. Valentia cried that night.

In the morning she found a note outside her door:

"Pardon me if I was rude, but I was not master of myself. I am going to Volendam; I hate Monnickendam."

VI

Ferdinand arrived at Volendam. It was a fishing village, only three miles across country from Monnickendam, but the route, by steam tram and canal, was so circuitous that, with luggage, it took one two hours to get from place to place. He walked over there with Valentia, and it had almost tempted them to desert Monnickendam. Ferdinand took a room at the hotel and walked out, trying to distract himself. The village consisted of a couple of score of houses, built round a semicircular dyke against the sea, and in the semicircle lay the fleet of fishing boats. Men and women were sitting at their doors mending nets. He looked at the fishermen, great, sturdy fellows, with rough, weather-beaten faces, huge earrings dangling from their ears. He took note of their quaint costume—black stockings and breeches, the latter more baggy than a Turk's, and the crushed strawberry of their high jackets, cut close to the body. He remembered how he had looked at them with Valentia, and the group of boys and men that she had sketched. He remembered how they walked along, peeping into the houses, where everything was spick and span, as only a Dutch cottage can be, with old delft plates hanging on the walls, and pots and pans of polished brass. And he looked over the sea to the island of Marken, with its masts crowded together, like a forest without leaf or branch. Coming to the end of the little town, he saw the church of Monnickendam, the red steeple half-

hidden by the trees. He wondered where Valentia was—what she was doing.

But he turned back resolutely, and, going to his room, opened his books and began reading. He rubbed his eyes and frowned, in order to fix his attention, but the book said nothing but Valentia. At last he threw it aside and took his Plato and his dictionary, commencing to translate a difficult passage, word for word. But whenever he looked up a word he could only see Valentia, and he could not make head or tail of the Greek. He threw it aside also, and set out walking. He walked as hard as he could—away from Monnickendam.

The second day was not quite so difficult, and he read till his mind was dazed, and then he wrote letters home and told them he was enjoying himself tremendously, and he walked till he felt his legs dropping off.

Next morning it occurred to him that Valentia might have written. Trembling with excitement, he watched the postman coming down the street—but he had no letter for Ferdinand. There would be no more post that day.

But the next day Ferdinand felt sure there would be a letter for him; the postman passed by the hotel door without stopping. Ferdinand thought he should go mad. All day he walked up and down his room, thinking only of Valentia. Why did she not write?

The night fell and he could see from his window the moon shining over the clump of trees about Monnickendam church—he could stand it no longer. He put on his hat and walked across country; the three miles were endless; the church and the trees seemed to grow no nearer, and at last, when he thought himself close, he found he had a bay to walk round, and it appeared further away than ever.

He came to the mouth of the canal along which he and Valentia had so often walked. He looked about, but he could see no one. His heart beat as he approached the little bridge, but Valentia was not there. Of course she would not come out alone. He ran to the hotel and asked for her. They told him she was not in. He walked through the town; not a soul was to be seen. He came to the church; he walked round, and then—right at the edge of the trees—he saw a figure sitting on a bench.

She was dressed in the same flowered dress which she had worn

when he likened her to a Dresden shepherdess; she was looking towards Volendam.

He went up to her silently. She sprang up with a little shriek.

"Ferdinand!"

"Oh, Valentia, I cannot help it. I could not remain away any longer. I could do nothing but think of you all day, all night. If you knew how I loved you! Oh, Valentia, have pity on me! I cannot be your friend. It's all nonsense about friendship; I hate it. I can only love you. I love you with all my heart and soul, Valentia."

She was frightened.

"Oh! how can you stand there so coldly and watch my agony? Don't you see? How can you be so cold?"

"I am not cold, Ferdinand," she said, trembling. "Do you think I have been happy while you were away?"

"Valentia!"

"I thought of you, too, Ferdinand, all day, all night. And I longed for you to come back. I did not know till you went that—I loved you."

"Oh, Valentia!"

He took her in his arms and pressed her passionately to him.

"No, for God's sake!"

She tore herself away. But again he took her in his arms, and this time he kissed her on the mouth. She tried to turn her face away.

"I shall kill myself, Ferdinand!"

"What do you mean?"

"In those long hours that I sat here looking towards you, I felt I loved you—I loved you as passionately as you said you loved me. But if you came back, and—anything happened—I swore that I would throw myself in the canal."

He looked at her.

"I could not—live afterwards," she said hoarsely. "It would be too horrible. I should be—oh, I can't think of it!"

He took her in his arms again and kissed her.

"Have mercy on me!" she cried.

"You love me, Valentia."

"Oh, it is nothing to you. Afterwards you will be just the same as before. Why cannot men love peacefully like women? I should

be so happy to remain always as we are now, and never change. I tell you I shall kill myself."

"I will do as you do, Valentia."

"You?"

"If anything happens, Valentia," he said gravely, "we will go down to the canal together."

She was horrified at the idea; but it fascinated her.

"I should like to die in your arms," she said.

For the second time he bent down and took her hands and kissed them. Then she went alone into the silent church, and prayed.

VII

They went home. Ferdinand was so pleased to be at the hotel again, near her. His bed seemed so comfortable; he was so happy, and he slept, dreaming of Valentia.

The following night they went for their walk, arm in arm; and they came to the canal. From the bridge they looked at the water. It was very dark; they could not hear it flow. No stars were reflected in it, and the trees by its side made the depth seem endless. Valentia shuddered. Perhaps in a little while their bodies would be lying deep down in the water. And they would be in one another's arms, and they would never be separated. Oh, what a price it was to pay! She looked tearfully at Ferdinand, but he was looking down at the darkness beneath them, and he was intensely grave.

And they wandered there by day and looked at the black reflection of the trees. And in the heat it seemed so cool and restful. . . .

They abandoned their work. What did pictures and books matter now? They sauntered about the meadows, along shady roads; they watched the black and white cows sleepily browsing, sometimes coming to the water's edge to drink, and looking at themselves, amazed. They saw the huge-limbed milkmaids come along with their little stools and their pails, deftly tying the cow's hind legs that it might not kick. And the streaming milk frothed into the pails and was poured into huge barrels, and as each cow was freed, she shook herself a little and recommenced to browse.

And they loved their life as they had never loved it before.

One evening they went again to the canal and looked at the water, but they seemed to have lost their emotions before it. They were no longer afraid. Ferdinand sat on the parapet and Valentia leaned against him. He bent his head so that his face might touch her hair. She looked at him and smiled, and she almost lifted her lips. He kissed them.

"Do you love me, Ferdinand?"

He gave the answer without words.

Their faces were touching now, and he was holding her hands. They were both very happy.

"You know, Ferdinand," she whispered, "we are very foolish."

"I don't care."

"Monsieur Rollo said that folly was the chief attribute of man."

"What did he say of love?"

"I forget."

Then, after a pause, he whispered in her ear:

"I love you!"

And she held up her lips to him again.

"After all," she said, "we're only human beings. We can't help it. I think—"

She hesitated; what she was going to say had something of the anticlimax in it.

"I think—it would be very silly if—if we threw ourselves in the horrid canal."

"Valentia, do you mean—?"

She smiled charmingly as she answered:

"What you will, Ferdinand."

Again he took both her hands, and, bending down, kissed them. . . . But this time she lifted him up to her and kissed him on the lips.

VIII

One night after dinner I told this story to my aunt.

"But why on earth didn't they get married?" she asked, when I had finished.

"Good heavens!" I cried. "It never occurred to me."

"Well, I think they ought," she said.

"Oh, I have no doubt they did. I expect they got on their bikes and rode off to the consulate at Amsterdam there and then. I'm sure it would have been his first thought."

"Of course, some girls are very queer," said my aunt.

FAITH

(1899)

I

The moon shone fitfully through the clouds on to the weary face of Brother Jasper kneeling in his cell. His hands were fervently clasped, uplifted to the crucifix that hung on the bare wall, and he was praying, praying as he had never prayed before. All through the hours of night, while the monks were sleeping, Brother Jasper had been supplicating his God for light; but in his soul remained a darkness deeper than that of the blackest night. At last he heard the tinkling of the bell that called the monks to prayers, and with a groan lifted himself up. He opened his cell door and went out into the cloister. With down-turned face he walked along till he came to the chapel, and, reaching his seat, sank again heavily to his knees.

The lights in the chapel were few enough, for San Lucido was nearly the poorest monastery in Spain; a few dim candles on the altar threw long shadows on the pavement, and in the choir their yellow glare lit up uncouthly the pale faces of the monks. When Brother Jasper stood up, the taper at his back cast an unnatural light over him, like a halo, making his great black eyes shine strangely from their deep sockets, while below them the dark lines and the black shadow of his shaven chin gave him an unearthly weirdness. He looked like a living corpse standing in the brown Franciscan cowl—a dead monk doomed for some sin to wander through the earth till the day, the Day of Judgment; and in the agony of that weary face one could almost read the terrors of eternal death.

The monks recited the service with their heavy drone, and the

sound of the harsh men's voices ascended to the vault, dragging along the roof. But Jasper heard not what they said; he rose and knelt as they did; he uttered the words; he walked out of the church in his turn, and through the cloister to his cell. And he threw himself on the floor and beat his head against the hard stones, weeping passionately. And he cried out:

"What shall I do? What shall I do?"

For Brother Jasper did not believe.

II

Two days before, the monk, standing amid the stunted shrubs on the hill of San Lucido, had looked out on the arid plain before him. It was all brown and grey, the desolate ground strewn with huge granite boulders, treeless; and for the wretched sheep who fed there, thin and scanty grass; the shepherd, in his tattered cloak, sat on a rock, moodily, paying no heed to his flock, dully looking at the desert round him. Brother Jasper gazed at the scene as he had gazed for three years since he had come to San Lucido, filled with faith and great love for God. In those days he had thought nothing of the cold waste as his eyes rested on it; the light of heaven shed a wonderful glow on the scene, and when at sunset the heavy clouds were piled one above the other, like huge, fantastic mountains turned into golden fire, when he looked beyond them and saw the whole sky burning red and then a mass of yellow and gold, he could imagine that God was sitting there on His throne of fire, with Christ on His right hand in robes of light and glory, and Mary the Queen on His left. And above them the Dove with its outstretched wings, the white bird hovering in a sea of light! And it seemed so near! Brother Jasper felt in him almost the power to go there, to climb up those massy clouds of fire and attain the great joy—the joy of the presence of God.

The sun sank slowly, the red darkened into purple, and over the whole sky came a colour of indescribable softness, while in the east, very far away, shone out the star. And soon the soft faint blue sank before the night, and the stars in the sky were countless; but still in the west there was the shadow of the sun, a misty gleam. Over the rocky plain the heavens seemed so great, so high,

that Brother Jasper sank down in his insignificance; yet he remembered the glories of the sunset, and felt that he was almost at the feet of God.

But now, when he looked at the clouds and the sun behind them, he saw no God; he saw the desert plain, the barrenness of the earth, the overladen, wretched donkey staggering under his pannier, and the broad-hatted peasant urging him on. He looked at the sunset and tried to imagine the Trinity that sat there, but he saw nothing. And he asked himself:

"Why should there be a God?"

He started up with a cry of terror, with his hands clasped to his head.

"My God! what have I done?"

He sank to his knees, humiliating himself. What vengeance would fall on him? He prayed passionately. But again the thought came; he shrieked with terror, he invoked the Mother of God to help him.

"Why should there be a God?"

He could not help it. The thought would not leave him that all this might exist without. How did he know? How could anyone be sure, quite sure? But he drove the thoughts away, and in his cell imposed upon himself a penance. It was Satan that stood whispering in his ear, Satan lying in wait for his soul; let him deny God and he would be damned for ever.

He prayed with all his strength, he argued with himself, he cried out, "I believe! I believe!" but in his soul was the doubt. The terror made him tremble like a leaf in the wind, and great drops of sweat stood on his forehead and ran heavily down his cheek. He beat his head against the wall, and in his agony swayed from side to side. . . . But he could not believe.

III

And for two days he had endured the torments of hell-fire, battling against himself—in vain. The heavy lines beneath his eyes grew blacker than the night, his lips were pale with agony and fasting. He had not dared to speak to anyone, he could not tell them, and in him was the impulse to shout out, "Why should there be?" Now he could bear it no longer. In the morning he

went to the prior's cell, and, falling on his knees, buried his face in the old man's lap.

"Oh, Father, help me! help me!"

The prior was old and wasted; for fifty years he had lived in the desert Castilian plain in the little monastery—all through his youth and manhood, through his age; and now he was older than anyone else at San Lucido. White-haired and wrinkled, but with a clear, rosy skin like a boy's; his soft blue eyes had shone with light, but a cataract had developed, and gradually his sight had left him till he could barely see the crucifix in his cell and the fingers of his hand; at last he could only see the light. But the prior did not lose the beautiful serenity of his life; he was always happy and kind; and, feeling that his death could not now be very distant, he was filled with a heavenly joy that he would shortly see the face of God. Long hours he sat in his chair looking at the light with an indescribably charming smile hovering on his lips.

His voice broken by sobs, Brother Jasper told his story, while the prior gently stroked the young man's hands and face.

"Oh, Father, make me believe!"

"One cannot force one's faith, my dear. It comes, it goes, and no man knows the wherefore. Faith does not come from reasoning; it comes from God. . . . Pray for it and rest in peace."

"I want to believe so earnestly. I am so unhappy!"

"You are not the only one who has been tried, my son. Others have doubted before you and have been saved."

"But if I died to-night—I should die in mortal sin."

"Believe that God counts the attempt as worthy as the achievement."

"Oh, pray for me, Father, pray for me! I cannot stand alone. Give me your strength."

"Go in peace, my son; I will pray for you, and God will give you strength!"

Jasper went away.

Day followed day, and week followed week; the spring came, and the summer; but there was no difference in the rocky desert of San Lucido. There were no trees to bud and burst into leaf, no flowers to bloom and fade; biting winds gave way to fiery heat, the sun beat down on the plain, and the sky was cloudless, cloudless—even the nights were so hot that the monks in their

cells gasped for breath. And Brother Jasper brooded over the faith that was dead; and in his self-torment his cheeks became so hollow that the bones of his face seemed about to pierce the skin, the flesh shrunk from his hands, and the fingers became long and thin, like the claws of a vulture. He used to spend long hours with the prior, while the old man talked gently, trying to bring faith to the poor monk, that his soul might rest. But one day, in the midst of the speaking, the prior stopped, and Jasper saw an expression of pain pass over his face.

"What is it?"

"Nothing, my son," he replied, smiling. . . . "We enter the world with pain, and with pain we leave it!"

"What do you mean? Are you ill? Father! Father!"

The prior opened his mouth and showed a great sloughing sore; he put Jasper's fingers to his neck and made him feel the enlarged and hardened glands.

"What is it? You must see a surgeon."

"No surgeon can help me, Brother Jasper. It is cancer, the Crab—it is the way that God has sent to call me to Himself."

Then the prior began to suffer the agonies of the disease, terrible pains shot through his head and neck; he could not swallow. It was a slow starvation; the torment kept him awake through night after night, and only occasionally his very exhaustion gave him a little relief so that he slept. Thinner and thinner he became, and his whole mouth was turned into a putrid, horrible sore. But yet he never murmured. Brother Jasper knelt by his bed, looking at him pitifully.

"How can you suffer it all? What have you done that God should give you this? Was it not enough that you were blind?"

"Ah, I saw such beautiful things after I became blind—all heaven appeared before me."

"It is unjust—unjust!"

"My son, all is just."

"You drive me mad! . . . Do you still believe in the merciful goodness of God?"

A beautiful smile broke through the pain on the old man's face.

"I still believe in the merciful goodness of God!"

There was a silence. Brother Jasper buried his face in his hands and thought broken-heartedly of his own affliction. How happy he could be if he had that faith. . . . But the silence in the room

was more than the silence of people who did not speak. Jasper looked up suddenly.

The prior was dead.

Then the monk bent over the body and looked at the face, into the opaque white eyes; there was no difference, the flesh was warm—everything was just the same, and yet . . . and yet he was dead. What did they mean by saying the soul had fled? What had happened? Jasper understood nothing of it. And afterwards, before the funeral, when he looked at the corpse again, and it was cold and a horrible blackness stained the lips, he felt sure.

Brother Jasper could not believe in the resurrection of the dead. And the soul—what did they mean by the soul?

IV

Then a great loneliness came over him; the hours of his life seemed endless, and there was no one in whom he could find comfort. The prior had given him a ray of hope, but he was gone, and now Jasper was alone in the world. . . . And beyond? Oh! how could one be certain? It was awful, this perpetual doubt, recurring more strongly than ever. Men had believed so long. Think of all the beautiful churches that had been made in the honour of God, and the pictures. Think of the works that had been done for his love, the martyrs who had cheerfully given up their lives. It seemed impossible that it should be all for nothing. But—but Jasper could not believe. And he cried out to the soul of the prior, resting in heaven, to come to him and help him. Surely, if he really were alive again, he would not let the poor monk whom he had loved linger in this terrible uncertainty. Jasper redoubled his prayers; for hours he remained on his knees, imploring God to send him light. . . . But no light came, and exhausted, Brother Jasper sank into despair.

The new prior was a tall, gaunt man, with a great hooked nose and heavy lips; his keen, dark eyes shone fiercely from beneath his shaggy brows. He was still young, full of passionate energy. And with large gesture and loud, metallic voice he loved to speak of hell-fire and the pains of the damned, hating the Jews and heretics with a bitter personal hatred.

"To the stake!" he used to say. "The earth must be purged of this vermin, and it must be purged by fire."

He exacted the most absolute obedience from the monks, and pitiless was the punishment for any infringement of his rules. . . . Brother Jasper feared the man with an almost unearthly terror; when he felt resting upon him the piercing black eyes, he trembled in his seat, and a cold sweat broke out over him. If the prior knew—the thought almost made him faint. And yet the fear of it seemed to drag him on; like a bird before a serpent, he was fascinated. Sometimes he felt sudden impulses to tell him—but the vengeful eyes terrified him.

One day he was in the cloister, looking out at the little green plot in the middle where the monks were buried, wondering confusedly whether all that prayer and effort had been offered up to empty images of what—of the fear of Man? Turning round, he started back and his heart beat, for the prior was standing close by, looking at him with those horrible eyes. Brother Jasper trembled so that he could scarcely stand; he looked down.

"Brother Jasper!" The prior's voice seemed sterner than it had ever been before. "Brother Jasper!"

"Father!"

"What have you to tell me?"

Jasper looked up at him; the blood fled from his lips.

"Nothing, my Father!" The prior looked at him firmly, and Jasper thought he read the inmost secrets of his heart.

"Speak, Brother Jasper!" said the prior, and his voice was loud and menacing.

Then hurriedly, stuttering in his anxiety, the monk confessed his misery. . . . A horror came over the prior's face as he listened, and Jasper became so terrified that he could hardly speak; but the prior seemed to recover himself, and interrupted him with a furious burst of anger.

"You look over the plain and do not see God, and for that you doubt Him? Miserable fool!"

"Oh, Father, have mercy on me! I have tried so hard. I want to believe. But I cannot."

"I cannot! I cannot! What is that? Have men believed for a thousand years—has God performed miracle after miracle—and a miserable monk dares to deny Him?"

"I cannot believe!"

"You must!" His voice was so loud that it rang through the cloisters. He seized Jasper's clasped hands, raised in supplication before him, and forced him to his knees. "I tell you, you shall believe!"

Quivering with wrath, he looked at the prostrate form at his feet, moved by convulsive weeping. He raised his hand as if to strike the monk, but with difficulty contained himself.

Then the prior bade Brother Jasper go to the church and wait. The monks were gathered together, all astonished. They stood in their usual places, but Jasper remained in the middle, away from them, with head cast down. The prior called out to them in his loud, clear voice:

"Pray, my brethren, pray for the soul of Brother Jasper, which lies in peril of eternal death."

The monks looked at him suddenly, and Brother Jasper's head sank lower, so that no one could see his face. The prior sank to his knees and prayed with savage fervour. Afterwards the monks went their ways; but when Jasper passed them they looked down, and when by chance he addressed a novice, the youth hurried from him without answering. They looked upon him as accursed. The prior spoke no more, but often Jasper felt his stern gaze resting on him, and a shiver would pass through him. In the services Jasper stood apart from the rest, like an unclean thing; he did not join in their prayers, listening confusedly to their monotonous droning; and when a pause came and he felt all eyes turn to him, he put his hands to his face to hide himself.

"Pray, my brethren, pray for the soul of Brother Jasper, which lies in peril of eternal death."

V

In his cell the monk would for days sit apathetically looking at the stone wall in front of him, sore of heart; the hours would pass by unnoticed, and only the ringing of the chapel bell awoke him from his stupor. And sometimes he would be seized with sudden passion and, throwing himself on his knees, pour forth a stream of eager, vehement prayer. He remembered the penances which the seraphic father imposed on his flesh—but he always had faith; and Jasper would scourge himself till he felt sick and faint, and,

hoping to gain his soul by mortification of the body, refuse the bread and water which were thrust into his cell, and for a long while eat nothing. He became so weak and ill that he could hardly stand; and still no help came.

Then he took it into his head that God would pity him and send a miracle to drive away his uncertainty. Was he not anxious to believe, if only he could?—so anxious! God would not send a miracle to a poor monk. . . . Yet miracles had been performed for smaller folk than he—for shepherds and tenders of swine. But Christ himself had said that miracles only come by faith, but—Jasper remembered that often the profligate and the harlot had been brought to repentance by a vision. Even the Holy Francis had been but a loose gallant till Christ appeared to him. Yet, if Christ had appeared, it showed—ah! but how could one be sure? It might only have been a dream. Let a vision appear to him and he would believe. Oh, how enchanted he would be to believe, to rest in peace, to know that before him, however hard the life, were eternal joy and the kingdom of heaven.

But Brother Jasper put his hands to his head cruelly aching. He could not understand, he could not know—the doubt weighed on his brain like a sheet of lead; he felt inclined to tear his skull apart to relieve the insupportable pressure. How endless life was! Why could it not finish quickly and let him know? But supposing there really was a God, He would exact terrible vengeance. What punishment would He inflict on the monk who had denied Him—who had betrayed Him like a second Judas? Then a fantastic idea came into his crazy brain. Was it Satan that put all these doubts into his head? If it were, Satan must exist; and if he did, God existed too. He knew that the devil stood ready to appear to all who called. If Christ would not appear, let Satan show himself. It meant hell-fire; but if God were, the monk felt he was damned already—for the truth he would give his soul!

The idea sent a coldness through him, so that he shivered; but it possessed him, and he exulted, thinking that he would know at last. He rose from his bed—it was the dead of night and all the monks were sleeping—and, trembling with cold, began to draw with chalk strange figures on the floor. He had seen them long ago in an old book of magic, and their fantastic shapes, fascinating him, had remained in his memory.

In the centre of the strange confusion of triangles he stood and

uttered in a husky voice the invocation. He murmured uncouth words in an unknown language, and bade Satan stand forth. . . . He expected a thunder-clap, the flashing of lightning, sulphurous fumes—but the night remained silent and quiet; not a sound broke the stillness of the monastery; the snow outside fell steadily.

VI

Next day the prior sent for him and repeated his solemn question.

"Brother Jasper, what have you to say to me?"

And, absolutely despairing, Jasper answered:

"Nothing, nothing, nothing!"

Then the prior strode up to him in wrath and smote him on the cheek.

"It is a devil within you—a devil of obstinacy and pride. You shall believe!"

He cried to monks to lay hold of him; they dragged him roughly to the cloisters, and, stripping him of his cowl, tied it round his waist, and bound him by the hands to a pillar. . . . And the prior ordered them to give Jasper eight-and-thirty strokes with the scourge—one less than Christ—that the devil might be driven out. The scourge was heavy and knotted, and the porter bared his arms that he might strike the better; the monks stood round in eager expectation. The scourge whizzed through the air and came down with a thud on Jasper's bare shoulders; a tremor passed through him, but he did not speak. Again it came down, and as the porter raised it for the third time the monks saw great bleeding weals on Brother Jasper's back. Then, as the scourge fell heavily, a terrible groan burst from him. The porter swung his arm, and this time a shriek broke from the wretched monk; the blows came pitilessly and Jasper lost all courage. He shrieked with agony, imploring them to stop.

But ferociously the prior cried:

"Did Christ bear in silence forty stripes save one, and do you cry out like a woman before you have had ten!"

The porter went on, and the prior's words were interrupted by piercing shrieks.

"It is the devil crying out within him," said the monks, gloating on the bleeding back and the face of agony.

Heavy drops of sweat ran off the porter's face and his arm began to tire; but he seized the handle with both hands and swung the knotted ropes with all his strength.

Jasper fainted.

"See!" said the prior. "See the fate of him who has not faith in God!"

The cords with which he was tied prevented the monk from falling, and stroke after stroke fell on his back till the number was completed. Then they loosed him from the column, and he sank senseless and bleeding to the ground. They left him. Brother Jasper regained slowly his senses, lying out in the cold cloister with the snow on the graves in the middle; his hands and feet were stiff and blue. He shivered and drew himself together for warmth, then a groan burst from him, feeling the wounds of his back. Painfully he lifted himself up and crawled to the chapel door; he pushed it open, and, staggering forward, fell on his face, looking towards the altar. He remained there long, dazed and weary, pulling his cowl close round him to keep out the bitter cold. The pain of his body almost relieved the pain of his mind; he wished dumbly that he could lie there and die, and be finished with it all. He did not know the time; he wondered whether any service would soon bring the monks to disturb him. He took sad pleasure in the solitude, and in the great church the solitude seemed more intense. Oh, and he hated the monks! It was cruel, cruel, cruel! He put his hands to his face and sobbed bitterly.

But suddenly a warmth fell on him; he looked up, and the glow seemed to come from the crucified Christ in the great painted window by the altar. The monk started up with a cry and looked eagerly; the bell began to ring. The green colour of death was becoming richer, the glass gained the fulness of real flesh; now it was a soft round whiteness. And Brother Jasper cried out in ecstasy:

"It is Christ!"

Then the glow deepened, and from the Crucified One was shed a wonderful light like the rising of the sun behind the mountains, and the church was filled with its rich effulgence.

"Oh, God, it is moving!"

The Christ seemed to look at Brother Jasper and bow His head.

Two by two the monks walked silently in, and Brother Jasper lifted up his arms, crying:

"Behold a miracle! Christ has appeared to me!"

A murmur of astonishment broke from them, and they looked at Jasper gazing in ecstasy at the painted window.

"Christ has appeared to me. . . . I am saved!"

Then the prior came up to him and took him in his arms and kissed him.

"My son, praise be to God! You are whole again."

But Jasper pushed him aside, so that he might not be robbed of the sight which filled him with rapture; the monks crowded round, questioning, but he took no notice of them. He stood with outstretched arms, looking eagerly, his face lighted up with joy. The monks began to kiss his cowl and his feet, and they touched his hands.

"I am saved! I am saved!"

And the prior cried to them:

"Praise God, my brethren, praise God! For we have saved the soul of Brother Jasper from eternal death."

But when the service was over and the monks had filed out, Brother Jasper came to himself—and he saw that the light had gone from the window; the Christ was cold and dead, a thing of the handicraft of man. What was it that had happened? Had a miracle occurred? The question flashing through his mind made him cry out. He had prayed for a miracle, and a miracle had been shown him—the poor monk of San Lucido. . . . And now he doubted the miracle. Oh, God must have ordained the damnation of his soul to give him so little strength—perhaps He had sent the miracle that he might have no answer at the Day of Judgment.

"Faith thou hadst not—I showed Myself to thee in flesh and blood, I moved My head; thou didst not believe thine own eyes. . . ."

VII

Next day, at vespers, Jasper anxiously fixed his gaze on the stained-glass window—again a glow came from it, and as he moved the head seemed to incline itself; but now Jasper saw it was only the sun shining through the window—only the sun! Then

the heaviness descended into the deepest parts of Jasper's soul, and he despaired.

The night came and Jasper returned to his cell. . . . He leant against the door, looking out through the little window, but he could only see the darkness. And he likened it to the darkness in his own soul.

"What shall I do?" he groaned.

He could not tell the monks that it was not a miracle he had seen; he could not tell them that he had lost faith again. . . . And then his thoughts wandering to the future:

"Must I remain all my life in this cold monastery? If there is no God, if I have but one life, what is the good of it? Why cannot I enjoy my short existence as other men? Am not I young—am not I of the same flesh and blood as they?"

Vague recollections came to him of those new lands beyond the ocean, those lands of sunshine and sweet odours. His mind became filled with a vision of broad rivers, running slow and cool, overshadowed by strange, luxuriant trees. And all was a wealth of beautiful colour.

"Oh, I cannot stay!" he cried. "I cannot stay!"

And it was a land of loving-kindness, a land of soft-eyed, gentle women.

"I cannot stay! I cannot stay!"

The desire to go forth was overwhelming, the walls of his cell seemed drawing together to crush him; he must be free. Oh, for life! life! He started up, not seeing the madness of his adventure; he did not think of the snow-covered desert, the night, the distance from a town. He saw before him the glorious sunshine of a new life, and he went towards it like a blind man, with outstretched arms.

Everyone was asleep in the monastery. He crept out of his cell and silently opened the door of the porter's lodge; the porter was sleeping heavily. Jasper took the keys and unlocked the gate. He was free. He took no notice of the keen wind blowing across the desert; he hurried down the hill, slipping on the frozen snow. . . . Suddenly he stopped; he had caught sight of the great crucifix which stood by the wayside at the bottom of the hill. Then the madness of it all occurred to him. Wherever he went he would find the crucifix, even beyond the sea, and nowhere would he be able to forget his God. Always the recollection, always the doubt,

and he would never have rest till he was in the grave. He went close to it and looked up; it was one of those strange Spanish crucifixes—a wooden image with long, thin arms and legs and protruding ribs, with real hair hanging over the shoulders, and a true crown of thorns placed on the head; the ends of the tattered cloth fastened about the loins fluttered in the wind. In the night the lifelikeness was almost ghastly; it might have been a real man that hung there, with great nails through his feet. The common people paid superstitious reverence to it, and Jasper had often heard the peasants tell of the consolations they had received.

Why should not he too receive consolation? Was his soul not as worth saving as theirs? A last spark of hope filled him, and he lifted himself up on tip-toe to touch the feet.

"Oh, Christ, come down to me! Tell me whether Thou art indeed a God. Oh, Christ, help me!"

But the words lost themselves in the wind and night. . . . Then a great rage seized him that he alone should receive no comfort. He clenched his fists and beat passionately against the cross.

"Oh, you are a cruel God! I hate you, I hate you!"

If he could have reached it he would have torn the image down, and beat it as he had been beaten. In his impotent rage he shrieked out curses upon it—he blasphemed.

But his strength spent itself and he sank to the foot of the cross, bursting into tears. In his self-pity he thought his heart was broken. Lifting himself to his knees, he clasped the wood with his hands and looked up for the last time at the dead face of Christ.

It was the end. . . . A strange peace came over him as the anguish of his mind fell away before the cold. His hands and his feet were senseless, he felt his heart turning to ice—and he felt nothing.

In a little while the snow began to fall, lightly covering his shoulders. Brother Jasper knew the secret of death at last.

VIII

The day broke slowly, dim and grey. There was a hurried knocking at the porter's door, a peasant with white and startled face said that a brother was kneeling at the great cross in the snow and would not speak.

The monks sallied forth anxiously, and came to the silent figure, clasping the cross in supplication.

"Brother Jasper!"

The prior touched his hands; they were as cold as ice.

"He is dead!"

The villagers crowded round in astonishment, whispering to one another. The monks tried to move him, but his hands, frozen to the cross, prevented them.

"He died in prayer—he was a saint!"

But a woman with a paralysed arm came near him, and in her curiosity touched his ragged cowl. . . . Suddenly she felt a warmth pass through her, and the dead arm began to tingle. She cried out in astonishment, and as the people turned to look she moved the fingers.

"He has restored my arm," she said. "Look!"

"A miracle!" they cried out. "A miracle! He is a saint!"

The news spread like fire; and soon they brought a youth lying on a bed, wasted by a mysterious illness, so thin that the bones protruding had formed angry sores on the skin. They touched him with the hem of the monk's garment, and immediately he roused himself.

"I am whole; give me to eat!"

A murmur of wonder passed through the crowd. The monks sank to their knees and prayed.

At last they lifted up the dead monk and bore him to the church. But people all round the country crowded to see him; the sick and the paralysed came from afar, and often went away sound as when they were born.

They buried him at last, but still to his tomb they came from all sides, rich and poor; and the wretched monk, who had not faith to cure the disease of his own mind, cured the diseases of those who had faith in him.

THE CHOICE OF AMYNTAS

(1899)

I

Often enough the lover of cities tires of their unceasing noise; the din of the traffic buzzes perpetually in his ears, and even in the silences of night he hears the footfalls on the pavement, the dull stamping of horses, the screeching of wheels; the fog chokes up the lungs so that he cannot breathe; he sees no longer any charms in the tall chimneys of the factory and the heavy smoke winding in curves against the leaden sky; then he flies to countries where the greenness is like cold spring water, where he can hear the budding of the trees and the stars tell him fantastic things, the silence is full of mysterious new emotions. And so the writer sometimes grows weary to death of the life he sees, and he presses his hands before his eyes, that he may hide from him the endless failure in the endless quest; then he too sets sail for Bohemia by the Sea, and the other countries of the Frankly Impossible, where men are always brave and women ever beautiful; there the tears of the morning are followed by laughter at night, trials are easily surmountable, virtue is always triumphant; there no illusions are lost, and lovers live ever happily in a world without end.

II

Once upon a time, very long ago, when the world was younger and more wicked than it is now, there lived in the West Country

a man called Peter the Schoolmaster. But he was very different from ordinary schoolmasters, for he was a scholar and a man of letters; he was consequently very poor. All his life he had pored over old books and musty parchments; but from them he had acquired little wisdom, for one bright springtime he fell in love with a farmer's daughter—and married her. The farmer's daughter was a buxom wench, and, to the schoolmaster's delight—he had a careless, charming soul—she presented him in course of time with a round dozen of sturdy children. Peter compared himself with Priam of Troy, with Jacob, with King Solomon of Israel, and with Queen Anne of England. Peter wrote a Latin ode to each offspring in turn, which he recited to the assembled multitude when the midwife put into his arms for the first time the new arrival. There was great rejoicing over the birth of every one of the twelve children; but, as was most proper in a land of primogeniture, the chiefest joy was the first-born; and to him Peter wrote an Horatian ode, which was two stanzas longer than the longest Horace ever wrote. Peter vowed that no infant had ever been given the world's greeting in so magnificent a manner; certainly he had never himself surpassed that first essay. As he told the parson, to write twelve odes on paternity, twelve greetings to the new-born soul, is a severe tax even on the most fertile imagination.

But the object of all this eloquence was the cause of the first and only quarrel between the gentle schoolmaster and his spouse; for the learned man had dug out of one of his old books the name of Amyntas, and Amyntas he vowed should be the name of his son; so with that trisyllable he finished every stanza of his ode. His wife threw her head back, and, putting her hands on her hips, stood with arms akimbo; she said that never in all her born days had she heard of anyone being called by such a name, which was more fit for a heathen idol than for a plain, straightforward member of the church by law established. In its stead she suggested that the boy be called Peter, after his father, or John, after hers. The gentle schoolmaster was in the habit of giving way to his wife in all things, and it may be surmised that this was the reason why the pair had lived in happiest concord; but now he was firm! He said it was impossible to call the boy by any other name than Amyntas.

"The name is necessary to the metre of my ode," he said. "It is

its very life. How can I finish my stanzas with Petrus or Johannes? I would sooner die."

His wife did not think the ode mattered a rap. Peter turned pale with emotion; he could scarcely express himself.

"Every mother in England has had a child; children have been born since the days of Cain and Abel thicker than the sands of the sea. What is a child? But an ode—my ode! A child is but an ordinary product of man and woman, but a poem is a divine product of the Muses. My poem is sacred; it shall not be defiled by any Petrus or Johannes! Let my house fall about my head, let my household goods be scattered abroad, let the Fates with their serpent hair render desolate my hearth; but do not rob me of my verse. I would sooner lose the light of my eyes than the light of my verse! Ah! let me wander through the land like Homer, sightless, homeless; let me beg my bread from door to door, and I will sing the ode, the ode to Amyntas. . . ."

He said all this with so much feeling that Mrs. Peter began to cry, and, with her apron up to her eyes, said that she didn't want him to go blind; but even if he did, he should never want, for she would work herself to the bone to keep him. Peter waved his hand in tragic deprecation. No, he would beg his bread from door to door; he would sleep by the roadside in the bitter winter night.

Now, the parson was present during this colloquy, and he proposed an arrangement; and finally it was settled that Peter should have his way in this case, but that Mrs. Peter should have the naming of all subsequent additions to the family. So, of the rest, one was called Peter, and one was called John, and there was a Mary, and a Jane, and a Sarah; but the eldest, according to agreement, was christened Amyntas, although to her dying day, notwithstanding the parson's assurances, the mother was convinced in her heart of hearts that the name was papistical and not fit for a plain, straightforward member of the church by law established.

III

Now, it was as clear as a pikestaff to Peter the Schoolmaster that a person called Amyntas could not go through the world like any other ordinary being; so he devoted particular care to his son's education, teaching him, which was the way of schoolmasters then

as now, very many entirely useless things, and nothing that could be to him of the slightest service in earning his bread and butter.

But twelve children cannot be brought up on limpid air, and there were often difficulties when new boots were wanted; sometimes, indeed, there were difficulties when bread and meat and puddings were wanted. Such things did not affect Peter; he felt not the pangs of hunger as he read his books, and he vastly preferred to use the white and the yolk of an egg in the restoration of an old leather binding than to have it solemnly cooked and thrust into his belly. What cared he for the ratings of his wife and the crying of the children when he could wander in imagination on Mount Ida, clad only in his beauty, and the three goddesses came to him promising wonderful things? He was a tall, lean man, with thin white hair and blue eyes, but his wrinkled cheeks were still rosy; incessant snuff-taking had given a special character to his nose. And sometimes, taking upon him the spirit of Catullus, he wrote verses to Lesbia, or, beneath the breast-plate of Marcus Aurelius, he felt his heart beat bravely as he marched against the barbarians; he was Launcelot, and he made charming speeches to Guinevere as he kissed her long white hand. . . .

But now and then the clamour of the outer world became too strong, and he had to face seriously the question of his children's appetites.

It was on one of these occasions that the schoolmaster called his son to his study and said to him:

"Amyntas, you are now eighteen years of age. I have taught you all I know, and you have profited by my teaching; you know Greek and Latin as well as I do myself; you are well acquainted with Horace and Tully; you have read Homer and Aristotle; and added to this, you can read the Bible in the original Hebrew. That is to say, you have all knowledge at your fingers' ends, and you are prepared to go forth and conquer the world. Your mother will make a bundle of your clothes; I will give you my blessing and a guinea, and you can start to-morrow."

Then he returned to his study of an oration of Isocrates. Amyntas was thunderstruck.

"But, Father, where am I to go?"

The schoolmaster raised his head in surprise, looking at his son over the top of his spectacles.

"My son," he said, with a wave of the arm; "my son, you have the world before you—is that not enough?"

"Yes, Father," said Amyntas, who thought it was a great deal too much; "but what am I to do? I can't get very far on a guinea."

"Amyntas," answered Peter, rising from his chair with great dignity, "have you profited so ill by the examples of antiquity, which you have had placed before you from your earliest years? Do you not know that riches consist in an equal mind, and happiness in golden mediocrity? Did the wise Odysseus quail before the unknown, because he had only a guinea in his pocket? Shame on the heart that doubts! Leave me, my son, and make ready."

Amyntas, very crest-fallen, left the room and went to his mother to acquaint her with the occurrence. She was occupied in the performance of the family's toilet.

"Well, my boy," she said, as she scrubbed the face of the last but one, "it's about time that you set about doing something to earn your living, I must say. Now, if instead of learning all this popish stuff about Greek and Latin and Lord knows what, you'd learnt to milk a cow or groom a horse you'd be as right as a trivet now. Well, I'll put you up a few things in a bundle as your father says and you can start early to-morrow morning. . . . Now then, darling," she added, turning to her Benjamin, "come and have your face washed, there's a dear."

IV

Amyntas scratched his head, and presently an inspiration came to him.

"I will go to the parson," he said.

The parson had been hunting, and he was sitting in his study in a great oak chair, drinking a bottle of port; his huge body and his red face expressed the very completest satisfaction with the world in general; one felt that he would go to bed that night with the cheerful happiness of duty performed, and snore stentoriously for twelve hours. He was troubled by no qualms of conscience; the Thirty-nine Articles caused him never a doubt, and it had never occurred to him to concern himself with the condition of the working classes. He lived in a golden age, when the pauper was

allowed to drink himself to death as well as the nobleman, and no clergyman's wife read tracts by his bedside. . . .

Amyntas told his news.

"Well, my boy"—he never spoke but he shouted—"so you're going away? Well, God bless you!"

Amyntas looked at him expectantly, and the parson, wondering what he expected, came to the conclusion that it was a glass of port, for at that moment he was able to imagine nothing that man could desire more. He smiled benignly upon Amyntas, and poured him out a glass.

"Drink that, my boy. Keep it in your memory. It's the finest thing in the world. It's port that's made England what she is!"

Amyntas drank the port, but his face did not express due satisfaction.

"Damn the boy!" said the parson. "Port's wasted on him. . . ." Then, thinking again what Amyntas might want, he rose slowly from his chair, stretching his legs. "I'm not so young as I used to be; I get stiff after a day's hunting." He walked round his room, looking at his bookshelves; at last he picked out a book and blew the dust off the edges. "Here's a Bible for you, Amyntas. The two finest things in the world are port and the Bible."

Amyntas thanked him, but without great enthusiasm. Another idea struck the parson, and he shouted out another question.

"Have you any money?"

Amyntas told him of the guinea.

"Damn your father! What's the good of a guinea?" He went to a drawer and pulled out a handful of gold—the tithes had been paid a couple of days before. "Here are ten; a man can go to hell on ten guineas."

"Thank you very much, sir," said Amyntas, pocketing the money, "but I don't think I want to go quite so far just yet."

"Then where the devil do you want to go?" shouted the parson.

"That's just what I came to ask you about."

"Why didn't you say so at once? I thought you wanted a glass of port. I'd sooner give ten men advice than one man port." He went to the door and called out, "Jane, bring me another bottle." He drank the bottle in silence, while Amyntas stood before him, resting now upon one leg, now upon another, turning his cap round and round in his hands. At last the parson spoke.

"You may look upon a bottle of port in two ways," he said;

"you may take it as a symbol of a happy life or as a method of thought. . . . There are four glasses in a bottle. The first glass is full of expectation; you enter life with mingled feelings; you cannot tell whether it will be good or no. The second glass has the full savour of the grape; it is youth with vine-leaves in its hair and the passion of young blood. The third glass is void of emotion; it is grave and calm, like middle age; drink it slowly, you are in full possession of yourself, and it will not come again. The fourth glass has the sadness of death and the bitter sweetness of retrospect."

He paused a moment for Amyntas to weigh his words.

"But a bottle of port is a better method of thought than any taught by the schoolmen. The first glass is that of contemplation—I think of your case; the second is apprehension—an idea occurs to me; the third is elaboration—I examine the idea and weigh the pros and cons; the fourth is realization—and here I give you the completed scheme. Look at this letter; it is from my old friend Van Tiefel, a Dutch merchant who lives at Cádiz, asking for an English clerk. One of his ships is sailing from Plymouth next Sunday, and it will put in at Cádiz on the way to Turkey."

Amyntas thought the project could have been formed without a bottle of port, but he was too discreet to say so, and heartily thanked the parson. The good man lived in a time when teetotalism had not ruined the clergy's nerves, and sanctity was not considered incompatible with a good digestion and common humanity. . . .

V

Amyntas spent the evening bidding tender farewells to a round dozen of village beauties, whose susceptible hearts had not been proof against the brown eyes and the dimples of the youth. There was indeed woe when he spread the news of his departure; and all those maiden eyes ran streams of salt tears as he bade them one by one good-bye; and though he squeezed their hands and kissed their lips, vowing them one and all the most unalterable fidelity, they were perfectly inconsolable. It is an interesting fact to notice that the instincts of the true hero are invariably polygamic. . . .

It was lucky for Amyntas that the parson had given him money, for his father, though he gave him a copy of the *Ethics of Aristotle*

and his blessing, forgot the quinea; and Amyntas was too fearful of another reproach to remind him of it.

Amyntas was up with the lark, and, having eaten as largely as he could in his uncertainty of the future, made ready to start. The schoolmaster had retired to his study to conceal his agitation; he was sitting like Agamemnon with a dishcloth over his head, because he felt his face unable to express his emotion. But the boy's mother stood at the cottage door, wiping her eyes with the corner of her apron, surrounded by her weeping children. She threw her arms about her son's neck, giving him a loud kiss on either cheek, and Amyntas went the round of his brothers and sisters, kissing them and bidding them not forget him. To console them, he promised to bring back green parrots and golden bracelets, and embroidered satins from Japan. As he passed down the village street he shook hands with the good folk standing at their doors to bid him good-bye, and slowly made his way into the open country.

VI

The way of the hero is often very hard, and Amyntas felt as if he would choke as he walked slowly along. He looked back at every step, wondering when he would see the old home again. He loitered through the lanes, taking a last farewell of the nooks and corners where he had sat on summer evenings with some fair female friend, and he heartily wished that his name were James or John, and that he were an ordinary farmer's son who could earn his living without going out for it into the wide, wide world. So may Dick Whittington have meditated as he trudged the London road, but Amyntas had no talismanic cat and no church bells rang him inspiring messages. Besides, Dick Whittington had had in him from his birth the makings of a lord mayor—he had the golden mediocrity which is the surest harbinger of success. But to Amyntas the world seemed cold and grey, notwithstanding the sunshine of the morning; and the bare branches of the oak trees were gnarled and twisted like the fingers of evil fate. At last he came to the top of a little hill whence one had the last view of the village. He looked at the red-roofed church nestling among the trees, and in front of the inn he could still see the sign of the "Turk's Head." A sob burst from him; he felt he could not leave

it all; it would not be so bad if he could see it once more. He might go back at night and wander through the streets; he could stand outside his own home door and look up at his father's light, perhaps seeing his father's shadow bent over his books. He cared nothing that his name was Amyntas; he would go to the neighbouring farmers and offer his services as labourer—the village barber wanted an apprentice. Ah! he would ten times sooner be a village Hampden or a songless Milton than any hero! He hid his face in the grass and cried as if his heart were breaking.

Presently he cried himself to sleep, and when he awoke the sun was high in the heavens and he had the very healthiest of appetites. He repaired to a neighbouring inn and ordered bread and cheese and a pot of beer. Oh, mighty is the power of beer! Why am I not a poet, that I may stand with my hair dishevelled, one hand in my manly bosom and the other outstretched with splendid gesture, to proclaim the excellent beauty of beer? Avaunt! ye sallow teetotalers, ye manufacturers of lemonade, ye cocoa-drinkers! You only see the sodden wretch who hangs about the public-house door in filthy slums, blinking his eyes in the glare of electric light, shivering in his scanty rags—and you do not know the squalor and the terrible despair of hunger which he strives to forget. . . . But above all, you do not know the glorious ale of the country, the golden brown ale, with its scent of green hops, its broad scents of the country; its foam is whiter than snow and lighter than the almond blossoms; and it is cold, cold. . . . Amyntas drank his beer, and he sighed with great content; the sun shone hopefully upon him now, and the birds twittered all sorts of inspiring things; still in his mouth was the delightful bitterness of the hops. He threw off care as a mantle, and he stepped forward with joyful heart. Spain was a wild country, the land of the grave hidalgo and the haughty princess. He felt in his strong right arm the power to fight and kill and conquer. Black-bearded villains should capture beautiful maidens on purpose for him to rescue. Van Tiefel was but a stepping-stone; he was not made for the desk of a counting-house. No heights dazzled him; he saw himself being made a peer or a prince, being granted wide domains by a grateful monarch. He was not too low to aspire to the hand of a king's fair daughter; he was a hero, every inch a hero. Great is the power of beer. Avaunt! ye sallow teetotalers, ye manufacturers of lemonade, ye cocoa-drinkers!

At night he slept on a haystack, with the blue sky, star-bespangled, for his only roof, and dreamed luxurious dreams. . . . The milestones flew past one another as he strode along, two days, three days, four days. On the fifth, as he reached the summit of a little hill, he saw a great expanse of light shining in the distance, and the sea glittered before him like the bellies of innumerable little silver fishes. He went down the hill, up another, and thence saw Plymouth at his feet; the masts of the ships were like a great forest of leafless trees. . . . He thanked his stars, for one's imagination is all very well for a while, and the thought of one's future prowess certainly shortens the time; but roads are hard and hills are steep, one's legs grow tired and one's feet grow sore; and things are not so rose-coloured at the end of a journey as at the beginning. Amyntas could not forever keep thinking of beautiful princesses and feats of arms, and after the second day he had exhausted every possible adventure; he had raised himself to the highest possible altitudes, and his aristocratic amours had had the most successful outcome.

He sat down by a little stream that ran along the roadside, and bathed his aching feet; he washed his face and hands; starting down the hill, he made his way towards the town and entered the gate.

VII

Amyntas discovered Captain Thorman of the good ship *Calderon* drinking rum punch in a tavern parlour. In those days all men were heroic. . . . He gave him the parson's letter.

"Well, my boy," said the captain, after twice reading it, "I don't mind taking you to Cádiz; I dare say you'll be able to make yourself useful on board. What can you do?"

"Please, sir," answered Amyntas, with some pride, "I know Latin and Greek; I am well acquainted with Horace and Tully; I have read Homer and Aristotle; and added to this, I can read the Bible in the original Hebrew."

The captain looked at him.

"If you talk to me like that," he said, "I'll shy my glass at your head." He shook with rage, and the redness of his nose emitted

lightning sparks of indignation; when he had recovered his speech, he asked Amyntas why he stood there like an owl, and told him to get on board.

Amyntas bowed himself meekly out of the room, went down to the harbour, and, bearing in mind what he had heard of the extreme wickedness of Plymouth, held tightly on to his money; he had been especially warned against the women who lure the unwary seaman into dark dens and rob him of money and life. But no adventure befell him, thanks chiefly to the swiftness of his heels, for when a young lady of prepossessing appearance came up to him and inquired after his health, affectionately putting her arm in his, he promptly took to his legs and fled.

Amyntas was in luck's way, for it was not often that an English ship carried merchandise to Spain. As a rule, the two powers were at daggers drawn; but at this period they had just ceased cutting one another's throats and sinking one another's ships, joining together in fraternal alliance to cut the throats and sink the ships of a rival power, which, till the treaty, had been a faithful and brotherly ally to His Majesty of Great Britain, and which our gracious king had abandoned with unusual dexterity, just as it was preparing to abandon him. . . .

As Amyntas stood on the deck of the ship and saw the grey cliffs of Albion disappear into the sea, he felt the emotions and sentiments which inevitably come to the patriotic Englishman who leaves his native shore; his melancholy became almost unbearable as the ship, getting out into the open sea, began to roll, and he drank to the dregs the bitter cup of leaving England, home, beauty —and *terra firma*. He went below, and, climbing painfully into his hammock, gave himself over to misery and *mal-de-mer*.

Two days he spent of lamentation and gnashing of teeth, wishing he had never been born, and not till the third day did he come on deck. He was pale and weak, feeling ever so unheroic, but the sky was blue and the ship bounded over the blue waves as if it were alive. Amyntas sniffed in the salt air and the rushing wind, and felt alive again. The days went by, the sun became hotter, and the sky a different, deeper blue, while its vault spread itself over the sea in a vaster expanse. They came in sight of land again; they coasted down a gloomy country with lofty cliffs going sheer into the sea; they passed magnificent galleons laden with gold

from America; and one morning, when Amyntas came on deck at break of day, he saw before him the white walls and red roofs of a southern city. The ship slowly entered the harbour of Cádiz.

VIII

At last! Amyntas went on shore immediately. His spirit was so airy within him that he felt he could hover along in the air, like Mr. Lang's spiritualistic butlers, and it was only by a serious effort of will that he walked soberly down the streets like normal persons. His soul shouted with the joy of living. He took in long breaths as if to breathe in the novelty and the strangeness. He walked along, too excited to look at things, only conscious of a glare of light and colour, a thronging crowd, life and joyousness on every side. . . . He walked through street after street, almost sobbing with delight, through narrow alleys down which the sun never fell, into big squares hot as ovens and dazzling, up hill and down hill, past ragged slums, past the splendid palaces of the rich, past shops, past taverns. Finally he came on to the shore again and threw himself down in the shade of a little grove of orange trees to sleep.

When he awoke, he saw, standing motionless by his side, a Spanish lady. He looked at her silently, noting her olive skin, her dark and lustrous eyes, the luxuriance of her hair. If she had only possessed a tambourine she would have been the complete realisation of his dreams. He smiled.

"Why do you lie here alone, sweet youth?" she asked, with an answering smile. "And who and what are you?"

"I lay down here to rest, lady," he replied. "I have this day arrived from England, and I am going to Van Tiefel, the merchant."

"Ah! a young English merchant. They are all very rich. Are you?"

"Yes, lady," frankly answered Amyntas, pulling out his handful of gold.

The Spaniard smiled on him, and then sighed deeply.

"Why do you sigh?" he asked.

"Ah! you English merchants are so fascinating." She took his hand and pressed it. Amyntas was not a forward youth, but he

had some experience of English maidens, and felt that there was but one appropriate rejoinder. He kissed her.

She sighed again as she relinquished herself to his embrace. "You English merchants are so fascinating—and so rich."

Amyntas thought the Spanish lady was sent him by the gods, for she took him to her house and gave him melons and grapes, which, being young and of lusty appetite, he devoured with great content. She gave him wine—strong, red, fiery wine, that burned his throat—and she gave him sundry other very delightful things, which it does not seem necessary to relate.

When Amyntas on his departure shyly offered some remuneration for his entertainment, it was with an exquisite southern grace that she relieved him of his ten golden guineas, and he almost felt she was doing him a favour as she carelessly rattled the coins into a silken purse. And if he was a little dismayed to see his treasure go so speedily, he was far too delicate-minded to betray any emotion; but he resolved to lose no time in finding out the offices of the wealthy Tiefel.

IX

But Van Tiefel was no longer in Cádiz! On the outbreak of the treaty, the Spanish authorities had given the Dutch merchant four-and-twenty hours to leave the country, and had seized his property, making him understand that it was only by a signal mercy that his life was spared. Amyntas rushed down to the harbour in dismay. The good ship *Calderon* had already sailed. Amyntas cursed his luck, he cursed himself; above all, he cursed the lovely Spanish lady whose charms had caused him to delay his search for Van Tiefel till the ship had gone on its eastward journey.

After looking long and wistfully at the sea, he turned back into the town and rambled melancholy through the streets, wondering what would become of him. Soon the pangs of hunger assailed him, and he knew the discomfort of a healthy English appetite. He hadn't a single farthing, and even Scotch poets, when they come to London to set the Thames on fire, are wont to put a half-crown piece in their pockets. Amyntas meditated upon the folly of extravagance, the indiscretion of youth and the wickedness of woman. . . . He tightened his belt and walked on. At last,

feeling weary and faint with hunger, he lay down on the steps of a church and there spent the night. When he awoke next morning, he soon remembered that he had slept supperless; he was ravenous. Suddenly his eye, looking across the square, caught sight of a bookshop, and it occurred to him that he might turn to account the books which his father and the parson had given him. He blessed their foresight. The Bible fetched nothing, but the Aristotle brought him enough to keep him from starvation for a week. Having satisfied his hunger, he set about trying to find work. He went to booksellers and told them his accomplishments, but no one could see any use in a knowledge of Greek, Latin, and the Hebrew Bible. He applied at shops. Growing bolder with necessity, he went into merchants' offices, and to great men's porters, but all with great civility sent him about his business, and poor Amyntas was no more able to get work than nowadays a professional tramp or the secretary of a trade's union.

For days he went on, trying here and trying there, eating figs and melons and bread, drinking water, sleeping beneath archways or on the steps of churches, and he dreamed of the home of roast beef and ale which he had left behind him. Every day he became more disheartened. But at last he rose up against Fate; he cursed it Byronically. Every man's hand was against him; his hand should be against every man. He would be a brigand! He shook off his feet the dust of Cádiz, and boldly went into the country to find a band of free companions. He stopped herdsmen and pedlars and asked them where brigands were. They pointed to the mountains, and to the mountains he turned his face. He would join the band, provoke a quarrel with the chief, kill him and be made chief in his stead. Then he would scour the country in a velvet mask and a peaked hat with a feather in it, carrying fire and desolation everywhere. A price would be set on his head, but he would snap his fingers in the face of the Prime Minister. He would rule his followers with an iron hand. But now he was in the midst of the mountains, and there were not the smallest signs of lawless folk, not even a gibbet with a skeleton hanging in chains to show where lawless folk had been. He sought high and low, but he never saw a living soul besides a few shepherds clothed in skins. It was most disheartening! Once he saw two men crouching behind a rock, and approached them; but as soon as they saw him they ran away, and although he followed them, shouting that they

were not to be afraid since he wanted to be a brigand too, they paid no attention, but only ran the faster, and at last he had to give up the chase for want of breath. One can't be a robber chief all by oneself, nor is it given to everyone in this world to be a brigand. Amyntas found that even heroes have their limitations.

X

One day, making his way along a rocky path, he found a swineherd guarding his flock.

"Good-morrow!" said the man, and asked Amyntas whither he was bound.

"God knows!" answered Amyntas. "I am wandering at chance, and know not where I go."

"Well, youth, stay the night with me, and to-morrow you can set out again. In return for your company I will give you food and shelter."

Amyntas accepted gratefully, for he had been feeding on herbs for a week, and the prospect of goat's milk, cheese, and black bread was like the feast of Trimalchio. When Amyntas had said his story, the herdsman told him that there was a rich man in the neighbouring village who wanted a swineherd, and in the morning showed him the way to the rich man's house.

"I will come a little way with you lest you take the wrong path. . . ."

They walked along the rocky track, and presently the way divided.

"This path to the right leads to the village," said the man.

"And this one to the left, swineherd?"

The swineherd crossed himself.

"Ah! that is the path of evil fortune. It leads to the accursed cavern."

A cold wind blew across their faces.

"Come away," said the herdsman, shuddering. "Do you not feel on your face the cold breath of it?"

"Tell me what it is," said Amyntas. He stood looking at the opening between the low trees.

"It is a lake of death—a lake beneath the mountain—and the roof of it is held up by marble columns, which were never wrought

by the hand of man. Come away! Do you not feel on your face the cold breath of it?"

He dragged Amyntas away along the path that led to the village, and when the way was clear before him, turned back, returning to his swine. But Amyntas ran after him.

"Tell me what they say of the accursed cavern."

"They say many things. Some say it is a treasure-house of the Moors, where they have left their wealth. Some say it is an entrance to the enchanted land; some say it is an entrance to hell itself. . . . Venturous men have gone in to discover the terrible secret, but none has returned to tell it."

Amyntas wandered slowly towards the village. Were his dreams to end in the herding of swine? What was this cavern of which the herdsman spoke? He felt a strange impulse to go back and look at the dark opening between the little trees from which blew the cold wind. . . . But perhaps the rich man had a beauteous daughter; history is full of the social successes of swineherds. Amyntas felt a strange thrill as the dark lake came before his mind; he almost heard the lapping of the water. . . . Kings' daughters had often looked upon lowly swineherds and raised them to golden thrones. But he could not help going to look again at the dark opening between the little trees. He walked back and again the cold breath blew against his face; he felt in it the icy coldness of the water. It drew him in; he separated the little trees on either side. He walked on as if a hidden power urged him. And now the path became less clear; trees and bushes grew in the way and hindered him, brambles and long creeping plants twisted about his legs and pulled him back. But the wind with its coldness of the black water drew him on. . . . The birds of the air were hushed, and not one of the thousand insects of the wood uttered a note. Great trees above him hid the light. The silence was ghastly; he felt as if he were the only person in the world.

Suddenly he gave a cry; he had come to the end of the forest, and before him he saw the opening of the cavern. He looked in; he saw black, stagnant water, motionless and heavy, and, as far as the eye could reach, sombre pillars, covered with green, moist slime; they stood half out of the water, supporting the roof, and from the roof oozed moisture which fell in heavy drops, in heavy drops continually. At the entrance was a little skiff with a paddle in it.

Amyntas stood at the edge. Dared he venture? What could there be behind that darkness? The darkness was blacker than the blackest night. He stepped into the boat. Should he go? With beating heart he untied the rope; he hardly dared to breathe. He pushed away.

XI

He looked to the right and left, paddling slowly; on all sides he saw the slimy columns stretching regularly into the darkness. The light of the open day grew dimmer as he advanced, the air became colder. He looked eagerly around him, paddling slowly. Already he half repented the attempt. The boat went along easily, and the black and heavy water hardly splashed as he drew his paddle through it. Still nothing could be seen but the even ranks of pillars. Then, all at once, the night grew blacker, and again the cold wind arose and blew in his face; everywhere were the ghastly silence and the darkness. A shiver went through him; he could not bear it; in an agony of terror he turned his paddle to go back. Whatever might be the secret of the cavern or the reward of the adventure, he dared go no further. He must get back quickly to the open air and the blue sky. He drew his paddle through the water. The boat did not turn. He gave a cry, he pulled with all his might, the boat only lurched a little and went on its way. He set his teeth and backed; his life depended upon it. The boat swam on. A cold sweat broke out over him; he put all his strength in his stroke. The boat went on into the darkness swiftly and silently. He paused a little to regain force; he stifled a sob of horror and despair. Then he made a last effort; the skiff whirled round into another avenue of columns, and the paddle shivered into atoms against a pillar. The little light of the cavern entrance was lost, and there was utter darkness.

Amyntas cowered down in the boat. He gave up hope of life, and lay there for long hours awaiting his end; the water carried the skiff along swiftly, silently. The darkness was so heavy that the columns were invisible, heavy drops fell into the water from the roof. How long would it last? Would the boat go on till he died, and then speed on forever? He thought of the others who had gone

into the cavern. Were there other boats hurrying eternally along the heavy waters, bearing cold skeletons?

He covered his face with his hands and moaned. But he started up, the night seemed less black; he looked intently; yes, he could distinguish the outlines of the pillars dimly, so dimly that he thought he saw them only in imagination. And soon he could see distinctly their massive shapes against the surrounding darkness. And as gradually the night thinned away into dim twilight, he saw that the columns were different from those at the entrance of the cavern; they were no longer covered with weed and slime, the marble was polished and smooth; and the water beneath him appeared less black. The skiff went on so swiftly that the perpetual sequence of the pillars tired his eyes; but their grim severity gave way to round columns less forbidding and more graceful; as the light grew clearer, there was almost a tinge of blue in the water. Amyntas was filled with wonder, for the columns became lighter and more decorated, surmounted by capitals, adorned with strange sculptures. Some were green and some were red, others were yellow or glistening white; they mirrored themselves in the sapphire water. Gradually the roof raised itself and the columns became more slender; from them sprang lofty arches, gorgeously ornamented, and all was gold and silver and rich colour. The water turned to a dazzling, translucent blue, so that Amyntas could see hundreds of feet down to the bottom, and the bottom was covered with golden sand. And the light grew and grew till it was more brilliant than the clearest day; gradually the skiff slowed down and it swam leisurely towards the light's source, threading its way beneath the horse-shoe arches among the columns, and these gathered themselves into two lines to form a huge avenue surmounted by a vast span, and at the end, in a splendour of light, Amyntas saw a wondrous palace, with steps leading down to the water. The boat glided towards it and at the steps ceased moving.

XII

At the same moment the silver doors of the palace were opened, and from them issued black slaves, magnificently apparelled; they descended to Amyntas and with courteous gestures assisted him out of the boat. Then two other slaves, even more splendidly at-

tired than their fellows, came down and led Amyntas slowly and with great state into the court of the palace, at the end of which was a great chamber; into this they motioned the youth to enter. They made him the lowest possible bows and retired, letting a curtain fall over the doorway. But immediately the curtain was raised and other slaves came in, bearing gorgeous robes and all kinds of necessaries for the toilet. With much ceremony they proceeded to bathe and scent the fortunate creature; they polished and dyed his fingernails; they pencilled his eyebrows and faintly darkened his long eyelashes; they put precious balsam on his hair; then they clothed him in silken robes glittering with gold and silver; they put the daintiest red morocco shoes on his feet, a jewelled chain about his neck, rings on his fingers, and in his turban a rich diamond. Finally they placed before him a gigantic mirror, and left him.

Everything had been conducted in complete silence, and Amyntas throughout had preserved the most intense gravity. But when he was alone he gave a little silent laugh of delight. It was obvious that at last he was to be rewarded according to his deserts. He looked at the rings on his fingers, resisting a desire to put one or two of them in his pocket in case of a future rainy day. Then, catching sight of himself in the mirror, he started. Was that really himself? How very delightful! He made sure that no one could see, and then began to make bows to himself in the mirror; he walked up and down the room, observing the stateliness of his gesture; he waved his hands in a lordly and patronising fashion; he turned himself round to look at his back; he was very annoyed that he could not see his profile. He came to the conclusion that he looked every inch a king's son, and his inner consciousness told him that consequently the king's daughter could not be far off.

But he would explore his palace! He girded his sword about him; it was a scimitar of beautiful workmanship, and the scabbard was incrusted with precious stones. . . . From the court he passed into many wonderful rooms, one leading out of the other; there were rich carpets on the marble floors, and fountains played softly in the centre, the walls were inlaid with rare marbles; but he never saw a living soul.

In the last hour Amyntas had become fully alive to his great importance, and carried himself accordingly. He took long, dignified steps, and held one hand on the jewelled hilt of his sword,

with his elbows stuck out at right angles to his body; his head was thrown back proudly and his nostrils dilated with appropriate scorn. At last he came to a door closed by a curtain; he raised it. But he started back and was so surprised that he found no words to express his emotions. Four maidens were sitting in the room, more beautiful than he had thought possible in his most extravagant dreams. The gods had evidently not intended Amyntas for single blessedness. . . . The young persons appeared not to have noticed him. Two of them were seated on rugs playing a languid game of chess, the others were lazily smoking cigarettes.

"Mate!" murmured one of the players.

"Oh!" sighed the other, yawning, "another game finished! That makes five million and twenty-three games against your five million and seventy-nine."

They all yawned.

But Amyntas felt he must give notice of his presence, and suddenly remembering an expression he had learnt on board ship, he put on a most ferocious look and cried out:

"Shiver my timbers!"

The maidens turned towards him with a little cry, but they quickly recovered themselves and one of them came towards him.

"You speak like a king's son, O youth!" she said.

There was a moment's hesitation, and the lady, with a smile, added, "Oh, ardently expected one, you are a compendium of the seven excellences!"

Then they all began to pay him compliments, each one capping the other's remark.

"You have a face like the full moon, O youth; your eyes are the eyes of the gazelle; your walk is like the gait of the mountain partridge; your chin is as an apple; your cheeks are pomegranates."

But Amyntas interrupted them.

"For God's sake, madam," he said, "let us have no palavering, and if you love me give me some victuals . . . !"

Immediately female slaves came in with salvers laden with choice food, and the four maidens plied Amyntas with delicacies. At the end of the repast they sprinkled him with rose-water, and the eldest of them put a crown of roses on his hair. Amyntas thought that after all life was not an empty dream.

XIII

"And now, may it please you, O stranger, to hear our story.

"Know then that our father was a Moor, one of the wealthiest of his people, and he dwelt with his fellows in Spain, honoured and beloved. Now, when Allah—whose name be exalted!—decreed that our nation should be driven from the country, he, unwilling to leave the land of his birth, built him, with the aid of magic arts, this palace. Here he brought us, his four daughters and all his riches; he peopled it with slaves and filled it with all necessary things, and here we lived in peace and prosperity for many years; but at last a great misfortune befell us, for our father, who was a very learned man and accustomed to busy himself with many abstruse matters, one day got lost in a metaphysical speculation—and has never been found again."

Here she stopped, and they all sighed deeply.

"We searched high and low, but in vain, and he has not been found to this day. So we took his will, and having broken the seal, read the following: 'My daughters, I know by my wisdom that the time will come when I shall be lost to you; then you will live alone enjoying the riches and the pleasures which I have put at your disposal; but I foresee that at the end of many years a youth will find his way to this your palace. And though my magic arts have been able to build this paradise for your habitation, though they have endowed you with perpetual youth and loveliness, and, greatest deed of all, have banished hence the dark shadow of Death, yet have they not the power to make four maidens live in happiness and unity with but one man! Therefore, I have given unto each of you certain gifts, and of you four the youth shall choose one to be his love; and to him and her shall belong this palace, and all my riches, and all my power; while the remaining three shall leave everything here to these two, and depart hence forever.'

"Now, gentle youth, it is with you to choose which of us four you will have remain."

Amyntas looked at the four damsels standing before him, and his heart beat violently.

"I," resumed the speaker, "I am the eldest of the four, and it is my right to speak first."

She stepped forward and stood alone in front of Amyntas; her aspect was most queenly, her features beautiful and clear, her eyes proud and fiery; and masses of raven hair contrasted with the red flaming of her garments. With an imperious gesture she flung back her hair, and spoke thus:

"Know, youth, that the gift which my father gave me was the gift of war, and I have the power to make a great warrior of him whose love I am. I will make you a king, youth; you shall command mighty armies, and you shall lead them to battle on a prancing horse; your enemies shall quail before your face, and at last you shall die no sluggard's death, but pierced by honourable wounds, and the field of battle shall be your death-bed; a nation shall mourn your loss, and your name shall go down famous to after ages."

"You are very beautiful," said Amyntas, "but I am not so eager for warlike exploits as when I wandered through the green lanes of my native land. Let me hear the others."

A second stepped forward. She was clad most gorgeously of all; a crown of diamonds was on her head, and her robes were of cloth of gold sewn with rubies and emeralds and sapphires.

"The gift I have to give is wealth, riches—riches innumerable, riches greater than man can dream of. Do you want to be a king, the riches I can give will make you one; do you want armies, riches can procure them; do you want victory, riches can buy it—all these that my sister offers you can I with my riches give you; and more than that, for everything in the world can be got with riches, and you shall be all-powerful. Take me to be your love and I will make you the Lord of Gold."

Amyntas smiled.

"You forget, lady, that I am but twenty."

The third stepped forward. She was beautiful and pale and thoughtful. Her hair was yellow, like corn when the sun is shining on it; and her dress was green, like the young grass of the spring. She spoke without the animation of the others, mournfully rather than proudly, and she looked at Amyntas with melancholy eyes.

"I am the Lady of Art; all that is beautiful and good and wise is in my province. Live with me; I will make you a poet, and

you shall sing beautiful songs. You shall be wise; and in perfect wisdom, O youth!, is perfect happiness."

"The poet has said that wisdom is weariness, O lady!" said Amyntas. "My father is a poet; he has written ten thousand Latin hexameters, and a large number of Greek iambics. . . ."

Then came forward the last. As she stood before Amyntas a cry burst from him; he had never in his life seen anyone so ravishingly beautiful. She was looking down, and her long eyelashes prevented her eyes from being seen, but her lips were like a perfect rose, and her skin was like a peach; her hair fell to her waist in great masses of curls, and their sparkling auburn, many-hued and indescribable, changed in the sunbeams from richest brown to gold, tinged with deep red. She wore a simple tunic of thin silk, clasped at her waist with a jewelled belt of gold.

She stood before Amyntas, letting him gaze; then suddenly she lifted her eyes to his. Amyntas's heart gave a mighty beat against his chest. Her eyes, her eyes were the very lights of love, carrying passionate kisses on their beams. A sob of ecstasy choked the youth, and he felt that he could kneel down and worship before them.

Slowly her lips broke into a smile, and her voice was soft and low.

"I am the Lady of Love," she said. "Look!" She raised her arms, and the thin, loose sleeves falling back displayed their roundness and exquisite shape; she lifted her head, and Amyntas thrilled to cover her neck with kisses. At last she loosened her girdle, and when the silken tunic fell to her feet she stood before him in perfect loveliness.

"I cannot give you fame, or riches, or wisdom; I can only give you Love, Love, Love. . . . Oh, what an eternity of delight shall we enjoy in one another's arms! Come, my beloved, come!"

"Yes, I come, my darling!" Amyntas stepped forward with outstretched arms, and took her hands in his. "I take you for my love; I want not wealth nor great renown, but only you. You will give me love-alluring kisses, and we will live in never-ending bliss."

He drew her to him, and with his arms around her, pressed back her head and covered her lips with kisses.

XIV

And while Amyntas lost his soul in the eyes of his beloved, the three sisters went sadly away. They ascended the stately barge which awaited them, and the water bore them down the long avenue of columns into the darkness. After a long time they reached the entrance of the cavern, and, having placed a great stone against it, that none might enter more, they separated, wandering in different directions.

The Lady of War passed through Spain, finding none there worthy of her. She crossed the mountains, and presently she fell in love with a little artillery officer, and raised him to dignity and power; and together they ran through the lands, wasting and burning, making women widows and children orphans, ruthless, unsparing, caring for naught but the voluptuousness of blood. But she sickened of the man at last and left him; then the blood he had spilt rose up against him, and he was cast down and died an exile on a lonely isle. And now they say she dwells in the palaces of a youth with a withered hand; together they rule a mighty empire, and their people cry out at the oppression, but the ruler heeds nothing but the burning kisses of his love.

The Lady of Riches, too, passed out of Spain. But she was not content with one love, nor with a hundred. She gave her favours to the first comer, and everyone was welcome; she wandered carelessly through the world, but chiefly she loved an island in the north; and in its capital she has her palace, and the inhabitants of the isle have given themselves over, body and soul, to her domination; they pander and lie and cheat, and forswear themselves; to gain her smile, they will shrink from no base deed, no meanness; and she, too, makes women widows and children orphans. . . . But her subjects care not; they are fat and well content; the goddess smiles on them, and they are the richest in the world.

The Lady of Art has not found an emperor nor a mighty people to be her lovers. She wanders lonely through the world; now and then a youthful dreamer sees her in his sleep and devotes his life to her pursuit; but the way is hard, very hard; so he turns aside to worship at the throne of her sister of Riches, and

she repays him for the neglect he has suffered, she showers gold upon him and makes him one of her knights. But sometimes the youth remains faithful, and goes through his life in the endless search; and at last, when his end has come, she comes down to the garret in which he lies cold and dead, and, stooping down, kisses him gently—and lo! he is immortal.

But as for Amyntas, when the sisters had retired, he again took his bride in his arms, and covered her lips with kisses; and she, putting her arms round his neck, said with a smile:

"I have waited for you so long, my love, so long!"

And here it is fit that we should follow the example of the three sisters, and retire also.

The moral of this story is that if your godfathers and godmothers at your baptism give you a pretty name, you will probably marry the most beautiful woman in the world and live happily ever afterwards. . . . And the platitudinous philosopher may marvel at the tremendous effects of the most insignificant causes, for if Amyntas had been called Peter or John, as his mother wished, William II might be eating sauerkraut as peacefully as his ancestors, the Lord Mayor of London might not drive about in a gilded carriage, and possibly even—Mr. Alfred Austin might not be Poet Laureate. . . .

DAISY

(1899)

I

It was Sunday morning—a damp, warm November morning, with the sky overhead grey and low. Miss Reed stopped a little to take breath before climbing the hill, at the top of which, in the middle of the churchyard, was Blackstable Church. Miss Reed panted, and the sultriness made her loosen her jacket. She stood at the junction of the two roads which led to the church, one from the harbour end of the town and the other from the station. Behind her lay the houses of Blackstable, the wind-beaten houses with slate roofs of the old fishing village and the red brick villas of the seaside resort which Blackstable was fast becoming; in the harbour were the masts of the ships, colliers that brought coal from the north; and beyond, the grey sea, very motionless, mingling in the distance with the sky. . . . The peal of the church bells ceased, and was replaced by a single bell, ringing a little hurriedly, querulously, which denoted that there were only ten minutes before the beginning of the service. Miss Reed walked on; she looked curiously at the people who passed her, wondering. . . .

"Good-morning, Mr. Golding!" she said to a fisherman who pounded by her, ungainly in his Sunday clothes.

"Good-morning, Miss Reed!" he replied. "Warm this morning."

She wondered whether he knew anything of the subject which made her heart beat with excitement whenever she thought of it, and for thinking of it she hadn't slept a wink all night.

"Have you seen Mr. Griffith this morning?" she asked, watching his face.

"No; I saw Mrs. Griffith and George as I was walking up."

"Oh! they are coming to church, then!" Miss Reed cried with the utmost surprise.

Mr. Golding looked at her stupidly, not understanding her agitation. But they had reached the church. Miss Reed stopped in the porch to wipe her boots and pass an arranging hand over her hair. Then, gathering herself together, she walked down the aisle to her pew.

She arranged the hassock and knelt down, clasping her hands and closing her eyes; she said the Lord's Prayer; and being a religious woman, she did not immediately rise, but remained a certain time in the same position of worship to cultivate a proper frame of mind, her long, sallow face upraised, her mouth firmly closed, and her eyelids quivering a little from the devotional force with which she kept her eyes shut; her thin bust, very erect, was encased in a black jacket as in a coat of steel. But when Miss Reed considered that a due period had elapsed, she opened her eyes, and, as she rose from her knees, bent over to a lady sitting just in front of her.

"Have you heard about the Griffiths, Mrs. Howlett?"

"No . . . ! What is it?" answered Mrs. Howlett, half turning round, intensely curious.

Miss Reed waited a moment to heighten the effect of her statement.

"Daisy Griffith has eloped—with an officer from the depot at Tercanbury."

Mrs. Howlett gave a little gasp.

"You don't say so!"

"It's all they could expect," whispered Miss Reed. "They ought to have known something was the matter when she went into Tercanbury three or four times a week."

Blackstable is six miles from Tercanbury, which is a cathedral city and has a cavalry depot.

"I've seen her hanging about the barracks with my own eyes," said Mrs. Howlett, "but I never suspected anything."

"Shocking, isn't it?" said Miss Reed, with suppressed delight.

"But how did you find out?" asked Mrs. Howlett.

"Ssh!" whispered Miss Reed—the widow, in her excitement, had raised her voice a little and Miss Reed could never suffer the least irreverence in church. . . . "She never came back last

night, and George Browning saw them get into the London train at Tercanbury."

"Well, I never!" exclaimed Mrs. Howlett.

"D'you think the Griffiths'll have the face to come to church?"

"I shouldn't if I was them," said Miss Reed.

But at that moment the vestry door was opened and the organ began to play the hymn.

"I'll see you afterwards," Miss Reed whispered hurriedly; and, rising from their seats, both ladies began to sing:

O Jesus, thou art standing
Outside the fast closed door,
In lowly patience waiting
To pass the threshold o'er;
We bear the name of Christians. . . .

Miss Reed held the book rather close to her face, being short-sighted; but, without even lifting her eyes, she had become aware of the entrance of Mrs. Griffith and George. She glanced significantly at Mrs. Howlett. Mr. Griffith hadn't come, although he was churchwarden, and Mrs. Howlett gave an answering look which meant that it was then evidently quite true. But they both gathered themselves together for the last verse, taking breath.

O Jesus, thou are pleading
In accents meek and low . . .

A—A—men! The congregation fell to its knees, and the curate, rolling his eyes to see who was in church, began gabbling the morning prayers—*"Dearly beloved brethren. . . ."*

II

At the Sunday dinner, the vacant place of Daisy Griffith stared at them. Her father sat at the head of the table, looking down at his plate, in silence; every now and then, without raising his head, he glanced up at the empty space, filled with a madness of grief. . . . He had gone into Tercanbury in the morning, inquiring at the houses of all Daisy's friends, imagining that she had spent the night with one of them. He could not believe that George Browning's story was true; he could so easily have been

mistaken in the semi-darkness of the station. And even he had gone to the barracks—his cheeks still burned with the humiliation—asking if they knew a Daisy Griffith.

He pushed his plate away with a groan. He wished passionately that it were Monday, so that he could work. And the post would surely bring a letter, explaining.

"The vicar asked where you were," said Mrs. Griffith.

Robert, the father, looked at her with his pained eyes, but her eyes were hard and shining, her lips almost disappeared in the tight closing of the mouth. She was willing to believe the worst. He looked at his son; he was frowning; he looked as coldly angry as the mother. He, too, was willing to believe everything, and they neither seemed very sorry. . . . Perhaps they were even glad.

"I was the only one who loved her," he muttered to himself, and, pushing back his chair, he got up and left the room. He almost tottered; he had aged twenty years in the night.

"Aren't you going to have any pudding?" asked his wife.

He made no answer.

He walked out into the courtyard quite aimlessly, but the force of habit took him to the workshop, where, every Sunday afternoon, he was used to going after dinner to see that everything was in order, and to-day also he opened the window, put away a tool which the men had left about, examined the Saturday's work. . . .

Mrs. Griffith and George, stiff and ill at ease in his clumsy Sunday clothes, went on with their dinner.

"D'you think the vicar knew?" he asked as soon as the father had closed the door.

"I don't think he'd have asked if he had. Mrs. Gray might, but he's too simple—unless she put him up to it."

"I thought I should never get round with the plate," said George. Mr. Griffith, being a carpenter, which is respectable and well to do, which is honourable, had been made churchwarden, and part of his duty was to take round the offertory plate. This duty George performed in his father's occasional absences, as when a coffin was very urgently required.

"I wasn't going to let them get anything out of me," said Mrs. Griffith, defiantly.

All through the service a number of eyes had been fixed on

them, eager to catch some sign of emotion, full of horrible curiosity to know what the Griffiths felt and thought; but Mrs. Griffith had been inscrutable.

III

Next day the Griffiths lay in wait for the postman; George sat by the parlour window, peeping through the muslin curtains.

"Fanning's just coming up the street," he said at last. Until the post had come old Griffith could not work; in the courtyard at the back was heard the sound of hammering.

There was a rat-tat at the door, the sound of a letter falling on the mat, and Fanning the postman passed on. George leaned back quickly so that he might not see him. Mr. Griffith fetched the letter, opened it with trembling hands. . . . He gave a little gasp of relief.

"She's got a situation in London."

"Is that all she says?" asked Mrs. Griffith. "Give me the letter," and she almost tore it from her husband's hand.

She read it through and uttered a little ejaculation of contempt —almost of triumph. "You don't mean to say you believe that?" she cried.

"Let's look, Mother," said George. He read the letter and he too gave a snort of contempt.

"She says she's got a situation," repeated Mrs. Griffith, with a sneer at her husband, "and we're not to be angry or anxious, and she's quite happy—and we can write to Charing Cross Post Office. I know what sort of a situation she's got."

Mr. Griffith looked from his wife to his son.

"Don't you think it's true?" he asked helplessly. At the first moment he had put the fullest faith in Daisy's letter, he had been so anxious to believe it; but the scorn of the others . . .

"There's Miss Reed coming down the street," said George. "She's looking this way, and she's crossing over. I believe she's coming in."

"What does she want?" asked Mrs. Griffith, angrily.

There was another knock at the door, and through the curtains they saw Miss Reed's eyes looking towards them, trying to pierce the muslin. Mrs. Griffith motioned the two men out of the room,

and hurriedly put antimacassars on the chairs. The knock was repeated, and Mrs. Griffith, catching hold of a duster, went to the door.

"Oh, Miss Reed! Who'd have thought of seeing you?" she cried with surprise.

"I hope I'm not disturbing," answered Miss Reed, with an acid smile.

"Oh, dear no!" said Mrs. Griffith. "I was just doing the dusting in the parlour. Come in, won't you? The place is all upside down, but you won't mind that, will you?"

Miss Reed sat on the edge of a chair.

"I thought I'd just pop in to ask about dear Daisy. I met Fanning as I was coming along and he told me you'd had a letter."

"Oh! Daisy?" Mrs. Griffith had understood at once why Miss Reed came, but she was rather at a loss for an answer. . . . "Yes, we have had a letter from her. She's up in London."

"Yes, I knew that," said Miss Reed. "George Browning saw them get into the London train, you know."

Mrs. Griffith saw it was no good fencing, but an idea occurred to her.

"Yes, of course her father and I are very distressed about—her eloping like that."

"I can quite understand that," said Miss Reed.

"But it was on account of his family. He didn't want anyone to know about it till he was married."

"Oh!" said Miss Reed, raising her eyebrows very high.

"Yes," said Mrs. Griffith, "that's what she said in her letter; they were married on Saturday at a registry office."

"But, Mrs. Griffith, I'm afraid she's been deceiving you. It's Captain Hogan . . . and he's a married man."

She could have laughed outright at the look of dismay on Mrs. Griffith's face. The blow was sudden, and, notwithstanding all her power of self-control, Mrs. Griffith could not help herself. But at once she recovered, an angry flush appeared on her cheekbones.

"You don't mean it?" she cried.

"I'm afraid it's quite true," said Miss Reed, humbly. "In fact I know it is."

"Then she's a lying, deceitful hussy, and she's made a fool of

all of us. I give you my word of honour that she told us she was married; I'll fetch you the letter." Mrs. Griffith rose from her chair, but Miss Reed put out a hand to stop her.

"Oh, don't trouble, Mrs. Griffith; of course I believe you," she said, and Mrs. Griffith immediately sat down again.

But she burst into a storm of abuse of Daisy, for her deceitfulness and wickedness. She vowed she should never forgive her. She assured Miss Reed again and again that she had known nothing about it. Finally she burst into a perfect torrent of tears. Miss Reed was mildly sympathetic; but now she was anxious to get away to impart her news to the rest of Blackstable. Mrs. Griffith sobbed her visitor out of the front door, but when she had closed it, dried her tears. She went into the parlour and flung open the door that led to the back room. Griffith was sitting with his face hidden in his hands, and every now and then a sob shook his great frame. George was very pale, biting his nails.

"You heard what she said," cried Mrs. Griffith. "He's married . . . !" She looked at her husband contemptuously. "It's all very well for you to carry on like that now. It was you who did it; it was all your fault. If she'd been brought up as I wanted her to be, this wouldn't ever have happened."

Again there was a knock, and George, going out, ushered in Mrs. Gray, the vicar's wife. She rushed in when she heard the sound of voices.

"Oh, Mrs. Griffith, it's dreadful! simply dreadful! Miss Reed has just told me all about it. What is to be done? And what'll the dissenters make of it? Oh dear, it's simply dreadful!"

"You've just come in time, Mrs. Gray," said Mrs. Griffith, angrily. "It's not my fault, I can tell you that. It's her father who's brought it about. He would have her go into Tercanbury to be educated, and he would have her take singing lessons and dancing lessons. The Church school was good enough for George. It's been Daisy this and Daisy that all through. Me and George have been always put by for Daisy. I didn't want her brought up above her station, I can assure you. It's him who would have her brought up as a lady; and see what's come of it! And he let her spend any money she liked on her dress. . . . It wasn't me that let her go into Tercanbury every day in the week if she wanted to. I knew she was up to no good. There you see what you've brought her to; it's you who's disgraced us all!"

She hissed out the words with intense malignity, nearly screaming in the bitterness she felt towards the beautiful daughter of better education than herself, almost of different station. It was all but a triumph for her that this had happened. It brought her daughter down; she turned the tables, and now, from the superiority of her virtue, she looked down upon her with utter contempt.

IV

On the following Sunday the people of Blackstable enjoyed an emotion; as Miss Reed said:

"It was worth going to church this morning, even for a dissenter."

The vicar was preaching, and the congregation paid a very languid attention, but suddenly a curious little sound went through the church—one of those scarcely perceptible noises which no comparison can explain; it was a quick attraction of all eyes, an arousing of somnolent intelligences, a slight, quick drawing-in of the breath. The listeners had heeded very indifferently Mr. Gray's admonitions to brotherly love and charity as matters which did not concern them other than abstractedly; but quite suddenly they had realised that he was bringing his discourse round to the subject of Daisy Griffith, and they pricked up both ears. They saw it coming directly along the highways of Vanity and Luxuriousness; and everyone became intensely wide awake.

"And we have in all our minds," he said at last, "the terrible fall which has almost broken the hearts of sorrowing parents and brought bitter grief—bitter grief and shame to all of us. . . ."

He went on hinting at the scandal in the matter of the personal columns in newspapers, and drawing a number of obvious morals. The Griffith family were sitting in their pew well in view of the congregation; and, losing even the shadow of decency, the people turned round and stared at them, ghoul-like. . . . Robert Griffith sat in the corner with his head bent down, huddled up, his rough face speaking in all its lines the terrible humiliation; his hair was all dishevelled. He was not more than fifty, and he looked an old man. But Mrs. Griffith sat next him, very erect, not leaning against the back, with her head well up, her mouth firmly closed, and she looked straight in front of her, her little eyes sparkling, as

if she had not an idea that a hundred people were staring at her. In the other corner was George, very white, looking up at the roof in simulation of indifference. Suddenly a sob came from the Griffiths' pew, and people saw that the father had broken down; he seemed to forget where he was, and he cried as if indeed his heart were broken. The great tears ran down his cheeks in the sight of all—the painful tears of men; he had not even the courage to hide his face in his hands. Still Mrs. Griffith made no motion, she never gave a sign that she heard her husband's agony; but two little red spots appeared angrily on her cheek-bones, and perhaps she compressed her lips a little more tightly. . . .

V

Six months passed. One evening, when Mr. Griffith was standing at the door after work, smoking his pipe, the postman handed him a letter. He changed colour and his hand shook when he recognized the handwriting. He turned quickly into the house.

"A letter from Daisy," he said. They had not replied to her first letter, and since then had heard nothing.

"Give it to me," said his wife.

He drew it quickly towards him, with an instinctive gesture of retention.

"It's addressed to me."

"Well, then, you'd better open it."

He looked up at his wife; he wanted to take the letter away and read it alone, but her eyes were upon him, compelling him there and then to open it.

"She wants to come back," he said in a broken voice.

Mrs. Griffith snatched the letter from him.

"That means he's left her," she said.

The letter was all incoherent, nearly incomprehensible, covered with blots, every other word scratched out. One could see that the girl was quite distraught, and Mrs. Griffith's keen eyes saw the trace of tears on the paper. . . . It was a long, bitter cry of repentance. She begged them to take her back, repeating again and again the cry of penitence, piteously beseeching them to forgive her.

"I'll go and write to her," said Mr. Griffith.

"Write what?"

"Why—that it's all right and she isn't to worry; and we want her back, and that I'll go up and fetch her."

Mrs. Griffith placed herself between him and the door.

"What d'you mean?" she cried. "She's not coming back into my house."

Mr. Griffith started back.

"You don't want to leave her where she is! She says she'll kill herself."

"Yes, I believe that," she replied scornfully; and then, gathering up her anger, "D'you mean to say you expect me to have her in the house after what she's done? I tell you I won't. She's never coming in this house again as long as I live; I'm an honest woman and she isn't. She's a ——" Mrs. Griffith called her daughter the foulest name that can be applied to her sex.

Mr. Griffith stood indecisively before his wife.

"But think what a state she's in, Mother. She was crying when she wrote the letter."

"Let her cry; she'll have to cry a lot more before she's done. And it serves her right; and it serves you right. She'll have to go through a good deal more than that before God forgives her, I can tell you."

"Perhaps she's starving."

"Let her starve, for all I care. She's dead to us; I've told everyone in Blackstable that I haven't got a daughter now, and if she came on her bended knees before me I'd spit on her."

George had come in and listened to the conversation.

"Think what people would say, Father," he said now; "as it is, it's jolly awkward, I can tell you. No one would speak to us if she was back again. It's not as if people didn't know; everyone in Blackstable knows what she's been up to."

"And what about George?" put in Mrs. Griffith. "D'you think the Polletts would stand it?" George was engaged to Edith Pollett.

"She'd be quite capable of breaking it off if Daisy came back," said George. "She's said as much."

"Quite right, too!" cried his mother. "And I'm not going to be like Mrs. Jay with Lottie. Everyone knows about Lottie's goings-on, and you can see how people treat them—her and her mother. When Mrs. Gray passes them in the street she always goes on

the other side. No, I've always held my head high, and I'm always going to. I've never done anything to be ashamed of as far as I know, and I'm not going to begin now. Everyone knows it was no fault of mine what Daisy did, and all through I've behaved so that no one should think the worse of me."

Mr. Griffith sank helplessly into a chair, the old habit of submission asserted itself, and his weakness gave way as usual before his wife's strong will. He had not the courage to oppose her.

"What shall I answer, then?" he asked.

"Answer? Nothing."

"I must write something. She'll be waiting for the letter, and waiting and waiting."

"Let her wait."

VI

A few days later another letter came from Daisy, asking pitifully why they didn't write, begging them again to forgive her and take her back. The letter was addressed to Mr. Griffith; the girl knew that it was only from him she might expect mercy; but he was out when it arrived. Mrs. Griffith opened it, and passed it on to her son. They looked at one another guiltily; the same thought had occurred to both, and each knew it was in the other's mind.

"I don't think we'd better let Father see it," Mrs. Griffith said, a little uncertainly; "it'll do no good and it'll only distress him."

"And it's no good making a fuss, because we can't have her back."

"She'll never enter this door as long as I'm in the world. . . . I think I'll lock it up."

"I'd burn it, if I was you, Mother. It's safer."

Then every day Mrs. Griffith made a point of going to the door herself for the letters. Two more came from Daisy.

I know it's not you; it's Mother and George. They've always hated me. Oh, don't be so cruel, Father! You don't know what I've gone through. I've cried and cried till I thought I should die. For God's sake write to me! They might let you write just once. I'm alone all day, day after day, and I think I shall go

mad. You might take me back; I'm sure I've suffered enough, and you wouldn't know me now, I'm so changed. Tell Mother that if she'll only forgive me I'll be quite different. I'll do the housework and anything she tells me. I'll be a servant to you, and you can send the girl away. If you knew how I repent! Do forgive me and have me back. Oh, I know that no one would speak to me; but I don't care about that, if I can only be with you!

"She doesn't think about us," said George, "what we should do if she was back. No one would speak to us, either."

But the next letter said that she couldn't bear the terrible silence; if her father didn't write she'd come down to Blackstable. Mrs. Griffith was furious.

"I'd shut the door in her face; I wonder how she can dare to come."

"It's jolly awkward," said George. "Supposing Father found out we'd kept back the letters?"

"It was for his own good," said Mrs. Griffith, angrily. "I'm not ashamed of what I've done, and I'll tell him so to his face if he says anything to me."

"Well, it is awkward. You know what Father is; if he saw her. . . ."

Mrs. Griffith paused a moment.

"You must go up and see her, George!"

"Me!" he cried in astonishment, a little in terror.

"You must go as if you came from her father to say we won't have anything more to do with her and she's not to write."

VII

Next day George Griffith, on getting out of the station at Victoria, jumped on a Fulham 'bus, taking his seat with the self-assertiveness of the countryman who intends to show the Londoners that he's as good as they are. He was in some trepidation and his best clothes. He didn't know what to say to Daisy, and his hands sweated uncomfortably. When he knocked at the door he wished she might be out—but that would only be postponing the ordeal.

"Does Mrs. Hogan live here?"

"Yes. Who shall I say?"

"Say a gentleman wants to see her."

He followed quickly on the landlady's heels and passed through the door the woman opened while she was giving the message. Daisy sprang to her feet with a cry.

"George!"

She was very pale, her blue eyes dim and lifeless, with the lids heavy and red; she was in a dressing gown, her beautiful hair dishevelled, wound loosely into a knot at the back of her head. She had not half the beauty of her old self. . . . George, to affirm the superiority of virtue over vice, kept his hat on.

She looked at him with frightened eyes, then her lips quivered, and, turning away her head, she fell on a chair and burst into tears. George looked at her sternly. His indignation was greater than ever now that he saw her. His old jealousy made him exult at the change in her.

"She's got nothing much to boast about now," he said to himself, noting how ill she looked.

"Oh, George . . . !" she began, sobbing; but he interrupted her.

"I've come from Father," he said, "and we don't want to have anything more to do with you, and you're not to write."

"Oh!" She looked at him now with her eyes suddenly quite dry. They seemed to burn her in their sockets. "Did he send you here to tell me that?"

"Yes; and you're not to come down."

She put her hand to her forehead, looking vacantly before her.

"But what am I to do? I haven't got any money; I've pawned everything."

George looked at her silently; but he was horribly curious.

"Why did he leave you?" he said.

She made no answer; she looked before her as if she were going out of her mind.

"Has he left you any money?" asked George.

Then she started up, her cheeks flaming red.

"I wouldn't touch a halfpenny of his. I'd rather starve!" she screamed.

George shrugged his shoulders.

"Well, you understand?" he said.

"Oh, how can you! It's all you and Mother. You've always hated me. But I'll pay you out, by God! I'll pay you out. I know what you are, all of you—you and Mother, and all the Blackstable people. You're a set of damned hypocrites."

"Look here, Daisy! I'm not going to stand here and hear you talk like that of me and Mother," he replied with dignity; "and as for the Blackstable people, you're not fit to—to associate with them. And I can see where you learnt your language."

Daisy burst into hysterical laughter. George became more angry—virtuously indignant.

"Oh, you can laugh as much as you like! I know your repentance is a lot of damned humbug. You've always been a conceited little beast. And you've been stuck up and cocky because you thought yourself nice-looking, and because you were educated in Tercanbury. And no one was good enough for you in Blackstable. And I'm jolly glad that all this has happened to you; it serves you jolly well right. And if you dare to show yourself at Blackstable, we'll send for the police."

Daisy stepped up to him.

"I'm a damned bad lot," she said, "but I swear I'm not half as bad as you are. . . . You know what you're driving me to."

"You don't think I care what you do," he answered, as he flung himself out of the door. He slammed it behind him, and he also slammed the front door to show that he was a man of high principles. And even George Washington when he said, "I cannot tell a lie; I did it with my little hatchet," did not feel so righteous as George Griffith at that moment.

Daisy went to the window to see him go, and then, throwing up her arms, she fell on her knees, weeping, weeping, and she cried:

"My God, have pity on me!"

VIII

"I wouldn't go through it again for a hundred pounds," said George, when he recounted his experience to his mother. "And she wasn't a bit humble, as you'd expect."

"Oh! that's Daisy all over. Whatever happens to her, she'll be as bold as brass."

"And she didn't choose her language," he said, with mingled grief and horror.

They heard nothing more of Daisy for over a year, when George went up to London for the choir treat. He did not come back till three o'clock in the morning, but he went at once to his mother's room.

He woke her very carefully, so as not to disturb his father. She started up, about to speak, but he prevented her with his hand.

"Come outside; I've got something to tell you."

Mrs. Griffith was about to tell him rather crossly to wait till the morrow, but he interrupted her:

"I've seen Daisy."

She quickly got out of bed, and they went together into the parlour.

"I couldn't keep it till the morning," he said. . . . "What d'you think she's doing now? Well, after we came out of the Empire, I went down Piccadilly, and—well, I saw Daisy standing there. . . . It did give me a turn, I can tell you; I thought some of the chaps would see her. I simply went cold all over. But they were on ahead and hadn't noticed her."

"Thank God for that!" said Mrs. Griffith, piously.

"Well, what d'you think I did? I went straight up to her and looked her full in the face. But d'you think she moved a muscle? She simply looked at me as if she'd never set eyes on me before. Well, I was taken aback, I can tell you. I thought she'd faint. Not a bit of it."

"No, I know Daisy," said Mrs. Griffith; "you think she's this and that, because she looks at you with those blue eyes of hers, as if she couldn't say boo to a goose, but she's got the very devil inside her. . . . Well, I shall tell her father that, just so as to let him see what she has come to. . . ."

The existence of the Griffith household went on calmly. Husband and wife and son led their life in the dull little fishing town, the seasons passed insensibly into one another, one year slid grad-

ually into the next; and the five years that went by seemed like one long, long day. Mrs. Griffith did not alter an atom; she performed her housework, went to church regularly, and behaved like a Christian woman in that state of life in which a merciful Providence had been pleased to put her. George got married, and on Sunday afternoons could be seen wheeling an infant in a perambulator along the street. He was a good husband and an excellent father. He never drank too much, he worked well, he was careful of his earnings, and he also went to church regularly; his ambition was to become churchwarden after his father. And even in Mr. Griffith there was not so very much change. He was more bowed, his hair and beard were greyer. His face was set in an expression of passive misery, and he was extremely silent. But as Mrs. Griffith said:

"Of course, he's getting old. One can't expect to remain young forever"—she was a woman who frequently said profound things —"and I've known all along he wasn't the sort of man to make old bones. He's never had the go in him that I have. Why, I'd make two of him."

The Griffiths were not so well-to-do as before. As Blackstable became a more important health resort, a regular undertaker opened a shop there; and his window, with two little model coffins and an arrangement of black Prince of Wales's feathers surrounded by a white wreath, took the fancy of the natives, so that Mr. Griffith almost completely lost the most remunerative part of his business. Other carpenters sprang into existence and took away much of the trade.

"I've no patience with him," said Mrs. Griffith of her husband. "He lets these newcomers come along and just take the bread out of his hands. Oh, if I was a man, I'd make things different, I can tell you! He doesn't seem to care. . . ."

At last, one day George came to his mother in a state of tremendous excitement.

"I say, Mother, you know the pantomime they've got at Tercanbury this week?"

"Yes."

"Well, the principal boy's Daisy."

Mrs. Griffith sank into a chair, gasping.

"Harry Ferne's been, and he recognised her at once. It's all over the town."

Mrs. Griffith, for the first time in her life, was completely at a loss for words.

"Tomorrow's the last night," added her son, after a little while, "and all the Blackstable people are going."

"To think that this should happen to me!" said Mrs. Griffith, distractedly. "What have I done to deserve it? Why couldn't it happen to Mrs. Garman or Mrs. Jay? If the Lord had seen fit to bring it upon them—well, I shouldn't have wondered."

"Edith wants us to go," said George—Edith was his wife.

"You don't mean to say you're going, with all the Blackstable people there?"

"Well, Edith says we ought to go, just to show them we don't care."

"Well, I shall come too!" cried Mrs. Griffith.

IX

Next evening half Blackstable took the special train to Tercanbury, which had been put on for the pantomime, and there was such a crowd at the doors that the impresario half thought of extending his stay. The Rev. Charles Gray and Mrs. Gray were there, also James, their nephew. Mr. Gray had some scruples about going to a theatre, but his wife said a pantomime was quite different; besides, curiosity may gently enter even a clerical bosom. Miss Reed was there in black satin, with her friend Mrs. Howlett; Mrs. Griffith sat in the middle of the stalls, flanked by her dutiful son and her daughter-in-law; and George searched for female beauty with his opera-glass, which is quite the proper thing to do on such occasions. . . .

The curtain went up, and the villagers of Dick Whittington's native place sang a chorus.

"Now she's coming," whispered George.

All those Blackstable hearts stood still. And Daisy, as Dick Whittington, bounded on the stage—in flesh-coloured tights, with particularly scanty trunks, and her bodice—rather low. The vicar's nephew sniggered, and Mrs. Gray gave him a reproachful glance; all the other Blackstable people looked pained; Miss Reed blushed. But as Daisy waved her hand and gave a kick, the audience

broke out into prolonged applause; Tercanbury people have no moral sense, although Tercanbury is a cathedral city.

Daisy began to sing:

I'm a jolly sort of boy, tol, lol,
And I don't care a damn who knows it.
I'm fond of every joy, tol, lol,
As you may very well suppose it.
Tol, lol, lol,
Tol, lol, lol.

Then the audience, the audience of a cathedral city, as Mr. Gray said, took up the refrain:

Tol, lol, lol,
Tol, lol, lol.

However, the piece went on to the bitter end, and Dick Whittington appeared in many different costumes and sang many songs, and kicked many kicks, till he was finally made Lord Mayor —in tights.

Ah, it was an evening of bitter humiliation for Blackstable people. Some of them, as Miss Reed said, behaved scandalously; they really appeared to enjoy it. And even George laughed at some of the jokes the cat made, though his wife and his mother sternly reproved him.

"I'm ashamed of you, George, laughing at such a time!" they said.

Afterwards the Grays and Miss Reed got into the same railway carriage with the Griffiths.

"Well, Mrs. Griffith," said the vicar's wife, "what do you think of your daughter now?"

"Mrs. Gray," replied Mrs. Griffith, solemnly, "I haven't got a daughter."

"That's a very proper spirit in which to look at it," answered the lady. . . . "She was simply covered with diamonds."

"They must be worth a fortune," said Miss Reed.

"Oh, I dare say they're not real," said Mrs. Gray; "at that distance and with the limelight, you know, it's very difficult to tell."

"I'm sorry to say," said Mrs. Griffith, with some asperity, feeling the doubt almost an affront to her, "I'm sorry to say that I *know* they're real."

The ladies coughed discreetly, scenting a little scandalous mystery which they must get out of Mrs. Griffith at another opportunity.

"My nephew James says she earns at least thirty or forty pounds a week."

Miss Reed sighed at the thought of such depravity.

"It's very sad," she remarked, "to think of such things happening to a fellow-creature. . . ."

"But what I can't understand," said Mrs. Gray, next morning, at the breakfast-table, "is how she got into such a position. We all know that at one time she was to be seen in—well, in a very questionable place, at an hour which left no doubt about her—her means of livelihood. I must say I thought she was quite lost. . . ."

"Oh well, I can tell you that easily enough," replied her nephew. "She's being kept by Sir Somebody Something, and he's running the show for her."

"James, I wish you would be more careful about your language. It's not necessary to call a spade a spade, and you can surely find a less objectionable expression to explain the relationship between the persons. . . . Don't you remember his name?"

"No; I heard it, but I've really forgotten."

"I see in this week's *Tercanbury Times* that there's a Sir Herbert Ously-Farrowham staying at the George just now."

"That's it. Sir Herbert Ously-Farrowham."

"How sad! I'll look him out in Burke."

She took down the reference book, which was kept beside the clergy list.

"Dear me, he's only twenty-nine. . . . And he's got a house in Cavendish Square and a house in the country. He must be very well-to-do; and he belongs to the Junior Carlton and two other clubs. . . . And he's got a sister who's married to Lord Edward Lake." Mrs. Gray closed the book and held it with a finger to mark the place, like a Bible. "It's very sad to think of the dissipation of so many members of the aristocracy. It sets such a bad example to the lower classes."

X

They showed old Griffith a portrait of Daisy in her theatrical costume.

"Has she come to that?" he said.

He looked at it a moment, then savagely tore it in pieces and flung it in the fire.

"Oh, my God!" he groaned; he could not get out of his head the picture, the shamelessness of the costume, the smile, the evident prosperity and content. He felt now that he had lost his daughter indeed. All these years he had kept his heart open to her, and his heart had bled when he thought of her starving, ragged, perhaps dead. He had thought of her begging her bread and working her beautiful hands to the bone in some factory. He had always hoped that some day she could return to him, purified by the fire of suffering. . . . But she was prosperous and happy and rich. She was applauded, worshipped; the papers were full of her praise. Old Griffith was filled with a feeling of horror, of immense repulsion. She was flourishing in her sin, and he loathed her. He had been so ready to forgive her when he thought her despairing and unhappy; but now he was implacable.

Three months later Mrs. Griffith came to her husband, trembling with excitement, and handed him a cutting from a paper:

We hear that Miss Daisy Griffith, who earned golden opinions in the provinces last winter with her Dick Whittington, is about to be married to Sir Herbert Ously-Farrowham. Her friends, and their name is legion, will join with us in the heartiest congratulations.

He returned the paper without answering.

"Well?" asked his wife.

"It is nothing to me. I don't know either of the parties mentioned."

At that moment there was a knock at the door, and Mrs. Gray and Miss Reed entered, having met on the doorstep. Mrs. Griffith at once regained her self-possession.

"Have you heard the news, Mrs. Griffith?" said Miss Reed.

"D'you mean about the marriage of Sir Herbert Ously-Farrowham?" She mouthed the long name.

"Yes," replied the two ladies together.

"It is nothing to me. . . . I have no daughter, Mrs. Gray."

"I'm sorry to hear you say that, Mrs. Griffith," said Mrs. Gray very stiffly. "I think you show a most unforgiving spirit."

"Yes," said Miss Reed; "I can't help thinking that if you'd treated poor Daisy in a—well, in a more *Christian* way, you might have saved her from a great deal."

"Yes," added Mrs. Gray. "I must say that all through I don't think you've shown a nice spirit at all. I remember poor, dear Daisy quite well, and she had a very sweet character. And I'm sure that if she'd been treated a little more gently, nothing of all this would have happened."

Mrs. Gray and Miss Reed looked at Mrs. Griffith sternly and reproachfully; they felt themselves like God Almighty judging a miserable sinner. Mrs. Griffith was extremely angry; she felt that she was being blamed most unjustly, and, moreover, she was not used to being blamed.

"I'm sure you're very kind, Mrs. Gray and Miss Reed, but I must take the liberty of saying that I know best what my daughter was."

"Mrs. Griffith, all I say is this—you are not a good mother."

"Excuse me, madam . . ." said Mrs. Griffith, having grown red with anger; but Mrs. Gray interrupted.

"I am truly sorry to have to say it to one of my parishioners, but you are not a good Christian. And we all know that your husband's business isn't going at all well, and I think it's a judgment of Providence."

"Very well, ma'am," said Mrs. Griffith, getting up. "You're at liberty to think what you please, but I shall not come to church again. Mr. Friend, the Baptist minister, has asked me to go to his chapel, and I'm sure he won't treat me like that."

"I'm sure we don't want you to come to church in that spirit, Mrs. Griffith. That's not the spirit with which you can please God, Mrs. Griffith. I can quite imagine now why dear Daisy ran away. You're no Christian."

"I'm sure I don't care what you think, Mrs. Gray, but I'm as good as you are."

"Will you open the door for me, Mrs. Griffith?" said Mrs. Gray, with outraged dignity.

"Oh, you can open it yourself, Mrs. Gray!" replied Mrs. Griffith.

XI

Mrs. Griffith went to see her daughter-in-law.

"I've never been spoken to in that way before," she said. "Fancy me not being a Christian! I'm a better Christian than Mrs. Gray, any day. I like Mrs. Gray, with the airs she gives herself—as if she'd got anything to boast about . . . ! No, Edith, I've said it, and I'm not the woman to go back on what I've said—I'll not go to church again. From this day I go to chapel."

But George came to see his mother a few days later.

"Look here, Mother, Edith says you'd better forgive Daisy now."

"George," cried his mother, "I've only done my duty all through, and if you think it's my duty to forgive my daughter now she's going to enter the bonds of holy matrimony, I will do so. No one can say that I'm not a Christian, and I haven't said the Lord's Prayer night and morning ever since I remember for nothing."

Mrs. Griffith sat down to write, looking up to her son for inspiration.

"Dearest Daisy!" he said.

"No, George," she replied, "I'm not going to cringe to my daughter, although she is going to be a lady; I shall simply say, 'Daisy.' "

The letter was very dignified, gently reproachful, for Daisy had undoubtedly committed certain peccadilloes, although she was going to be a baronet's wife; but still it was completely forgiving, and Mrs. Griffith signed herself, *"Your loving and forgiving mother, whose heart you nearly broke."*

But the letter was not answered, and a couple of weeks later the same Sunday paper contained an announcement of the date of the marriage and the name of the church. Mrs. Griffith wrote a second time.

MY DARLING DAUGHTER, I am much surprised at receiving no answer to my long letter. All is forgiven. I should so much like to see you again before I die, and to have you married from your father's house. All is forgiven. Your loving mother.

MARY ANN GRIFFITH.

This time the letter was returned unopened.

"George," cried Mrs. Griffith, "she's got her back up."

"And the wedding's to-morrow," he replied.

"It's most awkward, George. I've told all the Blackstable people that I've forgiven her and that Sir Herbert has written to say he wants to make my acquaintance. And I've got a new dress on purpose to go to the wedding. Oh! she's a cruel and exasperating thing, George; I never liked her. You were always my favourite."

"Well, I do think she's not acting as she should," replied George. "And I'm sure I don't know what's to be done."

But Mrs. Griffith was a woman who made up her mind quickly.

"I shall go up to town and see her myself, George; and you must come too."

"I'll come up with you, Mother, but you'd better go to her alone, because I expect she's not forgotten the last time I saw her."

They caught a train immediately, and, having arrived at Daisy's house, Mrs. Griffith went up the steps while George waited in a neighbouring public-house. The door was opened by a smart maid—much smarter than the Vicarage maid at Blackstable, as Mrs. Griffith remarked with satisfaction. On finding that Daisy was at home, she sent up a message to ask if a lady could see her.

The maid returned.

"Would you give your name, madam? Miss Griffith cannot see you without."

Mrs. Griffith had foreseen the eventuality, and, unwilling to give her card, had written another little letter, using Edith as amanuensis, so that Daisy should at least open it. She sent it up. In a few minutes the maid came down again.

"There's no answer," and she opened the door for Mrs. Griffith to go out.

That lady turned very red. Her first impulse was to make a scene and call the housemaid to witness how Daisy treated her own mother; but immediately she thought how undignified she would appear in the maid's eyes. So she went out like a lamb. . . .

She told George all about it as they sat in the private bar of the public-house, drinking a little scotch whisky.

"All I can say," she remarked, "is that I hope she'll never live to repent it. Fancy treating her own mother like that! But I shall go to the wedding; I don't care. I will see my own daughter married."

That had been her great ambition, and she would have crawled before Daisy to be asked to the ceremony. . . . But George dissuaded her from going uninvited. There were sure to be one or two Blackstable people present, and they would see that she was there as a stranger; the humiliation would be too great.

"I think she's an ungrateful girl," said Mrs. Griffith, as she gave way and allowed George to take her back to Blackstable.

XII

But the prestige of the Griffiths diminished. Everyone in Blackstable came to the conclusion that the new Lady Ously-Farrowham had been very badly treated by her relatives, and many young ladies said they would have done just the same in her place. Also Mrs. Gray induced her husband to ask Griffith to resign his churchwardenship.

"You know, Mr. Griffith," said the vicar deprecatingly, "now that your wife goes to chapel I don't think we can have you as churchwarden any longer; and besides, I don't think you've behaved to your daughter in a Christian way."

It was in the carpenter's shop; the business had dwindled till Griffith only kept one man and a boy; he put aside the saw he was using.

"What I've done to my daughter, I'm willing to take the responsibility for; I ask no one's advice and I want no one's opinion; and if you think I'm not fit to be churchwarden you can find someone else better."

"Why don't you make it up with your daughter, Griffith?"

"Mind your own business!"

The carpenter had brooded and brooded over his sorrow till now his daughter's name roused him to fury. He had even asserted a little authority over his wife, and she dared not mention her daughter before him. Daisy's marriage had seemed like the consummation of her shame; it was vice riding triumphant in a golden chariot. . . .

But the name of Lady Ously-Farrowham was hardly ever out of her mother's lips; and she spent a good deal more money in her dress to keep up her dignity.

"Why, that's another new dress you've got on!" said a neighbour.

"Yes," said Mrs. Griffith, complacently, "you see we're in quite a different position now. I have to think of my daughter, Lady Ously-Farrowham. I don't want her to be ashamed of her mother. I had such a nice long letter from her the other day. She's so happy with Sir Herbert. And Sir Herbert's so good to her. . . ."

"Oh, I didn't know you were. . . ."

"Oh yes! Of course she was a little—well, a little wild when she was a girl, but *I've* forgiven that. It's her father won't forgive her. He always was a hard man, and he never loved her as I did. She wants to come and stay with me, but he won't let her. Isn't it cruel of him? I should so like to have Lady Ously-Farrowham down here. . . ."

XIII

But at last the crash came. To pay for the new things which Mrs. Griffith felt needful to preserve her dignity, she had drawn on her husband's savings in the bank; and he had been drawing on them himself for the last four years without his wife's knowledge. For, as his business declined, he had been afraid to give her less money than usual, and every week had made up the sum by taking something out of the bank. George only earned a pound a week—he had been made clerk to a coal merchant by his mother, who thought that more genteel than carpentering—and after his marriage he had constantly borrowed from his parents. At last Mrs. Griffith learnt to her dismay that their savings had come to an end completely. She had a talk with her husband, and found out that he was earning almost nothing. He talked

of sending his only remaining workman away and moving into a smaller place. If he kept his one or two old customers, they might just manage to make both ends meet.

Mrs. Griffith was burning with anger. She looked at her husband, sitting in front of her with his helpless look.

"You fool!" she said.

She thought of herself coming down in the world, living in a poky little house away from the High Street, unable to buy new dresses, unnoticed by the chief people of Blackstable—she who had always held up her head with the best of them!

George and Edith came in, and she told them, hurling contemptuous sarcasms at her husband. He sat looking at them with his pained, unhappy eyes, while they stared back at him as if he were some despicable, noxious beast.

"But why didn't you say how things were going before, Father?" George asked him.

He shrugged his shoulders.

"I didn't like to," he said hoarsely; those cold, angry eyes crushed him; he felt the stupid, useless fool he saw they thought him.

"I don't know what's to be done," said George.

His wife looked at old Griffith with her hard grey eyes; the sharpness of her features, the firm, clear complexion, with all softness blown out of it by the east winds, expressed the coldest resolution.

"Father must get Daisy to help; she's got lots of money. She may do it for him."

Old Griffith broke suddenly out of his apathy.

"I'd sooner go to the workhouse; I'll never touch a penny of hers!"

"Now then, Father," said Mrs. Griffith, quickly understanding, "you drop that, you'll have to."

George at the same time got pen and paper and put them before the old man. They stood round him angrily. He stared at the paper; a look of horror came over his face.

"Go on! don't be a fool!" said his wife. She dipped the pen in the ink and handed it to him.

Edith's steel-grey eyes were fixed on him, coldly compelling.

"Dear Daisy," she began.

"Father always used to call her Daisy darling," said George; "he'd better put that so as to bring back old times."

They talked of him strangely, as if he were absent or had not ears to hear.

"Very well," replied Edith, and she began again; the old man wrote bewilderedly, as if he were asleep. "DAISY DARLING: . . . Forgive me! . . . I have been hard and cruel towards you. . . . On my knees I beg your forgiveness. . . . The business has gone wrong . . . and I am ruined. . . . If you don't help me . . . we shall have the brokers in . . . and have to go to the workhouse. . . . For God's sake . . . have mercy on me! You can't let me starve. . . . I know I have sinned towards you. Your broken-hearted . . . FATHER."

She read through the letter. "I think that'll do; now the envelope," and she dictated the address.

When it was finished, Griffith looked at them with loathing, absolute loathing—but they paid no more attention to him. They arranged to send a telegram first, in case she should not open the letter:

"Letter coming; for God's sake open! In great distress. FATHER."

George went out immediately to send the wire and post the letter.

XIV

The letter was sent on a Tuesday, and on Thursday morning a telegram came from Daisy to say she was coming down. Mrs. Griffith was highly agitated.

"I'll go and put on my silk dress," she said.

"No, Mother, that is a silly thing; be as shabby as you can."

"How'll Father be?" asked George. "You'd better speak to him, Edith."

He was called, the stranger in his own house.

"Look here, Father, Daisy's coming this morning. Now, you'll be civil, won't you?"

"I'm afraid he'll go and spoil everything," said Mrs. Griffith, anxiously.

At that moment there was a knock at the door. "It's her!"

Griffith was pushed into the back room; Mrs. Griffith hurriedly put on a ragged apron and went to the door.

"Daisy!" she cried, opening her arms. She embraced her daughter and pressed her to her voluminous bosom. "Oh, Daisy!"

Daisy accepted passively the tokens of affection, with a little sad smile. She tried not to be unsympathetic. Mrs. Griffith led her daughter into the sitting-room, where George and Edith were sitting. George was very white.

"You don't mean to say you walked here!" said Mrs. Griffith, as she shut the front door. "Fancy that, when you could have all the carriages in Blackstable to drive you about!"

"Welcome to your home again," said George, with somewhat the air of a dissenting minister.

"Oh, George!" she said, with the same sad, half-ironical smile, allowing herself to be kissed.

"Don't you remember me?" said Edith, coming forward. "I'm George's wife; I used to be Edith Pollett."

"Oh yes!" Daisy put out her hand.

They all three looked at her, and the women noticed the elegance of her simple dress. She was no longer the merry girl they had known, but a tall, dignified woman, and her great blue eyes were very grave. They were rather afraid of her; but Mrs. Griffith made an effort to be cordial and at the same time familiar.

"Fancy you being a real lady!" she said.

Daisy smiled again.

"Where's Father?" she asked.

"In the next room." They moved towards the door and entered. Old Griffith rose as he saw his daughter, but he did not come towards her. She looked at him a moment, then turned to the others.

"Please leave me alone with Father for a few minutes."

They did not want to, knowing that their presence would restrain him; but Daisy looked at them so firmly that they were obliged to obey. She closed the door behind them.

"Father!" she said, turning towards him.

"They made me write the letter," he said hoarsely.

"I thought so," she said. "Won't you kiss me?"

He stepped back as if in repulsion. She looked at him with her beautiful eyes full of tears.

"I'm so sorry I've made you unhappy. But I've been unhappy too—oh, you don't know what I've gone through . . . ! Won't you forgive me?"

"I didn't write the letter," he repeated hoarsely; "they stood over me and made me."

Her lips trembled, but with an effort she commanded herself. They looked at one another steadily, it seemed for a very long time; in his eyes was the look of a hunted beast. . . . At last she turned away without saying anything more, and left him.

In the next room the three were anxiously waiting. She contemplated them a moment, and then, sitting down, asked about the affairs. They explained how things were.

"I talked to my husband about it," she said; "he's proposed to make you an allowance so that you can retire from business."

"Oh, that's Sir Herbert all over," said Mrs. Griffith, greasily—she knew nothing about him but his name!

"How much do you think you could live on?" asked Daisy.

Mrs. Griffith looked at George and then at Edith. What should they ask? Edith and George exchanged a glance; they were in agonies lest Mrs. Griffith should demand too little.

"Well," said that lady, at last, with a little cough of uncertainty, "in our best years we used to make four pounds a week out of the business—didn't we, George?"

"Quite that!" answered he and his wife, in a breath.

"Then, shall I tell my husband that if he allows you five pounds a week you will be able to live comfortably?"

"Oh, that's very handsome!" said Mrs. Griffith.

"Very well," said Daisy, getting up.

"You're not going?" cried her mother.

"Yes."

"Well, that is hard. After not seeing you all these years. But you know best, of course!"

"There's no train up to London for two yours yet," said George.

"No; I want to take a walk through Blackstable."

"Oh, you'd better drive, in your position."

"I prefer to walk."

"Shall George come with you?"

"I prefer to walk alone."

Then Mrs. Griffith again enveloped her daughter in her arms, and told her she had always loved her and that she was her only daughter; after which, Daisy allowed herself to be embraced by her brother and his wife. Finally they shut the door on her and watched her from the window walk slowly down the High Street.

"If you'd asked it, I believe she'd have gone up to six quid a week," said George.

XV

Daisy walked down the High Street slowly, looking at the houses she remembered, and her lips quivered a little; at every step smells blew across to her full of memories—the smell of a tannery, the blood smell of a butcher's shop, the sea-odour from a shop of fishermen's clothes. . . . At last she came on to the beach, and in the darkening November day she looked at the booths she knew so well, the boats drawn up for the winter, whose names she knew, whose owners she had known from her childhood; she noticed the new villas built in her absence. And she looked at the grey sea; a sob burst from her; but she was very strong, and at once she recovered herself. She turned back and slowly walked up the High Street again to the station. The lamps were lighted now, and the street looked as it had looked in her memory through the years; between the Green Dragon and the Duke of Kent were the same groups of men—farmers, townsfolk, fishermen—talking in the glare of the rival inns, and they stared at her curiously as she passed, a tall figure, closely veiled. She looked at the well-remembered shops, the stationery shop with its old-fashioned, fly-blown knick-knacks, the milliner's with cheap, gaudy hats, the little tailor's with his antiquated fashion plates. At last she came to the station, and sat in the waiting-room, her heart full of infinite sadness—the terrible sadness of the past. . . .

And she could not shake it off in the train; she could only just keep back the tears.

At Victoria she took a cab and finally reached home. The servants said her husband was in his study.

"Hulloa!" he said. "I didn't expect you to-night."

"I couldn't stay; it was awful." Then she went up to him and looked into his eyes. "You do love me, Herbert, don't you?" she said, her voice suddenly breaking. "I want your love so badly."

"I love you with all my heart!" he said, putting his arms around her.

But she could restrain herself no longer; the strong arms seemed to take away the rest of her strength, and she burst into tears.

"I will try and be a good wife to you, Herbert," she said, as he kissed them away.

CUPID AND THE VICAR OF SWALE

(1900)

Swale is a place of many advantages. It is strikingly picturesque and eminently respectable; the people who live in it excite the admiration of the world in general, not only by their affluence, but by their gentility also, and in these degenerate days the one does not always accompany the other. They inhabit mansions overgrown with creepers, and they all keep a carriage. Here and there a few poor people live in artistic cottages for the special conveniences of the young ladies, who paint in water-colours. But the poor people, even, are of the nicest class, the class that looks so pleasant in Academy pictures. Alas! it is a type that is fast disappearing in England. Now the labourer is an independent creature with no feelings of gratitude; he does not touch his hat to the parson, and his wife drops no curtsey to the squire; he is full of new-fangled Radical notions, and neither looks nice in pictures nor in reality. He has become distinctly vulgar. But Swale is still different, and long may it keep free from the corruption of external influence! As I said, the cottages are delightful, with little leaded windows admitting neither light nor air—but that is a detail; they are most pleasing to the fair sketcher; honeysuckle and roses climb about the doorway, many of the roofs are thatched, and the whole appearance is exquisitely dilapidated.

One landlord, in a thoughtless moment, decided to pull down those on his own estate, and erect new ones with sanitary conveniences, and all kinds of modern improvements; but an indignation meeting was held, and a deputation of ladies called upon him to protest against the desecration. Being quite a plebeian

creature, the only person in Swale history whose breeding was not irreproachable, he would not listen to their arguments on abstract beauty, and they did not even convince him by showing that he would utterly ruin the type of good honest English peasant. They appealed to his patriotism: the English countryman was the backbone of the British Army, and how could he be expected to retain his native candour, his obedience and deference to his betters, if he were born and bred, not in a picturesque old cottage covered with honeysuckle, but in a new-fangled place with a bath-room? But fortunately, Mr. Simpson, the owner of the estate in question, was called to a world where it is to be hoped horrid Radicals are in the minority, and his daughters were comparatively innocuous. The poor of Swale were left in peace and quietness, to their own content, for they looked upon it as somehow a merciful dispensation of Providence that every winter their children should die of diphtheria or typhoid. For many centuries they had been used to look upon themselves as different beings from the gentry, and they were not going to begin now to give themselves airs. The gentry were the gentry: they were only common people whose part in life it was to minister to their betters' needs, and there was an end of it. It must be said that the richer inhabitants of Swale behaved very well in any calamity. They showered jellies and port-wine and coals upon the indigent, and read the Bible to them for hours.

Now, when the old Vicar of Swale departed the life which he had thoroughly enjoyed for hard upon eighty years, there was much perturbation in the parish over the choice of his successor.

"We don't want somebody too strenuous," said Lady Proudfoot, the widow of Sir George Proudfoot, who had been given his K.C.B. after bungling some important affair in the Colonies.

Mrs. Strong was taking a cup of tea with Lady Proudfoot, while the latter's daughters were playing tennis. Mrs. Strong, having arrived perilously near the age of forty, had given up violent exercise; she thought it ugly enough for a young girl to get red in the face, but for a woman of her years, unpardonable. Besides, she did not take heat becomingly. In her youth Mrs. Strong had been rather overpowering. Her six feet of height and her generally massive proportions made her seem almost mountainous, and when she gambolled, she reminded one of a young elephant. But years had brought their chastening influence. She was still massive, but the effect now was magnificent. She was sedate, admirably self-pos-

sessed, a type of the British matron. The literary young ladies of Swale said she reminded them of Boadicea. She was undoubtedly a very fine woman, with well-cut features and clear, steady eyes. The only fault to be found with her was that, though her teeth were obviously perfect, she need not have shown them quite so much; but as she was a very good-natured creature, with an uncommon sense of humour, her constant smiles may have been due to a cause other than vanity.

"Of course," said Lady Proudfoot, "there are so many different sorts of clergymen."

"Yes," replied Mrs. Strong, smiling, "there are the parsons who are Christians, the parsons who are gentlemen, and the parsons who are neither."

"Well, the chief thing is that he should be a gentleman," said Lady Proudfoot. "If he's been to Oxford and taken his degree he'll be quite Christian enough for us."

"It would certainly be terrible if we had an eager little man with a wife and a red nose."

"To say nothing of fifteen children, my dear," cried Lady Proudfoot. "And the wives that those sort of clergymen choose are too impossible; Heaven only knows where they find them! No, the fact is, Edith, that if we have a horrid creature who wants to reform everything, it will simply be the ruin of Swale. We get along very well as we are, and I'm certain that no one could find anything seriously wrong with us."

"We go to church regularly in the newest of bonnets," interrupted Mrs. Strong, "and when we call ourselves miserable sinners we know it's merely a *façon de parler*."

"If we have a vicar who wants to have Mothers' Meetings and Bands of Hope and all that rubbish, I really don't know what will become of us."

"Yes," replied Mrs. Strong, with a drawl which might have been sarcastic, "as long as he can play tennis and behave decently at a dinner-party, our souls can take care of themselves."

"Well, the living's worth six hundred a year and the house is in excellent condition, so I really think we ought to get some one nice."

Lady Proudfoot, and the inhabitants of Swale in general, had every reason to be pleased with the bishop's choice. The Rev. Robert Branscombe was evidently a gentleman—he was, indeed,

second cousin to a peer, which necessarily inspired his parishioners with confidence. He was a bachelor, and forty years of age, tall, good-looking, with a fine presence. In ten years his presence would perhaps be a little too fine, already he gave signs of future corpulence; but at the period of which I write it was most striking. He was clean-shaven, and dressed in the latest clerical fashion. I need only add that he was High Church, as befitted so respectable a place as Swale, and had charming manners. He talked a great deal, in a loud voice and in a slightly magisterial manner. His conversation was easy, and could be understood by a child. The latest novel, the local rose-show, dances, and dinner-parties formed sufficient ground for the display of his powers. He rarely spoke of parish matters, considering it bad form to talk shop. Finally, he had a passion for Tennyson, which in a person of his cloth is a proof of much candour and purity of soul. The ladies pronounced him charming, and when an unsympathetic man suggested that his conceit was phenomenal, waxed mighty wroth in the vicar's defence.

"What *I* like in him," said Lady Proudfoot, "is that except for the clothes he wears, you'd never think he was a clergyman."

It was obvious that the Vicar of Swale ought to marry, and during the two years of his incumbency, the parishioners had done nothing but concoct schemes to that end. Mr. Branscombe was to the tips of his fingers a marrying man. But the choice in Swale was limited, and lay, in fact, between Mrs. Strong and Jane Simpson. The latter was the eldest daughter of the horrid Radical whom death only had prevented from disfiguring the landscape in the manner I have related. She was a rather homely young woman of nine and twenty, and harmless enough to have gained the sufferance of the other inhabitants of Swale, though they could not be expected to forget that her father had made his money in the city. Her matrimonial desires were obvious, and Lady Proudfoot was disgusted at the way in which she behaved with Mr. Branscombe. Of course she did nothing indecorous—she was the quietest and most modest of young persons—but she turned pale at his approach, and blushed at every word he said to her. She was evidently dying of love, and every one knew that he need only ask to be accorded her hand and fortune, which was at least one hundred thousand pounds in solid securities.

But the match was looked upon with disfavour, and his pa-

rishioners found much comfort in the thought that Mr. Branscombe was not mercenary. Yet though he would not marry Jane Simpson for her money, he was, after all, only human, and could not be expected to remain insensible to her evident adoration. The hopes of the ladies of Swale were centred entirely upon Mrs. Strong, whom the Fates had not favoured only in looks. Mrs. Strong was not only handsome, but a widow with fifteen hundred a year as well. Her age, appearance, and station made her appear designed by higher powers to share with Mr. Branscombe this life of woe. She was a fascinating woman, and the vicar harboured for her the sincerest admiration. The matter would doubtless have been settled in the first year of his residence at Swale, if Miss Simpson, by her sighs and blushes, had not a little disconcerted him. He was really a kind man, and did not wish to break the poor thing's heart. And the attitude of Mrs. Strong was a little embarrassing. She smiled at him, asked him to dinner, and callers found him constantly taking a cup of tea with her. She seemed to think it quite natural that amiable hostesses at luncheon parties should always pair them off together. The difficulty was that Mrs. Strong was equally amiable with every one she met, and though she evidently liked the Vicar of Swale, she had given no particular signs of desiring him to be her husband. The Rev. Robert Branscombe had too much dignity and too fine a presence to undergo the humiliation of a refusal—so he hesitated. Of course the ladies of Swale saw how things were, and they did everything to help him—but still he hesitated.

"Upon my word," said Lady Proudfoot, "I don't know what more encouragement he can want. He can't expect Edith to propose to him herself."

Lady Proudfoot, more than any one else in Swale, was concerned with the matrimonial affairs of Robert Branscombe. She was of the opinion that it was as improper for a clergyman to be unmarried as for a doctor, and, besides that, Mrs. Strong was her bosom friend. She knew very well in what state of mind the vicar was, and decided at length to speak with Mrs. Strong on the subject. One day she attacked her by leading the conversation to Jane Simpson.

"I really don't see why she shouldn't marry Mr. Branscombe if she wants to, poor thing," said Mrs. Strong. "She's a nice quiet girl, and she'd make an admirable wife for a clergyman."

"My dear Edith," rejoined Lady Proudfoot, "I think it would be most disagreeable for all of us. You know she's inclined to be frightfully religious already."

"Oh, six months of marriage with the vicar would quite cure her of that."

"Besides, I don't think she's the sort of wife for Mr. Branscombe. He likes to have everything so nice, and she's terribly homely. I noticed last time I called there that she—that she wore knitted stockings, my dear."

Mrs. Strong laughed, showing her beautiful teeth. "I dare say the poor girl's circulation is bad and she has cold feet."

"I have no patience with you, Edith," said Lady Proudfoot, abruptly coming to the point. "Can't you see that he wants to marry *you?*"

Mrs. Strong was not at all disconcerted. "He has never said so."

"I wish you would make up your mind. I think it's absurd for a woman like you, without any encumbrances, to remain unmarried." Mrs. Strong made no answer, and Lady Proudfoot added, "I wonder if you'd accept him if he proposed?"

"Has he commissioned you to find out?"

"Not directly," said Lady Proudfoot; "I know he thinks you very charming."

"I'm afraid I don't think him very courageous."

"That sounds like encouragement."

"It does a little," agreed Mrs. Strong, smiling.

Lady Proudfoot rose to go, and kissed her friend.

"I dare say he'll come and see you to-morrow," she added.

Mrs. Strong was not particularly anxious to get married. The Vicar of Swale was rather a pleasant man, and it was flattering to know that he wished to make her his wife. She wondered that he had not already become engaged to Jane Simpson. Anyhow, he might come; she had committed herself to nothing, and would listen to what he had to say.

Next day at three o'clock the Rev. Robert Branscombe was shown into her boudoir. Mrs. Strong received him with her usual easy amiability, and his self-assurance did not desert him. There was nothing in their behaviour to show that either was love-sick; so far as concerned the man, his presence was the only sign that Lady Proudfoot had delivered any message. His confidence slightly

irritated Mrs. Strong. She wished he were a little less at ease. She offered him some tea, which he refused.

"Of course," she thought, "he has too much humour to be sentimental with a cup of tea in his hand."

Meanwhile Mr. Branscombe talked of the weather.

"It really is very hot," he said. "Everything in the vicarage garden is quite parched. You've not seen it since I altered the path on the west side, have you?"

Mrs. Strong divined at once that he was leading the conversation to the vicarage in order to suggest that she should become its mistress. She took a malicious pleasure in veering away. Mr. Branscombe was very self-assured, and she felt it her duty to show him it was not so easy as he thought to win such a charming woman as herself.

"Oh yes," she replied. "Miss Simpson told me you'd been making alterations. I see they're rebuilding the lodge at Manor House." She plunged into a description of the operations.

But Mr. Branscombe did not lose his self-possession. He conversed fluently of the lodge at Manor House.

"It's a charming old place," he said, when the conversation of itself gave him the opportunity. "But of course I like nothing better than my own vicarage."

He had brought his own house up again. Mrs. Strong commented upon the unoriginality of man; but with a beautiful smile, like a hare doubling, broke into an account of a delightful vicarage she had taken one summer at Blackstable. It was rather exciting to see Mr. Branscombe driving steadfastly to one point, while she did her best to keep away from it. But at last she was cornered.

"Are you fond of vicarages?" he asked.

The question was inane, but required an answer.

"Passably."

"How do you like mine," he asked.

Such an inquiry insisted on a civil answer. "Of course it's charming." It amused her to know herself caught.

"It would be ten times more charming if—if you adorned it." He was distinctly clumsy. Mrs. Strong expected better things of clerical gentlemen of forty.

"Would you put me in a niche in the wall like an Italian saint?"

"You wilfully misunderstand me," he replied with a gently patronising smile.

"I'm so sorry," she murmured.

He looked at her for one moment, and Mrs. Strong thought that his appearance was too impressive for any one less than an archdeacon.

"Lady Proudfoot sent for me yesterday," he said. "And—she told me I might call upon you."

"I didn't know you required permission to do that," she said with her frank smile, looking steadily at him without the least embarrassment. He was not embarrassed either. He smiled back upon her benignly.

"Will you share my vicarage with me, Mrs. Strong?"

He had evidently made up his mind beforehand how to express himself, and he could not allow the accidents of social chatter to disturb his ordered course. "I've come here to-day," he added, raising his voice a little and speaking with the same solemnity as he used in church on Sundays—"I have come here to-day to ask you to become my wife."

Mrs. Strong looked down. After what Lady Proudfoot had told him it would be ridiculous to seem surprised. She was not certain that so matter-of-fact a proposal pleased her. Notwithstanding her massive proportions, she had a certain tenderness for sentiment, and she would have liked him to hesitate bashfully. A spark of poetry would not have been out of place, nor even some indication of suppressed passion. His certainty of success in the suit was irritating. She felt inclined to refuse him to see how he would take it.

"I feel very much flattered, Mr. Branscombe," she said slowly, to gain time.

"Won't you call me Robert?" he said, patting her hand.

Mrs. Strong looked up quickly, and, bending over, the clergyman kissed her on the cheek.

"I thank you with all my heart," he said. "I will endeavour to perform my duty to you as a Christian husband."

Mrs. Strong was surprised. He evidently was under the impression that she had accepted him, and she was still considering whether she should or not. Surely when you tell a man that his offer flatters you, it is not equivalent to an acceptance? But there was no doubt in Mr. Branscombe's mind. He even asked her to name the day upon which he would become the happiest of men. He vowed he must immediately impart the good news to Lady Proudfoot.

"What an excitement it will cause in the parish," he said, laughing. When he was going away he urged her again to fix a day for the ceremony.

"Till then," he said, "you will find me a most impatient man."

"It's nice of you to be so eager," she said, showing her beautiful teeth. "But you know there is no end of legal things which will want settling." It seemed as if she had definitely surrendered.

"If there is anything I can do to help you," he replied gallantly, "command me."

"How kind you are! You know I have an income of fifteen hundred a year."

"My dear Edith!" He waved his hand in deprecation. He was not the man to listen to gross monetary details.

"I think it right to tell you at once," she said, in answer to his gesture. "My income—is contingent on my widowhood."

"I beg your pardon?" he said.

She smiled. "It ceases on my marrying again."

She watched him closely as she made the statement. Mr. Branscombe started; but his discomposure was momentary.

"My dear Edith," he said, "you will be more precious to me with the thought that I alone am providing for you. If I have hesitated to ask you to become my wife, it was because your greater income might have—cast suspicion on the purity of my motives."

He kissed her gravely on the forehead and went away.

"I wonder," said Mrs. Strong, "how he'll get out of it?"

Next day Mr. Branscombe came to luncheon. He advanced to Mrs. Strong solemnly and kissed her forehead. He was not a very ardent lover.

"Did you pass a good night?" he asked.

"Oh yes," she replied, smiling. "I always do."

"Ah!" He paused, and then with a slight effort broke into ecstasies with the view from Mrs. Strong's windows.

"I can never be sufficiently grateful to you for abandoning all this for my humble vicarage."

"I'm not cynical," said Mrs. Strong. "I believe in love in a cottage."

"Ah well, it has its disadvantages."

Mrs. Strong had never realised before that her fiancé's conversation was sometimes painfully obvious. They went in to lunch-

eon, and the presence of the butler confined them to commonplaces. But Mrs. Strong was in high spirits. She saw that Mr. Branscombe was somewhat embarrassed. She had never seen him in such a condition before, and it delighted her.

"You know," he said, when they retured to the drawing-room, "life will be very different for you as chatelaine of Swale Vicarage. I'm afraid we shall not be able to afford a carriage."

"Oh, a pony-cart fulfils all my aspirations."

"What a charming character you have," he said.

He was becoming more and more ill at ease. Mrs. Strong's humourous eyes were upon him, and he was afraid of looking foolish. He made an effort to be gallant.

"I've never seen any one with such beautiful hair as you have," he said.

She laughed, and he felt his remark absurd.

"Have you told Lady Proudfoot of our engagement?" she asked.

At last he positively blushed. "No. On second thoughts I fancied I had better not. After all, it's no business of hers. And besides, the date of our marriage is so very uncertain, isn't it?" Mrs. Strong had the charity not to look at him. But he took his courage in both hands. "I won't conceal from you that what you told me yesterday has made some alteration in the matter—not in my feelings, of course; your poverty can only make my love the greater."

Now Mrs. Strong looked at him, and he faltered. She at last had seen the Rev. Robert Branscombe lose his self-assurance.

"Of course," he said, "I know my behaviour is liable to misconstruction. It looks as if—as if I were mercenary. Yesterday I asked you to marry me as quickly as possible. I know it sounds funny when I ask you to-day to wait."

"Oh, not at all," said Mrs. Strong, encouragingly.

He took her hands, but Mrs. Strong gently withdrew them. He was talking very quickly, nervously.

"I feel," he said, "that my duty to you counterbalances everything. I hope you understand that it's entirely for your sake that I want you to wait."

"Oh, you want me to wait?"

"In three or four years all sorts of things may happen. I have a good deal of influence in clerical quarters, and I have been given

to understand that I'm my Uncle George's sole heir. Of course he's only sixty-five. He may live another ten years; but even then I should only be fifty." He took her hand again. "I know I'm asking a great deal; but will you wait for me, Edith, say five years? I'm certain to get a better living by then."

"Are you sure," she asked quietly, "that you wouldn't prefer not to be bound by an engagement? As you suggest, so much may happen in five years."

"Oh, Edith, surely you have not so poor an opinion of me as to suppose me capable of breaking off our engagement because—because—"

"You know, Robert, you are a young man, and in ten years you'll only be fifty; but I shall be fifty too! And you have a great future before you. I'm sure you'll end up as a bishop. A man of your calibre is wasted on a little country parish. I don't feel myself justified in hampering you."

"I should be contemptible if I asked you to give me back my word." The Vicar of Swale was genuinely disturbed; he was a gentleman, and he could not stoop to a discreditable action.

"But it is I who ask you, Robert. I do not feel myself justified in standing in your way. It is no sacrifice to me when I think of your future."

"I can't accept your sacrifice," he said solemnly. "I should feel such a—such a cad."

"Nonsense," said Mrs. Strong, changing her tone. "We will forget our interview of yesterday. You may be quite certain that I will say nothing about it."

"Ah, Mrs. Strong, you are a truly Christian woman."

The Vicar of Swale was humbled, but Mrs. Strong was a woman, and she could not let him go without a small revenge.

"I hope," she murmured with a smile, as she shook his hand, "I hope I haven't made you feel very ridiculous? I really haven't tried to."

Next morning Lady Proudfoot rushed into Mrs. Strong's drawing-room.

"Oh, Edith, what have you done?"

"Good Heavens! what's the matter?"

"I've just had a letter from Mr. Branscombe, and he tells me—"

"What?" Surely the Vicar of Swale had not betrayed their secret.

"He tells me that he's engaged to Jane Simpson."

Mrs. Strong did not move a muscle.

"Oh, is that all?" she said. "I knew he meant to propose to her. He came to see me two days ago, and I told him she'd make a pattern wife."

"But he wanted to propose to you."

"Oh, dear no. You're completely mistaken," she replied, calmly. "He thinks I'm really too Low Church."

She smiled her most fascinating smile.

"You certainly have got beautiful teeth," said Lady Proudfoot, rather sourly.

LADY HABART

(1900)

I

Ever since Lady Habart had been able to look in a mirror, and she was a precocious child, she had been a warm admirer of her personal appearance; and long before mastering the multiplication table she had become convinced of her own abnormal cleverness. She was indeed excessively clever; she was one of those persons who can multiply by thirteen as easily as the common herd by two; but a gift for mathematics is fatal to a woman, her skill in the manipulation of figures and her jugglery with accounts invariably land her in the Bankruptcy Court. Lady Habart was no exception to the rule, and of late her thoughts had often wandered to future interviews with the Official Receiver; she had considered the explanations she would offer to that most pertinacious of enquirers. This was the first occasion in her life upon which she had shunned publicity, and she came to the conclusion that it was scandalous to allow the newspapers to publish details about the private affairs of widowed gentlewomen. Her mind was also disturbed by the vague prospect of dreadful penalties if she contracted debts for more than twenty pounds; it seemed so vulgar not to get one's discharge.

The most casual observer would have noticed how distressed was Lady Habart, for she had overpowdered her nose; and she was too true a gentlewoman ever to commit such an enormity, except when suffering from the very greatest perturbation of spirit. . . . Lady Habart had realised early in life that woman is essentially artificial, and consequently that artifice can always heighten the charms of even the most beautiful; so she lent a

delightful wave to the straightness of her hair, and altered the cold brown with which Nature had endowed her to a delicate reddish gold that exactly suited her great blue eyes and her rose-like mouth. She had never seen a mouth she preferred to her own. She was a consummate artist, and few men noticed that the lady's pencilled eyebrows and long black lashes owed half their beauty to her exquisite taste; and if they did they cared not. They saw that Lady Habart was charming and did not mind how she came by her advantages; when pressed by their womankind, they acknowledged that she was made-up; but so were many other people, and she certainly made up uncommonly well. Lady Habart's enemies said her clothes were outrageous, but that was solely her misfortune, for she was the type of woman who would have looked overdressed apparelled in nothing more elaborate than fig-leaves. She was exactly the woman whom one would suspect of wearing artificial jewellery, and her bosom friends whispered that the suspicion had grounds—but this was generally disbelieved. It is best to keep to solid fact, and it was as plain as a pikestaff that Lady Habart was very delightful when she liked, that she was beautiful and under thirty.

Lady Habart was in her boudoir reading Mrs. Humphry Ward's latest novel. Being a widow, she thought it the proper thing to do. She was also dining that very evening with some literary people—there are literary folk who give dinner-parties to which quite nice persons go—and her inner consciousness told her that this particular work would undoubtedly be discussed. Now, one can never feign such ignorance of a book as when one has read it, and she understood that the men who talked would be much annoyed if she knew all about it. . . . But it was impossible for her to fix her attention, her heart beat uncomfortably, and at every sound she started. She put her book down, and, taking out her handkerchief, withdrew from it a little flat powder-puff and passed it over her face. . . . At last the door opened and a young man entered, tall, good-looking, fair, and resembling Lady Habart. He was her brother. He was one of those men whom one sees everywhere, and who always have ample ready money, although no one can imagine where the deuce they get it. Guy Cherriton was the son of a general on half pay who had left a very small fortune, and Guy appeared every year to spend at least half his capital. He was al-

ways well dressed, well groomed, and well behaved. People supposed he would eventually marry an heiress and settle down.

"Well?" said Lady Habart eagerly.

"He won't hear of it," answered her brother.

"Oh!" she cried. "You are so hopelessly stupid!"

As I have hinted, Lady Habart was up to her eyes in debt; her brother, Guy, had been to a money-lender, trying to get time for the payment of old debts, and if possible to contract a new one. But money-lenders have lost their faith in countesses.

"Did you tell him that I simply couldn't pay?" she asked distractedly.

"He said you'd have to. If you don't fork out within a week he'll make you bankrupt."

"What a loathsome brute he is! I wish I'd never had anything to do with him. I wish I'd gone to a Jew instead of to a Christian. Christians always swindle one more."

She walked up and down the room, and in her agitation put more powder on her face. She stopped suddenly in front of her brother.

"Why d'you stand there like an owl? Why on earth don't you do something?"

"What the dickens can I do!" he said crossly. "I haven't got any damned money."

"Oh, it's no good beginning to swear—that won't help me. And besides, it's bad form."

"How about your diamonds?"

"Oh, really, Guy, you are really too idiotic. You must know that I've been wearing paste for the last two years. . . . What's to be done! Nobody will trust me now. I can't get any clothes unless I pay ready money—tradesmen nowadays are so disgustingly independent. . . . Did you tell Smithson that I'd sign anything?"

Smithson was the Christian money-lender.

"Oh, I said we'd both sign anything, and he told me it was no good wasting clean paper on such a pair as us."

"Why didn't you knock him down?"

Brother Guy shrugged his shoulders, while Lady Habart stood in front of a looking-glass, frowning.

"I do look frightful," she said. She arranged the curls of her fringe; then her features relaxed and she slowly smiled at herself.

Her teeth were perfect. She assumed a languorous expression, and her blue eyes became very caressing.

"I think," she said softly, "I'll go and see him myself."

"Oh, you won't be able to bamboozle him," said her brother, immediately divining.

She assumed an air of great dignity. "I shall merely state the facts, and I have no doubt that he'll be reasonable. He's a very gentlemanly man really."

Her brother shrugged his shoulders again. Lady Habart was not a woman with whom one could argue; reason is always the undoing of her sex, and she was too clever to listen to it.

She rang the bell to order the carriage, and, going to her room, began to dress. She discussed within herself whether she should go in the simplest costume possible to show the disordered state of her mind, or whether she should clothe herself magnificently to prove her great importance. It was a very difficult question, but eventually she decided on the latter, thinking to impress the money-lender. She dressed as carefully as if she were about to visit her dearest enemy, and finally surveyed herself in the glass. But then she changed her mind.

"He's sure to have lots of actresses who go to him frightfully dressed up. It'll be far nicer to be quite simple."

She was very pleased with the idea and smiled contentedly as she caused her maid to robe her in a gown the simplicity of which was only equalled by its costliness. And it was grey, that which no colour suited her better. In her carriage she looked at herself in a little mirror.

"I really don't look more than three and twenty," she murmured.

II

Lady Habart was shown into a gorgeous waiting-room.

"Captain Smithson will see you in two minutes," said an attendant, who looked like a butler in a family that came over with the Conqueror.

Once upon a time money-lenders were unwashed Hebrews in shabby clothes, malodorous, speaking English with an abominable accent; and the newspapers tell us that even now there flourishes a worthy Pole who answers more or less to this description. But

Captain Smithson—of the Militia—was a gentleman to the tips of his fingers. He had been to a public school and afterwards to Oxford, where he had distinguished himself by his classical attainments. He always had a box at the opera for the season, and every morning could be seen in the park riding a horse which had obviously cost a fortune. He once thought of taking over the Exshire hounds, for he was as sportsman-like as he was gentlemanly. He was the sort of man of whom one might swear that he would invariably do the right thing at the right moment. Captain Smithson did not use a poky and ill-smelling office in the city, but received his clients in a palatial suite of chambers not three minutes' walk from Piccadilly.

After a very short time Lady Habart was invited to step into Captain Smithson's private room. It was decorated with priceless china, with mezzotints and Chippendale furniture; nothing could be more chastely elegant. He came to the door to meet her—a handsome man of thirty with an excessively military appearance; his fine moustache was carefully waxed, he wore an eyeglass, and his clothes fitted perfectly. He was dressed with the absolute irreproachableness of a tailor in Savile Row and an haberdasher in Bond Street. He was justly proud of his figure.

"I'm so sorry I kept you waiting," he said with a slight drawl, shaking Lady Habart's hand. "So good of you to take the trouble to come and see me."

"Oh," she replied, with her most gracious smile, "I'm always pleased to come here, you have such lovely things; I simply adore china."

"Yes, I know you do," he replied enthusiastically. "Now just look at these two plates that I got at Christie's yesterday—look at the drawing of those figures and the colour."

"Perfectly exquisite," replied Lady Habart, whom nothing bored so much as porcelain. "How clever of you to have picked them up."

"But do sit down."

"You're very kind."

Captain Smithson stroked his moustache, waiting for the lady to speak.

"I expected to find my brother with you," she said, with her usual air of veracity. "We arranged to meet here, you know."

"I'm sorry, he left an hour ago."

"Did he really," cried Lady Habart, with the utmost surprise, rising from her seat. "How very annoying!"

"Oh, don't go, Lady Habart. Do sit down."

Lady Habart seated herself immediately. "Did he talk to you about—about that loan of mine?" she asked.

"Let me see," said the money-lender, as if he were thinking. "I think he did. I dare say you remember that the money is due on Monday next."

"Oh, well, Captain Smithson," said Lady Habart, with a sweetly innocent laugh, "I can't pay it."

Captain Smithson smiled, but his smile was merely a clever facial contortion; his eyes were quite grim, no one could have seen in them the least trace of amusement.

"I'm afraid you'll have to, dear Lady Habart," he said.

"Come now," she said, putting her pretty hand on his arm. "You're not an ordinary business man, you're one of us, aren't you?"

"I must have the money next Monday," he replied shortly. He was becoming grave.

Lady Habart began to think him singularly ill-bred.

"I think you're very unkind," she murmured, and looked at him languishingly. "You know I'm absolutely in your power. . . . I think you might treat me as a friend."

There was a sofa in the room, and Lady Habart wished they were sitting on it side by side. It is impossible for a woman to be really nice to a man who is ensconced in a writing-chair two feet away from her. A writing-chair is a very chilling thing. She drew her seat a little closer to his. Captain Smithson watched her with amusement. She could not guess that fair ladies went through the same pantomine seven times a day.

"I wish you'd come and see me and talk about it comfortably over a cup of tea," she said. She smiled bewitchingly. "There are many men who'd give their heads to get such an invitation out of me."

Captain Smithson looked at his nails, thinking he must go to the manicurist when he had dismissed his visitor.

"I don't think that would be any use," he remarked gently. "I must have the money on Monday."

"Beast!" said Lady Habart under her breath, and aloud: "But

my dear Mr. Smithson, I haven't got three thousand pounds in the world!" Her voice broke and her eyes filled with tears.

"A woman in your position can always get money."

"You are cruel!" she cried, putting her handkerchief to her eyes. "I feel so faint," she sobbed.

Captain Smithson smiled.

"If you put your head down—between your legs—the faintness will pass off immediately. It's merely a question of driving the blood back to the brain."

Then Lady Habart lost her temper. She had been as seductive as she knew how, and the vulgar creature had declined to be seduced. She was about to put her handkerchief away, and tell the wretch in sarcastic language what she thought of him; but she restrained herself. It was no good making an enemy. She lowered her veil and in faltering accents bade him farewell.

"When are you going to file the petition?" she asked.

"Oh, you'll find the money," he said.

III

Lady Habart's carriage was waiting half-a-dozen doors lower down at a very smart dressmaker's. People recognising it would naturally suppose the owner within, trying on expensive costumes. Lady Habart stepped in and ordered the coachman to drive her home. She was furious. She was clever enough to see that the money-lender had been laughing at her, and she saw now that she had made herself ridiculous. She felt no particular humiliation, but she could not make up her mind whether Captain Smithson was a brute or a fool.

"I should have thought any man would see that I'm not exactly hideous. Perhaps he's got some odious wife hidden away somewhere. I dare say Jews are better after all."

The remarks that Lady Habart made to herself often sounded inconsequential, but in her own mind the meaning was always clear. . . . She drove along in a storm of indignation, railing against the fate which had caused her invariably to come across in this world persons of egregious stupidity. If her husband had not been a drivelling fool he would never have broken his silly neck in the hunting-field. Thousands of men rode to hounds every winter,

and it was so unnecessary for a man who practically could not leave his wife a penny to go and kill himself. She got on so well with her spouse that it was most irritating of him to come to a premature end: for a month the defunct earl had adored his countess, for six months he had loathed her, and for the remainder of their two years of married life had been completely indifferent, which is the most comfortable situation for married couples. She had looked upon him as a rather disagreeable acquaintance, but except when she was not feeling very well had always treated him politely.

Her only consolation in the fact that Lord Habart had been unable to will away a penny of his property was that at all events he had not enjoyed the spiteful pleasure of leaving it to a charity, and cutting her off with his blessing. She knew that such a form of humour would have thoroughly appealed to his limited intelligence.

But her carriage was blocked in Piccadilly, and quite close was a man in a hansom, looking at her. She seemed to know the face, but for the moment could not recollect who the creature was; she had not decided whether she should bow when her horses moved on. Then she remembered.

"Good Heavens, how lucky I was not to recognise him—he might have cut me!"

She looked at herself hurriedly in the mirror and was pleased to see that, notwithstanding her past emotions, she did not appear at all discomposed. On getting home she telephoned at once for her brother.

"It's no good," she cried. "I can't get anything out of Smithson. It was absurd of you to make me go to him. He's simply a vulgar beast."

"I told you it was no good going."

"You always say, 'I told you so'; you can never help bringing that in. . . . I want to know how I'm going to live?"

It is rather a bore, when you have preyed all your life on society, that society should eventually turn upon you. In the five years of her widowhood Lady Habart had mortgaged her annuity, and for the last eighteen months had lived entirely on usurers and confiding tradesmen. She loathed them for wanting their money.

"It's some comfort that they'll only get about sixpence in the pound," she said. "I shall be even with them there."

It never occurred to her that they had any legitimate cause for complaint against her. . . . She looked at her brother reading a paper.

"I wish you wouldn't read that odious sporting rag," she remarked. "You never get the least good out of it—all the horses that you tell me to back come in nowhere, or break their legs or do anything but win."

She smelt her salts, then the bottle in which they were reminded her of the giver.

"Oh, Guy, d'you know whom I saw to-day? Freddy Ramsden."

"He's been in town some time."

"Why on earth didn't you tell me?"

Guy shrugged his shoulders. The fact was that Freddy Ramsden had been engaged to Lady Habart when she was nothing more than pretty Dolly Cherriton, and she had jilted him as soon as the late lamented Habart hove in sight. One does not by preference talk to women either of the lovers they have jilted or the husbands they have divorced.

"Oh, of course I jilted him. He was only the younger son of a country squire with twopence halfpenny a year, and Habart had twenty thousand. I didn't know it was all tied up in that ridiculous fashion."

"You'd have been better off if you had married Freddy," said Guy.

"Don't be odiously moral, Guy, for Heaven's sake! How could I know his eldest brother was going to die and leave him the estate; you do irritate me. . . . I've been frightfully unfortunate; it's always the people I wanted to live who died, and those who might do me some good by dying simply live on forever. . . . I rather wish I hadn't cut him. I really didn't recognise him at first, he's frightfully altered."

"You'd better marry him now," said her brother.

"My boots are so pointed," he replied, "they rather amused me."

"Don't be brutal, Guy; I can never forget poor Habart."

Guy lit a cigarette with a smile.

"What are you sniggering for in that idiotic manner," asked Lady Habart sharply. "One would think you had good teeth."

"You needn't tell lies. I hate people who are not frank. You know quite well that I was awfully cut up when they brought

poor Habart home on a stretcher. It was on the very day of the St. Olphert's ball."

For a moment Lady Habart gave herself up to the painfulness of her recollections, then passed the cunning powder-puff over her nose.

"I wore mourning for longer than any one I know," she murmured, "and black doesn't suit me a bit. . . . Is he still unmarried?"

"Who—Freddy Ramsden?"

"D'you think I'm talking of the Emperor of China?" replied the lady with asperity.

"I say, Dolly, your temper to-day is angelic; no wonder Habart took to riding bolters."

"I wish you'd answer my questions, instead of trying to say silly smart things. Can't you see that I'm perfectly distracted? What am I to do? They'll make me bankrupt, and I shall have to go and live in poky lodgings in the country on two hundred a year; and I sha'n't see any one except a lot of disgusting country people. Fancy me drinking a dish of tea with the wife of the local doctor and having to go to church every Sunday." She smelt her salts. "Why don't you tell me if Freddy's married?"

"No, of course he isn't." He looked at his sister a little and said quietly: "Your only chance is to get married again. If you were engaged Smithson would let the matter stand over."

"It wasn't my fault that I got into debt," she said plaintively. "Decent people have to keep up appearances, and it's simply impossible to do that without going bankrupt, unless you're a soap-boiler, or something equally horrible."

"My dear girl, I'm not reproaching you."

To reproach her was the last thing her brother would think of doing—but Lady Habart was in a quarrelsome mood.

"Oh no, you're not reproaching me in so many words," she said, "but you look as if you thought I was to blame. I'd much sooner you said it outright than keep hinting at it, and looking at me like a dissenting minister. You look perfectly awful to-day; you're as yellow as a Chinaman; you look as if you took too much to drink last night."

She began to cry, for she felt miserable, and the world was treating her very harshly.

"You're awfully unkind," she said to her brother. Then, after a

pause: "But it's no good making myself look frightful. Haven't you got anything to say?"

She had an idea in her mind, but she had no wish to utter it, and waited for Guy to do so. The idea was Freddy Ramsden. But her brother appeared to have entirely forgotten her old lover, and again she inveighed against the stupidity of man.

"I believe Freddy will come and call," she said at last, driven for once into frankness; "I don't think he could keep away."

Guy sprang up. "If you can get engaged to him before next Monday, you're saved."

A flush came over Lady Habart's face, and she clenched her pretty hand. "I can't make him call. I don't care if he hates me or loves me, if he'll only come and see me."

"I don't believe Freddy Ramsden is the sort of man to get over anything of that sort."

"He always used to say he'd love me forever," she murmured pensively, "but then—so used I."

"He was terribly cut up when you—er, chucked him over for Habart."

"I wish you wouldn't talk of it like that, you know I wasn't to blame. I was a wretchedly innocent girl and he'd only got twopence halfpenny a year. You all insisted on my giving him up. Papa wouldn't hear of it. . . . I was perfectly heart-broken."

Guy did not think his sister expressed the facts very exactly, but he was far too discreet to remind her of past events. She had a truly feminine way of putting on other people the blame of all her mistakes, of all her actions which seemed discreditable; and she invariably took to herself the whole credit of the good deeds with which she was at all connected. For much that she did was highly creditable to her sex and station; she was deeply interested in the reclaiming of bad characters, and her name was printed in large type on the prospectus of many charitable institutions. Now that certain ill-considered individuals are beginning to cast aspersions upon the press, suggesting (most unjustly, of course) that it is slanderous, narrow-minded, and stupid, that it panders to all the worst instincts of the mob—it must be counted for righteousness in Lady Habart that she recognised its profound usefulness, and constantly sent to the papers details of her comings and goings, of the functions she gave, and the various deeds of mercy she performed.

"It shows what sort of a chap Freddy is that he should have spent five years abroad," said Guy after a pause.

"It shows that, like all men, he's very unoriginal. How absurd it is for a man to go and shoot things in the Rockies just because his engagement's broken off. It's such bad taste."

"What would you have him do?" asked Guy.

"Announce it in the *Morning Post* and behave reasonably. They say women have no sense for comedy—men have only the sense for melodrama."

"I'm afraid I must go," said Guy. "I've got to dine with some people, and I must get home to dress."

"Oh, but it's not six yet!" replied Lady Habart.

"I have a long way to get, they live at Dulwich."

"Oh! I shouldn't have thought it was worth your while to know people who live in the suburbs. I thought in those parts they always dined in the middle of the day. Can't you wire that you're ill? You see that I'm not in a fit state to be left alone."

"Well, I hardly know the people."

"Oh, of course, I can't expect you to show the least indulgence to me. If you're going, go at once and let me have a little peace."

"If you really wish me to stay—"

"No, I don't! I shouldn't dine with you in any case, I'm far too ill to sit up. I shall go to bed and have dinner in my room. I only thought it might be convenient to have you in the house in case I wanted anything."

Lady Habart looked at herself in the glass when her brother had gone. She felt sure Freddy Ramsden would come. . . . People said his father had fifteen thousand a year, and all that was his now; of course men's incomes were always exaggerated. She knew that by sad experience in the case of her lamented husband; he had not half the fortune attributed to him; but then the Ramsdens were bankers, and Habart had been merely a landowner.

"I wonder if he loves me still," she said. There was a look in his eyes when he gazed at her that betokened something. But what was it? She did not care so long as he came, and she felt certain he would be unable to stay away. He had loved her too passionately to forget her; in those days she had been the mistress of his whole soul. He would have done anything for her sake, he adored her like a goddess. . . . She brushed a little fluff off the end of her nose.

"I hate new powder-puffs," she muttered, "they always come off on you."

She arranged a wisp of hair at the back of her head and passed a hand over her ear. She knew her ears were not good, and covered as much of them as possible with her hair.

"I wish I had really beautiful ears," she said, looking at them for a moment; they were too large, the lobe was not detached from the face. She gave a little shudder and hid them again. She took up her book and began to read—but still her mind wandered.

"If I can get engaged by Monday, I'm saved." The thought seized her that he might be no longer free. "He's the sort of man to fall in love with the typical creamy English girl. Thank God I was never that."

The butler opened the door, and even before his announcement, before she saw the incomer, she knew who it was.

"Mr. Ramsden."

He was a big, broad-shouldered fellow, with grayish hair and a heavy moustache; he was deeply bronzed, and his swartness was emphasized by the whiteness of his collar. He wore his frock-coat a little uneasily, as if he were used to freer things. Lady Habart noticed at once that he gave as little attention to his clothes as when she had known him years before. He had always the look of the countryman, and mentally she decided that such a man should never go to places where he could not wear knickerbockers and a Norfolk jacket. He was the sort of man of whose gentility dowagers are not perfectly assured till they know he has a very handsome fortune; he was the sort of man whom everybody else would have called at once a thoroughly good sort.

Ramsden came forward, and Lady Habart rose from her chair.

"How nice of you to come and see me," she said. "I felt sure you would."

"How strange," he answered. "I felt sure you would not expect me."

His reply was a little disconcerting, but Lady Habart remembered that it was an old habit of his to say unnecessarily frank things, and ignored it.

"Do have some tea," she murmured. "Do you still take it without sugar?"

The tea had stood some time, but Lady Habart supposed Freddy's agitation such that he would not notice the difference.

The very suddenness of Ramsden's arrival upon her thoughts had a little embarrassed the charming woman, but she was recovering herself; she assumed her armour of bewitching glances and sugary smiles; she asked herself why he came and what were his sentiments. She watched him like a cat, but there was nothing in her exterior to betray the excitement of her mind; she was playing admirably the part of the accomplished hostess. It could not fail to strike him after his long sojourn in foreign lands.

"Do you still take tea without sugar?" she repeated, as he watched her pour it out and did not reply.

"It is very polite of you to remember," he said dryly.

"After so long?" she gave a little silvery laugh and turned upon him the light of her blue eyes. She knew how caressing they were. Years ago, their glance would have made his heart beat strangely. . . . "You've been away shooting, haven't you?"

"I've been in Africa," he replied.

"Yes, so Guy told me." She mentally reviled her brother for telling her that Ramsden was in America: she might have made so awkward a slip. "That's why you're so brown," she added with another smile. "But you haven't changed a bit. You're just the same Freddy Ramsden I used to know."

"Why did you cut me to-day?" he asked with what Lady Habart considered a rather disagreeable smile.

"I thought you didn't recognise me," she replied promptly. "You looked at me in exactly the way people look when they're wondering who on earth you are. And I should have felt so ridiculous if I'd bowed and you'd taken no notice."

He paused, looking at her somewhat critically. Lady Habart was pleased to think her frock fitted so perfectly, and she was sitting with her back to the light, so the closest scrutiny was supportable.

"Are you very surprised that I should call on you, Lady Habart?" he asked.

The lady's heart gave a little beat; at last it was coming; she set all her nerves taut for the fray. The approaching battle exhilarated her; for all her delicate exterior, she was a fighting woman, and never felt herself living so intensely as when she had to martial the whole array of her wits against those of another.

"Oh no; I'm not a bit surprised. I'm very pleased."

"I imagined that you would not greatly care to see me," he

answered. "One naturally dislikes the person one has treated vilely."

"I really don't understand what you mean," she cried, with a pretty expression of injured innocence.

"If you remember that I take my tea without sugar, you can hardly have forgotten that—that once you were engaged to marry me."

She vaguely thought it was rather bad taste in Freddy to put the matter so brusquely; but he was always rather abrupt. She looked down at the tips of her shoes as she had seen actresses look down on the stage when they were representing high-born damsels of three and twenty: that was her favourite age.

"Are you still angry?" she asked in a low and effective voice—it should, perhaps, have been a little more husky.

"Not in the slightest," he answered, smiling.

Lady Habart looked at him quickly—he seemed amused.

"Why have you come here to-day if you don't care for me any more?"

"How do you know that I no longer care for you?"

"If you did, you would still be angry." She came to the conclusion that a semblance of perfect frankness would be most useful.

"One gets over things, you know," he replied, with a shrug of the shoulders.

"I'm sorry I made you suffer." Her heart was beating, and she with difficulty repressed her delight; she knew she was acting the comedy perfectly—her voice and manner came to her without the smallest effort. Like every great actress, she almost felt the emotions she represented, and the pathos of her voice very nearly brought tears to her eyes. "I'm sorry I made you suffer."

"It was salutary," he said, smiling, but she noticed that the smile was a little painful. "If you had not behaved as you did, I might have gone on loving you to the end of my life. And that, I feel, would have been the most intense degradation that I could suffer."

"You are hardly polite."

"Shall I go?"

"No!"

"Oh, I can't be polite," he cried. "I have suffered too much. D'you know that out in Africa in my solitude, for months I thought of you. I remembered every word you had ever said, every look of your eyes, and I saw that you were selfish, and cold-hearted,

and cruel. At first I hated you with all the strength with which I'd loved you. But afterwards—afterwards, I saw how paltry and mean you were, and I only despised you. I longed to be face to face with you so that I might tell you how I loathed you."

"Is that why you came to-day?" she asked.

"Yes."

He rose to go, but she took no notice of his movement.

"You don't despise me one half so much as I despise myself."

He looked at her in silence, with a look of contempt upon his face.

"D'you think I was happy after I married?"

"You were a countess, and had twenty thousand a year. What more could you want?"

"He puts things in such an inexpressibly vulgar way," said Lady Habart mentally, while out loud she murmured: "You have a right to be hard upon me."

"You made me fall in love with you; and you know how passionately I adored you. You promised to marry me, and when you met Habart you threw me over without a thought but of yourself."

"I am very sorry," she said.

Ramsden gave a laugh. "What is the good of being sorry? Do you know what you made me suffer? Can you imagine my bitter agony while I tried to forget you? Oh, I hate you with all my heart."

Lady Habart gave a little cry, not of pain, or horror, but of exultation; for she knew suddenly that he still loved her; she had been right in all her suppositions. Her heart swelled with pride and pleasure, with keen appreciation of her own cleverness. He was looking at her with flaming eyes, and he muttered again: "I hate you."

Then she tried a bold stroke. "But I—I love you all the same, Freddy."

"You are excessively clever, Lady Habart." His passion was dissipated, and he spoke now with the calm appreciation of the dilettante. Lady Habart considered him neither clever nor polite.

"Oh, it is you who are heartless now," she cried, with a finely dramatic gesture. "I suffered also—I suffered too much for my fault." She put her hands to her head and her voice trembled; perhaps she forced the note a little. "I was mad. Of course I was wrong. I know I behaved vilely to you. When Habart came down

to Blueriver he turned my head. I was so young then, I was only a child. I didn't love him. I confess I married him for—oh, it's too horrible to think of, it's too inexpressibly vulgar. But I loved you, Freddy," she concluded, with a heart-rending sigh. "I can't call you Mr. Ramsden; I've always thought of you as Freddy."

"I'm glad you suffered."

If the note was forced, Ramsden had not perceived it.

"I used to be always thinking of you, Freddy. And the more I was with him the more I loathed him, the more I regretted what I had lost. Don't you believe I love you, Freddy?"

"No!" He looked at her angrily; she knew she was stirring in his heart all the old emotions; the passion of the old days was returning to him like an overwhelming flood.

"And then I knew you were unhappy, and I knew it was my fault. I repented bitterly."

"I should have thought your house in Park Lane and your castle in the country would have silenced the qualms of your conscience. It must be more obstinate than I suspected."

"If he only knew," she murmured to herself in the same distracted tones, "how out of repair the town-house was, and how old-fashioned the furniture. . . . I had looked forward to it all so much," she cried; "and then when I had it— Oh, I longed to be back again in the country, in your arms, Freddy; and I longed for your simple, frank old smile."

They paused, buried in contemplation. Lady Habart had forgotten that she was acting a part, and now believed every word she said. It would have been wonderful if her passionate accents had not affected Ramsden, for her they touched profoundly. She felt herself the most ill-used of distressed females, and she had not much ground to traverse before thinking Freddy Ramsden vastly to blame for leaving her to the tender mercies of her late husband. Lady Habart turned towards her visitor the best side of her profile.

"Was Habart good to you?" asked Ramsden at last.

"He loved me very much," replied Lady Habart, heaving a sigh. But that was so frank a misrepresentation of her husband's feelings that she almost smiled; she was a woman of humour. "Oh, Freddy, my life was awful; sometimes I felt I couldn't go on with it. I was so unhappy. Often I was on the verge of running away and following you."

"You have lied to me so much."

Immediately she spoke her last words she knew that they did not ring true. He withdrew himself into his shell.

"Don't you believe what I say?" she sighed. "But why should you? I know you'll never believe in me again—I don't deserve that you should. . . . Oh, but forgive me, Freddy." She put out in supplication her bejewelled hands: as she had told her brother, the rings were mostly paste. "Forgive me before we part forever."

"Would my forgiveness do you any good?"

"You're going to be married soon, aren't you? I do hope you'll be happy—I'd willingly give my life to know you completely happy."

"I shall never get married," he replied.

Lady Habart looked up quickly.

"Oh, but Guy told me you were engaged to a Miss—I forget the name. I thought you'd only come from abroad to get married."

"I have only been engaged once."

"Oh, well, I'm glad. I don't want you to get married; I don't want you to forget me. . . . Oh, I don't know what I'm saying—I wish you didn't hate me!"

"Do you think I have no cause, Lady Habart?"

"You used to call me Dolly—don't you remember?"

"I have no right to, now."

"It would make me a little happier, if you did." She had again lost herself in her part and she was living, not acting. She really felt very miserable and the strain upon her nerves began to tell on her. She could not restrain the real tears that came to her eyes, and she put her handkerchief up, sobbing quietly. It was tremendously effective, and she could not help perceiving it. "I'm so unhappy—I want some one so badly in whom I can trust."

"I will do anything I can to help you," he whispered; he could not trust himself to speak aloud. Few men can stand a woman's tears.

"What can you do! I'm so frightfully unhappy. You don't know what it is to be utterly alone in the world with nobody to stand by one—with nobody to love one."

"Ah, Dolly, I would have loved you all my life if you had let me."

"It's too late now," she sighed, drying her tears. "I feel that my life is finished—I'm quite young and I feel so old." She remembered that in artificial light she did not look more than twenty-three.

"Sometimes I think I should like to lie down and die. . . . I used to be beautiful when you knew me, Freddy."

"To me you are always beautiful."

She smiled at him painfully, thinking the style of his remark more applicable to a woman of at least forty. Her eyes, wandering over Freddy's head, caught sight of one of the water-colours of her school-days.

"Do you remember how we used to wander about the fields together at home, when we were boy and girl? And on Sunday evenings when we walked home from church you used to put your arm round my waist. And we used to sit under the big trees and smoke cigarettes."

"Ah, Dolly," he cried, as the recollections crowded back upon him, "how could you treat me as you did!"

"And we used to play tennis together. D'you remember how frightfully cross you used to get when I beat you?"

He laughed in his old boyish manner, forgetting suddenly all that had gone between. "You only won when I didn't play up."

"Oh, what nonsense! You always used to say that just to aggravate me, but it wasn't true. . . . And afterwards you used to lie down on the grass and smoke, while I made you lemon-squashes."

"D'you remember how sick your first cigarette made you?"

"Oh, it was horrible!"

"You wouldn't speak to me for days afterwards, and you made me give you my knife to make it up."

"But you took it back again next day," she said, laughing.

"It seems to me that then there were no rainy days. Our whole life was warm and sunny and beautiful."

"And d'you remember that day I nearly fell in the lake? I was so frightened and you kissed me. You were always kissing me."

"You drive me perfectly mad," he said. "Oh, I know you loved me then, Dolly. Why didn't you let that sweet life go on forever!"

She put her hands to her eyes. Surely now he would spring forward and clasp her in his arms, vowing he adored her; she would sink her beautiful head upon his bosom and burst into another flood of tears; she would offer her rose-like mouth to his kisses.

But he uttered a cry and it made Lady Habart start and look rapidly at him.

"What a fool I am!" he said. "You took me in like a child. You've been humbugging me all through."

"Freddy," she cried, springing up. "What d'you mean? You're mad."

She could not understand the sudden change. What error had she committed? It was incomprehensible.

"You humbug!" he repeated.

"Freddy!" A look of genuine horror came into her eyes. How had he seen?

He took up his hat and walked out of the room without another word. Lady Habart sank back into her chair, half-fainting. Had she lost him? But why, why? Oh, it was impossible.

"Oh no, he'll come back," she muttered. At the first moment she was overcome, but her confidence quickly returned. She knew he loved her passionately, he couldn't help himself; he was like a fish with the hook in its mouth, struggling to get free. Every toss and turn forced the steel deeper in, and she smiled at the thought of the bleeding gills. She looked at the time. She had intended to send a note to the people with whom she was dining to say she was seriously indisposed and could not possibly come; but the matter had gone out of her head and now it was, perhaps, a little late. She was restless and excited, inclined to go out, experiencing a need for speech and admiration. She was so sure of her triumph that she could afford to dismiss the subject from her thoughts. There was now really nothing to ruffle her temper, and already she began to feel herself looking more beautiful than an hour ago.

She went to her room in the highest of good humours, and chose to wear her most extravagant costume. Looking at herself in the glass, she thought she had never appeared more fascinating. For once she did not ask herself whether her hair should not be golden red rather than reddish gold—a momentous question which had given her many troubled moments. Her neck was adorable, her eyes flashed, and she felt sure of repeating in a different way her triumph of the afternoon. Finally she descended to her carriage; certainly she was overdressed, but then no one could have been more fashionable. She wondered whether after dinner Freddy Ramsden would walk up and down beneath her windows; he was a sentimental creature, and she thought it very probable. Her absence, however, made such a performance distinctly ridiculous.

"Poor Freddy," she murmured, "he's so naïf."

Next day Lady Habart was somewhat meditative. She sat in her boudoir awaiting Freddy's inevitable visit; her old knowledge of him told her that he had been counting the hours which passed before he could decently present himself again. She had closed her door to every one but him, even to her brother; for she felt certain that Ramsden had prepared some speech or other with which to break in upon her, and the presence of a third party would possibly be disastrous. Poor Freddy was so melodramatic; Lady Habart had a very low opinion of masculine good taste; judged by the standard of her own exquisite *savoir faire,* all men were just a little vulgar.

A servant brought her coffee—it was after luncheon—and said that Captain Smithson had called.

"What on earth can he want?" she asked herself. The servant added that the money-lender had particularly asked to see her, and on being told she was out had inquired when she would be at home, and then said he would come again a couple of hours later. Lady Habart was still wondering why Captain Smithson should want so particularly to see her, when Ramsden was shown in. Lady Habart sprang up.

"Freddy!" she cried with astonishment. "I expected never to see you again."

"I ought not to have come. I am not—I am not worthy to see you. I have come to beg your pardon."

Lady Habart looked at the pattern of her carpet. "It is not you who should do that—I beg your pardon, Freddy, with all my heart for all I have done."

"I spoke to you like a cad yesterday; I had thought out long ago what I wanted to say to you. When I saw you I felt I couldn't, but—I forced myself."

"You said nothing that I did not deserve," she replied in a low voice, with a humble bend of the head.

"I've come to-day to ask you to forgive me. And," he hesitated, colouring, then with an obvious effort, "and I've come to ask you to marry me. Yesterday I accused you of being insincere, I thought you were humbugging me; but when I accused you—forgive me, I was mad—a look of horror came over your face that has been haunting me all the night. That look showed me that I wronged you." He came forward and took her hands, pleading. "Will you marry me, Dolly?"

Then an inspiration came to her. She restrained the joyful *"Yes"* that was forcing itself from her lips against her will. If she accepted him, and he discovered her penniless condition, he would understand that she had been indeed playing the fool with him. She dared not risk it; he would surely make inquiries about her. It was safer to tell him first. She disengaged her hands.

"I can't," she whispered. "Oh! God help me! I can't. I thank you all with my heart for what you have said; but it's impossible, Freddy. I'm so sorry; I think I could have made you happy."

"What do you mean?" he cried. "Yesterday you swore you loved me."

She passed her hand over her forehead. "Don't you know? I thought all the world knew. I'm hopelessly in debt, and I'm going to be made bankrupt."

"What! But Habart—"

"He left me nothing. Everything was tied up. I had a little, but—oh, I don't know what happened. I got into the hands of the money-lenders. One of them has just been here clamouring for his money. Oh, God, I don't know what I shall do. Everything will be sold, and I shall be a beggar."

"Oh, Dolly, I love you with all my heart."

He clasped her in his arms, but she pushed him away.

"Oh no," she cried, "don't humiliate me. Don't you see that I can't marry you; it wouldn't be honourable. My name will be dragged through the dust. People will say that I married you for your money."

"What does it matter what people say!"

"Oh, I couldn't bear it. I love you too much."

"But if you're in trouble let me stand by you. Oh, now, you must marry me. You owe it to me, I have suffered and loved so much."

"I daren't. Don't tempt me. I should like to so much, but I'm afraid. Afterwards, when you thought of it, you'd believe also that I married you for your money. And if I saw that thought in your eyes I'd kill myself. If I don't marry you it means hopeless ruin and disgrace. You'd think I inveigled you into marriage. I've got to pay Smithson four thousand pounds next Monday, and I can't, I can't."

She finished by burying her head on his bosom, while he kissed her repeatedly.

"Say 'Yes,'" he said; "say 'Yes.'"

And at last she cried: "Oh, I can't help it, I love you too much. Take me and do what you will with me."

Freddy Ramsden had not enjoyed such bliss for many years. He pressed her to marry him quickly, and she did not resist.

"And now I want you to do something for me," he said at last. "Will you promise—on your word of honour?"

"Yes," she replied, smiling through her tears.

"I want you to let me give you a cheque to pay that money-lender with. You promised," he added, as she started, and he saw she meant to tell him such a thing was impossible. "You promised."

"You are too good to me," she murmured. She thought herself very clever for having put an extra thousand on to the sum; it would be mightily useful for incidental expenses. She quickly ran up in her mind which bills she was bound to pay immediately. It seemed as if Freddy could not tear himself away; but at last he left her, promising to return for dinner, and then Lady Habart hurriedly slipped the cheque into an envelope and sent it to her bank. Four thousand pounds! She gave a little cry of delight. She telephoned for her brother.

The moment he appeared she burst into a torrent of explanation. Never in her whole life had she felt more pleased with herself; the triumph of Habart's proposal had been nothing to this, for he had been but a second and better string to her bow. Ramsden never knew that she had written him his letter of dismissal two hours after accepting the earl. . . . Lady Habart had never felt herself so entirely spiritual as at this moment; never had she been more convinced of the superiority of mind over matter, of man over beast, of herself over everybody else. Though she was a pious woman and fervently thanked her Maker for her success, she thanked her own intelligence more.

"Oh, I was splendid," she cried to her brother. "If I weren't going to be married, I'd go on the stage. What a success I should be!"

She could not contain herself, and she repeated half-a-dozen times every detail of the two interviews with Ramsden. She could scarcely understand that her mind should be so remarkable—she wondered whence her talent came; certainly neither her father nor her mother had ever shown such diabolical cleverness. It

flattered her to think herself Mephistophelian. Then in unwonted generosity she began telling Guy all she would do for him—his circumstances had been no better than hers, but his debts were infinitesimal, since no one had ever been so foolish as to trust him. She said she would find him a rich wife—that was self-help after the most approved pattern of the excellent Samuel Smiles; it would provide for him also without any expense to herself or dear Freddy. Dear Freddy's money she now looked upon as her own and meant to be careful with it. Of course, Freddy would go into Parliament—it would give him something to do, and keep him out of the way, and he'd be quite at home among all those old fogies. She would write his speeches herself; she had always had an inclination for public life, and henceforward she would go in for problems, model dwelling-houses, old-age pensions, temperance, and all that sort of thing. Guy listened meekly to all she was going to do for him, for Freddy, and for Freddy's wife. In his heart of hearts he did not greatly believe in any one benefiting enormously by her efforts besides herself. He had for her a very great affection, but few illusions.

But the butler interrupted Lady Habart with the announcement that Captain Smithson was again below, insisting on seeing Her Ladyship.

"What a rude man he is," said Lady Habart. "Isn't it a shame that I should have to pay him the money!"

"I'd better go and see what he wants, hadn't I?" said Guy.

"Yes, do go; and be as rude to him as you possibly can. Treat him like the cad he is. If you get the ghost of a chance, kick him downstairs."

Guy laughed, and was proceeding to carry out the lady's gentle wish, when she stopped him.

"No, don't go: I want to be rude to him myself. He was simply insolent when I called on him."

"Well, I'll get out of the way," said Guy.

"No, stop here and read the paper. Take no notice either of him or me," she replied, touching the bell for the captain to be sent up.

Lady Habart sat down at a writing-table, and began writing a note to a duchess of her acquaintance. The expression on her face was not amiable. The door was opened, and the butler announced the name. Captain Smithson stalked forward with his

fashionable gesture, holding the shiniest of top-hats. He stopped as Lady Habart did not rise to take his outstretched hand, and for once was a little embarrassed. Laby Habart had been right in supposing Guy's presence would add to the humiliation. A man can sometimes bear a woman's snub, but never if a second man is present. Guy went on reading his paper and Lady Habart continued her letter.

"Er—Lady Habart"; he thought that they possibly had not heard his entrance.

Lady Habart half-turned her head. "Oh, is that you, Smithson?" she said. "I'll attend to you in one minute."

Captain Smithson looked at her quickly and then glanced at Guy; he could not understand. They did not offer him a chair, but he sat down to show he was at his ease; but then, sitting away from the others, he felt himself ridiculous, and he marched up to Guy.

"Anything in the paper?" he asked in as natural a tone as he could assume.

"What?" said Guy, looking up.

Captain Smithson repeated his question.

"Absolutely nothing," answered Guy, and at once buried his head behind it again. Captain Smithson frowned; he was not a patient man and he was quite unused to such treatment.

"I would be obliged if you could give me your attention immediately, Lady Habart; I'm very busy."

"Really?" said Lady Habart, looking at him for one moment, contemptuously.

He could think of nothing further to say and he waited. He swore he would make her pay for her behaviour; of course, she had the money, otherwise she would never have altered her behaviour so markedly. Lady Habart finished the letter with great deliberation.

"Now, my good man, what can I do for you?" she said at last. She left him standing, as being more menial and humiliating. Captain Smithson was in rather an awkward position. He had come to her with a proposition to delay calling in his money for another three months, on terms extremely advantageous to himself. He knew that if the worst came to worst the present holder of the title would pay the lady's debts and there was no need to press her too hard. But evidently she had the money

and his errand had lost its object. Lady Habart impatiently tapped the ground with her foot.

"Please state your business at once."

"I came to see you about our conversation of yesterday afternoon."

"Oh, indeed!"

"Well, the fact is—"

"But really, I don't understand what right you have to come to my house and insist on being shown in. I look upon it as a piece of the grossest impertinence."

"You forget that you invited me to take tea with you, Lady Habart," he said, flushing.

"I?" said Lady Habart indignantly. "The man's mad. Did you ever hear such a thing, Guy!"

Guy raised his eyebrows and looked at the money-lender as if he were some wonderful beast.

"Your Ladyship has a very bad memory," said the captain sarcastically.

"You are very impertinent. Please ring the bell, Guy."

"You know what to expect if you don't pay me my money, Lady Habart."

"I am under the impression that it is not due till Monday. Oh, Russell," she added to the butler, "you will show this man to the door, and if he comes again you will call the police."

Captain Smithson was going to speak, but there were three pairs of eyes upon him; also Guy was obviously athletic and would love an opportunity to throw him downstairs. He walked out like a lamb. When the door was closed behind him, Lady Habart smiled and kissed her brother.

PRO PATRIA

(1903)

I

Mr. John Porter-Smith was a "carpet-bagger"—which means, of course, a candidate who has no connection with the place he wishes to represent; and arrives to catch the electors' votes with no more unwieldy luggage than a carpet bag. But Mr. Porter-Smith, though his constituency had certainly heard nothing of him till he was sent down from headquarters to contest the seat, came by no means with exiguous baggage. On the contrary, he brought with him a reassuring quantity of personal effects, a motor-car, and postilions in handsome red coats. These, it should be added, he did not use with the motor-car, but in a magnificent and highly varnished carriage, which dashed continually up and down the streets behind four equally magnificent horses. An election is perhaps the only occasion on which an ordinarily modest Englishman may give rein to his tastes for eccentricity and grandiloquence; and these are qualities which fifty years of repression have done little to extinguish. It is only the mortal fear of ridicule which has bullied the Briton of to-day out of the bottle-green frock-coat of Disraeli and the pompous phrases of Bulwer-Lytton: when he can offer his patriotism as an excuse, even the quietest will rival the Salvation Army in the gaudiness of his costume and of his rhetoric. Mr. Porter-Smith, indeed, went on further than to exhibit in every shop-window his photograph as an Imperial Yeoman, but outriders and postilions sufficiently made up for the deficiency; and his speeches were models of rodomontade. The fact that he was perfectly unknown to the electors was counterbalanced by the happy circumstance that Mr. Porter-Smith had not only fought for his king in South Africa, but had even shed

his red blood for that gracious personage. He had been scratched on the hand and obliged for three days to wear a bandage; but the exact nature of his injury was by himself and by his more enthusiastic supporters rightly considered a matter of no consequence. The latter drew lurid pictures of Mr. Porter-Smith lying wounded on the field of battle, silent, uncomplaining, heroic, bleeding his life's blood, ready to die for his country; and when the candidate himself unassumingly said it was nothing, that he had only done his duty, the electors cheered to the echo at such a noble mingling of manly sentiment and of intrepid modesty.

II

A couple of days before the election Mr. Porter-Smith went to his committee-rooms in the morning, overflowing with high spirits. He had driven up with his four horses; and the attention he created, with the scarlet outriders and the postilions, always elated him.

"Well," said he, "they seem more enthusiastic than ever."

"Enthusiasm be hanged!" said Major Long, a jovial, red-faced man, who, with the Reverend Septimus Cameron, was Porter-Smith's most influential supporter.

And the agent, who was sitting with him, looked as if he fully agreed with the rather forcible expression.

"What's the matter?" asked Porter-Smith, looking with surprise at their gloomy faces.

"Cameron has been here."

"What, the worthy Septimus?" replied the candidate, flippantly. "Has he had his hair cut?"

The Rev. Septimus Cameron was the leader of the Low Church Party in the constituency; and a man not only of irreproachable character, which might have been unimportant, but of overpowering influence as well, which made his principles things to be treated with respect. The Radical candidate was a Roman Catholic, and the Rev. Septimus looked upon him consequently as little better than Satan. Porter-Smith, who knew nothing about the questions which agitated the Low Church Party and the Nonconformists, and cared less, cheerfully pledged himself to support the measures favoured by those respectable factions. Likewise, when they set

him a long string of questions about his beliefs and his attitude towards certain matters, he did not hesitate to answer them all in the way his agent suggested.

"If you get the Low Church vote and the Nonconformists, the election is yours," said the agent: and that for Mr. Porter-Smith settled the matter.

But this morning neither the agent nor Major Long was inclined to take things lightly.

"The fact is," said the agent, "that Mr. Cameron has been here this morning to say he can't vote for you. He's going over to the other side. He'll take all the Low Churchmen, and the Dissenters will go with him."

"And you won't have a ghost of a chance of getting in," added Long.

Porter-Smith for a moment was speechless. "Good Lord," he said, "the old chap must be off his head! Haven't I given enough pledges? What does he want now? I'll give him more pledges, if he likes."

"It's not pledges he's after now," said Major Long, "it's morals."

"Well, ain't I moral enough?" said Porter-Smith. "After all, I have fought for my country, and been wounded. For us who have lain on the field of battle—"

"Yes, I know, I know," interrupted Long impatiently, recognising the candidate's favourite point with an unruly audience. "Where's your wife, man?"

"My wife? What does old Cameron want with my wife?"

"I think you should know that certain reports are being circulated," said the agent.

"And they've got to old Cameron; and he came here in a towering rage, said you'd deceived him, and that you weren't fit to go into Parliament. And he's going to write a public letter to you explaining his reasons for not voting for you. And it's something about a governess."

"It's an infernal lie!" said Porter-Smith, indignantly.

"That's what we told him; and he promised to wait till to-night to give you a chance of clearing yourself."

There was to be a great meeting that evening in the Town Hall, and it was for this, apparently, that the excellent clergyman was laying his plans.

"How the dickens am I to clear myself?" said Porter-Smith,

walking up and down. "I think it's disgusting to bring personalities into elections; besides, there's no truth in the story."

"Well, now, how are you going to prove that?"

Porter-Smith looked at his supporter helplessly. "The fact is," he said at last, "there *is* a certain amount of truth."

"Ah!" said the agent and Major Long in one breath.

"You needn't look as if you knew it all along. And besides, I did nothing I'm ashamed of. It was only a little mistake."

"If it loses us the election, you'll find it a very big mistake," said Long, grimly.

"It wasn't my fault at all." Porter-Smith looked from one of his auditors to the other; then, in a burst of confidence: "The fact is, my wife and I were staying at her sister's, and she had a governess. Well, one day when I was taking a stroll with the governess she slipped, and I put out my arm—to save her from falling. And somehow she fell into my arms, and then, without thinking what I was doing, I kissed her. My wife happened to come along at the very moment, and of course she misconstrued the whole thing. She wouldn't let me explain. I told her it was the first time, but he said it was very unlikely."

"It was—very. It sounds fishy."

"It's an accident that might happen to any one," said Porter-Smith, in an aggrieved tone. "It was idiotic of her to go up to London and say she wasn't coming back. I said I was sorry, and that it shouldn't occur again. Women are so beastly unreasonable."

"How old was the governess—middle-aged?"

"No, of course not."

"And how long ago did this take place?"

"Why, just before the war. I thought if I volunteered it would bring Fanny to her knees. But I don't believe she cared a straw. I shall never forgive her now."

The agent considered a moment. "There's only one thing Mr. Porter-Smith can do. He must produce his wife, and she must deny the whole story."

"Oh, but that's impossible," the candidate said hurriedly.

"Where's your wife?" asked Major Long.

"I don't know. Besides, I refuse to bring private matters into the contest. What have my relations with my wife got to do with the beastly voters? I've not seen my wife for more than a year; and she's behaved shamefully to me."

"If you don't contradict the story authoritatively this evening, you may as well pack up your things and retire," said the agent. "And you might have consideration upon us! How many meetings have I harrowed by saying that you separated yourself from all you loved—even from your wife—to fight the enemies of your country; and now you tell us that you and your wife are not upon speaking terms! You must go and see her at once, and bring her down here."

"She won't come," said Porter-Smith irritably. "You don't know her; and I tell you I don't know where she is."

"You say she went to her mother's; she's probably there still. You must go up and eat humble pie, and ask her to forgive you."

"I wouldn't for a thousand pounds," cried Porter-Smith.

"It will cost you more than that if you don't," said the agent. "You're very much mistaken if you think you'll get out of the election under fifteen hundred."

"Parliamentary candidates shouldn't kiss governesses," said Major Long.

Meanwhile the indispensable agent had been looking out the trains, and announced that Mr. Porter-Smith could catch one to London within half an hour. Major Long elicited the address of Mrs. Porter-Smith's mother, and wrote out a telegram: *Must see wife, matter of life and death, arriving 2.30.* And between them they bustled the unlucky husband to the station; for greater safety Long accompanied him to town.

"You might have given me time to change my clothes," said Porter-Smith, looking at his irreproachable suit: "I'm not fit to be seen."

"Nonsense! You look as if you'd come out of a bandbox."

"I wish the train didn't go so quickly," said Porter-Smith presently; then, looking nervously at his supporter: "I say, Long, you won't leave me, will you?"

"Bless you, I'll put a string on to you if you like."

III

They arrived at the house of the candidate's mother-in-law, a well-set-up mansion in South Kensington, exuding respectability

from every brick. The peccant husband was as white as a sheet, and all his jauntiness had deserted him.

"She won't even see me," he said, standing irresolutely on the doorstep.

"Don't be a fool!" said Long, brushing past and ringing the bell.

They were shown into the drawing-room, and Porter-Smith introduced his friend to a tall, buxom woman of fifty, with fair hair and a comfortable smile.

"Major Long—Mrs. Mahon."

Porter-Smith had usually a ready flow of conversation, but at the present moment his brain was painfully blank; and he looked at his supporter with beseeching eyes.

"Is Mrs. Porter-Smith quite well?" asked Long.

"Quite well."

"I hope she'll be able to see us."

"She declares that nothing on earth shall induce her to do so," replied Mrs. Mahon, smiling. "And she's gone to put a new frock on!"

Major Long then explained the circumstances to Mrs. Mahon, who replied that she had no influence on her daughter.

"I knew she wouldn't see me," said Porter-Smith.

"I only know that she *says* she won't see you," replied Mrs. Mahon.

"She never changes her mind," said the husband.

"Then she's the most extraordinary woman in the world," said the mother.

At that moment the door opened, and Mrs. Porter-Smith came in: quite a ravishing person, slender, delicate, dressed with the utmost care. She made a slight bow to her husband, and sat down with an assumption of complete indifference. Major Long and the mother noticed that her cheeks were flushed and her eyes shone. There was a momentary silence, and Mrs. Mahon suggested: "Major Long and I will go and look at the conservatory; I dare say you two have plenty to talk about."

"Oh no, that's not necessary at all," said the married couple with one breath; and while Mrs. Porter-Smith suddenly became perfectly white, her husband blushed a deep and healthy red.

"I'm sure John and I have nothing to say to one another that can't be said before witnesses."

Long and Mrs. Mahon resumed their seats. Mrs. Porter-Smith sat as far as possible from her husband, and, although she pretended not to look at him, turned to his inspection the best side of her face. She knew he had always admired her profile; and the position gave her the opportunity of looking at him very carefully without the least appearance of so doing. Mrs. Mahon now took up the matter, and explained to her daughter the circumstances.

"When people do shameful things," said Mrs. Porter-Smith, "they mustn't complain when they're found out."

The candidate opened his mouth to make a somewhat heated rejoinder, when Long broke in with a long plea; but Mrs. Porter-Smith interrupted him.

"Do you mean to say you want me to go down and tell this Cameron man that the story isn't true?"

"Precisely!"

"I shall do no such thing," replied the lady, rising from her chair.

"Don't be unreasonable, Fanny," said her mother.

"Mamma," replied Mrs. Porter-Smith, indignantly, "he's asking me to tell a lie!"

"Only a very little one," interrupted Major Long, impetuously. "And for a good cause. Think of your husband going out to fight for his country. Don't you think that he has made up for a momentary lapse? He was severely wounded, you know."

"It said 'slightly' in the paper," replied Mrs. Porter-Smith, stiffly.

"It bled a great deal," said the candidate.

Mrs. Porter-Smith looked at him sideways, from under her long eyelashes, and she really thought that he looked uncommonly pale and thin. Major Long caught the glance, and pursued his advantage.

"Think of him lying on the battlefield all the night through, silent, uncomplaining, heroic, bleeding his life's blood, ready to die for his country." Long quoted the most effective passage of his speech.

"I only did my duty," said Mr. Porter-Smith.

"Do you know he might have been killed?" asked Major Long, with hushed voice.

"He behaved shamefully with the governess," said Mrs. Porter-

Smith, after a pause. "I could never have believed it if I hadn't seen it with my own eyes. And then he tried to make me believe it was an accident. I shouldn't have minded so much if he'd frankly confessed everything."

"But there was nothing to confess," said Porter-Smith.

"I shall *never* believe that."

Then Major Long played his last card. "Have you no patriotism?" he cried indignantly. "Your husband fought for his country like a man; and you stay at home at ease. When you're asked to do the smallest thing for your country, you refuse."

And in reply to Mrs. Porter-Smith's look of astonishment he added: "Don't you see that if you won't come down we shall lose the election? It means a dreadful blow to the Unionist cause; one can't tell what effects it may have on the country. Of course the loss of a seat counts only two on a division, but the moral effect is incalculable. Do you take no interest in your country's welfare?"

"I'm a Primrose Dame," answered Mrs. Porter-Smith, with pardonable satisfaction.

"And yet you throw a seat into the hands of the Little Englanders! It's your duty to sacrifice your private feelings. Surely your king and your country come before a wretched family difference?"

Major Long wiped his brow, overcome by his own eloquence. Mrs. Porter-Smith sat bolt upright, and a noble quiver passed through her as she saw herself in the character of a Roman matron.

"It shall never be said that I shrink from doing my duty," she said at last. "If every one were as scrupulous as I, this difficulty wouldn't have arisen."

"You'll come?" asked Long eagerly. The candidate himself wisely held his tongue.

"Yes," said Mrs. Porter-Smith, with a freezing look at her husband. "But on the condition that John lays no claim to me afterwards. Until the election is over I will live in the same house with him: of course Mamma will come; but the day after I shall come back to town. What I do is for the sake of my country, and John isn't to look upon it as a condonation of his behaviour. His conduct was scandalous, and I shall never forgive him."

IV

Mrs. Porter-Smith aggressively read the papers during the journey, sitting, of course, as far from her husband as the size of the carriage permitted; and when they arrived eventually at the Unionist committee rooms they found the Rev. Septimus Cameron waiting to see the candidate.

"He has assured me," said the agent, "that unless you give him full satisfaction he will make a complete explanation at the meeting to-night. He's going to say that no honest man can decently vote for you."

Porter-Smith muttered words of wrath in his moustache, but Major Long was jubilant.

"Come alone," he said: "we'll sit on him for all we're worth."

Porter-Smith went into the private room, and the reverend gentleman bowed coldly to him, resolutely keeping his hands behind his back. The candidate by now had regained his breezy good-humour.

"Well, Mr. Cameron, what's all this I hear? You surely don't believe every scandal that the Rads. invent!"

"I tried not to, Mr. Porter-Smith, but I'm afraid the evidence is overwhelming."

"But here is my wife." And Mrs. Porter-Smith, accompanied by her mother, was ushered in by Major Long.

Mrs. Porter-Smith stared coldly at Mr. Cameron in answer to his bow, and sat down. "I understand," she said, "that certain reports have arisen concerning the relations between my husband and myself?"

The Rev. Septimus Cameron bowed.

"Well, I think it's scandalous," she said, her cheeks flushing brightly. "I adore my husband, and he's the best man that ever lived, and I'm the last woman to suffer disloyalty. If he had done what you suggest, I would never speak to him again. Oh, it's too cruel to sully the purity of our married life with such base insinuations."

"That ought to satisfy you, Mr. Cameron," said Major Long.

"And if you knew what I suffered when he went to South

Africa, and I thought he might be killed!" Mrs. Porter-Smith's voice broke, and she put her handkerchief to her eyes.

"'I could not love you, dear, so much, loved I not honour more,'" quoted Major Long.

Mrs. Porter-Smith's sobs became audible, and the clergyman went up to the candidate and shook his hand. "Of course, after this there's nothing more to be said," he added. "I need not tell you how glad I am to find these charges untrue."

Mrs. Porter-Smith removed her handkerchief. "I think it's shameful that you should ever have believed them. You're a clergyman, and you ought to set a better example."

The others were aghast at this vehement little speech, for Mr. Cameron was influential and he was unused to reproof.

"Fanny, Fanny!" said Porter-Smith: "Mr. Cameron was only doing his duty. He acted from the highest motives."

But Mr. Cameron was disposed to be magnanimous, even though he had proved himself to be in the wrong. "My dear lady, you're quite right: I humbly beg your pardon and your husband's. And since there have been rumours in the constituency, I will make it my business to-night at the meeting to give them the very strongest contradiction."

Mrs. Porter-Smith rose and stretched out her hand, smiling. "I'll forgive you," she said, "and you must get my husband elected."

"I'll do my best."

But immediately the clergyman had gone, Porter-Smith sprang forward gratefully. "You *are* a brick, Fanny!" he said.

Mrs. Porter-Smith drew herself to her full height. "You need not thank me," she said icily. "I did it for my country."

V

Mrs. Porter-Smith, vowing that the election did not in the least interest her, stayed reading a book at home while the count was being made. But presently she heard a great noise, and, springing to the window, saw her husband waving his hat from the carriage, which was drawn by a band of zealous supporters: cheer upon cheer rang through the air.

"He's won," she said to herself, and her heart began to beat

rapidly. But, hearing the front door open, she quickly returned to her chair and began unconcernedly to read her book. Porter-Smith rushed in, wildly excited. "We've won, Fanny! We've won!"

"Have you?" she said coolly.

"Come to the balcony," he cried.

He took her by the arm, notwithstanding her slight resistance, and they stepped out. They were met by rapturous cheers.

"Three cheers for Mrs. Porter-Smith!" cried some one, and the air was rent by the yells of enthusiasm.

Mrs. Porter-Smith bowed and smiled, and the beating of her heart became tumultuous; the excitement was gaining upon her, and, looking round to her husband, she found him gazing at her with manifest pleasure. The crowd withdrew at last, and the happy couple returned to the drawing-room.

"Why, where's your mother, Fanny?" he asked. It was the first time he had found himself alone with her since the reunion.

Mrs. Porter-Smith hesitated a moment. "She's gone up to town," she said at last.

"Why?"

"She says—she says I'm a ridiculous fool."

Porter-Smith began to laugh.

"I don't see anything to laugh at," remarked his wife. "I shall go up tomorrow. I suppose you'll take a house in town now?"

"Yes; I thought of Grosvenor Square. Of course I shall have to entertain a great deal."

Mrs. Porter-Smith glanced at him, but said nothing.

"There's a very nice house in Grosvenor Square to be let now," she murmured, after a pause.

He was standing very close to her, and his eyes were fixed upon her with singular intensity.

"I suppose you wouldn't come and play hostess sometimes, when I'm giving a function?" he asked.

"It's quite out of the question," she said, but very indecisively. She could not help thinking that it would be pleasant to give large parties in Grosvenor Square.

"I'm thinking of going to Paris for a fortnight to rest," he said.

"Are you?" she replied. *"I've* been thinking of going to Paris to get some new things."

"Of course I shan't be able to do much. I'm rather exhausted after the election, and I've been so seedy lately."

She turned her eyes on him again, and he approached a little closer.

"Were you very bad in South Africa?" she asked.

"I was bad because I hadn't you with me," he said.

"If you'd really cared for me you wouldn't have gone."

Her voice broke, and when her husband put his arm round her waist she had not strength to resist.

"I thought you'd be glad," he said.

"You knew I should be miserable. When I saw you had volunteered I knew you were pleased to have got rid of me."

"You said you would never come back to me; or I shouldn't have gone."

"You might have given me time to change my mind."

"Fanny!"

He put both arms round her now, and unreasonably she began to cry.

"Your behaviour was scandalous, wasn't it?" she asked tearfully, as if she were no longer quite certain.

"Utterly!"

"Well, if you'll confess that, I'll confess that I behaved like a fool. When I'd got to Mamma's I was ashamed to come back again; and you wouldn't own that you were wrong."

"Then you'll forgive me everything?"

"I'm not sure that there was anything to forgive." She raised her face, and when he kissed her she whispered: "You know it was quite true when I told old Cameron that I adored you, and you were the best man in the world."

"We'll never quarrel again, will we?"

"Never!"

And so far they haven't; but then the election only took place the other day.

A POINT OF LAW

(1903)

When I feel more than usually poor, (on a rainy day, for instance, when opulent stockbrokers roll swiftly in electric broughams, or when some friend in bleak March weather tells me he is starting that very night for Monte Carlo), I make my will; it gives me a peculiar satisfaction to leave my worldly goods, such as they are, to persons who will not in the least care to receive them, and I like the obsequious air of the clerk who blows my name up a tube to the family solicitor. It is an amusement which costs me nothing, for Mr. Addishaw, the senior partner in the eminently respectable firm of Addishaw, Jones, and Braham, knows my foible; he is aware also that a solicitor's bill is the last I should ever pay, and I have warned him that if ever he sends it I will write a satiric story which shall hold him up to the ridicule of all his neighbours on Brixton Hill. What accounts he prepares after my demise do not in the smallest degree perturb me; my executors and he may fight it out between them.

One day, then, I walked down the Strand, feeling very wretched after a cheap luncheon in a crowded Italian restaurant (a crust of bread and a glass of water may be rendered appetizing by hunger and a keen sense of the romantic, but who can survey without despondency a cut off the joint, half cold and ill-cooked, and boiled potatoes?), and, jostled by hurrying persons, I meditated on the hollowness and the folly of the world. I felt certain that Mr. Addishaw at this hour would be disengaged, and it seemed an occasion upon which his services were eminently desirable; it would comfort me just then to prepare for the inevitable dissolution. I turned the corner and soon found myself at the handsome edifice, with its array of polished brass plates

and its general look of prosperity, wherein the firm for many years had rented offices.

"Can I see Mr. Addishaw?" I inquired.

And in a moment I was shown upstairs into the sumptuous apartment which the good gentleman inhabited. He had evidently just lunched, and with him the meal had without doubt been satisfactory; for he sat in the arm-chair generally reserved for clients, toasting his toes at the cheerful fire, and with great content smoked his cigar. There was so much self-satisfaction about his red face that the mere sight of him cheered me; and the benevolence of his snowy whiskers impressed me more than ever before with a sense of his extreme worth.

"You look as if you read the Lessons in church every Sunday morning, Mr. Addishaw," I said, when I shook hands with him. "I've come to make my will."

"Ah, well," he answered, "I have nothing to do for ten minutes. I don't mind wasting a little time."

"You must sit at your desk," I insisted, "or I shan't feel that I'm getting my money's worth."

Patiently he changed his seat, and with some elaboration I gave a list of all the bequests I wished to make.

"And now," said I, "we come to my wines, spirits, and liqueurs."

"Good gracious me!" he cried. "I didn't know that you had started a cellar. You are becoming a man of substance. I will tell my wife to ask for your new book at Mudie's."

"Your generosity overwhelms me," I retorted. "Some day, I venture to hope, you will go so far as to buy a second-hand copy of one of my works. But I have no cellar. The wine in my flat is kept in a cupboard along with the coats and hats, the electric meter, my priceless manuscripts, and several pairs of old boots. I have no wines, spirits, and liqueurs, but I wish to leave them to somebody, so that future generations may imagine that writers in the twentieth century lived as luxuriously as butchers and peers of the realm and mountebanks."

Somewhat astonished at this harangue, Mr. Addishaw wrote as I desired; then a pale young clerk was sent for and together the legal gentlemen witnessed my signature.

"And now," said I, "I will light a cigar to complete the illusion that I am a man of means, and bid you good afternoon."

Mr. Addishaw returned to his arm-chair by the fire and, feeling

apparently very good-humoured, asked me to remain for a few minutes; he had taken the only comfortable seat in the room, but I drew up the writing-chair and sat down.

"Wills are odd things," said Mr. Addishaw, in a meditative manner. "Only the other day I had to deal with the testament of the late Lord Justice Drysden; and it was so ill-composed that no one could make head or tail of it. But his eldest son happened to be a solicitor, and he said to the rest of the family: 'I'm going to arrange this matter as I consider right, and if you don't agree I'll throw the whole thing into Chancery and you'll none of you get a penny!' The family were not too pleased, for their brother thought fit to order the affair in a manner not altogether disadvantageous to himself; but I advised them to submit. My father and my grandfather were solicitors before me, so I think I have law more or less in the blood; and I've always taught my children two things. I think if they know them they can't come to much harm in the world."

"And what are they?" I asked.

"Never tell a lie and never go to law."

Mr. Addishaw rose slowly from his chair and went to the door.

"If anyone wishes to see me, Drayton, say that I shall be disengaged in a quarter of an hour," he called to his clerk.

Then, with a little smile which sent his honest red face into a number of puckers, he took from a cupboard a bottle, well coated with dust, and two wine-glasses.

"What is this?" I asked.

"Well, I'm an old man," he answered, "and I keep to some customs of the profession which these young sparks of to-day have given up. I always have a bottle of port in my room, and sometimes when I don't feel very well I drink a glass or two."

He poured out the wine and looked at it with a smile of infinite content. He lifted it to his nose and closed his eyes as though he were contemplating some pious mystery. He sipped it and then nodded to me three times with a look full of meaning.

"And yet there are total abstainers in the world!" he exclaimed.

He emptied the glass, sighed, refilled it, and sat down.

"Talking of wills, I said the last word in a matter this morning which has interested me a good deal; and, if you like, I will tell you the story, because it shows how sometimes by pure chance

that ass, the law, may work so as to protect the innocent and punish the contriving.

"One of the oldest clients of my firm is the family of Daubernoon, North Country squires, who have held immense estates in Westmorland since the good old days of King Henry VIII. They were not a saving race, so that in personalty they never left anything worth speaking of, but they always took care to keep the property unencumbered; and even now, when land is worth so little and the landlord finds it as difficult as the farmer to make both ends meet, their estates bring in the goodly income of six thousand a year.

"Roger Daubernoon, the late squire, injured his spine in a hunting accident, and it would have been a mercy if he had killed himself outright, since he lingered for twenty years, a cripple and an invalid who required incessant care. His wife died shortly afterwards and he was left with an only daughter, in whose charge he placed himself. A man used to an active, busy life, in illness he grew querulous and selfish, and it seemed to him quite natural that Kate Daubernoon, then a girl of twenty, should devote her life to his comfort. A skilful nurse, she became so necessary to him that he could not face the thought that one day she might leave him; he was devoured by the fear that she would marry, and he refused, pretexting his ill-health, to have visitors at the manor. He grew petulant and angry if to go to some party she abandoned him for a couple of hours, and finally Miss Daubernoon resigned herself to a cloistral life. Year in, year out, she remained in close attendance on her father, partly from affection, but more for duty's sake; she looked after the house, walked by the squire's bath-chair, read to him, and never once left home. She saw no one but the villagers, by whom for her charitable kindness she was adored, the parson and his wife, the doctor, and twice a year myself.

"And she grew old. Miss Daubernoon had never been beautiful, she had never been even pretty; and the stealthy years, the monotonous life, robbed her of the country freshness which in early youth had made up for other deficiencies. As year by year I went up to Westmorland to see Mr. Daubernoon, I was distressed to note the difference in his daughter; and before her time she grew prim and old-maidish. She ceased to regret the joyous life of the world, growing so accustomed to the narrow circle wherein vegetably she existed that I think nothing at last would have induced

her to withdraw from it. Finally, when I was staying in the house at Christmas, two years ago, the village doctor came privately to see me. He told me that Miss Daubernoon had been ill through the autumn and now, to his dismay, he had discovered that she was phthisical.

"'You know what our winters are here,' he said to me; 'if she does not go away it will probably kill her.'

"I went to her at the doctor's request, and used the persuasions which with him had been quite useless. But she would listen to nothing.

"'I know that I am ill,' she answered, 'but I cannot leave my father. Do you see no change in him since you were last here?'

"I was obliged to confess that I did; the long years of suffering had broken down at last that iron frame, and even the most inexperienced could see that now the end could not be far off.

"'It would kill my father at once to move him. It would kill him also if I went away.'

"'But do you think you have a right to place your own life in such danger?'

"'I am willing to take the risk.'

"I knew her obstinate character, and I felt I could never induce her to change her mind, so I went straight to Mr. Daubernoon himself.

"'I think you should know that Kate is dangerously ill,' I said. 'She has consumption, and the only thing that can save her is to winter abroad.'

"'Who says so?' he asked.

"There was no astonishment in his manner, so that I wondered whether he had divined the illness of Miss Daubernoon, or whether in his utter selfishness he was indifferent to it. I mentioned Dr. Hobley's name.

"'Twenty years ago he said I couldn't live six months,' answered Mr. Daubernoon. 'He's a nervous old woman. Kate's as strong and well as you are.'

"'Would you like a specialist to come from Liverpool to see her?'

"'Oh, those doctors always back one another up. A specialist would only frighten Kate.'

"I saw that he would never allow himself to be persuaded that his daughter needed attention, and I spoke more sternly to him.

"'Mr. Daubernoon,' I said, 'if your daughter dies the responsibility will be yours.'

"Then a cruel look came into his worn, thin face—a look I had never seen before—and a hardness filled his eyes that was horrible.

"'After all, I can only last six months. When I'm dead she can do what she likes. *"Aprés moi le déluge."*'

"I did not answer, appalled by the sick man's cruel selfishness; the poor girl had sacrificed her youth to him, her hopes of being wife and mother; and now he wanted her very life. And she was ready to give it.

"Mr. Daubernoon lived four months longer than he said, for the autumn had arrived when a telegram came saying that he was dead. It was sent by Dr. Hobley, who bade me come to Westmorland at once.

"But when I arrived it was the change in Miss Daubernoon that shocked me most. Those final months had worked havoc with her, so that it was impossible not to see that she was very ill. She was thin and haggard, her hair was streaked with grey, and she coughed constantly. She seemed ten years older than when I had last seen her, and, though she was no more than forty, looked almost an elderly woman.

"'I'm very much alarmed at the change in Miss Daubernoon,' I told the doctor. 'What do you think?'

"'She's dying, Mr. Addishaw,' he answered; 'she can't live another year.'

"'Fortunately, now she can go away.'

"'She can do that, but it won't save her. It's too late.'

"After the funeral Miss Daubernoon came to me and said she wished to have a talk on business matters.

"'Never mind about business,' I said; 'I can arrange all that. What you must do is to get down to Italy before the cold weather comes.'

"'That is what I mean to do,' she answered. 'I think I should tell you'—she hesitated and looked down, a faint blush colouring her pallid cheeks—'I think I should tell you that I am going to be married at once.'

" 'What!' I cried. 'But you're not fit to marry; you're as ill as you can be.'

" 'I think I have six months to live. I want to be happy. It's only because I'm so ill that I cannot wait. We are to be married in London in a week.'

"For a moment I was silent, not knowing what to say. Then I asked to whom she was engaged.

" 'Mr. Ralph Mason,' she answered, shortly. 'You met him last time you were here. We have been devoted to one another for the last two years.'

"I could not remember anyone of that name, and I inquired, somewhat curtly, when I should have the pleasure of renewing my acquaintance with this gentleman.

" 'He's now coming towards us,' she said, and a look of radiant happiness came into her face.

"I saw walking along the garden path, through which we sauntered, a tall young man in a frock-coat, a tall hat, and patent-leather boots. In a moment I recognised him.

" 'But that is the land-agent's clerk?'

" 'Yes,' she said.

"He was certainly a very handsome man, with a beautiful moustache and the dashing air of a counter-jumper trying to ape the gentleman. I should think he was fifteen years younger than Miss Daubernoon, and this was enough to surprise me; but the most amazing part of it all was that her pride—you know what the pride is of people in that particular class of life—should have allowed her to think of marriage with such a person. And when I knew him better I found to my dismay that there was in him no redeeming trait; he was merely a very ordinary, common, provincial tradesman, with nothing but his rather vulgar good looks to recommend him. And when I compared his strapping vigour with Miss Daubernoon's old, sickly weakness, I could not doubt that he was merely an adventurer of the very worst class. I said nothing at the time, but later, finding myself alone with her, I did not hesitate to speak plainly.

" 'Why do you suppose Mr. Mason wishes to marry you?' I asked.

"A painful, timid look came into her eyes, so that I almost repented my words, but it seemed a duty to be outspoken at all costs to save her much future pain.

"'I think he loves me,' she answered.

"'My dear, I don't want to hurt you, but I must tell you the truth. You can't believe that this young man really cares for you. You're very ill.'

"'I'm dying,' she interrupted.

"'You're ever so much older than he is. Good Heavens! look at yourself in the glass. Ask yourself if he can possibly have fallen in love with you. And there's one palpable reason why he wishes to marry you. Can't you see that it's your money he wants, and for your money's sake he's willing to—to put up with you?'

"Hot tears ran down her cheeks, so that I felt hatefully cruel, but something had to be done to stop such an insane marriage.

"'Don't remind me that I'm old and plain,' she said. 'Do you think I can't feel it? But I know he loves me for myself, and even if he doesn't I will marry him. The only thing that has kept me alive is my love for him, and, after all, I have such a little while to live that you might let me spend it as happily as I can.'

"'And do you think you can be happy with him? Do you think he'll have the patience to wait for your death? My poor lady, you don't know what may be in store for you. At present he's nice enough to you, and apparently you don't mind if he's common and vulgar; but when you're once safely married do you think he'll take the trouble to pretend he loves you? You must be mad.'

"She began to cry, silently, so that for the life of me I could not go on, and I resolved instead to speak with Ralph Mason himself. I made inquiries in the neighbouring market-town, and I was scarcely surprised to discover that his character was thoroughly bad. He was known to be a hard drinker, violent in temper, unscrupulous; his friends said he was a good sportsman, which meant, apparently, that he attended all the race-meetings he could and betted more heavily than his means allowed. A sort of provincial Lothario, various tales were brought me of his exploits; and his good looks, his supercilious charm of manner, appeared to make women an easy conquest. I cannot tell you how alarmed I was when I learnt for what sort of a man it was that Miss Daubernoon had conceived such a passionate infatuation; but his very depravity made it just possible that he would accept certain proposals that I had in mind. I telegraphed to Robert Daubernoon, an officer on half-pay with a large family, a cousin

of the late squire's, and Kate's only relative and natural heir; and on receiving his answer invited Ralph Mason to call on me.

"'I want to talk to you as a business man,' I said. 'When Miss Daubernoon told me she wished to marry you, I ventured to make certain inquiries; and I have heard a good deal about you.'

"He was going to speak, but I begged him to listen quietly till I had finished. With scoundrels I have always found it best to speak to the point; a certain cynical frankness often puts them at their ease, so that much time and verbiage are spared.

"'You know as well as I do that Miss Daubernoon is dying, and I dare say you will not think it necessary to pretend to me that you are in love with her. You cannot seriously wish to marry her, and I am authorized to offer you an annuity of two thousand a year if you will put off your marriage indefinitely.'

"He looked at me and stroked his handsome moustache, and presently he gave a mocking smile.

"'You are a solicitor, Mr. Addishaw?' he asked.

"'Yes.'

"'And presumably a man of business?'

"I was inclined to call him an impertinent jackanapes, but refrained.

"'And granting that all you say is true, and I don't love Kate Daubernoon, and wish to marry her solely because I think she can only live a few months, at the end of which I shall find myself a rich man—do you think I should be such a fool as to accept your offer?'

"'I thought it possible, when you considered that the money was as safe as the Bank of England, while otherwise you are dependent on your wife's will, which may be altered.'

"'I'm not afraid of that.'

"'And also that you would be behaving more or less like a gentleman. Her own doctor has told me that marriage is bound to kill her almost at once. Don't you think what you're doing is very cruel?'

"'I'm a business man too, Mr. Addishaw,' he answered.

"He broke off the conversation abruptly, and I felt I had done harm rather than good, for soon I found that Miss Daubernoon knew what I had said. I do not know what account of the affair Ralph Mason gave her, but I can imagine that my behaviour was painted in the darkest colours, while his own shone with all

the heroic virtues. Miss Daubernoon, harassed by her father's death and funeral, for two or three days was too ill to leave her room, and only Ralph Mason was allowed to see her. She wrote me a note.

"'I did not mind what you said to me,' she wrote, 'but I am indignant and deeply distressed that you should have attempted to turn Ralph from me. I think your interference impertinent. I address you now no longer as a friend, but merely as my solicitor, and I beg you to prepare at once, for my signature, a will leaving absolutely everything of which I die possessed to Ralph Mason.'

"I dare say I am not a man of very easy temper, and with some heat I replied that she might get another solicitor to prepare this will for her; I would have nothing to do with it. And that evening, without seeing her again, I started for London.

"Three days later I heard from Dr. Hobley that they had left Daubernoon, though Kate was much too ill to travel; they were married at a registry office in Marylebone, and next day crossed the Channel on their way to Italy.

"There was a good deal of work connected with the estate of the late Roger Daubernoon. He had left rather a large legacy to his cousin Robert and smaller sums to various servants and dependents, so that practically all his personalty was absorbed. Stocks and shares had to be sold; consequently I was in somewhat frequent correspondence with Mrs. Mason, but her letters were always very short, referring merely to the business on hand, so that I could not tell whether she was ill or well, happy or wretched. I hoped with all my heart that these last months of her life went smoothly, I hoped the man was kind to her, and at least took the trouble to conceal from his wife that he waited impatiently for her death. Poor thing, I trust she preserved to the last the illusion which had given her the only joy her life had known; I was no longer angry with her, but very, very sorry.

"Then one day, in the spring, my clerk whistled up that Mr. Ralph Mason wished to see me. I knew at once that the poor woman was dead. He came in; and though in the country he had dressed himself preposterously in a frock-coat and a tall hat, now he wore a rather loud check suit and a bowler; a black tie was his only sign of mourning. And I had never felt such an antipathy for this swell-mobsman. I hated his handsome military bearing, his smart counter-jumper looks, and the scent on his

handkerchief. There was a superciliousness in his manner which told me I should have to pay for all I had said of him; he, of course, was now the squire, and I was a humble solicitor. I knew I should not long keep the business of the house of Daubernoon, and upon my word I was not sorry. I had no wish to deal with a man of that stamp.

"I did not rise from my chair as he came in.

" 'Good morning,' I said. 'Pray be seated.'

" 'I have come to see you on business,' he answered, insolently. 'My wife died in Rome on the twenty-fourth of last March, and you are executor of her will.'

"I felt expressions of regret would be out of place, and I could imagine the satisfaction the man took in his freedom.

" 'I hope you were not unkind to her,' I said.

" 'I told you I'd come solely on business. I have brought the will in my pocket. It was by my wish that you were appointed executor.'

"I understood what a revengeful pleasure he took in the thought that I must deliver over to him the vast estates of the Daubernoons. Silently I took the will, which was very short, written on a sheet of note-paper.

" 'I, Kate Daubernoon, of the Manor, Daubernoon, hereby revoke all former wills and testamentary dispositions made by me, and declare this to be my last will and testament. I appoint James Addishaw, of 103, Lancaster Place, London, to be the executor of this my will. I give all my real and personal property whatsoever to Ralph Mason. In witness whereof I have set my hand to this my will the 10th day of September, 1902.

KATE DAUBERNOON

"It was written in her own hand and duly witness by two servants at the manor. I could hardly believe my eyes.

" 'How did you get the form?' I asked.

" 'I have some knowledge of law,' he answered.

" 'That I can scarcely believe.' My heart beat with excitement, but I did not wish to let him see my triumph too quickly. 'Is this the only will your wife made?'

" 'Yes.'

" 'Are you sure there is no later one?'

" 'Absolutely positive.'

" 'Have you observed the date? Three days before your marriage.'

" 'The will was made on the very day that you sent for me and offered me two thousand a year to give her up.'

"There was a ring of exultation in his voice, but I answered very quietly, 'You would have been wise to accept it.'

" 'Do you think so?' he laughed.

" 'Because this will is invalid. Marriage annuls all testamentary dispositions previously made, and this piece of paper is absolutely worthless.'

"I shall never forget the look that came into his face, the green pallor that spread across his cheeks, discolouring his very lips; at first he could not understand, the blow was too unexpected.

" 'What do you mean?' he cried. 'It's not true.'

" 'You may take the will to any solicitor you choose.'

" 'You old wretch!' he hissed.

" 'If you're not civil I shall send for my clerks to kick you downstairs.'

"He reached out his hand for the will and I handed it to him; he read it through once more.

" 'Do you mean to say I get nothing?'

" 'Not exactly. Your wife died intestate; her real property goes to Robert Daubernoon, the heir-at-law. You, as her husband, get the personalty.'

" 'But she meant to leave me everything.'

" 'I dare say. But the fact remains that she left you nothing at all.'

" 'I get the money and the furniture of the manor. I shall go there at once.'

" 'Pardon me; I shall telegraph to the servants not to admit you. The house has no longer anything to do with you. And as for the furniture, I should remind you that there your wife had only a life interest; her father never expected her to marry, and, anxious that it should not be disturbed, left it to Robert Daubernoon.'

"As I spoke I thought how Ralph Mason must have looked at the old pictures and seen them going one by one under the hammer at Christie's; they would have fetched a goodly sum. I think this last shock broke him, for he asked me in quite another tone how much money there was.

" 'You know that as well as I do,' was my reply. 'Mr. Daubernoon's legacies took a great deal. There can be very little left. You may feel sure that what there is shall be duly handed to you.'

"I stood up and opened the door for him to go out. He looked up defiantly.

" 'Well, I'll fight you,' he said.

" 'You'll find no one fool enough to take up the case,' I answered scornfully.

"He looked at me as though gladly he would have seized me by the throat; he glanced round the room for something on which to wreak his passion, but apparently nothing offered, and with a kind of stifled groan he went out. And he departed to think over the utter frustration of all his schemes, a bad man and a clever man, and that ass, the law, had beaten him.

"I settled up everything as quickly as I could. I found a good many bills owing, and these I paid; the journey to Italy had cost a great deal, and my own account was not a small one. There was even less money due to the estate than I expected, for Mrs. Mason had died immediately before quarter-day. This morning I was able to write to her husband, sending him a cheque for the amount, less legacy duty, to which he was entitled. I can imagine his feelings when he looked at it, for the exact sum was forty-three pounds seven shillings and threepence halfpenny."

AN IRISH GENTLEMAN

(1904)

I

When mine host of the Golden Eagle took the visitors' book to a foreigner lately arrived by diligence in the little capital of the Principality of Wartburg-Hochstein, the newcomer, in a flourishing hand, described himself as Robert O'Donnel, gentleman, aged twenty-eight; and when the innkeeper, curious to know his guest's history, made discreet inquiries, he added to these brief facts the information that he travelled through Germany in pursuit of artistic emotion, had visited the galleries of Dresden and Berlin, and now, on his way to Munich and Italy, proposed in the town of Wartburg to sort his ideas and bring his journal up to date. For in those early years of Queen Victoria's reign no person of culture went abroad without a copious note-book; and Mr. O'Donnel had already covered a vast number of pages with the ecstasies occasioned in his enthusiastic bosom by the palaces of Potsdam, the Madonna Sistina, the castles of the Rhine; and for his own edification had added thereto sundry philosophic reflections and poetical ideas.

He was a handsome man, with a florid complexion, white teeth, and bold eyes; the Byronic frenzy still reigned supreme, and his hair was worn in admired but careful disorder; of his whiskers he was inordinately vain. His dress, flamboyant even for those days, when young bloods sought systematically to astound the vulgar, excited a flattering attention; his loose collar exhibited the fine contour of his neck, his satin stock contrasted vehemently with the extravagance of his waistcoat, and his tall hat was worn with a rakish swagger achieved by none but him. The innkeeper

thought him a surprising creature, but was charmed by the assurance with which in a rich brogue he discoursed fluently in abominable German; and his good-humoured, gallant ease made the German suspect that he must be some English noblemen of great wealth, till Mr. O'Donnel assured him he was greater than that, bedad, for he was an Irish gentleman in whose veins ran the blood of innumerable kings. It never occurred to him to add that his family had fallen upon evil days, and the five notes in his pocket-book formed the entire capital of this scion of an ancient race.

For many years Mr. O'Donnel had lived adventurously on his wits, turning his quick intelligence to whatever offered the chance of honest gain; he had taught ignorant boys Latin, played the grave-digger in *Hamlet,* written for booksellers, gambled, enjoyed every minute of his life; and now, having by lucky chance made a hundred pounds by backing an outsider, was carrying out an old-cherished dream to visit the romantic lands whereon his fancy had so long battened. His good spirits had borne him through many vicissitudes, his sense of honour had kept him, even in the direst straits, from any action unbecoming his royal forebears, and his charm of manner had secured him a multitude of friends from whom, at an extremity, he could always borrow a guinea.

Things looked brighter for him in London at last, and it seemed possible that he could attain a position of some ease; but a life of humdrum prosperity was the last to attract him, and no sooner had he this round sum in his pocket than he flung his prospects to the wind, and with *Virgil* in one pocket and *Childe Harold* in the other set out on a tour of adventure. He reckoned that his money would last till he came to Rome, where he had friends and could wait till something happened; there perhaps some cardinal might want a secretary, a war would break out wherein volunteers were needed, an expedition might be formed to discover the North Pole, some nobleman might desire a tutor for his son. Anyhow, the future must look after itself; Mr. O'Donnel could only attend to the present.

The day after his arrival at Wartburg he set out to visit the castle, celebrated for its romantic history and its dungeons; he observed everything with eager eyes, and afterwards, wandering in the princely forest, his imagination all aflame, invented thrilling adventures wherein he, a gallant hero, rescued from those dark walls fair damsels in distress.

Suddenly he saw coming towards him a young girl on horseback, at terrific speed. She pulled the reins with all her might, obviously terrified, but with no effect; and he saw that she had entirely lost control over the steed she rode. Mr. O'Donnel was strong in the arm and brave; he flung himself in the way, seized the bridle, for some yards was dragged along, but succeeded eventually in stopping the horse. The lady slipped from the saddle and fainted in his arms; he was sufficiently versed in the literature of the day to know how to revive her, and, carrying her to the neighbouring brook, bathed her temples with cold water. Presently she opened her eyes, smiled gently, and blushed.

"I think you've saved my life," she murmured.

"Madam, for that I would willingly have given mine own," he replied, gallantly.

But before the conversation could proceed an older lady and two gentlemen cantered up, dismounted quickly, and surrounded the fair equestrian with anxious demands.

"I'm not hurt, I'm not frightened," she said. "This gentleman came to my rescue."

The elder woman thanked him elaborately, and one of the gentlemen stepped forward, a wizened man with a skin of parchment.

"Sir, allow me to present myself—Count Peter von Graban."

"My name is Robert O'Donnel, your very humble servant."

"You have done an inestimable service to Her Serene Highness the Princess Mary of Wartburg-Hochstein."

Mr. O'Donnel swept the ground with his tall hat, and the girl, with a smile, held out her hand.

"How can I thank you?"

He kissed the proffered hand and placed his own on his heart.

"Madam, it is I who owe you thanks."

II

A few hours later Mr. O'Donnel was writing in his journal a glowing account of the whole affair, with such information as he had gathered concerning the hereditary prince whose daughter he had so romantically assisted. It appeared that John-Adolphus of Wartburg-Hochstein was a most despotic ruler, and Mr. O'Don-

nel's liberal soul revolted against the accounts of his tyranny; feared by all that came in contact with him, seldom seen to smile, he rarely spoke save to command. He seemed altogether a person of few amenities. Mr. O'Donnel drew a flowery picture of this martinet chastising his people with scorpions, of the constant terror wherein they lived, and asked in flowing periods when the spirit of liberty would awake these sluggard Teutons to a sense of the nobility of man.

There was a knock at the door and the innkeeper, with wondering visage, announced that the court chamberlain, Count Peter von Graban, desired to see him.

"Show him in," said Mr. O'Donnel.

"I am commanded by His Serene Highness to thank you for the service you rendered the princess this morning and to give you this small return."

The little old man produced a pocket-book and counted a number of bank-notes.

"In English money you will find it amounts to fifty pounds."

Mr. O'Donnel reddened to the very roots of his hair, for such an insult had never been offered him before; then grew extremely pale. He paused for one moment to consider his reply.

"I beg you to tender my most respectful thanks to His Serene Highness. I am extremely grateful for this mark of his favour. At the same time, may I ask you whether there is not in the town some charity in which the princess is interested?"

"Certainly. The orphanage for daughters of poor noblemen is under her special protection."

"Then perhaps she will permit me to subscribe to so admirable an object this sum, and to add thereto another fifty pounds of my own."

Mr. O'Donnel unlocked his box, took out his five English notes, and gravely handed the whole to the astonished chamberlain.

"You will be so good as to see to this matter for me."

"But, sir, I do not know what the prince will say to such a proceeding. You still leave His Serene Highness under a great obligation to you."

Mr. O'Donnel raised himself to his full height and struck a magnificent gesture.

"Sir, King William IV, before he ascended the throne, once borrowed a guinea from your humble servant and never repaid

it. I shall be charmed to add the name of your master to the sovereigns in my debt."

"The prince will never permit it."

"Then let Her Serene Highness his daughter give me the glove which I had the honour to touch with my lips this morning, and I shall feel myself amply repaid."

The court chamberlain stared at him with helpless amazement; in his long experience he had never come across anyone whose manner was so magnificent, whose glance was so haughty, and whose German so imperfect.

"But you don't know what sort of a man the prince is. If I go back to him with such a message, he's capable of hitting me with his riding-whip. He'll look upon this reply as an insult—his temper is ungovernable. I won't answer for the consequences to yourself."

Then Mr. O'Donnel held his tongue no longer.

"And how dare he insult me! Who does he think I am that he should send me fifty pounds as though I were a lackey? Go, sir, and tell your master that he must have the soul of a flunkey to use an Irish gentleman with such indignity."

Mr. O'Donnel flung open the door, and the Count Peter von Graban was so taken aback that, without another word, he walked out. Then the Irishman rubbed his hands.

"Robert, me boy, you acted with spirit," he said to himself, contentedly. "I'm proud of ye."

But then he sat down to think, for his generosity, though apposite to the occasion, had left him—penniless. His wanderings in North Germany had cost half the sum at his disposal, and the fifty pounds he had just given away were all he had. He did not regret his munificence, but it forced upon him a hateful subject, the future; the most he could do was to get away decently from Wartburg, and then he must trust to luck. For one hour he was immensely despondent, but then an idea struck him; he would get as far as Baden, and then it was strange if he found no one from whom he could borrow ten guineas to try his luck at the tables. Already he saw a shining pile of gold in front of him, and, feeling that his journey to Italy was after all assured, he went down to dinner in the highest spirits. The state of his finances was such that economy was entirely out of the question, and he ordered the innkeeper to bring the best bottle of wine in his cellar. The news of

his adventure had quickly spread, and the various persons at the *table d'hôte* were anxious to hear details; but with a wave of the hand Mr. O'Donnel put them off, giving them to understand that it was his habit to stop runaway horses every day of his life. He had not finished dinner when the maid entered to say that the chamberlain was again desirous to see him.

"Will no one rid me of this pestilent fellow?" cried Mr. O'Donnel, with irritation. "Say that I'm dining, but shall be glad if he will drink a glass of wine with me."

The innkeeper, marvelling at his guest's independent spirit, himself carried the message, and Count Peter walked in. Somewhat curtly he signified his desire to speak with the Irishman alone, and in a moment the pair were left to themselves. For a while he hesitated awkwardly, sipping the wine which Mr. O'Donnel insisted he should take.

"You must wonder why I intrude myself upon you again to-day," he said at last, abruptly.

"Not at all. I can quite understand that the pleasure of my company has drawn you hither."

The count frowned, unused to such flippancy, and irritably drummed the table with his fingers.

"I am the bearer of an apology. His Serene Highness commands me to express his regrets and my own for the insult that was offered you."

Mr. O'Donnel nodded.

"Was he in a passion?"

"The saints preserve us!" cried the old man, throwing up his hands. "He raged and stormed and fumed. You don't know what a man he is; he was within an ace of having me arrested. . . . He wishes to know how he can acknowledge the great service you have done him."

"Let him do me the honour of dining with me to-morrow," answered Mr. O'Donnel, without hesitation.

"Are you mad, sir? Do you not know that John-Adolphus is the proudest prince in Germany? He would no more eat with you in an inn than—than—"

The chamberlain sought for some monstrous comparison, but found nothing. He repeated that such a thing was impossible; the prince would look upon the invitation as the height of impudence;

he might very well cause the Irishman to be conducted across the frontier.

"Which would certainly save the expense of the diligence," interrupted Mr. O'Donnel, with a smile.

The count reasoned, argued, persuaded, but the other was immovable. He wanted nothing on this earth save the company at dinner of His Serene Highness Prince John-Adolphus of Wartburg-Hochstein. At length the chamberlain departed, saying, grimly, that the answer would be brought next day by a troop of soldiers. Mr. O'Donnel shrugged his shoulders, and, presently going out, composed the first verses of a ballad suggested by the dungeons of Wartburg-Hochstein. In the morning an equerry brought the reply that His Serene Highness would be pleased to dine with Mr. O'Donnel that afternoon.

III

Mr. O'Donnel told his landlord that he expected a distinguished person to dinner, and himself went to the cellar to choose the wines that pleased him. He interviewed the cook, and impressed her vastly by the subtlety of his knowledge. He was something of an artist in culinary affairs, and with his own hands prepared a dish which the greatest epicures of London had pronounced incomparable. At the appointed hour, to the innkeeper's confusion and amazement, the prince himself drove up in full uniform, blazing with decorations. He was a huge man, with grey hair and a grey moustache, with bushy eyebrows and scowling eyes. He gave the impression of imperious temper and of violent disposition. Mr. O'Donnel received him with courteous ease, and, as though he had known him for years, led him into the private room made ready for their meal.

"I thought you wanted to show me off at the *table d'hôte,"* said the prince, grimly.

"By no means. Had it been possible I should have begged you to come incognito."

They sat down and dinner was served. Mr. O'Donnel was always good company, but on this occasion he surpassed himself; he was humorous, fantastical, witty; he would have kept a whole table in a roar of laughter, but the prince never smiled. He

watched his companion gravely, apparently indifferent both to the brilliant conversation and the excellent dinner. Still Mr. O'Donnel was not put out of countenance, and exerted himself to amuse and divert his royal guest. At last the prince rose to his feet.

"Now we are quits," he said.

"On the contrary, I am eternally your debtor for the entertainment you have given me in these two hours."

The prince looked at him grimly, and perhaps the shadow of a smile twinkled behind his heavy eyebrows; but he said nothing, and, turning to the door, ordered his carriage.

"I do not understand you," he said, as he stepped in. "What have you gained by this?"

"The pleasure of a brief acquaintance with Your Serene Highness."

The prince grunted fiercely and drove off. Mr. O'Donnel went to his room, flung himself on the bed, and cried: "Now, how the deuce am I going to pay the bill?"

Somewhat ruefully he counted the loose change in his pocket, which formed the entire capital at his command. Nothing was left but to pawn his ring, which he valued immensely, since it was a present from the great Count d'Orsay, and when it grew dark he set out to find a jeweller. On second thoughts, considering it unlikely that he would ever again set foot in this unlucky town, Mr. O'Donnel offered it for sale, and though the man was willing to give but half its value he had not the face to haggle. The sum suggested was large enough to get him safely to Baden, and he accepted thankfully. Next morning he paid his bill and set out with the diligence.

Mr. O'Donnel, light of heart once more, observed the scenery with as much enthusiasm as though there were no uncertainty about his dinner on the following day. At the frontier horses for the second time were changed and, somewhat to the passengers' surprise, passports demanded. An officer carefully examined the Irishman's and looked at him with great suspicion.

"Have you any fault to find with this important document?"

"You did not have it *visé* when you arrived at Wartburg."

"Upon my soul I had better things to do than to trouble myself with needless formalities."

"I can't allow you to leave the principality. You must go back to Wartburg."

"What do you mean, sir?" cried Mr. O'Donnel, in a fury. "I shall do no such thing, and I'll see you—further."

The officer briefly motioned to his men, and before the other knew what they were about he found himself seized and pinioned. He struggled with all his might, but they had taken him unawares and he was helpless; he could only vent his wrath in a copious flow of language, and he expressed himself with a force and vigour which would have astonished a Billingsgate fishwife. The officer was entirely indifferent, and ordered him to be taken into a room of the inn at which the diligence had stopped till a carriage could be got ready to take him back to Wartburg. In half an hour all arrangements were complete, and Mr. O'Donnel, fuming and mystified, found himself traversing the country he had admired during the day.

"Will you undo my arms?" he asked, savagely. "If I've got to spend the night in this jolting carriage I may as well make myself as comfortable as possible."

This was accordingly done, and Mr. O'Donnel, having come to the conclusion that he had been arrested by some mistake which would be explained as soon as he got to Wartburg, soon recovered his equanimity. He was in search of adventure, and here was one which would make an admirable story for his friends in London; he began already to surround it with humorous details. So passed the night, and in the morning the carriage seemed to ascend a steep hill, and it flashed across the Irishman's mind that he was being taken to the castle of Wartburg. He chuckled when he thought of meeting the prince again under such different circumstances. The carriage stopped.

"Now I must blindfold you," said the officer.

"What ridiculous folly is this?" cried Mr. O'Donnel, losing his temper again. "I've never been treated so ignominiously in my life. I shouldn't like to stand in your shoes when I tell the prince how you have used me."

"Everything that has happened to you is by express command of His Serene Highness."

The Irishman was too staggered by this to answer, and helplessly allowed his eyes to be bandaged. He was led along passages, through courtyards, down stairs, till a greater chill told him he was underground. The handkerchief was removed, and with a cry Mr.

O'Donnel saw he was in one of those historic dungeons which two days before had so excited his romantic fancy.

"Upon my soul," he cried, "this is beyond a joke."

IV

With creaking of locks and drawing of rusty bolts the heavy door was closed and the Irishman was left in absolute darkness; for a while he could see nothing, and it seemed to him the dungeon was darker than the darkest night he had ever known. But presently through a narrow chink he discerned a faint glimmer of light, and, his eyes growing used to the obscurity, he saw that he was in a small chamber with stone walls, slimy and wet. In one corner was a plank bed, and opposite the light was dimly seen a crucifix. He started when something crossed his foot, and with beating heart recognised the scampering of rats. Besides this, all that broke the oppressive silence was a continual drip, drip, as water fell slowly from the damp roof.

Mr. O'Donnel sat on the bed to think what this might mean; the whole thing was so improbable that he was utterly dumfounded; a hundred explanations ran through his mind, but each seemed absurd. He passed from amazement to despondency, from terror to rage. At last, growing desperately hungry, he made the tour of his cell, and discovered in a recess a jug of water and some coarse black bread. This assuaged his hunger, but scarcely his passion, and the more he thought of what had happened the more indignant he grew. Then he heard sounds; the door was ponderously unlocked and two soldiers entered with candles, which they set on a ledge, thus illuminating for the prisoner's edification all the discomfort of that place. They retired, and in a moment there appeared—John-Adolphus, Hereditary Prince of Wartburg-Hochstein.

"Good morning, my friend," he said, coolly. "I hope you've made yourself at home."

For an instant Mr. O'Donnel was too much taken aback to reply, but, recovering himself, broke forthwith into an indignant harangue, wherein he threatened the prince with the most horrid revenge, and demanded explanations for the infamous treatment

to which he had been subjected. John-Adolphus shrugged his shoulders.

"You entertained me so well that I desired to continue our acquaintance. It seemed the only way to gain once more the pleasure of your conversation was to arrest you before you crossed the frontier."

"But I will never suffer such an indignity. I will appeal to the English Ambassador, and you shall learn what it means to trifle with the liberty of an English subject."

"Nonsense, my dear sir. It will never get to the ears of your ambassador that I have taken you prisoner. I can detain you for thirty years without the smallest risk to myself."

"My disappearance will be remarked and commented upon."

"I doubt it. I can scarcely think anyone will much trouble himself with the whereabouts of an obscure Irishman who travels with ten thalers in his pocket."

"How do you know that?"

"You forget that you were searched. Your luggage was examined, and I arrived at the conclusion that you were nearly penniless. By the way, that was a singularly unflattering description you drew of me in your journal—and somewhat treasonable to boot."

"Treasonable it may have been," returned Mr. O'Donnel, "but by all the saints of Heaven it was not unflattering."

"I am anxious to know why you gave your entire fortune to a charitable institution and then sold your ring to pay for my dinner."

With a grim smile the prince held out his hand, on the little finger of which Mr. O'Donnel observed the ring which two days before he had left with the jeweller. He was about to burst out again angrily when the twinkling eyes of the prince suggested to him that the whole thing was an elaborate practical joke.

"Upon my soul," he cried, "Your Serene Highness has the oddest sense of humour that ever I saw."

The prince chuckled: it was the first time Mr. O'Donnel had seen in him any signs of amusement.

"You had your little jest with me, Mr. O'Donnel—you must not mind if I have mine. I could not resist the temptation to see how you would like the dungeons about which you raved so poetically when you only knew them from the outside. Let us make friends and go to our dinner, which is just now ready."

"Faith, I shall be able to do justice to it," answered the other, still very sore, but determined to make the best of things, "for your prison fare is not calculated to stay a man's appetite."

It seemed like a story from the *Arabian Nights* when Mr. O'Donnel found himself half an hour later seated at table between John-Adolphus and his daughter the Princess Mary. The prince was quite a different creature from the sullen, haughty officer who came to the Golden Eagle, and evidently could enjoy a joke as well as any man. The Irishman, flushed with wine, finding his audience appreciative, gave of his best, and poured forth the full stream of his rollicking fun; there was no restraint to his audacity, to the quaint turns of his humour, to his boisterous anecdote. The prince and his daughter held their sides with laughter. Tears streamed from their eyes, and the grim stone walls of Wartburg had not for years heard such loud hilarity.

But with his spirits Mr. O'Donnel had recovered his sense of the effective; he knew his success was unparalleled, and he did not mean to spoil it by lingering on the scene of his triumph. Admirable actor as he was, he knew the value of a striking exit. No sooner was dinner ended than he rose to his feet.

"It grows late, and I must reach Baden quickly. Have I Your Serene Highness's permission to retire?"

"To-night?" cried the prince. "Of course, if you wish it, I say nothing; but is there not something I can do before you go to show my appreciation of your wit and good-humour?"

"Certainly," returned Mr. O'Donnel, promptly. "Your Serene Highness remembers that my means are small. If the carriage that brought me back here may take me again to the frontier you will overwhelm me with benefits."

"But you have no money at all. Surely now you will accept something from me?"

"The saints preserve me!" cried Mr. O'Donnel, with a wave of the hand. "Have you more charities that you want to benefit?"

The prince shook his head, more mystified than ever by this eccentricity. He could not understand that to the Irishman, rollicking and romantic, feather-brained and heroic, a fine phrase or a striking attitude was more than all the treasure of this world. At length he had a sensible idea.

"Mr. O'Donnel, I am going to keep this ring with which you paid for my dinner. In return I crave your acceptance of mine."

He took a splendid diamond from his finger.

"But beside this mine is quite worthless," cried Mr. O'Donnel.

"Pray take it. You may find it useful when next you entertain royal personages at dinner."

Mr. O'Donnel hesitated no longer, but with profuse thanks slipped the ring on his finger. Then the princess stepped forward.

"I, too, have a present for you. I wish you to keep it in remembrance of the service you did me. It is of no value at all."

She handed him the glove which he had before gallantly asked for.

"On the contrary," he said. "It is ten times more valuable than the ring, for *you* have worn it."

He bent down and kissed her hand. The carriage was at the door, and, waiting only to launch one parting jest, Mr. O'Donnel took advantage of their laughter to bow and retire. From the window, laughing still, the prince and his daughter watched him drive out into the night, with ten thalers in his pocket and on his hand a ring worth two hundred pounds.

"Is he a mountebank or is he a hero?" she asked. "I've never met such a man."

"English and Irish, they're all mad," answered John-Adolphus; "that's why they conquer the world."

Meanwhile, Mr. O'Donnel, immensely pleased with himself, without a thought of the difficult future, composed himself to sleep as comfortably as though he lay on a feather bed.

FLIRTATION

(1906)

I

At the age of forty Bertie Shenton was still a young man about town, and flattered himself that with the light behind him he could yet pass for five and twenty; clean-shaven and slight of build, with a quick eye and a laughing mouth, there was nothing to betray advancing years.

He felt younger than ever, and looked without envy at the youths of twenty who seemed in every way vastly older than himself; he saw no reason why he should ever give way to middle age, for his income was sufficient, his desires easily attainable, and his digestion perfect.

He knew a host of people, whom he kept perpetually amused by his flippant conversation and his good nature; he was the sort of man whom everyone after half-an-hour's acquaintance calls by his Christian name, and he had scores of intimate friends whom he did not even know by sight.

When he drove to Lady Mereston's party he was as usual in the best of spirits, and the world seemed an excellent place; the night was warm, the house he was bound for pleasant, and the women without doubt would be pretty. With a smile he greeted the little lady who stepped out of her carriage immediately before himself, and, having given up his hat and coat, waited for her on the stairs.

"I'm lying in wait for you, Mrs. Parnaby," he cried when she appeared.

He noticed with discreet admiration the beauty of her gown, and he thought the pretty widow had never looked better than that evening. She gave him a quick glance.

"Make it," she said, imperiously.

"What?"

"The compliment that's on the tip of your tongue."

He laughed and asked her to give him that dance.

"Very well," she answered, "but we must sit down. I'm perfectly exhausted. I've just come on from the Lemaines. Let's go somewhere and talk sensibly."

"Ah, you want to flirt with me," he laughed, as they went into the conservatory. "It's what a woman always means when she asks you to talk sensibly."

She looked at him calmly. "The only reason I like you, Bertie, is that you don't make love to me. When you're an eligible widow you get so tired of it. Men are such bores; I can't think why they want to make things worse by becoming husbands."

"You have such odd ideas about my sex."

"Not at all—only it must be obvious to you that man is an inferior creature. He's so weak. He has no wiles. When a male thing sees a brick wall it never occurs to him that there's anything on the other side."

"You mean he has certain elementary ideas about truthfulness."

"Poor thing, he has to be truthful, he lies so badly," returned Mrs. Parnaby, with a shrug of her dainty shoulders. "You know, I'm longing to find the man that I can't turn round my little finger."

Bertie Shenton got up and made an elaborate bow. "Madam, your very humble servant."

"My dear Bertie! I could make you do anything I like," she laughed. "I could make you propose to me in five minutes."

"My dear lady, it's been tried too often. I flatter myself I'm a difficult fish to catch."

"I detest a man who thinks every woman is in love with him."

"Bless you, I don't think that. I only think a great many want to marry me. After all, with the sort of people we know, marriage is still the only respectable means of livelihood for a really nice girl. However old, ugly, and generally undesirable a man is, he'll find heaps of charming girls who are willing to share with him a house in Portman Square and a comfortable income."

"But, my dear Bertie, if a woman really makes up her mind to marry a man nothing on earth can save him."

"Don't say that," cried he, "you terrify me."

She looked at him for one moment and smiled. "You need not be in the least alarmed, because I shall refuse you."

"Thanks," he answered; "it's a bargain, but I don't think I'll risk a proposal."

"Oh yes, you will. I feel absolutely certain. I'll give you a fortnight."

He shook his head, laughing. "I'm not at all nervous."

"My dear man, your only safety is in instant flight. You're doomed. I've made up my mind that you shall propose to me."

"I bet you a pair of gloves I don't."

"Very well."

Mrs. Parnaby nodded to a young man who passed them, and eagerly he came up.

"I've been hunting for you everywhere," he said. "I was hoping to get a chance of speaking to you."

"That's the beauty of a crowd," she answered, "it gives such opportunities for a tête-à-tête."

Mrs. Parnaby directed these words to Bertie Shenton with such mockery in her eyes, such a malicious curl of the lip, that he could not help taking the hint.

"Let me give up my seat," he said. Oddly enough, to do so made him rather cross.

"Remember that the gloves are sixes," she remarked as he went.

"I fancy there are others to whom that information will be more useful," he retorted, with a glance of some annoyance at the intruder.

Mrs. Parnaby laughed. She knew very well that Bertie Shenton was devoted to her, but their relations were so pleasant that it had never occurred to her till that moment to make any change in them. He had never shown the least inclination to marry her, and each loved liberty too well to give it up freely. But the thoughtless bet, made lightly on the spur of the moment, set her thinking, and she chuckled to herself at the idea of winning it.

II

Her plan of campaign was quickly made, and for the rest of the evening she avoided Bertie systematically; but whenever his eyes rested upon her pretended to be much engrossed in her partner.

A dozen young men found her more charming than ever before, and each one concluded that he had made something of an impression; in their vanity it never struck them that these charms and graces were displayed only for the purpose of vexing a gentleman of forty, who watched irritably from the other side of the room. These tactics were apparently successful, for Bertie called upon her next day while she was out. She gave orders that he was not to be admitted, and when next he came he had the satisfaction of hearing her play the piano, while a third time on looking up he saw her calmly watching from the window. He smiled drily to himself, and with a little shrug of resignation went to a milliner's to buy a pair of gloves.

After a week he met her at luncheon, and though he was rather sulky she greeted him with the most malicious good humour; but during the meal, though they sat together, she addressed her conversation exclusively to her other neighbour in a manner which Bertie Shenton thought was as marked as it was disagreeable. When she bade her hostess farewell he rose also.

"Shall I drive you home?" he asked.

"I'm not going home. But if you like to drive me to Curzon Street you may; I have an appointment there at four."

"Very well."

They went out, stepped into a cab, and quite coolly Bertie told the driver to go to Hammersmith.

"What are you doing?" she cried.

"I want to have a talk with you."

"I'm sure that's charming of you," she answered, "but I shall miss my appointment."

"That's a matter of complete indifference to me." He paused, smiled, and took from his pocket the gloves he had bought. "You'll find they're sixes. If you're going to make yourself systematically disagreeable unless I marry you—I suppose I must marry you."

"Is that the proposal?" she asked gaily.

"Name the day, Mrs. Parnaby, and the lamb shall be ready for the slaughter."

"But that won't do at all. I must have it in proper terms. First you go on your bended knees."

"I really can't in a hansom cab."

"Then you say you're entirely unworthy of me."

"Women have such a passion for the commonplace," he sighed; "besides, I'm not at all unworthy of you. After all, only four words are needed: Will you marry me?"

She was putting on the gloves he had given her, and held out her hand for him to do up the buttons.

"Then I give you my answer in one: No."

"I beg your pardon?" he cried in surprise.

"The reply is in the negative. . . . I promised I'd refuse you."

"Oh, but I'll absolve you from your promise."

"The answer is still the same. I will be a sister to you."

"But good Heavens, why?"

"I don't want to marry you in the least. D'you want to marry me?"

"I suppose I do—more or less," he returned doubtfully. "It's a chance that will never recur, you know."

"I hope you agree now that any woman can make any man propose to her within a fortnight."

"D'you mean to say you've been trifling with my feelings?"

"Yes."

He looked at her, and broke into a smile. "Well, then, we're square, aren't we? I thought you'd be so amused if I proposed." He saw the look of surprise that came over her face. "I've not taken you in, have I? By Jove! I was awfully afraid that you'd accept."

"Didn't you want me to?" she cried.

"I don't know what I should have done if you had. It was rather risky, wasn't it?"

"You absolute brute," she exclaimed. She looked at him doubtfully, and then, seeing his amusement, "You did mean it, Bertie—I know you did."

"I will be a brother to you, Mrs. Parnaby."

"Oh, I will punish you for this," she answered, laughing in spite of herself.

"I shall be on my guard."

She opened the trap and told the cabman to drive back to Curzon Street. It was very hard to bear Bertie's triumph, for she had meant to give him a fall, and it looked much as though she had suffered one instead.

"Good-bye," she said, when they arrived at the door of the house into which she was going. "When shall I see you again?"

"Oh, very soon, I hope."

III

Somewhat to her surprise she heard him direct the cabman to Cook's office in Piccadilly, and when she was told two days later that he was gone to Homburg, Mrs. Parnaby wondered what he meant. His journey did not much disturb her, for she soon concluded he had done it merely to annoy, and within a week would be home again clamouring at her door. But the week passed, and there was no sign of him. Mrs. Parnaby asked herself if he had taken her refusal seriously. A second week went by, and she missed him more than she would have thought possible; a third week, and she grew very cross; a month, and she discovered to her consternation that she could think of nothing but Bertie Shenton. She had meant to amuse herself, and, behold, she was head over ears in love; it was very inconvenient and very absurd, and she did not know what to do. She tormented herself with all sorts of reasons to explain his absence, and once or twice, like the spoilt child she was, cried. But Mrs. Parnaby was a sensible woman, and soon made up her mind that if she could not live without the man she had better take steps to procure his presence. She wired to ask if she might come to tea at his house on the following Friday; he answered that he would be away; but, nothing daunted, she telegraphed again, more peremptorily this time, to announce her fixed determination to drink tea with him on the day mentioned. She duly went, and, of course, found him waiting for her. "So you've come back," she said, as she shook hands with him.

"I was just passing through town," he answered coldly.

"From where to where?"

"From Homburg to the Italian Lakes."

"Rather out of your way, isn't it?"

"Not at all," he replied. "If I were going from Liverpool to Manchester I should break the journey in London. That's one of my hobbies."

"Why d'you think I telegraphed to you the other day?"

"Because you're the most disgraceful flirt I've ever seen in my life," he answered promptly.

She opened her eyes very wide. "My dear Bertie, have you never contemplated yourself in a looking-glass?"

"You're not a bit repentant of the harm you've wrought."

She did not answer, but looked at him with a smile so entirely delightful that he cried out irritably: "I wish you wouldn't look like that."

"How am I looking?"

"To my innocent and inexperienced gaze very much as if you wanted to be kissed."

"You brute! I'll never speak to you again."

"Why d'you make such rash statements? You know you couldn't hold your tongue for two minutes together."

"I never can get a word in edgeways when I'm with you. You're such a chatterbox," she answered, crossly.

"Upon my word, I don't see why you should pretend to have a grievance," he said. "It's I who ought to be furious."

"You behaved very unkindly to me a month ago," she complained, trying to prevent a smile.

"You don't think of my injured feelings. You forget that for the last four weeks I've been laboriously piecing together the fragments of a broken heart."

"It was entirely your fault," she laughed. "If you hadn't been so conceited and certain that I was going to accept you I should never have refused. I couldn't resist the temptation of saying no just to see what you did."

"I flatter myself that I took it very well."

"You didn't," she answered. "You showed an entire lack of humour. You might have known that a nice woman doesn't accept a man the first time he asks her. It was very silly of you to go off to Homburg as if you didn't care. How was I to know that you meant to wait a month before asking me again?"

"I haven't the least intention of asking you again."

"Then why on earth did you invite me to come and have tea?"

"May I respectfully remind you that you invited yourself?" he protested.

"Don't go into irrelevant details," she commanded.

"Now, don't be cross with me."

"I shall be cross. You're not being at all nice."

He looked at her thoughtfully for a little while, and his eyes twinkled.

"Do you know what I'd do if I were you?"

"No, what?"

"Well, I can't suffer the humiliation of another refusal. Why don't you propose to me—just for a change?"

"What cheek!" Their eyes met, and she smiled. "What will you say if I do?"

"That depends on how you do it."

"I don't know how."

"Yes, you do," he insisted. "You gave me an admirable lesson. First you go on your bended knees and then you say you're quite unworthy of me."

"You are the most spiteful creature I've ever known. You're just the sort of man who'd beat his wife."

"Every Saturday night regularly," he agreed.

She hesitated, but saw in him no signs of yielding.

"Bertie, I am a widow, twenty-nine years of age, extremely eligible. My maid is a treasure, my dressmaker is charming, I'm clever enough to laugh at your jokes, and not so learned as to know where they come from."

"Really you're very long-winded. I said it all in four words."

"So could I if I might write it down." She stretched out her hands and he took her in his arms. "You might let me off, Bertie."

"No, I won't," he laughed.

"You know I don't really want to marry you a bit. I'm only doing it to please you. . . . You will say yes if I ask you, won't you?"

"I'll see when the time comes."

"Will you marry me?"

She said it quite indifferently as though she were asking what o'clock it was.

"Of course, I will, you silly," he answered.

"I never saw any one make such a fuss about so insignificant a detail as marriage."

She tried to draw away from him, but he held her fast, and, smiling, took a ring from his pocket.

"I've got a little present for you. I bought it this morning."

She looked at him.

"Then you meant to ask me all the time?"

"Yes."

"Oh, I wish I'd known that before."

He laughed, and the rest of their conversation concerns nobody.

THE FORTUNATE PAINTER

(1906)

"Let the great book of the world be your principal study." —*Chesterfield.*

There were times when Charlie Bartle could take his straitened circumstances with a light heart. When the sky was blue and the air of Paris, keen yet balmy, was more exhilarating than wine, his studio in the Rue Breda lost its shabbiness. On such days as these he went down into the street and watched gay ladies make their purchases for luncheon. The disarray of their costume in the morning contrasted with the splendour with which he had seen them emerge from their houses the night before. They lingered on the door of greengrocers, bargaining for their vegetables with the strenuousness of model housewives. Several had sat for him, and with these he exchanged the gossip of the quarter. Then, his eyes filled with the vivacity of that scene, he returned to his studio, and sought to place on canvas the dancing sunlight of the Parisian street. He felt in him the courage to paint masterpieces. But when grey clouds and rain made the colours on his palette scarcely distinguishable from one another, his mood changed. He could scarcely bear the dingy shabbiness of his studio. He looked with distaste at the picture on which he had been working for a month, and saw that it was bad. His poverty appalled him.

It was on such an occasion that Charles Bartle sat, pipe in mouth, contemplating with deep discouragement the work of his hands. He smoked gloomily. Presently, with a sigh, he took a

palette-knife and prepared to scrape down all that he had done. There was a knock at the door.

"Come in," cried Charlie, looking round.

It was slowly opened by a little old man, with a bald head, a hooked nose of immense size, and a grey beard. He was shabbily dressed, but the rings on his finger, the diamond in his tie, and his massive watch-chain suggested that it was not from poverty.

"Monsieur Leir!" said Charlie, with a smile. "Come in. I'm delighted to see you."

"I knew you couldn't paint in this weather, so I thought I shouldn't be in your way."

He came into the room and looked at Bartle's unfinished canvas. The painter watched him anxiously, but no change in the Frenchman's expression betrayed his opinion.

"Do you think it's utterly rotten?" asked Charlie.

"My dear fellow, you young men are so impatient. You buy a canvas, and you buy paints, and you think you can produce marvels immediately. You won't give time to it, and you won't give patience. The old masters weren't in such a hurry. Read Vasari and you'll see how they worked."

Charles Bartle impatiently threw aside his palette-knife.

"I wish I'd been a crossing-sweeper rather than a painter. It's a dog's life that I lead. I do without everything that gives happiness, and I don't even do work that's fit to look at."

Monsieur Leir sat down, took from his waistcoat pocket the stump of an unfinished cigar, rubbed the charred end with his finger, and lit it. He smoked this with apparent satisfaction. In his day he had known many painters. Some had succeeded, but most had failed, and he knew that the profession, even for the fortunate, was very hard. Genius itself starved at times, and recognition often did not arrive till a man was too embittered to enjoy it. But he liked artists, and found a peculiar satisfaction in their society. And this was only natural, for they had made his fortune. Monsieur Leir was a dealer. He had early seen the merit of the impressionists, had bought their pictures systematically, thus saving many of them from disaster and, at the same, benefiting himself, and finally sold them when the world discovered that Manet, Monet, and Sisley were great painters. His only daughter had married Rudolf Kühn, a dealer in New York, so Monsieur Leir felt justified in spending the years that remained to him in a con-

dition of opulent idleness. But he flattered himself that the painters whose works he had bought for a song were his friends as well as his customers, and it pleased him still to potter about the studios of those who yet lived. When Charlie Bartle settled in the house in which he himself had an apartment, Monsieur Leir gladly made his acquaintance. The young man was delighted to hear stories of the wild life they led in Montmartre in the 'seventies, and he was taken, too, by the kindliness of the retired dealer. There was an unaffected amiability in Monsieur Leir's manner, which led the foreigner quickly to pour into his sympathetic ear his troubles and his ambitions. The dealer was a lonely man, and he soon began to feel a certain affection for the young painter. Now that he was no longer in the trade, he could afford to put charms of manner before talent, and the mediocrity of his friend's work touched his gentle old heart.

"It's one of your bad days, *mon vieux,*" said the dealer.

"I wish to goodness I was a dealer, like you," laughed Charlie. "At least I shouldn't be worried to death by the approach of quarter-day."

"The picture-trade is no place for an honest man now," returned Monsieur Leir, reflectively. "It was all very well in the old days, when we had it in our own hands. We drove hard bargains, but it was all above-board. But now the Christians have taken to it, there's a good deal too much hocus-pocus."

"I simply can't go on this way. I have to pay three hundred francs for my rent to-morrow, and I shan't have a penny left to buy myself bread and butter for the next month. No one will buy a picture."

Monsieur Leir looked at him with good-natured eyes, but he said nothing. Charlie glanced at the portrait of a very pretty girl, which stood in solitary splendour, magnificently framed, on the chimney-piece.

"I had a letter from Rosie this morning. Her people want her to give me up. They say there's not the least chance of my ever earning any money."

"But will she do that?" asked the dealer.

"No, of course not," answered Charlie, with decision. "She's a good girl. But it means waiting, waiting, waiting; and our youth

is going, and we shall grow sore with hope deferred. When at last we marry we shall be disillusionised and bitter."

He sighed deeply. He brooded with despair on the future, and the old man did not venture to disturb him. He watched the painter with compassion. At last, however, he spoke.

"What are the exact conditions on which the father of your fiancée will allow you to marry her?"

"They're insane. You see, she has five thousand pounds of her own. He refuses to consent to our marriage unless I can produce the same sum or show that I am earning two hundred and fifty a year. And the worst of it is that I can't help acknowledging he's right. I don't want Rosie to endure hardships."

"You know that my daughter's husband is a dealer in New York," returned Monsieur Leir, presently. "I vowed when I sold off my stock that I would never deal in pictures again, but I'm fond of you, my friend, and I should like to help you. Show me your stuff, and I'll send it to Rudolf; he may be able to sell it in America."

"That would be awfully good of you," cried Charlie.

The dealer sat down while Bartle placed on his easel one after the other his finished pictures. There were, perhaps, a dozen, and Monsieur Leir looked at them without a word. For the moment he had gone back to his old state, and he allowed no expression to betray his feelings. No one could have told from that inscrutable gaze whether he thought the painting good or bad.

"That's the lot," said Charlie, at length. "D'you think the American public will seize their opportunity, and allow us to marry?"

"What is that?" asked the dealer quietly, pointing to the last canvas, its face against the wall, which Bartle had not shown him.

Without a word the painter produced it and fixed it on the easel. Monsieur Leir gave a slight start, and the indifference of his expression vanished.

"Watteau!" he cried. "But, my dear fellow, how did you get that? You talk of poverty and you have a Watteau. Why, I can sell that for you in America for double the sum you want."

"Look at it carefully," smiled Charlie.

The dealer went up to the picture and peered into it. His eyes glittered with delight. It represented a group of charming persons by the side of a lake. It was plain that the ladies, so decadent and

dainty, discussed preciously with swains, all gallant in multi-coloured satins, the verses of Racine or the letters of Madame de Sévigné. The placid water reflected white clouds, and the trees were russet already with approaching autumn. It was a stately scene, with its green woodland distance, and the sober opulence of oak and elm; and it suggested ease and long tending. Those yellows and greens and reds glowed with mellow light.

"It's one of the few Watteaus I've ever seen with a signature," said the dealer.

"You flatter me," said Charlie. "Of course, it's only a copy. The original belonged to some old ladies in England whom I knew; and last summer, when it rained, I spent my days in copying it. I suppose chance guided my hand happily; everyone agreed it was not badly done."

"A copy?" cried Monsieur Leir. "A copy? Where is the original? Would your friends sell it?"

"The ruling instinct is as strong as ever," laughed the painter. "Unfortunately, a month after I finished this the house was burnt down, and everything was destroyed."

The dealer drew a deep breath, and for a moment meditated. He looked at Charlie sharply.

"Didn't you say you wanted three hundred francs for your rent?" he asked, very quietly. "I'll buy that copy off you."

"Nonsense, I'll give it you. You're taking no end of trouble for me, and you've been awfully kind."

"You're a fool, my friend," answered Monsieur Leir. "Write me out a receipt for the money."

He took from his pocket-book three bank-notes and laid them on the table. Bartle hesitated for an instant, but he wanted the money badly. He shrugged his shoulders. He sat down and wrote the receipt. But as he was about to give it, an idea came to him and he quickly drew it back.

"Look here, you're not going to try any hanky-panky tricks, are you? I won't sell you the copy unless you give me your word that you won't try and pass it off as an original."

A quiet smile passed across the dealer's lips.

"You can easily reassure yourself. Just paint out the signature and put your name on the top of it."

Without a word, Bartle did as the old man suggested, and presently his own name was neatly painted in place of the master's.

"I don't mistrust you," he said, as he handed the receipt, "but it's well not to put temptation in the way of wily dealers."

Monsieur Leir laughed as he pocketed the document and took the Watteau in his hand. He pointed with a slightly disdainful finger at Bartle's pictures.

"I'm going to take the copy along with me, and I'll send my *femme de ménage* for the others," he said. But at the door he stopped. "I like your pictures, my friend, and when Rudolf knows that I take an interest in you, I dare say he'll be able to sell them. Don't be surprised if in another month I come and tell you that you can marry your fiancée."

Monsieur Leir packed the Watteau with his own hands, and despatched it without delay. He wrote a discreet little letter to his son-in-law announcing its immediate arrival, and suggesting that they should share the profits of its sale. It was growing late, so he went to his café and drank the absinthe with which he invariably prepared for the evening meal. Then, with a chuckle, he wrote the following note:

To the Chief Officer, U.S.A. Customs, New York. Sir, An attempt will shortly be made to pass through the Customs a copy of a picture by Watteau. It is signed Charles Bartle. If, moreover, you scrape away the name, you will find the signature of the French painter. I leave you to make what inferences you choose.

Yours faithfully,

AN HONEST MAN

Less than this was necessary to excite the suspicions of the least trusting section of mankind. It was scarcely to be wondered at, therefore, that when Rudolf Kühn went to the Customs House at New York to pass the picture that had been sent him, he was received with incredulity. He asserted with conviction that it was only a copy, and produced the receipt which Monsieur Leir had been so cautious as to send him. But the official who saw him merely laughed in his face. He was quite accustomed to the tricks whereby astute dealers in works of art sought to evade the duty.

"I suppose you'd be surprised if I told you that the picture was signed by Antoine Watteau," he said, with a dry smile.

"More than that. I should be amazed beyond words," answered Rudolf Kühn, confidently.

Silently the customs officer took a palette-knife, scraped away

the name of Charles Bartle, and there, sure enough, was the French artist's signature.

"What have you got to say now?" he asked in triumph.

A curious light passed through the dealer's eyes as he stared at the canvas, but he made no other sign that Monsieur Leir's astuteness had suddenly flashed across him.

"Nothing," he replied.

With meekness he paid duty on the estimated value of an original Watteau, and a very heavy fine into the bargain for his attempt to defraud the customs. He took the picture away. But when he reached home that night he kissed his wife on both cheeks with unusual warmth.

"Your father's still the smartest dealer in Europe, Rachel," he said. But when she asked for some explanation of his words, he merely shook his head and smiled.

In New York the newspapers learn everything, and perhaps it was not strange that within four and twenty hours of these events, an important journal had an amusing account of how Rudolf Kühn, the well-known dealer, had been foiled in his attempt to pass through the customs, as a copy by some obscure painter, a very perfect example of the art of Watteau. It was a triumph for the officials, and the newspaper gibed freely because they had got the better of a wily Hebrew. Now Rudolph Kühn had a client who chose to spend much of his vast wealth in the acquisition of Old Masters; and no sooner had he read these entertaining paragraphs than he hurried to the dealer's shop. When he saw the picture he burst out laughing.

"I like your darned impudence, trying to pass that off as a copy."

"I showed them the receipt," smiled Rudolph, with a deprecating shrug of the shoulders. "I propose to sell it as a copy. It was sold to my representative in Paris as such."

The millionaire looked at the dealer and chuckled. "Well, Uncle Sam's customs are good enough guarantee for me. I'll give you fifty thousand dollars for it."

"I'll take sixty," answered the other, quietly.

"Not bad for a copy," smiled the buyer. "I'll have it at that."

He carried the picture off, and with it the various documents which the Customs House had delivered to Rudolf Kühn in proof

that he had paid both duty and fine. In face of these it would have been a sceptic indeed who doubted the authenticity of so delightful a work.

* * * * *

Some weeks later Monsieur Leir again knocked at Charlie Bartle's door. He advanced into the middle of the studio, and without a word counted out fifty English bank-notes of a hundred pounds each.

"What the dickens are you doing?" cried Bartle, who thought he had suddenly taken leave of his senses.

"Five thousand pounds," said the old man. "I thought you'd like to see the money actually before you, so I changed it into these notes."

"What do you mean?"

"It's your share of the profit on the sale of your pictures, and you may marry your Rosie whenever you choose."

Bartle stared at Monsieur Leir, helplessly. He thought it must be some heartless jest, but the old man's eyes gleamed with their usual kindliness. He rubbed his hands joyfully as he gloated over the painter's utter consternation. At last he vouchsafed to explain. Bartle understood vaguely that a California millionaire had bought his picture, all his pictures, and this money was the result. He wanted to write to this amiable and discerning patron, but Monsieur Leir hastily told him that was impossible. The Californian had bought the pictures and taken them away without leaving his address. Monsieur Leir assured him that the American millionaires were notoriously eccentric. Bartle drew a long breath and looked at the pile of notes.

"Take them to the bank, my boy," said the old dealer, enchanted with the young man's pleasure, "and send a wire to a certain lady."

He made the notes into a bundle, and put them in Bartle's pocket, and led him out of the house. The painter walked as though he were in a dream. But when Monsieur Leir had seen the young man safely on his way to the bank, he went to his own apartment. He took out Charlie's pictures, which had remained in the safe obscurity of a well-locked cupboard. One by one he ripped them off their stretchers, and one by one he put them in the fire.

He laughed as he saw them crackle in the flames. Then he took a hatchet and cut up the stretchers neatly.

"Here is some excellent firewood," he chuckled, as he gave the bundle to his maid.

He rubbed his hands when he thought that thus he saved several coppers. It had slipped his memory completely that he had just made his friend a present of five thousand pounds.

A MARRIAGE OF CONVENIENCE

(1906)

I don't know why the desire seized me once, in my youth, to take a voyage on a Spanish cargo-boat. I was staying at Cádiz, with nothing in the world to do—O most delectable condition!—and, going down one day to the harbour, saw a rather shabby steamer loading vast bales of merchandise. I began to talk with a sailor-man who lounged idly on the quay, and learned that she was bound for Valencia, Tarragona, and Tunis. The blue of the sea was as deep as the blue of the heavens, and Romance, that jade of flattering insincerity, put out a beckoning finger. Before I knew what had happened my soul was aflame with the desire for unknown lands, and when the second mate—for such I discovered was the garrulous seaman—told me they sometimes took passangers, I made up my mind to take the journey. My traps were soon gathered together, my passage booked, and next morning we started on our leisurely tour of the Spanish coast. For some time things went well enough. I spent the day reading such books as I had, and the evening playing cards with the skipper. We stopped at one port after another, loading and unloading with truly Spanish deliberation. Presently, leaving the shores of Spain, we crossed to Africa, and one morning, very early, when I got up I found that we had cast anchor in the harbour of an island off the coast of Tunis. The sun shone with dazzling brilliancy upon the white houses of a little town, and here and there tall palm-trees rose into the air. We were to stay but a few hours, for the place was not on the steamer's route; and the captain called there only by chance, to execute some commission. I had determined not to go

on shore, but I know not what there was in the smiling, sunny town that exerted on me an odd fascination; the more I looked at it the greater was my desire not only to visit it, but to stay there. In all probability the immortal gods would never again bring me to that island, and I dared not risk the regrets which must be mine if I missed the present opportunity. I discussed the matter with the captain, who assured me I should only be disappointed: the town had nothing to attract travellers, and the only Europeans were the French Consul with his wife, a sergeant, and a dozen soldiers. I looked across the harbour once more, and the white houses seemed to whisper a welcome to me; I felt on a sudden that I was transported to the *Arabian Nights,* and this was a magic isle from which wonderful things might be expected. Hitherto my journey had been very barren of the romance I sought, for nothing could be more matter-of-fact than the cargo-boat in which for three weeks I had lived; but here surely was the real thing: here lived enchanted damsels singing sadly to their lutes, and the very beggars were kings fallen from their high estate. I shut my ears to the skipper's admonitions, packed my things hastily, and summoned a boat from the shore. My friends on board, thinking me mad, shook my hand, with solemn warnings that I should regret my folly, and in a quarter-of-an-hour I found myself landed, with all my belongings, on the beach.

I was at once surrounded by a score of swarthy Arabs, who apparently discussed me and my concerns with considerable interest, and one, who spoke broken French, asked if I wished to see the consul.

"No," I said; "I want to go to the hotel."

I confess I was a little dismayed when he answered that there was no such thing in the place, but now I would not for worlds have returned, crest-fallen, to the steamer; and I asked if I could nowhere get lodgings. The Arab, with much gesticulation, talked the matter over with his friends, and presently suggested the house of a certain lady whose name I have forgotten. He shouldered my bag, and I followed him down one winding, narrow street after another till we arrived at a little white house at which he stopped. He knocked repeatedly, and at last a woman opened. When he explained what I wanted, she looked at me curiously, but in due course agreed to let me have a room. I bargained for the price and entered.

Having made myself as comfortable as possible—which was not much—I sauntered down to the shore and watched my good cargo-boat set out to sea. I was alone on a foreign island, where I knew no soul, and the weekly packet that ran between the little town and the mainland was not due for five days. Presently, while I watched the sea, smoking a cigarette, I saw my friend of the morning in conversation with a Frenchman, who, I surmised at once, was the sergeant of whom I had heard. They came up to me, and the sergeant, saluting politely, began to talk. Somewhat to my amusement, I found that he regarded me with considerable suspicion, and he asked me question after question. I did not gather the general drift of his inquiries, but answered everything readily enough.

"But frankly," he asked for the tenth time, "why have you come here at all?"

"A mere whim, *cher monsieur,*" I answered. "Curiosity, nothing else."

He evidently found my explanations unsatisfactory, and I cannot say that I took much trouble to make my motives clear. He informed me at last that he would report my presence to Monsieur le Consul.

"By all means," said I. "And pray add that I shall give myself the pleasure of calling on him tomorrow if my throat is not cut tonight in the unsavoury den which appears to be your only substitute for a hotel."

He left me, and I spent the rest of the day in wandering about the Arab streets, looking at the people, and feeling, indeed, something of that thrill I had expected. At night my hostess provided me with food, of which it could only be said that it performed the first office of edible substances—it allayed the pangs of hunger. But beside it the dinners on the cargo-boat, and they had seemed bad enough in all conscience, were toothsome and sumptuous. I was very tired, and, going to my little dark room, surveyed, not without misgiving, the bed on which I was to spend five nights. I was just beginning to undress when I heard a great knocking at the street door. In a moment my room was burst violently into, and before I had realised what on earth was happening, I found myself seized by two soldiers, while the sergeant, so friendly and polite in the day, looked upon me with triumph. I was really so

taken aback that for a moment I had nothing to say; then with some irritation I asked him what in Heaven's name he was up to.

"Monsieur le Consul has ordered me to arrest you. You will be lodged in the goal to-night, and to-morrow morning he will examine you himself."

"But it's absurd," I answered, and I could not help laughing at my ridiculous situation.

"It's no laughing matter, monsieur," he said sternly.

"You need not be disagreeable about it," I remarked. "Tell these men to let go of me and I will accompany you wherever you like. I am quite willing to spend the night in your prison if it amuses you, and I feel sure the bed with which you intend to provide me will be no more objectionable than this."

The sergeant hesitated for an instant, and then seemed to make up his mind that I did not look a very dangerous ruffian.

"Very well," he said. "Take your hands off Monsieur. Follow me."

There was no one about to see the edifying spectacle which I presented as I marched through the streets, thus escorted, to the local gaol. They put me in quite an agreeable little cell, locked the door ponderously, and so left me to my own reflections. I admit that the night seemed endless. It was very dark, and I felt that horrible things were crawling over me. There was a fetid, oppressive smell. I sought in vain for the diverting side of the incident, but I was too uncomfortable, and I freely cursed my craving for the romantic, which had driven me to this inhospitable place. I cared no longer for the lovely damsels whom my fancy had presented plaiting their long black tresses or darkening their eyes with kohl; and if there were any in the neighbourhood I only wished they would free me from the cruel beasts that were biting, biting. But in the morning a soldier brought me some excellent coffee, and I induced him to get me also the wherewithal to wash and a barber to shave me. These things performed, feeling fresher and more contented, I looked forward to my interview with the consul with curiosity and interest. I was told this official would see me at half-past ten, and then I should discover for what monstrous crime I was thus evilly entreated.

In due course the sergeant came with two soldiers and told me I must now go to the consulate. Between them, doing my best to look accustomed to the process, I stalked through the winding

alleys till we came to a long, low, handsome building with a verandah, neat iron railings, and a charming garden. At the gate stood a sentry, and above waved the tricolour; upon my word, except for the Arab gardener busily at work, I might have been suddenly transported to France. I was taken into a large, cool room, barely furnished, but with masses of flowers everywhere. They suggested a woman's taste and forethought. At a desk, littered with papers, sat a little man with grey hair, cut very short, and a large grey moustache, excessively fierce and bristling; he was dressed in white, dapperly, and his figure was trim and neat. I found afterwards that his eyes were very alert, and he gesticulated in conversation with much vivacity. He was writing as I entered, and did not look up when the sergeant duly announced me. He passed his hands impatiently through the many papers, looking for the sergeant's official account of my arrival and arrest.

"Approchez," he said, then glanced at me quickly. But the glance lengthened into a stare, his face fell; and then, recovering himself, his eyes began to twinkle.

"But Monsieur isn't a spy, sergeant," he cried.

"Is that it?" I said, and began to chuckle.

I don't know why my amusement should have had such an effect on the consul, but immediately he burst into a roar of laughter; he threw himself back in his chair and held his sides. But though he evidently found it a huge joke, the sergeant's face grew longer and longer. "Monsieur's conduct has been most suspicious," he said. "He walked round the town yesterday and was seen to make notes of all he saw."

The sergeant produced my note-book and gravely handed it to the consul.

"Will you allow me to look at it?" asked he politely.

"By all means," I answered, somewhat surprised that he understood English.

And while he turned over the pages the sergeant repeated every one of my movements on the preceding day. It was unheard of that an Englishman should arrive in a Spanish ship and come on the island to stay. What could be my motives except to discover whether it was fortified and if men-o'-war could enter the harbour with safety. Without the shadow of a doubt I was a spy of the most dangerous class, and Monsieur le Consul would regret that he

had not listened to the sergeant when the British fleet bombarded the town.

"But, Sergeant," answered the consul, "it will not assist the English admiral in the least to learn from this gentleman's notes that the women here have magnificent eyes and that the Jews are as picturesque as they are dirty."

"Monsieur has, no doubt, written his observations in cypher," said the sergeant.

The consul turned to me.

"Would you be so obliging as to tell me your name?"

I said it, and he repeated it thoughtfully.

"I wonder where I've heard that? Ah!" He gave a cry and seized a number of the *Journal des Débats* which lay on the table. "Is this you?" He passed over the paper, and, to my great joy, I saw an article on a little book of mine.

I acknowledged that I was the blushing author of that work, and, with a bound, the consul sprang up, dashed round the table, and, seizing both my hands, wrung them violently.

"But I'm delighted to make your acquaintance. My wife is devoted to English novels—she's Swiss, you know, she comes from Geneva—the best place in the world to find a wife, a hive of young ladies, my dear fellow—and she loves your English novels because they're so pure. She will be charmed to see you and you shall talk English to her. My wife is a linguist, monsieur, a wonderful linguist. And there is the luncheon bell. Excellent! Come to luncheon."

I was perfectly overwhelmed by this stream of verbosity hurled at me in one breath, and before I could answer the consul had turned to the sergeant, who stood helplessly by.

"You are an idiot. You, with your mania for finding spies all over the place. Monsieur is not a spy any more than you are. He is a man of letters, and my wife has read a book that he has written. You are an imbecile, Sergeant. Come, monsieur, or the eggs will be cold."

He seized my arm and dragged me away, leaving the sergeant and his myrmidons astounded and perplexed. The consul led me to a charming dining-room where stood a tall, rather stout lady of forty-five. Her hair, of a pleasant brown, was very simply arranged; her features were placid and handsome; her soft grey eyes suggested infinite good nature. She was by no means beautiful,

but gave one the impression that advancing years had only added to her attractiveness, and there was about her a staid gracefulness which was very comforting and restful.

"Allow me to present you to my wife, Madame de Pornichet," said the consul with a flourish.

In one breath, voluble as ever, he related the whole story of my misadventure, told her who I was, and added that he had asked me to stay at the consulate for the rest of my visit to the island. This was the first I had heard of such an invitation, but when it was seconded by the amiable, stately lady, I made no difficulty in gratefully accepting. It was as delightful as it was unexpected to eat in that distant spot an admirable French luncheon; and everything was so fresh, so clean, so dainty, that I felt amply rewarded for my trivial sufferings. My hostess was not talkative, nor was this strange, since her husband monopolised the conversation; but now and then she put in a little kindly word, whereupon he stopped suddenly and looked at her as though some precious feast of wit had fallen from her lips. And while he rolled out anecdote after anecdote, fact upon fact (all of which I discovered later was highly unreliable), with regard to the island he governed, her eyes rested upon him with a tender smile of almost maternal affection.

Coffee and liqueurs were brought in, and we lit our cigars.

"I'm sure it's very good of you to be so hospitable," I said. "I was looking forward to abominable discomfort on this island."

"Good!" cried the consul. "You don't know how pleased I am to have a civilised man to entertain my wife. I always fear that she will be bored to death, for there is no one here to amuse her but myself."

"And I'm sure you do it very well," I answered.

Madame de Pornichet gave me a radiant smile of gratitude.

"Ah, you are right," she said. "No one could be bored in Lucien's company."

"Come, come, my dear," said the consul, deprecatingly but delighted.

She stretched out her hand, and most gallantly he kissed it.

"Mon petit chou," she said, and tears of happy love actually glistened in her eyes. She turned to me. "You see, love sometimes comes before marriage, and sometimes after. But when it comes after it lasts till death."

"Sophie, ma chère enfant," said the consul, and it was rather amusing that he should so address her, for she was a great deal bigger and more imposing than he. "I must tell Monsieur how I had the good fortune to make your acquaintance."

"It is insupportable," she answered, to me, smiling. "He tells this story to everyone he meets."

It was evident, however, that Madame de Pornichet was not unwilling I also should hear it, and the consul settled himself more comfortably in his chair.

"Well, you must know that the best years of my life were spent with our Colonial Army in Algeria, in Senegal, in Tonquin; and I was successively lieutenant, captain, and major. But, my dear friend, I succumbed at last to a pestiferous climate, and at the age of forty-five my health forced me to leave the service. That was twelve years ago, and I am still an active man, not unfit for work nor unused to it. I applied for a colonial appointment, I had some influence, and in due course the minister sent for me to offer the governorship of this island. The post was one that exactly suited me, the salary was adequate, and it was not so far from civilisation that I should feel myself cut off from all my friends. I accepted there and then, and told the minister I was ready to start whenever he chose.

" 'Very well,' he said. 'You will take up your duties in six weeks from now. That will allow your wife time to make all needful preparations.'

" 'But I have no wife,' I said. 'I am a bachelor.'

" 'What?' cried the minister. 'But that is very unfortunate, for I make a point of never sending an unmarried man to such a place. For a hundred reasons it is essential that you should be married.'

" 'I regret enormously,' I answered.

" 'I am afraid I cannot break an important and salutary rule. You must marry at once.'

" 'I?'

"You can imagine my consternation, for nothing of the sort had ever entered my head, and I ventured mildly to expostulate. But the minister would not listen to a word.

" 'Voyons,' he said, 'you have six weeks. In that time you can easily find a wife.'

"He dismissed me and I walked away sorely troubled. On the

one hand I was delighted with my good fortune in getting precisely the post of all others which I should have chosen: on the other I was dismayed at the thought of marriage. An old bachelor of my age would have great difficulty in changing his habits to those of a matrimonial life. Fortunately, I met an old friend of mine, a professor at the Sorbonne, a native of Geneva, and I told him at once of my great perplexity.

"'But don't hesitate, my friend,' he said. 'Of course you must marry. *Du reste,* at your age it is fit that a man should settle down and live a respectable life.'

"'But, *mon Dieu,* where am I to find a wife in six weeks? You cannot expect me to advertise in the *Figaro.*'

"'Why not? It is as good a way as another.'

"The result of this conversation was that within twenty-four hours an advertisement appeared in that widely circulated paper, stating my age and position, income, and giving as flattering an account as I honestly could, of my personal attractions. Then began my troubles. I went to the office of the *Figaro* next day to call for any replies that might have come, and the clerk brought me a sack—a large sack, sir.

"'Here are the answers to your advertisement, monsieur,' he said, with a malicious grin.

"I staggered, and gave a cry of horror. However, in a moment I regained my self-possession, seized the sack, and, laden like a coal-heaver, hailed a cab. I drove to my hotel, and once in my room emptied it out on the floor. Monsieur, seven hundred and forty-eight ladies desired to marry me. I spent two days reading the letters, in which they described their charms, and examining the photographs, which, according to my request, they had sent me. They were of all years, from sixteen to those who described themselves as of a certain age; they were fat, they were thin, they were dark or blond, they were of every station, from sempstresses to the widows of noblemen. They were single, or divorced, or widows; and some were betwixt and between. But all offered a loving heart and a sincere devotion. At the end my brain reeled. My Swiss friend came to see me, and when he saw the piles of letters, the piles of photographs, he laughed as though he would never stop.

"'But it is a serious matter,' I said. 'Time is flying and I have but five weeks and four days to marry a wife. You cannot

expect me to interview seven hundred and forty-eight blushing ladies. I cannot raise hopes, only to crush them, in seven hundred and forty-seven palpitating hearts.'

"'What will you do, then?'

"'I will send back all their photographs, and write to the minister that what he asks is impossible. I must lose my island.'

"'Now listen,' answered the professor. 'You know I was born in Geneva, and I have relations living there. It has suddenly occurred to me that my cousin Sophie Vienqué would exactly suit you. She is no longer quite young; nor are you, my friend; she is thirty, of pleasing appearance, and unmarried.'

"'But what makes you think she would marry me?'

"He shrugged his shoulders.

"'I do not see why she shouldn't. She has had time to grow bored with a single life, and I dare say will be pleased with the thought of an establishment of her own. You have much to offer. I can say without flattery that you are an agreeable man, robust still, and not lacking in intelligence. Anyhow, you can try.'

"'But, *mon cher,* how can I see her? On what pretext? I cannot call upon your cousin and take stock of her as though I were buying a horse.'

"The professor meditated for two minutes.

"'I have it. You will go to Geneva and offer her a box of chocolates from me. That will be an introduction. You can talk to her, and if she does not please you, all you have to do is to go your way. She will think you have merely come to make a trifling present on my behalf, and no harm will be done. On the other hand, if you like her it is easy for you to prosecute the acquaintance.'

"I was delighted with the idea. We went out at once, bought the chocolates, and I took the next train to Geneva. I assure you a lover of eighteen could not have been more excited than I was. I arrived early in the morning, and, having attended to my appearance at the hotel, went about ten o'clock, the box of chocolates in my hand, to the address my friend had given. I was so fortunate as to learn that Mademoiselle Vienqué was at home, and, being shown into the drawing-room, found myself in the presence of a very fine young woman. *Tenez*—I need not describe her, for there she sits before you; and, though twelve years have passed since then, she has altered only to become more ravishing each day."

"Voyons, Lucien," expostulated Madame de Pornichet. "Monsieur will think you perfectly ridiculous."

"Well, I executed my commission, received her thanks, and told her the professor was in the best of health. We began to chat, and the conversation went so easily that I was astounded when the clock struck eleven. I said to myself at once that if this charming lady was able to talk for an hour to a perfect stranger so that it seemed to him no more than five minutes, on closer acquaintance she could not fail to be entertaining during a lifetime. Everything about her pleased me. She was evidently fitted for the duties of a consul's wife: her attractive person, her amiable conversation—"

"How often have I told you, Lucien," interrupted his wife, "that you talked so incessantly on that occasion that I was not able to make *one* observation?"

He smiled and patted her hand.

"I rose to my feet," he continued, "and addressed her as follows: 'Mademoiselle, it will have occurred to you that I did not take the long journey from Paris to Geneva merely to present you with a box of chocolates.'

" 'Evidently,' said she.

" 'I came, in point of fact, to make you an offer of marriage.'

"Before she recovered from her astonishment I explained the circumstances, told her my position, and so far as possible sketched my character and my idiosyncrasies. Finally, I proposed that we should be married in a week from that day.

" 'But, monsieur, I don't know you,' she said.

" 'You will have abundant opportunities of making my acquaintance when we are settled on our island. There will be nothing else to do.'

"I saw that she did not dislike the idea, and I ventured a little to insist.

" 'Well, I will consult my father,' she said at last.

" 'But, mademoiselle, though Monsieur your father is without doubt an excellent man, it is not he whom I wish to marry, but you. Do I displease you?'

" 'No,' she admitted, 'not precisely.'

" 'Then why should you refuse me?'

" 'Give me till to-morrow to think it over.'

" 'I regret infinitely, dear lady, but as I tell you, my time is excessively limited. I beseech you to give me an answer now.'

" 'This minute?'

" 'This very minute.'

"She smiled and reached out her hand. 'Very well, monsieur, since you insist—I accept.' "

The consul drank a glass of wine.

"Monsieur, fourteen days after my visit to the minister, I was a married man, and I discovered that I had never known happiness before. My wife is a treasure, a jewel, and I think she loves me."

"Mon petit chou," said Madame de Pornichet tenderly.

"And if you are a bachelor, monsieur, go to Geneva. I assure you it is a beehive, a veritable beehive of young ladies."

The consul thus ended his story; and, I who had come to this curious island searching for romance, felt that I had found it, and, of all places, in a marriage of convenience.

GOOD MANNERS

(1907)

I

Most people thoroughly enjoyed the little dinners which Augustus Breton gave to his friends, for the company was always well chosen, the meats carefully ordered, and the wines unparalleled in the county. He was an epicure without grossness, who cultivated a delightful urbanity far from towns, living a hermit life by aid of the resources of civilisation and the consolations of philosophy. He was a recluse, dwelling among his books on the land he had inherited from his fathers, a student of men who prosecuted his inquiries by preference among the Kentish yokels and the squireens of that fertile county. A man with a certain ironic taste for self-analysis, he liked to observe himself against the background of the unsophisticated; and he practised, as a contrast to rustic manners, a courtesy which reminded you of the elaborate breeding of the eighteenth century. Augustus Breton's peculiar standpoint might be imagined by the stately air of his Georgian house, filled with the graceful furniture of Chippendale and of Sheraton, with mezzotints, and with exquisite silver; and his appearance fitted the frame with a perfection that suggested the studied pose. He was a man of scarcely middle size, slender notwithstanding his fifty years, with small hands and small feet, of which perhaps he was immoderately proud; he wore his grey beard cut in the fashion of gentlemen in the reign of Elizabeth, and his well-shaped aquiline nose, his pale blue eyes recalled the ancestral portraits which adorned his walls. He preferred, without actually stating it as a fact, to give the impression that all the beautiful things in his house had been handed down to him, but in truth he himself had bought the

great majority; he was an enthusiastic collector, talking most willingly of the great masters of mezzotint, of the marks and style of silver, of various cabinet-makers dead but still remembered; and during his rare visits to London, most of his time was spent where such things are bought and sold.

One evening I dined with him, to meet the rector, a youngish man with iron-grey hair and an ascetic manner, whom my host treated always with a peculiar deference; and a lieutenant in the Navy, who appeared to me to have been asked for his breezy ways and his adventurous air of having surpassed many strange perils. I felt sure Augustus Breton saw in him no ordinary young seaman, but an Elizabethan sailor who had passionate tales to tell of exploits on the Spanish Main. Our host liked to keep the conversation well in hand, and, with his exquisite politeness, took care that each guest in turn should speak of what most concerned him; he managed us with a lightness of touch that was admirable, talking himself but little, and then with a kind of grave wit, merely to change a topic that seemed to have been long enough debated, or to throw out a suggestion which might revive a languishing interest. We dealt with the rector, of vacant bishoprics and the influence of the Church in rural parts; with the sailor, of British armaments and the chance of war; and at last the admirable dinner was ended and port was set upon the table. Politely as ever at this stage, Augustus Breton inquired after the rector's wife; he could never forget that at the beginning of the acquaintance, when dining with him, she had ventured to eat an orange while drinking her port; and though he had borne the affront with unexampled civility, the lady had not again been invited to his house.

"This is an admirable wine," said the parson, who, for all his ascetic look, knew good port from bad.

"Yes," said his host, holding it meditatively to the light, "I have only just now begun to drink it. It has been in my cellar for some years, and this, in point of fact, is the first bottle I have tried. I will acknowledge that, besides wishing for the pleasure of your company, I asked you to be so good as to dine with me so that you might give me your opinion."

The rector, flattered that such a master in these affairs should challenge his praise, slowly inhaled the exquisite aroma.

"It is something really most remarkable," he said.

"My dear Rector," answered Augustus Breton, "your virtues are so signal that I am quite overwhelmed."

"How did you get hold of it?" I interrupted, to stop the interchange of compliments which I foresaw.

"Ah, that is a story which may interest you."

We begged him to tell it, and, evidently not unwilling, he began in these words.

II

"Of course you know Graveney Hall, the largest house in this neighbourhood, a magnificent place which even an auctioneer could scarcely describe in exaggerated terms. But it was very much too fine for its owners, who have been going downhill steadily for a century and a half; the beautiful gardens were neglected, and even the most needful repairs were left undone; and at length, with a remnant of good sense, they made up their minds that it must be let. They put it in the hands of various agents; but it was not an easy place to deal with, since it is so far from a station that none but a man of leisure would care to live there, and none but a man of means could afford it. Finally, however, they discovered a certain Baron von Bernheim, who came to see the house, fell in love with it there and then, and at once arranged to take it on a long lease. The Graveneys were in the seventh heaven of delight. He was a millionaire, currently reported to have made a vast fortune in South Africa, and without doubt his liberality with the Graveneys pointed to wealth easily acquired: he was ready to do all they asked and to pay all they demanded.

"The arrival of Herr von Bernheim made a certain stir in the neighbourhood, partly owing to the disappearance of the Graveneys, who, after all, have been the chief persons in this part for more than four hundred years; but still more because in every surrounding village is abject poverty, and it was generally felt that this new wealth would be freely scattered. The dormant countryside woke up, and a feverishness seized all and sundry at the thought of this amassed gold; in a smaller way it resembled those manias that took hold of people in the days of the South Sea Bubble, when nothing in life seemed desirable but money. When the German arrived, already half the quietness of this Kentish corner was

gone, and, from squire to ploughman, everyone was on the alert for gain. I hated the stranger. I am a lover of ancient ways, and I was ashamed that the Graveneys should live in future in a villa at Regent's Park, while this interloper occupied their stately home; and I felt that the old-world air I had striven so hard to maintain in this bit of country would vanish before the vulgar opulence of the upstart baron.

"My neighbours thought it civil to call upon him, but I, notwithstanding the entreaties of my old friend, Lady Elizabeth, refused to go. I would not know this man for whom the old-fashioned carriages of the Graveneys did not suffice, but who scoured the country in a new-fangled brake, painted bright yellow, behind horses whose value was preposterously obvious. And when I found he was taking great interest in village affairs, I hated him still more. I heard he was getting the postal service improved—in the old days we were content to receive letters once a day. He laid the first stone for a cottage hospital, and, worst of all, headed a deputation to the railway directors to make a station near Graveney; he subsidised schools—before his arrival it had been my boast that, notwithstanding all the laws they made at Westminster, not half the population could read or write; and consequently our people were better mannered, better workmen, and better satisfied."

The rector opened his mouth to combat this heresy, but good-humouredly Augustus Breton begged to be allowed to continue his story; and the parson held his tongue.

"Lady Elizabeth asked me why I would not make acquaintance with a man whom everyone thought charming.

" 'I'm sure you'd like him,' she said. 'Of course, he's fabulously rich, but not in the least purse-proud. He's very amusing. I believe you dislike him because he gives better dinners than you do.'

"Now, I will confess that it is my pride to treat my guests so that they may be pleased to come to me. With a little care it is possible to devise in the country a pleasanter meal than anyone can get in London, and I have no sympathy with certain neighbours of mine who give you slovenly viands with the excuse that nothing better can be got in this distant village; and it is possible that when Lady Elizabeth, with her accustomed enthusiasm, described the banquets that Baron von Bernheim gave at Graveney Hall, a faint tinge of jealousy did pass through me.

"But, at all events, I was content to do without the millionaire's lavish hospitality. It appeared that everyone found him as charming as Lady Elizabeth, for the county took him to its bosom, and wherever I went, his praises were dinned into my ears. The pleasure which all took in his friendship, the callous way in which people congratulated themselves that he had taken the Graveneys' place—for the Graveneys were too poor to take any part in the festivities of the county—irritated me still more, and I even went out of my way to avoid him. But I cannot deny that I was a little flattered when I heard that the German, at whose head the whole countryside with indecent haste had thrown itself, was making every endeavour to strike up an acquaintance with me. He went so far as to send a message through Lady Elizabeth, our common neighbour, to ask whether he might call on me, and I was obliged to pretext indifferent health to avoid the honour. Lady Elizabeth in her sprightly way called me all manner of things, but I was determined not to be forced into friendship.

"When he found his efforts were useless, Baron von Bernheim adopted a bold course. He came to my house one morning, just before luncheon, and asked whether I would subscribe to the restoration of the church. I refused somewhat curtly, for in the first place I hate this modern craze for meddling with old buildings, and I will never give a penny to restore anything—I know too well what it means; and secondly, I thought it impertinent that Herr von Bernheim should himself come to me. He took my refusal good-naturedly and walked towards the door; I had not asked him to sit down.

" 'You have some very charming things here,' he said.

" 'It is kind of you to say so,' I answered drily.

"He was passing out when his eye caught a mezzotint which has a peculiar history. It is the portrait of a lady, of great beauty and of exquisite workmanship. I had paid one hundred and fifty pounds for it, but on bringing it home was seized with an odd misgiving that it was counterfeit. No expert had discovered it.

"If a forgery, it was wonderfully done, and I tried to persuade myself that it was nothing of the kind, for all the evidence was in favour of its genuineness; but still I had an uneasy suspicion. I saw the baron stop in front of this picture, look quickly at me; and then the shadow of a smile played on his lips. I was astounded, for evidently he had no doubt that this was a reprint; but that

he should have discovered it with one rapid glance proved not only that he was a connoisseur, but that he had an innate genius in these things. A man who could tell real from false as if by intuition was remarkable. But I could not let him go without a word; for it was as bad as wearing false pearls, to hang on my walls a picture which was valuable if genuine, but otherwise worthless.

" 'You're looking at my reprint,' I said, casting all doubt behind me. 'I keep it because I think it such a wonderful example.'

" 'It is so good,' he replied, smiling, 'that I wondered if you knew it was not authentic. Of course, you know the man in Paris who makes these things?'

"I felt I had escaped a great peril, and to make sure that he did not think I had been foolishly deceived, I insisted on taking down the picture and bringing it to the window. We discussed it, and the baron for the second time took his leave. I had looked at him closely while he examined my hapless mezzotint, and was surprised to find his appearance not unattractive. His dress was very simple, and his manner restrained and unaffected; he was almost a good-looking man, with slightly mournful brown eyes and a singularly persuasive voice, which gave all he said a peculiar charm. I could well understand why women found him so fascinating. But as he shook hands with me, his eye fell on my greatest treasure, a jar in *famille verte* of such beauty that, though it has been always in my possession, I can never see it without a thrill of delight and of surprise. The sight of it makes my heart beat as might the sight of a beloved woman; but no human being had ever that exquisite grace of form, that soft brilliancy of colour.

"The baron took it in his hands. 'But about this there is no doubt,' he said, and he looked at it with dilated pupils. And when I saw him handle the jar, when I saw the caress of his fingers, the delicate, loving way with which he held it—as a proud mother might pass her hands over the silken hair of an only child—I knew, notwithstanding all my petulant complaints, that this was a kindred soul. Here was a man with whom I could talk of all my treasures, and who would understand me.

" 'It is just luncheon-time,' I said, somewhat confused, I admit. 'It would give me very great pleasure if you would stay and share my modest meal.'

"He seemed not in the least astonished, but very naturally, as

though we were already old friends, accepted. Perhaps it is one of my failings to imagine that at my own table I arrange the conversation so that my guests may speak of things that specially concern them; but on this occasion I found that I myself was led; and with infinite tact the baron arranged our talk so that I was carried away, and spoke not only more than is decent in a host, but of topics which I am unaccustomed to discuss with all and sundry. The German knew human nature, and in consequence I found him a most agreeable fellow. With quiet humour he bantered me good-naturedly on my opposition to his many schemes, and at length I was forced to confess that I had looked upon him always with great disfavour.

"'On acquaintance, I hope you will alter your opinion,' he said.

"And I, embarrassed: 'I have altered it already. And I feel bound to ask your pardon for my bearishness.'

"Then he asked to what I particularly objected; and when I told him it was the proposed station, he offered to take no further steps to secure it. I was a little overwhelmed, for I dared not prevent an innovation which might bring a new prosperity to these parts; but when he said he did not himself much care for the railway to come so near Graveney, I felt a great load fall from my mind. A few days later, I received an invitation to dine at the Hall, and with alacrity—anxious to atone for past impoliteness—I accepted.

"In truth, Von Bernheim's hospitality was lavish, and I freely acknowledged to Lady Elizabeth, who teased me because I had succumbed at last to the millionaire's fascination, that I was able to offer my guests nothing to equal it. I found the Graveneys' precious things arranged with ten times more taste than they had ever had, and the house, instead of being a sad mixture of beauty and tawdriness, was now wholly delightful. Herr von Bernheim had put few of his own things there, but these were so exquisite that any museum would have been proud to possess them.

"Lady Elizabeth drove me home afterwards, and when we were comfortably settled in the carriage, she cried: 'Now, honestly, don't you think he's perfectly enchanting?'

"'I do,' I answered. 'I withdraw all I said against him. He is an excellent host, and he has every virtue. But there is one thing which is quite beyond praise—I have never drunk better port in

my life. Good Heavens! where did the man get it? I would give my soul to own a wine half as good.'

"Lady Elizabeth laughed, and evidently repeated what I said to the German, for two days later, to my amazement, I received six bottles of this priceless wine, with a very civil note saying that he had noticed my appreciation, and begged I would accept those few bottles. To me, who fancy myself something of a judge in such matters, the gift was magnificent, and I knew not how adequately to express my gratitude. I went into my garden and cut some dahlias.

"'My dear Baron,' I wrote, 'you were so good the other day as to say that Graveney Hall could not show such dahlias as grew in my poor little garden, and I venture to send you some in return for your gift of wine.'

"The little present pleased him apparently, for next time we met, he thanked me as profusely as if my flowers had been of serious value, and he apologised for sending so few bottles of port, saying that he had only five dozen left. And from this beginning we grew into fast friends. I found his knowledge of the arts was deep and enthusiastic; he was able to tell me a thousand things I did not know before, and never a week passed when he was in the country that he did not lunch at my house, or that I did not dine at his. But the Baron von Bernheim was a singular man; we never heard of his doings in London, knowing vaguely only that he was concerned in vast undertakings. For all his friendliness, everyone was kept at a certain distance, and even I, after three years of constant communication, knew not a whit more of him than I had learnt on the first day of our acquaintance. He seemed to me the subtlest observer, but also the most careful, impenetrable man that I had ever met; he must have known every detail concerning every important inhabitant of the county, but of himself no one knew anything.

III

"His influence in this part of the country increased rapidly. The place awoke from its dull sleepiness, and everyone became strangely alert and active. Even I, though now I am ashamed to confess it, felt that I had somehow wasted the peaceful years

spent happily in my little house, and that I should have done more with my life. Lady Elizabeth was quite carried away, and under the baron's direction launched into such small speculations as she could afford. It was imagined that the baron, now a naturalised Englishman, would stand for Parliament; and the farmers, at the thought of all he would do for them, dreamed pleasant dreams of a new prosperity.

"One morning I was taking a walk along the road that runs past my house, when I met Lady Elizabeth in her dog-cart. She stopped, and I saw at once that something extraordinary had happened.

"'I was just coming to see you,' she cried. 'I've been to Tercanbury this morning and I've heard the most awful thing.'

"'What do you mean?'

"She looked quickly at her groom, gave him the reins, and stepped down. We walked till we were out of earshot, and then very anxiously she spoke.

"'Everyone in Tercanbury is full of Baron von Bernheim. They say he isn't a baron at all, but a well-known Continental swindler called Johann Herz. He's been carrying on some gigantic swindle in England, and now a warrant is out for his arrest. Isn't it dreadful? And he has five hundred pounds of mine.'

"I turned pale.

"'It can't be true!'

"'I've been to the bank, and the manager tells me he's arrested by now. There seems no doubt about it.'

"'But he was engaged to lunch with me to-day,' I said.

"'Well, he won't come,' she answered. 'Come to luncheon with me, and we'll talk it over.'

"'No,' I said, 'I must go in. He may come, and I should be there to receive him.'

"'You don't mean to say you're going to give him luncheon. He's a most desperate criminal. You must be mad. But of course he won't come. He's either arrested or fled.'

"'If he comes, I shall remember he's my guest, and I shall take care in no way to show that I have heard anything to his discredit.'

"'You're an old fool, Mr. Breton!' exclaimed Lady Elizabeth almost angrily. 'Of course he won't come; but if he does, you must send for the police.'

"I went home, more distressed by the news than I can possibly say. Lady Elizabeth seemed so positive that I could not doubt it was true, and somehow I was scarcely surprised; the German had been always so silent about his antecedents; and for all his apparent heartiness, there had ever seemed in him something that he concealed. But, after all, I had invited him to luncheon, and I determined to make no change in my arrangements.

" 'I shall not wait for Herr von Bernheim after ten minutes past two,' I told my servant, without giving any explanation.

"I looked at the clock with some nervousness, and in a moment it struck the hour.

" 'Am I too punctual?' cried a voice through my open window, and, turning around with a start, I saw Baron von Bernheim himself.

" 'I came round by the garden,' he added, walking in. 'I thought you would not mind.'

"For a moment I was taken aback. He was as calm and self-assured as ever I had seen him, immaculately dressed; and I had never been more impressed by his perfect ease of manner. He saw my confusion and asked whether I expected him.

" 'Of course,' I said, recovering myself. 'Let us go in to luncheon.'

"I cannot say I enjoyed the meal. I was very nervous. I wondered whether the whole story were untrue. I watched the windows anxiously for detectives. It would be horrible if the man were arrested at my very table. Then I asked myself whether the German did not know that a warrant was issued for his arrest, and almost with agony I wondered what I should do. But he was imperturbable. With his accustomed brilliant knowledge, he spoke of early Italian art, criticising the various schools with the acumen of a connoisseur and the enthusiasm of an artist. My own powers of conversation failed me, and all my efforts were centred on preserving the politeness due to a guest; but the baron did not seem to observe my awkward silence; he went on eloquently discoursing, till at last it was all I could do to prevent myself from crying out: 'Good Heavens, man! is it true? Don't you know that all the police in Kent are on your track?' Since then it has always been my consolation that I bore myself to the end courteously, and none could have seen that my guest was most unwelcome and I in a pitiful state of anxiety. We had just finished when I heard wheels on the gravel outside my door, and I started.

" 'What is that?' I cried, disconcerted.

"He looked at me calmly, and an ironic smile broke on his lips.

" 'It must be my trap,' he said. 'I gave orders that I was to be fetched at three. You will forgive me if I run away so quickly, but I must go to Scotland to-night, and the trains are so inconvenient from here, I can only just manage it.'

"He shook hands with me and, without the slightest sign of haste or anxiety, walked out. I watched him take the reins and drive away.

"Next morning the whole thing was in the papers. It was a most heartless, cruel swindle that the baron had devised, and for three years it had gone successfully; hundreds of people were ruined, and the sensation throughout the whole country was immense. But Johann Herz—for that indeed was his real name—had entirely disappeared; I was the last person who had seen him. He had gone off in the little sailing-boat he kept, none knew whither; all the ports on the Continent were watched, but he was not found. Then long accounts appeared of his previous history, and it appeared that he had gone under a dozen names, all somewhat high-sounding, for a pretence of nobility appeared his chief weakness; and it was known that, wherever he settled, he loved to adopt the airs of the country gentleman. But what interested me most was that he seemed notorious as a forger of works of art; nearly every high-priced imitation of oil-paintings, mezzotints, or porcelain had come from his workshops. He set his great talents to work on every artistic thing that became fashionable, and in this it appeared his keen sense of beauty, his vast knowledge, were extremely valuable. He had so much ability that he could have earned an honest livelihood with the greatest ease, but apparently there was some kink in his nature which made him unable to resist the strange fascination of crime. And even when I knew his whole history, I could not help admiring the bravado with which he had come to my luncheon; it was really magnificent, the coolness he had shown and the consummate daring. I confess I hoped he would escape—this was too picturesque a ruffian to fall into the law's iron hands; he was a hero living out of his time. In the fifteenth century, with such courage, resource, and wit, he would have founded a dynasty.

"And my heart sank when I read in the paper, fully three

months after the flight, that Johann Herz had been arrested in Naples. It was by the merest chance; all his precautions had been carefully thought out, and it seemed as if Fortune alone had been against him. He was brought to England, tried, convicted, and sentenced to seven years penal servitude."

Augustus Breton sank back in his chair and sighed.

"But how is this connected with your port?" I asked, at length.

"There was a sale at Graveney Hall of the baron's effects," answered our host, "and sadly I went to it. The curious had assembled in numbers, wishing to see where the notorious criminal had lived, but the bidding was bad. We were all very much ashamed of ourselves, and I noticed that those who had profited most by the German's splendid hospitality were most bitter in their denunciation of his character. They all said that they had never liked him, and had always thought there was something shady about him. I watched the scene with a certain melancholy, hardly attending to the bidding, when suddenly, by chance, I heard the auctioneer put up a small quantity of port. This must be the celebrated wine of which the Baron had given me six bottles at the beginning of our acquaintance. I thought I would buy it as a memento of my friend. I bid, and in a minute the wine was mine."

"But why have you kept it so long?"

"Ah, my friend, I hadn't the heart to drink it while the possessor of so delicate a palate was living on convict fare in Portland Prison. It would have been really in very bad taste. So I waited till his sentence had expired. I found out that to-day the convict was to be released, and I asked you all to come here so that the port might be solemnly drunk. Gentlemen, I ask you to drink to the health of Herr Johann Herz."

COUSIN AMY

(1908)

Amy is the daughter of my grandmother's nephew by marriage. I cannot imagine that she is any relative of mine; but she insists that we are cousins, and we call one another by our Christian names. Her idea of the connection is that she should treat me with all the unpleasant frankness of a close relation, while on my side there should be the extreme politeness, the flattering attentiveness, of a distant acquaintance. This was all very well when I was eighteen and Cousin Amy twenty-six; but now I am five and thirty, and Cousin Amy has ceased to count her birthdays. She does not realise that this makes all the difference in the world; and I have never been able to find the exact words in which to frame so delicate a statement. Cousin Amy lives in the country, and I was much surprised to meet her face to face in Piccadilly. She shook me warmly by the hand.

"How nice to see you after all these ages! We *must* have a talk, mustn't we?"

I replied that it would be very agreeable.

"Well, I'm only here for twenty-four hours," she pursued. "Are you doing anything this evening?"

"No, I'm not," I replied with alacrity.

I thought it would be pleasant to dine for once in a way at Cousin Amy's expense. In years gone by she had been apt to presume too far on the privilege (which her sex has never shown any wish to dispute with mine) of paying the bill.

"That's capital!" she said. "Then you can take me out to dinner."

"The prospect fills me with enthusiasm," I retorted icily.

"You know I've become a food reformer?"

"This is nuts," I murmured softly to myself, considering that the fruit in question was reported to be not only nutritious, but cheap. I went on with more earnestness: "And where does one eat reformed food?"

"Oh! anywhere," she answered airily. "I'm not a faddist, you know. Now I'm going to tell you something extraordinary: I've never dined at the *Ritz*."

There was a pause, during which you might have heard a pin drop in Piccadilly. But Amy broke it gaily.

"Well, I'll meet you there at eight, shall I? And don't order anything beforehand, since I eat next to nothing, you know."

This, at any rate, was consoling, for I had been saving up my money in order to spend a week in Paris and improve my mind. Amy tripped lightly away; and I, finding I had but a couple of pounds in my pocket, thought it would be wise in case of emergency to change a cheque.

When we sat down in the evening, Cousin Amy put her gloves on the table and looked round with a happy smile. "I know we're going to have a charming dinner," she said.

The waiter handed me the menu; but Cousin Amy is a practical woman.

"Now, you'd far better let me order my own dinner," she said. "I only want a snack; and you see, as I can't eat dead beasts, I'd better choose what I can eat."

The proposal seemed eminently reasonable.

Amy cast her eyes down the menu. "At all events, we can start with some *hors d'oeuvres*," she said. "Oh! and how delicious! There's *potage bisque*."

I had observed in my glance at the bill-of-fare that this was the most expensive soup on the list; but Cousin Amy never noticed these things. I wondered acidly how she had reached the quite mature age which I positively knew was hers without acquiring the elements of common decency. I ordered the *hors d'oeuvres* and the *potage bisque*.

"What fish, sir?" said the waiter.

Cousin Amy frowned at the menu. "It seems very extraordinary that you have no salmon," she said, in the arrogant way in which women generally address their inferiors. "It *must* be in season."

"Well, we have some, madam, but we haven't put it on the card. This is the first we've had."

"There!" said Cousin Amy in triumph. "You see, you can always get things if you ask for them."

I shuddered to think of the price I should have to pay for salmon which had only come on the London market that morning. I made up my mind that I should have to choose a cheaper hotel in Paris than the one upon which I had fixed. I pointed out to Amy that no woman who respected herself could eat a red fish after a red soup.

"Yes, I know that. I do feel rather a barbarian; but I must eat salmon, as it's full of proteids."

"But surely," I protested, "you told me that you never ate horrible dead beasts."

Amy opened her eyes wide. "Oh! that only applies to warm-blooded creatures; otherwise I couldn't have eaten the soup."

"It's lucky there's not whale on the menu," I murmured, as I meekly ordered the salmon.

I was beginning to think that one did oneself rather well on reformed food.

The *hors d'oeuvres* were set on the table; and Amy, explaining that she had to eat what she could, emptied the entire contents of three dishes on her plate. I thought they looked rather nice myself, but I hadn't the face to ask the waiter for more.

Then another waiter brought me a list of wines. This was my opportunity, and I seized it like a man. Cousin Amy was certainly growing uncommonly stout; and it is well known that obesity is best treated by abstention from liquid for two hours after the repast.

"As a food reformer, I take it that you only have a cup of coffee after eating," I said. "*I* shall have a whisky-and-soda."

"How did you get such a ridiculous idea into your head?" she answered briskly. "On the contrary, my doctor has ordered me to drink wine. You see, I have to keep myself up."

"Ah! what will you have?" I said gloomily.

"Oh! I don't really mind, so long as it's very dry."

I looked at Cousin Amy. "Do you remember the story of the man who was taking a pretty American out to dinner? He asked her what she would drink. 'I guess I'll have champagne,' she said. 'Guess again,' he answered."

"What a sell!" cried Amy, laughing merrily.

I have read somewhere that women have a greater delicacy of perception than men. I certainly never knew any one slower than Cousin Amy to take a hint.

She watched me turn over the pages. "If you really have no preference," she said, "I think I would like Veuve Cliquot. I always feel that we women ought to stand together."

It appeared that Cousin Amy was a suffragist as well as a food reformer; and after I had ordered the champagne which accorded with her principles, she favoured me with her views on the cause. Amy thoroughly enjoyed the *potage bisque,* and she positively gloated over the salmon. The obsequious waiter came for further orders.

"Now you see what an economical person I am to have to dinner," said Amy. "Any one else would ask for entrées and roasts and all kinds of abominations like that. But I only want a couple of vegetables, and I've done."

"I remember your saying you only wanted a snack."

She turned to the waiter. She thinks it is so nice to get on friendly terms with a waiter. She likes him to take an intelligent interest in her food.

"Now I'll tell you what I want: you know those great big asparagus, as large round as your arm? Well, I want some of them."

"Very good, madam," said he.

"It's so lucky I came up to town just when things I really like are in season," she reflected. "In the country we shall have to wait another three months for asparagus and green peas. You will order some peas, won't you?"

"Certainly, if you think you can eat them," I said politely.

"Ah! now you see what a difference it makes to eat in a rational manner. I can eat anything, my dear boy—anything!"

"I'm quite willing to believe it," I retorted.

She looked at me and smiled broadly.

"But I don't want you to sacrifice yourself on my account. I'm not narrow-minded, and if you want some flesh I have no objection to your having it."

A pile of asparagus and a great many green peas were set before us, and I knew they were worth their weight in gold. I began to feel more than doubtful about my trip to Paris.

"It's very kind of you," I answered; "but I seldom have more than a steak for dinner; and after devouring the meal you've ordered I shall feel like a boa-constrictor."

"You see, one has to get the proper amount of proteids in," Amy replied calmly, as she ate the giant asparagus.

I ate one or two myself, but I was no match for Amy. I no longer wondered that she was growing stout; and I thought that if anybody did marry her, he should be warned in time that to feed a food reformer is no joking matter.

When there was one long monster left on the dish, she seized it deliberately.

"I must eat that one," she said. "It means a handsome husband and five thousand a year."

"He'll want it," I replied.

"I thought I should only spoil my dinner if I had tea," she murmured reflectively.

"That was very considerate of you," I answered.

She leaned back with a sigh and looked at me.

"How pleased I am to have caught you before you went to Paris!"

"I very much doubt whether I shall be able to afford to go," I said.

Cousin Amy is an optimist.

"After all, there's no place like home," she answered cheerily. "If you go to Paris you'll probably get typhoid, and you'll certainly spend much more money than you can afford."

Cousin Amy has often besought me to be economical. She takes a cousinly interest in my finances.

At last she finished the peas; and I felt that *I* could eat nothing more for a week. Amy was in high spirits.

"Now a little sweet and a little dessert, and I'm done."

I began to admire Amy. I should have liked to introduce the fat boy of Peckham to her.

"Poires à la Melba," she ordered, with one glance at the menu.

With unerring instinct she had hit upon the specialty of the house. I decided definitely not to go to Paris after all.

"Delicious, aren't they?" she said.

We reached the dessert, and I became weak and silly when she said she had not had strawberries and cream that year. Neither had many other people. Strawberries and cream were brought,

mixed together in a huge bowl, and for a fixed sum—a rather large sum, it seemed to me—you could eat as many as you liked.

It was some consolation to me that Amy certainly had her money's worth. When she had done, she leaned back.

"After all one misses a great deal if one is a food reformer; but one has the consciousness that one is advancing a good cause. And besides, in Lent one has the advantage of killing two birds with one stone."

We had coffee, and I discovered that Amy had a fine taste in liqueur brandy. She told me her doctor wouldn't let her drink it unless it was very old. When the bill came—I congratulated myself on the fact that Amy had only wanted a snack, for if she had been really hungry I don't know what I should have done.

When we parted, she shook hands with me. "I *have* enjoyed myself," she said. "I'm so sorry I'm not staying in town longer, but you must come and lunch with *me* to-morrow. My system is chop for chop you know."

This was new in Cousin Amy, and I put the change down to the advance of years, which have a soft logic of their own.

"I shall be delighted!" I answered promptly. "Where shall we go?"

She looked at me with the utmost effrontery.

"What do you say to the Eustace Miles Restaurant? I should so much like to show you what a vegetarian restaurant is really like."

I have no presence of mind in emergencies, and I accepted Cousin Amy's invitation. But as I wandered away in the rain (I really couldn't afford a hansom) a sadder, poorer, wiser, and much overeaten man, I murmured to myself:

"She may call it chop for chop, if she likes. I call it carrot soup for *potage bisque*."

THE HAPPY COUPLE

(1908)

Miss Ley, the most delightful of old maids, having no engagements on hand, took a cottage on the river for the fortnight round Whitsuntide. The weather promised to be fine, and she had found a secluded spot in which she could enjoy the beauties of early summer to her heart's content. She was a woman who loved cities, but it pleased her at times to bury herself in the country, where, apart from men, she could collect herself and set her ideas in order. She was exhausted after a winter in London, and looked forward with pleasure to the peacefulness of the Valley of the Thames. With more books than she could possibly read in six months there was no chance of dulness, and the roses in the cottage garden offered all the companionship she needed. But her interest in her fellow-creatures was overwhelming, and she made the discovery in a day or two, not without satisfaction, that her neighbours in the next cottage were worthy of study. She had no wish to know them, since it amused her far more to divine what sort of folk they were from their appearance, and she did not want to be bothered with the trivialities of social intercourse. But they were plainly as disinclined as herself to strike up the acquaintance which was almost indicated by the fact that they lived constantly in one another's sight and met half a dozen times a day; and Miss Ley's mind, momentarily perturbed by the fear of an attempt upon her privacy, regained its usual serenity. She set herself to weave fancies about them. Miss Ley was not inquisitive and preferred to draw her imaginary portraits without the aid of disturbing information, and the details gathered by her maid were sufficiently scanty to leave scope for any amount of invention. The neighbours were a Mr. and Mrs. Craig, persons

apparently of some means, who had taken the cottage for the whole summer. It was evident that the man had no calling, for he spent all day at home. Miss Ley surmised that they had not been long married; they had a baby which was little more than a year old; and this surprised her, since both were middle-aged.

Craig was a handsome man, with a red, honest face, a grey moustache, and thin grey hair. He held himself well, and there was a bluff heartiness about him which suggested that he might be a retired soldier. His wife was a woman hard of visage, tall, and of a masculine appearance, with unattractive fair hair, a large nose, a large mouth, and a weather-beaten skin. She was not only plain, but grim. Her clothes were pretty, flimsy, and graceful. But they sat oddly upon her, for they would better have befitted a girl of eighteen; and Mrs. Craig was certainly forty. Miss Ley noticed that they were the work of an excellent dressmaker.

But though her appearance was unprepossessing and her manner hard, Miss Ley was curiously drawn towards her by the affection which she lavished upon her husband and her child. From her verandah Miss Ley could see the pair constantly walking up and down the lawn of their garden, arm in arm; they did not talk, but it was because they were happy to be together; and it was touching to observe the submissiveness with which the dour, unsympathetic woman treated her good-natured husband. She seemed to take a pleasure in doing his bidding. She looked for occasions to prove that she was his willing slave. And because they were no longer young, their mutual devotion seemed all the more charming. It was a pretty sight to observe Mrs. Craig brush an invisible speck of dust off the man's coat, and Miss Ley was convinced that she purposely made holes in his socks in order to have the pleasure of darning them. To watch this matrimonial felicity made the old maid more contented with herself and with the world in general. She christened the couple forthwith Edwin and Angelina.

But the most agreeable thing of all was to watch them with their baby. A nurse took it out every morning in a perambulator, but before this father and mother spent an ecstatic quarter of an hour in teaching it to walk. They stood a few yards apart and urged the child to flounder from one to the other, and each time it tumbled into the parental arms it was lifted up and

rapturously embraced. And when finally it was tucked up in the smart little cart, they hung over it with charming baby talk, and watched it out of sight as though they could not bear to let it go. Miss Ley had never seen a pair so devoted to one another, and so enchanted with their offspring.

She made up a little story about them. She was certain that they had fallen in love with one another years before—perhaps twenty years—when Angelina, a young girl then, had the fresh grace of her teens, and Edwin was a brave youth setting out joyously on the journey of life. And since the gods habitually ignore practical matters, it was evident that they had not a penny between them. To marry at once was impossible, but they had courage, hope, and confidence. The young man made up his mind to go out to the Colonies, make his fortune, and return to marry the girl who had patiently waited. It could not take him more than two or three years, and what is that when one is twenty and the whole of life is before one?

Angelina meanwhile would live with her widowed mother.

But things did not pass exactly as they had expected. Edwin found it more difficult than he thought to make a fortune. It was hard enough to keep himself from sheer starvation, and only Angelina's love and her tender letters gave him the heart to go on. The three years passed which he had given himself, and he was no more able to marry than before. Angelina's mother lived still, and it was impossible for the dutiful daughter to leave her. They must put aside all thought of marriage for the present. And so the years passed slowly; and Edwin's hair grew grey, and Angelina became grim and haggard. Hers was the harder lot, for she could do nothing but wait. The cruel glass showed such charms as she had once possessed slip away from her one by one, and at last she discovered that youth, with a mocking laugh and a pirouette, had left her for good; her sweetness grew bitter from long tending of a querulous invalid; her mind was narrowed by the society of the small manufacturing town in which she lived. Her friends married and had children; but she remained a solitary prisoner.

Often she despaired. She wondered if Edwin still loved her. She wondered if he would ever come back. Ten years went by, and fifteen, and twenty. At last Edwin wrote to say that his affairs were settled, he had made enough for them to live on at their

ease, and if she were still willing to marry him he would return at once. When they met after the long separation Angelina saw with dismay that Edwin, apparently no older, was as handsome as ever; the good-looking youth was become a good-looking man, and that was all. He was in the flower of his age. She felt suddenly very old. She was conscious of her narrowness compared with the breadth long sojourn in foreign countries had given him. He was joyous and breezy as of old, but all her spirit was crushed. The bitterness of life had warped her soul. She could not do otherwise than offer him his release; it seemed monstrous to bind that charming creature to her by a promise twenty years old. For a moment he thought she had ceased to care for him, and she saw the utter dismay of his face. She realised on a sudden—O rapture!—that to him, too, she was just the same as she had ever been. He had thought of her always as she was; her portrait had been, as it were, stamped on his heart, so that now, when the real woman stood before him, he did not see her. To him she was still eighteen. So Edwin and Angelina were married.

"I'm sure it's all true," Miss Ley said to herself. "And I'm convinced they'll live happily to the end of their days. Their love was founded on illusion, perhaps, but since it had to them all the appearances of reality, what did it matter?"

Now Miss Ley's greatest friend was Frank Hurrell, a man of half her age, who was assistant physician at St. Luke's Hospital; and when he suggested coming to see her on Whit Sunday she was very willing to forego for a while the delights of solitude. He arrived in time for luncheon, and they discussed, with pleasure at seeing one another again after a week's separation, the many interests they had in common. Frank was amused with Miss Ley's rural attitude, and asked her, smiling, how on earth she occupied her time. Miss Ley immediately gave him a catalogue of the various pursuits which filled the day, and she did not omit to mention her interest in the Craigs. She told him the story which she had invented to account for their middle-aged affection, and bore with equanimity his laughter. But while they were talking of him Miss Ley was able to point out Edwin in the flesh, for, apparently having finished his luncheon, he came out to smoke a pipe in the garden. Miss Ley and Frank were sitting on the verandah and had a full view of their neighbour's lawn.

"This is the first time I've ever seen him in the garden without

Angelina hanging on his arm," smiled Miss Ley. Frank looked at him carelessly, but in a moment his glance grew more intent.

"I seem to know his face," he said.

"If you say he's a widower with seventeen children and this is his second wife, I'll never forgive you."

"I can't remember anything about him. I'm convinced I've seen the man somewhere, but I can't put a name to him."

Then the nurse brought the baby out, and the happy father's face lit up.

"Come along, youngster," he said, as he took it from the nurse's arms.

He began to lift it as high as he could in the air, while the baby crowed gleefully; and when it had the chance, tugged at his moustache.

"He has such kind, good eyes," said Miss Ley. "I'm sure he's a perfectly charming creature."

Presently she proposed that they should take a stroll, and they wandered along the tow path, watching the gay crowds on the river. They talked of many things. But at last Miss Ley, looking at her watch, suggested that they should turn back. They had not gone far when she espied suddenly Edwin and Angelina walking towards them. It was the obvious walk for a Sunday afternoon, and it was not strange that the Craigs had chosen it as well as themselves.

"Now you'll be able to see her," said Miss Ley, quite interested in her little romance. "Their devotion is all the more touching because the poor thing's so plain."

They came closer, and Frank watched them with smiling eyes. In a moment they were face to face. Frank uttered a low exclamation, but it was enough to attract to him the glance of the happy couple. They stared at him for a moment. Then an extraordinary thing happened. They stood stock still and instinctively came close together, as though seeking for mutual protection. The man's red face was suddenly darkened by a purple flush, his eyes appeared almost to start out of his head; he seemed to have a difficulty to get his breath. All the colour fled from Mrs. Craig's sallow cheeks; her face in a moment grew drawn and haggard. And her eyes, too, were filled with indescribable terror. A convulsive trembling seized them, and Frank thought the woman would faint. He had never seen such frightful dread expressed on a human countenance.

They lost all semblance of mankind; they wore the look of hunted beasts. It was horrible to behold them. Suddenly, with a jerk, Craig seized his wife's arm and dragged her on. Miss Ley walked a few steps, filled with blank amazement. When she looked back she saw that Angelina had fainted.

"Won't you go to her?" she asked Frank.

"Goodness, no! She doesn't want me. Besides, the man's a doctor. He'll do all that's necessary."

"What on earth does it mean?" asked Miss Ley.

"Well, I do know them. As soon as I saw the woman I recognised her, and it's obvious enough that they recognised me."

"And who are they?"

Frank gave a grim little laugh.

"I'm afraid the story you made up about them is rather far from the truth. Do you remember the Wingfield murder?"

"No."

"Perhaps you were abroad at the time. It stirred the whole country." Frank paused a moment. "Miss Wingfield was a rich spinster of mature age, who lived in the country with a companion. Presently she died and was buried. It was found that she had left everything to this companion. She had been a strong, healthy woman, and no one expected her death. Various rumours were spread abroad, and at last the authorities ordered the body to be exhumed. The result of this was that the companion was arrested and charged with poisoning her employer. I was one of the medical experts called in by the prosecution. The chief witness in her favour was Miss Wingfield's doctor, a man called Brownley. The things that came out during the trial are indescribable. The accused woman must have been a monster of wickedness and cruelty. Personally I had no doubt about her guilt, but she was cleverly defended, and the jury disagreed. A new trial was ordered.

"In the meanwhile, the police gathered fresh evidence, and next time Dr. Brownley was put beside her in the dock. The prosecution sought to prove that the companion and the doctor were madly in love with one another, and had done the poor old lady to death so that they might marry on the fortune which the companion had caused to be left to her. The whole case hung together in such a way that it seemed impossible they should get off, and the judge summed up dead against them. But they were defended by the same man—that trial made his name for him,

and he'll be Lord Chief Justice before he dies—and he managed somehow to instil a doubt in the jury's minds. I shall never forget the suspense of waiting for the verdict. I was so interested in the case that I remained in court. At last the jury came in, and to the consternation of everyone, said that again they couldn't agree. The authorities decided not to prosecute a third time and the scoundrels—for that's what they are—were let out. A week afterwards an evening paper got hold of the news that they had been married that morning."

Frank stopped, and a shiver passed through Miss Ley.

"The real names of Edwin and Angelina are Dr. and Mrs. Brownley, and I haven't the shadow of a doubt that they committed between them a particularly cruel and heartless murder."

"But—good Heavens! How can they be so happy?" said Miss Ley.

"I don't think they're very happy at this moment," said Frank, quietly.

The friends returned to the cottage, and in the evening Frank went back to London. Miss Ley saw nothing of her neighbours. The night was beautiful and warm, but they did not appear as usual on their lawn; and the windows of the house were kept shut. Miss Ley wondered what they were feeling.

Next day her maid came to her in great excitement. The neighbouring cottage was empty. Its inhabitants had disappeared in the night, without a sound, without a word to anyone. They had fled like thieves, but nothing in the furnished house was missing. Their boxes were gone, heaven only knew how they had been taken away, and there was no trace of them. A pile of tradesmen's books had been left on a table, with money to pay them. No one had heard them go. No one had seen them. They had vanished like persons in a dream. And that for Miss Ley was the end of Edwin and Angelina.

Y0-DBT-367